THE SOUND OF
ONE HEART BEATING.
FASTER AND FASTER . . .

Spike Halleck is thirty-four years old. If you believe the actuaries, he has over forty years of blindness left. What the hell good is a blind man, he keeps asking himself? A blind man can't even pick out sleeping pills from a drugstore shelf to kill himself.

But suddenly, with Ellie's call, everything changes. Suddenly, with a conviction as clear as any image his sighted eyes had ever seen, he realizes that he might be the best, maybe even the only, chance to keep Janey alive. And Janey, Spike knows, is worth saving. . . .

Now that Spike Halleck has a good enough reason to live, he knows that there's nothing he can't handle. He really believes that—even if nobody else in the world will. . . .

SIGHT UNSEEN

To
Laura and Emily

"The eye, the window of the soul, is the chief means whereby the understanding can most fully and abundantly appreciate the infinite works of nature, and the ear is second."

—*Leonardo da Vinci*

Halleck never heard the sharp crack until the bullet knocked him over. Lying bleeding and sightless, the brittle shards of snow gale-driven on his skin, another cold stabbed through him as he heard the little girl cry out.

Instinctively, numb with the wind and frozen with fear, he lifted his head, drew in a breath, and yelled, "Stay down." Then he prayed that if there was a God she would stay down, that she would not get up, let herself into the deadly cross hairs that found him, that she at least would survive.

At the same moment, as he felt his shoulder, the warm blood cooling in the gelid December blasts, he doubted that she could. Somewhere out there, up to half a mile away, hidden, unseen, and unhurried, an expert sniper was lining up his next shot. He did not want Halleck. His bullets were not for him. They were for Janey. And unless he could think of something in the next three seconds, one of those bullets would find her, exploding her little head like a dropped melon.

Cold and powdery, the swirling snow had gathered knee-deep around him, miring him down. Throbbing in his shoulder, the pain, first hot and sharp, was strangely dull. Not cold, he knew, but shock. And suddenly, unexpectedly, terrifyingly, he felt faint, dizzy.

Not now, he thought, please not now. Lifting his head again, exposing himself too much, he shouted, "Stay down, Janey. I'm coming."

As he pulled himself toward her, another shot rang out.

1

Both men towered over the swarm of school children passing beneath them. Their eyes kept sifting through the swirling, shrieking crowd, ignoring the docent's departing speech, "Hope to see you back here, soon. Bring your parents and show them how much you learned." Ignoring their teachers' shepherding arms, their scolding words and anxious glances. Ignoring the boys, all of them. Alert for one little girl only.

The one looking like a bathroom attendant butted out his cigarette, now down to an inch of ash, turned and posted a sign, TEMPORARILY CLOSED, on the women's room behind him, intercepting an urgent-looking kid, maybe nine, who whined, "Mister, I can't hold it no more!"

"Use the room down the stairs," he said, not meeting her eyes. His own were hidden by Ray-Bans, as were his partner's. Together they kept searching, playing across the surging crowd for the one face they had burned into their memories.

"Maybe she ain't here no more," said the attendant.

The other, posted just outside the men's room, looked away as if they weren't acquainted and muttered back, "She's here. We saw her come in, didn't we?"

"Yeah." A few seconds later he added, "Got the cloth?"

The other nodded, kept scanning, suddenly froze on an image. "There's her teacher. Here comes the class. You ready?"

"What if she doesn't—"

The other man silenced him with a turn of his head, exposing his partner to his own image in the mirrored

11

sunglasses, saying evenly, as one of these teachers might to a child, "Be cool. We'll be home soon."

"There she is," he whispered.

Craning his head around, the other man, dressed immemorably in a white and beige ski parka, chinos, and cheap running shoes, said only, "I see her. Be cool."

"She's too—"

"Eyes front."

"What if—"

The glare again shut him up.

Janey Granville pulled up the shoulder strap on her plaid pinafore, turned impatiently, posted her hands on her hips in exasperation, and called out, "Todd Atkinson, you always get lost! Now get up here right away."

Todd looked back and sneered, not about to be bossed around by any *girl*, instantly returning his full attention to the blackened bronze nude, a life-sized nymph from the neoclassical Italian Renaissance. Disgusted at his preoccupation, she marched back, away from her class, and grabbed his hand. "Stop looking at that!" she demanded, unable to understand why Todd Atkinson always acted so perverted. "And get back with the class!"

"Can't," he said, playing his eyes over the figure.

"We're *leaving*, Todd."

"I dropped my scarf," he said, yawning.

Janey Granville shook her head, again in disgust, wondering what God put in boys' heads instead of the brains. "Where?" she sighed.

He pointed back toward the museum gallery exit, kept fondling the statue with his eyes.

"You stay right here," she told him, "while I find your scarf. Then we'll catch up with Mrs. Blanchard. You understand?"

Todd nodded and made what sounded like a gurgling noise, but kept his eyes pinned on the metal nipples.

She took his shoulder and shook it. "Stop staring at her tits, Todd! Promise me you won't move. You're always getting lost!"

Todd lowered his eyes from the magic baubles, filled them with disdain, and stuck his tongue out.

Janey shook her head, snorted, and marched off to retrieve the scarf. She knew it would be easy to find, even with all the people, because it was the ugliest thing she had ever seen, a broad band of twisting fluorescent stripes of chartreuse and vermillion that would stop a descending meteor. She had to wonder how his parents let him wear it, unless it helped them pick him out anywhere, even at a Chinese food riot.

Now where was it?

Her eyes snapped around, seizing on a far corner near the gallery exit, where another class was now pouring into the lobby of the Chicago Art Institute. Fighting her way through, looking back to check on Todd, whose eyes were still lasered on the bronze boobs, she shook her head, leaned down, and snatched it from the floor.

Turning quickly she saw the man in gray coveralls, tall and suspicious-looking. His eyes wouldn't let her go. At first she thought it might be one of those perverts they warned about, until he said, "That your scarf, kid?"

"No, it's—"

"Not your scarf, we're gonna have to take it to Lost and Found."

"It's Todd's," she whined, scowling. "Todd Atkinson's. You see, he gets lost—"

"Come with me, kid."

"I have to tell Mrs. Blanchard!"

"Bring the scarf . . ."

Janey turned, saw a flood of children walling her off from Todd, from Mrs. Blanchard, from the bus, turned and looked at the man with cold gray eyes piercing her, the strange, evil smile forming on his narrow lips. Right then she felt like running, started to when the huge hand scythed around her, covered her mouth before the scream could get out, covered it with something soft and wet and sickeningly sweet. With her last effort she lashed out as the attendant moved between her and Todd, Mrs. Blanchard and the bus. She tried to smash the toes behind her with her heel, pull away and run, but was held motionless as she watched the gray in the attendant's eyes melt into a pool that swallowed the world.

* * *

13

The crowd stopped and looked, curious, as the little girl collapsed. The attendant who caught her said to the man beside him, "Don't worry, sir, a doctor's coming."

"My little girl!" the man in the ski parka said, sobbing.

"We've got to get her to an office, mister."

Together they carried her off. Everyone seemed glad that help was on its way.

Mrs. Blanchard looked up, then down, as Todd Atkinson swept past her onto the bus. Clucking and shaking her head, then sighing and turning to the bus driver, she said, "Well, if Todd's on, you can be sure that's everyone. I'm always terrified he'll get lost."

Suddenly over the last few days, just as everything was beginning to seem normal, Spike Halleck felt a despair descend that left him desperate for the conviction that he really mattered, that he cared enough about life itself to keep on living. What he needed was a mission, a quest. Failing that, he wasn't quite ready to suck the muzzle of a .44 Magnum. So instead he slept, escaping the demons that haunted his waking hours. In sleep he found refuge, sometimes even peace, all because of the dream.

Although he could never know it, a smile was spreading across his face as he began slipping into REM sleep. Across the screen of his subconscious, THE dream had just begun to roll. In it he was seated in the back of a small, weathered dingy, casting off from a white-hot beach into a pristine lagoon. Almost as if he were actually stepping he felt the sparkling grains of sand ooze between his toes as he ambled, in no real hurry, to join the long-haired girl who waited smiling, ready to row. Just beyond the gently lapping waves, foaming and hissing on the beach, came the crisp sounds of oars dipping and plopping, sculling and dripping, as she held the boat ready for him, and as he stepped through the shallow water over the stern, where sun-parched letters spelled out FRENCH LEAVE.

The dream was always the same, as it was always different. When it began two years ago, the pastel images of swaying palms, surging waves, and pinking sky were impossibly vivid and laser-sharp, whereas over time the hues had come to seem washed, the objects blurred. Yet the sounds and odors and textures, originally background, now seemed to take over, to be so undeniably real that he was almost sure it wasn't a dream at all.

In this twilight illusion, he sat down in the boat, his rolled-up cuffs draining saltwater, and seized the gunnels, feeling every weathered grain, every knot, every splinter, and even swayed with the rocking hull beneath him. When he settled in, leaning back, letting the wind take his hair, the laughing dark-eyed woman hiked her worn skirt, flashed a slender, sunbaked thigh, and leaned into the oars. Rhythmically she leaned, moaned at her effort, pulled and fell back, her bare feet now raised and braced on the creaking thwart between them, her knees spread, breasts swelling, bursting, spilling nipples over the stretched and dipping neckline of the blouse. This was the place when it always began getting good.

Suddenly, undreamlike, came a jangling.

What?

The screen fuzzied, the old pitching boat and placid turquoise sea and haunting coral sky, never more than faded, began to gray and darken, then . . .

Then he was awake.

Without parting his eyelids he reached his hand out and grabbed the handset on the first snatch. No fumbling, no uncertainty. It was where it should be.

Bringing the mouthpiece to his lips, he rasped, "Spike Halleck."

Ellie's voice, shuddering and sobbing, cut through his stupor. "It's Janey, Spike. She's been kidnapped. Oh, God!"

Halleck sat straight upright, felt himself gasp. "Are you sure?"

"They left a message on the machine. I—"

"Have you called the police?"

"I don't know, Spike, they said—"

"Brian knows?"

"I just called. He's flying back from Seattle on the next plane out. Still, he won't be here till . . ."

"I'll be right there," he said, finding the white cane at the bedside.

"No. I'll pick you up in—"

"Stay there, Ellie. I'll join you as soon as I can. Stay put."

Fifteen months and a lifetime ago, Jack Halleck, known to his friends and associates as Spike, was standing at ground level looking at a sprawling sound stage for a movie that would eventually be called *MIRAGE*. It was the last thing he would ever see. Yet he would remember those last images with indelible certainty. Unlike the dream, where colors seemed to bleed away, imagined shapes to melt, his last sighted memories remained hauntingly clear.

In accepting it, he could not rationalize that it was just a freak accident, that he had been at the wrong place at the wrong time when the wrong thing happened. No. He had been there because he wanted to be there, and because he loved doing what he was doing. He was never out of work, never worked on what didn't interest him.

He did sound effects.

Sound effects are the most invisible of Hollywood magic. And they are invisible, Halleck knew, for the very seductive and convenient reason that the audience can never *see* them. But if the magic of sounds accompanying the pictures is any less than perfect, the spell is broken, as often, is the film. That's why Halleck had to be there, to see what the audience would see, to hear the original sounds and to make sounds that are more real, more gripping, more devastating, more horrifying or more pleasing than what the boom mikes ever picked up. Nothing recorded during filming is heard in the theaters. Every sound is recreated from scratch, often using tricks secret to the high priests of the art. Halleck was the best.

So he stood, arms folded, script in hand, looking up. The set replicated a hotel lobby, swept by cantilevered terraces and transparent walkways, tier after tier with glassed-in shops poised on the brink of the abyss, as if gravity had vanished so the guests could walk on air.

The script scheduled the set for wholesale destruction

in the last scene. The timing and sequences had been discussed and reworked, the action planned with greater precision than the raid on Entebbe, easy enough when you know what the bad guys will do.

The bad guys were going to kill the presidents of the United States and the Supreme Soviet, who had been lured by disarmament to Helsinki. The preceding scene, involving the gang rape of both first ladies, proved the terrorists intended to off both leaders of the superpowers and that they deserved the fate that was waiting them.

That brought everyone on the set to the last scene, designed to escalate the cinematic art of cataclysm. Enter the good guys, disguised as Jesuit priests who infiltrate the Papal suite, where his holiness was stopping en route to the Vatican.

That was the situation.

Halleck was glad, still, that he didn't have to face the critics. It wasn't his job. His job was to make it seem more real, by making the noises on the sound track seem more real than the actual noises. It had occurred to him that life is disappointing to many people because the movies have developed unrealistic expectations for experience. Reality can only fail because it had been so stunningly glossed in celluloid fraud.

But that wasn't his responsibility either.

His job this day was to see how he could make the glassy apocalypse boom and tinkle and whoosh and scream like a clarion for exhuming the dead on Judgment Day.

The accoustical reality was never that great. Only by Mount Saint Helens was he completely outclassed, and then he could come close. That's why they hired him.

And that's why he was on the set rather than waiting for the film to leak through the cutting room before thinking about the dubs. He wanted to feel what it should sound like, and he could only do that by seeing the whole panoramic sweep, not just what the cameraman would frame.

First they had to get some shots of the hotel lobby with *real* glass, which is the best substance for making the images on film look sharp, clear, and sparkling. Then, after that was done yesterday, came the change-out guys, who replaced all the glass with a crystalline sugary substitute. Now when the explosives went off, the shards, sounding about as much like real glass as putty, would bounce harmlessly off the stunt men.

They had been doing this in Hollywood for almost forty years.

So Spike Halleck stood close, folded his arms, and watched the last scene he would ever see.

"Places," said the director.

Actors and stunt men scurried about, ready for what they heard next.

"Action."

A moment of silence followed as the cameras began to grind, another reason the stage sound track would never work.

Then the protagonist, a familiar if miscast actor with piercing blue eyes, spat his line into a telephone, "Screw the KGB! If we don't move now, both of them are dead."

Halleck would be responsible for controlling the sound level and modulation of the telephone response, which was, "Then go."

The actor looked up, waved a hand, heard the director say, "Cut," then got his two-million-dollar-a-film body out of the way of what would happen next.

"Places," the director said again. "And everybody on the countdown," one of his favorite theatrical devices. "Four, three, two, *now.*"

Never one, zero. Halleck smiled. Always now.

On *now*, four stuntmen crashed through windows on reinforced nylon climbing ropes, landing together on a catwalk, scattering to the nearest terrace. The bad guys, hearing the noise, thinking, as the audience knew they were supposed to, "What the fuck?" appeared with stunned and angry faces, brandishing Uzis filled with an impossible number of blanks. The firing noises everyone heard in the theater would be made by Spike Halleck.

The bad guys cut loose with a volley of popping blanks.

The charges set by special effects blew out the sugary glass.

The good guys fired back, mowing down terrorists,

who fell with screams that sounded like they had twisted an ankle. It didn't matter. All Spike Halleck needed was the shape of their mouths. He would find a perfect scream for these dying men and make it work.

On the balcony, a particularly sinister-looking terrorist threw a hand grenade into the central chandelier. None of the screenwriters seemed to have a good explanation why he would do this, except to shrug and suggest that he might have been trying to kill the hero, who had phoned for help. But why not just lob the grenade down directly?

More shrugs. "It's a fucking visual medium, Halleck. A spectacular effect."

No doubt. The chandelier began to fall, with Spike Halleck the closest of anyone, including the stuntmen. He just watched it, nearly twenty feet in diameter, stretch and burst away from its suspension and fall, in what seemed, perhaps because of its size, like slow motion, taking on a slow rotation as it plummeted down, actually whistling air as it fell faster and faster. There would be a lot of sugar to clean up from this, he thought. The place will be sticky for months.

Except it wasn't sugar.

He could tell that from the sound, which is where he was the best. By then it was too late. Shattering glass has the terrifyingly numbing high-pitched hissing ring, the hiss from so many places the air was being cut to pieces at once, the ring, ring, ring for each explosion. Before he could duck, the shock front had peppered his face. When they got to him, the man who made sounds more real was making no sound at all. Bleeding, dazed, unable to see, he was in shock. What had gone wrong?

What had gone wrong?

In an industry that prided itself on detail, someone had forgotten one. Simple as that.

Spike Halleck did not sue.

Spike Halleck did not complain.

Spike Halleck did not blame.

He did not even quit.

He finished the job, the way they wanted him, too. Using an assistant, he developed better techniques for sequencing sounds, like using a recording optical microdensitometer to insert machine-gun noises, timing each burst on the sound track to the instant of maximum intensity of light bursting from the gun muzzle. But it was his last job. He was blind.

The studio gave him a generous pension and forgot.

It was an accident.

Accidents happen.

It was too bad but they couldn't do anything about it.

Spike Halleck was thirty-four years old. If you believe the actuaries, he had over forty years of blindness left. Now what the hell good was a blind man? he kept asking himself. A blind man can't even pick out sleeping pills from a drugstore shelf to kill himself.

But suddenly, with Ellie's call, everything had changed. Suddenly, in a conviction as clear as any image his sighted eyes had ever seen, he realized that he may be the best—maybe even the only—chance to keep Janey alive. And Janey, Spike knew, was worth saving. Janey was . . .

Janey was more than a cute face, and less. He could only believe his sister Ellie that she was cute. Spike had seen only pictures of Janey. But that didn't matter. It didn't matter because Janey had shown him presence, the way a person, even a little person, can step forward in the darkness and shine. Not a week ago, he had been playing chess with her.

He sat there, making a mental picture of the board, concentrating, listening to her say, "I moved my horse up two and one to the side."

"Which side?" Halleck asked, revising his mental picture. "To your right or your left?"

A moment of silence, then this, "I can't tell right or left."

"Did you move the knight—the horse—to the side of the board nearest the hand you draw with?"

Silence again. He could almost hear her mind turning. "No," she sighed, "to the other side."

"Then it's the right. The hand you draw with is your left."

"How come?"

"How come what?"

"How come they call the hand I draw with my left?"

"Because it is."

"But it's the same hand I write with, so why isn't it called my write hand?"

"Because it isn't."

"Your move, Spike."

"I know."

"How do you remember where all the pieces are if you can't see 'em?"

"I make a picture in my head."

"And you, like, redraw the picture every time I make a move?"

"Yeah."

"Wow."

"Not so wow, really. You can do it."

"Nah, I can't."

"Sure you can. It's the way you keep from tripping over Chombo when you go to the bathroom at night. You know where he is."

"Nah. I never go at night. I learned to hold it in till morning."

"Come on!"

"Really. I feel it's more ladylike."

"I see."

"No you don't, Spike. You're *blind*!"

"It's an expression."

"You used to be able to see. Before the accident."

"That's right."

Silence. Halleck could hear the gears turning, almost feel the smile that infected the next question. "What if I actually put the horse in a different place, to mess you up?"

"I'd get you."

Janey giggled. "How?"

"I'd get you. I'd tickle you until your teeth fell out."

"I'd run."

"I'd catch you."

"No you wouldn't. You can't see me."

"But I can hear you. And you giggle. Even if you didn't, I'd hear everything—your steps, your breathing. I'd know just where you were."

21

And he remembered all that with all the clarity and more of having seen it, which he didn't, but having once seen he could now accurately project the positions of objects in space from the projection points of noises and even, recently, from the reflections and echoes. It was a talent like a strange and beautiful flower that blossomed only in darkness. But having spent ten years where his life depended on knowing exactly what sounds any object made, and how much they seemed to sound like other objects, made him perhaps the most observant blind man alive.

Even if he wasn't, he felt that he had what it took to determine exactly where Janey was. What was it she had said? You can't see me. No, I can't. But nobody can now. So the only way we can tell where you're hidden is to look very carefully into the one clue we have, the ransom calls.

The one who planned it looked through the door to check on the kid. She was still under, the chloroform still holding. He wanted to make sure her breathing got back to normal before he gagged her, so she didn't suffocate. But even now her wrists were bound, her eyes blindfolded. She wasn't going anywhere or seeing anything.

The parents would want to talk to her.

He had figured on that.

Closing the door, he returned to the connecting room, where his partner stared at the TV, snapping back and forth to different channels. "This is shit," he said. "I'm goin' out for a video."

"You got a card?"

"Fran gave me one."

"Don't use your own."

"What, you think I'm stupid?"

He let that go.

The other zipped up his jacket, headed for the door. Turning, he smiled. "Hey, you wanna pop the kid?"

"What?"

"You wanna bust 'er cherry?"

"Get your video."

"Uncle a mine said he had a Cong girl 'bout her age in Vietnam, said they're real tight, a real turn-on."

"Pay cash."

"Sure. Hey, I'll let you, too, if you want."

"Go."

And the other left. No need to fight, no need for anger, to reveal that the thought of fucking a six-year-old kid sickened him. He wouldn't stand for that, even if she only had three days left to live.

Spike whisked through the hotel lobby. From the vacuum motor he could tell they were cleaning. Harold, the doorman, said, "Good evening, Mr. Halleck," with enough in the sound of those words to tell him that Harold was a disenchanted early middle-aged Pole, largely unread, probably with a wife he hated and a few children he felt ambivalent about. He worked as much as he could because he hated being home. And because tips never showed up as salary, so his old lady'd never see it.

"Taxi, Mr. Halleck?" Spike was close enough now to smell the cheap bourbon.

"Why don't I try to catch it myself?"

"Tough getting 'em to stop. They go right by, who knows why?"

Which was Harold's way of saying that if they do go right by, there's no way a blind man would ever know, was there? So why not give me a five for saving you the trouble of making an ass of yourself, you damn cripple?

"Why don't I just try?" Halleck repeated.

"Lotta hacks see someone looks a little funny, y'know, they think, well, maybe they think it's some kinda, whatdayacallit, like a trick. Like you're gonna get in there, pull those glasses off, put a gun the back'a their head and, y'know, blow their brains out or somethin'. Can hardly blame 'em for not stoppin', unless they know someone they're familiar with and all that."

Meaning Harold.

"If I have trouble, I'll ask you, and only you, to help me out. Okay?"

"Sure. Oh, Mr. Halleck, let me get the hinged door, here. Revolving one's busted or somethin'."

Spike moved a little to his right, found the revolving door, pushed on one of its panels. It turned. Looking exactly where he knew Harold to be, he said, "Looks like it fixed itself."

"Well, whatayaknow? Looks like it's your lucky day."

Spike stood down from the curb and raised his cane, looked to his left. The wind off Lake Shore Drive was blowing in, cutting down the concrete valleys, scudding newspapers along the sidewalk behind him, fluttering the scalloped canvas awning on the canopy leading down to the street. From the sounds, all the sounds he heard, Spike studiously reconstructed the corresponding three-dimensional reality. To keep oriented, he rebuilt the sight he had lost from the hearing he had not. In order to survive and remain independent, he imagined each instant the camera shot that belonged to the sound effects around him. Instead of working forward, adding sound to pictures, he now worked in reverse. At first it had been hard, and humbling. But like anything, it improved with practice.

He heard the cab pull up, the hack get out, say, "Let me help you here."

"It's all right," Halleck said, opening the door for himself.

"That's the front seat," the hack said.

"I know," he said. "I won't get thrown around so much up here."

"Whatever you say."

"1435 Oakvale, Lake Forest."

"Got it."

When the cab pulled up outside his sister's house, Halleck asked, "What's the fare?"

"Seventeen thirty-five."

He reached into his wallet, pulled out bills.

The cabbie cleared his throat. "Why don't we have someone inside come out, make sure it's right."

Halleck held four fresh fives like a fan of cards and directed his dead eyes right to the spot he knew the man must be sitting. "What's your name, friend?"

"Like it says on the license here, Malone."

Cute. "Malone what?"

"Gerry Malone. So what's it to you?"

"All right, Gerry." Halleck thrust the bills right under the driver's nose. "Here's twenty. Keep the change."

"How do you know it's right? Could be ones, right?"

"Four fives. Twenty."

"Listen, you can't know it's twenty, buddy."

"It's twenty."

"Let's get someone out here to help you out."

"When I need help, I ask for it. When I don't, I won't. Right now I don't. So let's do business in a way we can agree." Halleck slipped the fives back in his billfold, tucked it neatly into his suitcoat pocket, and told the hack, "Open your hand."

"What the fuck you talkin' about?"

Halleck snapped out his hand and shackled the cabbie's wrist. The man tried to pull away but couldn't budge.

"Just open your hand." Halleck could feel from the tendons in the man's wrist that the fingers were extended. Then he fished in his pocket and pulled out a quarter. Using his free hand he pressed it into the cabbie's palm. "Let's start by agreeing that's a quarter."

"Sure it's a quarter."

"Close your hand. Make sure. Hold onto what you've got."

The driver did it.

Halleck put his hand over the driver's and began to squeeze.

"Hey," the guy grunted. "Leggo."

"You know why I call a quarter jerkoff money?"

"I don't know," the man squirmed as Halleck squeezed tighter. "Why?"

"Because if I know someone is trying to rip me off because he knows I can't see the bills, he gets paid off in quarters. It works like this: You don't like my fives, all right. We go to a little bill-changing machine I know, a couple of blocks from the Loop. I put in the bill. If it's a one, like you say, I'll get four quarters in the change dish. But if I'm right and it's a five, I get twenty quarters in the dish. Whichever way, we stand there feeding the machine until you get your fare—but no tip—in quarters. And since we seem to be able to agree what a quarter is, there's no argument. Comprende? But if you're wrong, and you're just trying to boost the fare, you drive me back here free."

Halleck could hear the man breathing hard with pain as he squeezed on his hand.

"Deal?"

"Okay. Just leggo, buddy. Your money's good."

"Apologize."

"What?"

"Apologize. Say, I'm sorry."

"I'm sorry for Chrissake. Now leggo."

Halleck relaxed his grip. "And don't ever try to take advantage of a blind person again."

"Jesus, buddy, you're fucking crazy."

"Believe it."

Halleck stepped out and made his way up the flagstone path to the house.

Not a second passed between the instant he rang the doorbell and the moment he heard it open, felt the wave of heated air wash over him, felt Ellie's desperate hug and, "I'm so glad you're here. I've been going crazy." Her body was trembling, her voice broken.

Putting his hand on her shoulders, he backed her off.

"When will Brian get back?"

"Nine-thirty. O'Hare."

"Call the airline. Leave a message at the arrival gate that he's to take a cab home. You don't want him driving with this on his mind. Have you called the police yet?"

"Brian wanted me to, but I told him he had to hear what the tape said first."

"Where's the tape?"

"Still in the machine."

"Put a new tape in the answering machine. Let's hear the message on the stereo deck."

Knowing the house, he followed Ellie as she went to the answering machine and pulled the tape. "Here."

"Let's hear it."

"Spike, I can't listen. I just can't. It's too upsetting."

"Then just let me listen. And I'll need to take a copy."

"But it's evidence, Spike."

"Once I've made a copy, you can give the original to the police."

"But why?"

Halleck had to explain the obvious. "Ellie, listen to me. Maybe you call the police. I hope you do. We're going to need their help. But there are some things they can't, or won't do, some things that maybe, just maybe, I can do."

"Spike, for God's sake! Janey's been kidnapped! You're blind! What goddamn good is it going to do for you to have a copy of the tape! If we can't get her back—"

"That's exactly what I'm trying to do."

"What?"

"The tape, every tape, has a lot of information nobody ever notices. You, the police, listen to the words, maybe analyze the voice of the kidnapper, maybe set up a plan to pick him up when you make the drop, which means, at best, you get the kidnapper. What you really want is Janey, isn't that right?"

"Of course." Ellie's voice was still cracking with despair.

"That means you've got to locate her, not the kidnappers, before the time runs out."

"I don't see how the tape will give you that."

"Because *every* sound within the frequency range and pickup sensitivity of a telephone is on that tape right now. *Every* sound. Cars, buses, trains, airplanes. *All* on schedules. If we know the time the call came in—"

"No, Spike. I was away. There's no time."

"Or range of times, even, we could pinpoint almost exactly the location by identifying the specific sound with its source."

"You think?" Weak voice, a little hope.

"What else do we have?"

"Spike, I don't know. This seems . . ." He could hear her breathing, shaking her head. "There could be dozens of those kinds of sounds in a city like Chicago. I mean—"

"And there could be only one place where a helicopter with a specific kind of rotor noise was even in the air at that time of day."

He could hear her click the tapes into the stereo deck, press the buttons, and say, "I can't listen to this. Not again. Not until Brian gets here." Then he heard the door slam as she left through the porch into the backyard.

Halleck listened intently as the tape rolled through the prerecorded message.

"If you dialed correctly, you want to talk to us. We're the Granvilles, Brian and Ellie, and, yes, Janey, too. And if you leave your name, telephone number, the time you called, and a brief message, we'll get back to you as soon as we can. Just wait for the beep."

After the beep came another message, this one in a deep, gravelly voice, in heavy cadenced breathing and nasal, midwestern accent.

"We got your kid, folks. We kinda thought you should know so ya don't worry."

Here came a cough, another, then

"Well, you ain't home, so we can't tell ya nothin' yet about when we want the cash or nothing, 'cept that it should be small bills, nothin' as stupid as ta think about markin' 'em or nothin'. But it's gonna be, say two hundred thousand, that's cheap for a big banker, a course. Time and place later. I don't want to hurt the kid— she's cute—so don't do nothin' stupid like callin' the cops. Just think a this as a business deal. Maybe take her college money'ur somethin'—I don't know—if ya don't get 'er back, what hell good is it?"

A click yielded to a dial tone, then nothing. The tape ended with a message, they had Janey, a promise, to call back for arrangements, and a threat, not to involve the police. They had already made one mistake, Halleck thought. By not leaving enough information for the parents to focus on a time and date for return, the kidnappers had created enough uncertainty to force the police in. Panic would drive Ellie and Brian that way. And he couldn't tell them it was wrong, however he felt. It wasn't his kid, so it wasn't his call. Still, the police, and next the FBI, could never do one thing as well as he could. They could never tell exactly what the place where Janey was being kept sounded like. And there was only one place in Chicago, if they still were in Chicago, that sounded like that. And Halleck bet his life, and Janey's, that he could tell exactly where that was. The only question was, how long did he have?

He walked out through the screened-in porch, out the door, down the three steps, into the backyard, over the brick walkway, to where he could hear Ellie sobbing. It tore him to hear her, but he had to put all that away and master his feelings with his thoughts. Putting his hand exactly where he could tell her shoulder was, he said, calmly as he could, "Don't answer the phone again. Let the machine take everything until either the police or I can get it wired. It's a toss-up who can get it set up first. Still it's time we called them in. FBI, too."

"Call them," she said.

"You've got to do it. I can't make the report. Only you can, Ellie. You or Brian. Do it now."

She got up. "All right." Firmer, better. She was no longer waiting, no longer victim.

"Then get off the phone."

"You think the kidnappers will know?"

"No way. I'm not concerned about them right now. I just have a call of my own to make."

He could feel her looking at him strangely, in the strange way he had learned that contextual silence gives a blind person eyes. And he knew that she must have thought he was crazy until he said, "I have to call Midway Electronics to get what I need. They are the only people I know who deliver. I'll need your American Express card."

"Let me tell you the number," she said.

"Never mind. Just make your call and give me the card. I can feel them." In fact he could feel more than that. Having once heard the kidnapper's voice, he could already feel something about him, from the way he talked and what he said, he could tell something about the way the kidnapper thought. And he could feel more than that, too. Without hearing anything, he felt time working against him.

2

Sergeant Janowski of the Chicago Police was a huge man with a slow, methodical manner who ate garlic at lunch and was late for dinner. Halleck could tell all that without seeing him, from the smell of his breath, the rumbling of his stomach, and from the sounds he made after he walked through the door of Ellie's house. His ear had been that good even before he was blinded. At home in Palos Verdes, he used to sit in his study overlooking the Pacific and close his eyelids to extinguish the visual distractions so he could concentrate exclusively on sound, on what sounded exactly like something else and what, if any, differences there were between the two sounds. Not that those differences mattered much on film. On film if the action was fast and if the created sound was very close to the actual sound, it would always create the desired illusion. But Halleck himself could always tell the difference. And he had learned early, from friends who blindfolded him at parties, that he had a talent not only for identifying sounds but gleaning detailed information from them.

Like Sergeant Janowski's voice. The basso profundo meant a large larynx, hence, a large man. Not only that. When Ellie circled behind him to hang up his coat, the intensity of her voice dropped as she passed. Janowski was a big object, maybe tall, maybe just fat. In either case, wide.

Halleck could hear him dig into his sport coat, smell the sweat waft through the foyer, then hear the rustle of paper pages on a small notepad. He had been around screenplays so long that it didn't surprise him to hear

31

what Janowski said. "Mrs. Granville, where is it you think your daughter was abducted?"

"She was with a group at the Chicago Art Institute. They were all holding hands and"—Halleck heard Ellie sob, Janowski pat her on the back—"she was the last one, the most responsible, always made sure everybody else was safely on the bus back. I can't figure what really happened. Maybe there was a crush of people going out, they lost sight of her, then she was gone."

"So they didn't report it?"

"They didn't know, still don't. After the call I got so terrified for Janey that I didn't call anyone but her father and uncle."

"So you figure she was taken about when? Three-thirty?"

"I guess. They left the Institute then."

"And you got the call?"

"When I got in about four forty-five. I was supposed to pick her up myself at five."

"And the call came, when?"

"I don't know. They didn't say when."

"So the school group never noticed she was missing?"

"No. I guess that Mrs. Blanchard, the leader, thought that I picked up Janey when everybody else got off the bus."

"But that's not the way they usually do it?"

"Some parents do, if they're in a hurry."

Janowski was getting all this down. Halleck could hear the pencil, probably a gold pencil, scurrying over the small pad.

"Now I'd like to hear the call you got, Mrs. Granville," Janowski said, breathing heavily through his mouth. Allergy or asthma, maybe compounded by a cold. Could be out of shape. If fat, that made sense. It all had to add up.

"Spike has it," Ellie said. He could almost feel her point. Janowski's eyes turned his way.

The sergeant lumbered over, shuffling over the Perisan carpet that graced the foyer in a pattern Halleck would never again see. When Halleck could hear that the policeman was an arm's length away, he held out his hand to shake. The policeman enveloped it in one of those huge, meaty hands that dwarfed normal ones. But Halleck, as the cabbie had discovered, was very strong, and returned the pressure.

"You got the tape?"

Halleck nodded. "And I got Midway Electronics to rig the phone for recording."

"We got our own unit to do that. Should be here soon."

"I suggest leaving the one I have on."

Halleck's voice was firm, full of confidence and authority, but his tone remained only suggestive. The silence that greeted him extended coldly before Janowski said, "We gotta have the trace on it."

Halleck didn't know how to approach this. He knew that a trace could be run both remotely and automatically, on command, for every incoming call, using a distant switching station actuated by the local number. But saying that would make him seem like a smartass. Being a police officer allowed Janowski to make the decision. It could be a stupid decision, an ignorant decision, an impulsive and logically ridiculous decision, but once made it would be almost impossible to get reversed. And Janey had no time for Halleck to wage war on City Hall.

Instead he said, "Why not run the trace from an upstairs extension?"

He heard the tweed sport coat, with its characteristic bristle, shift as Janowski's shoulders shrugged, then, "Why?"

"Because we can get more information on where Janey is being kept if we use the equipment that's already hooked up."

"Whaddyatalkin'about?"

Knowing the floor plan and furnishings intimately, Halleck got up and swept across the foyer, into the living room, probably confusing Janowski, who was used to seeing blind folks tapping their white canes along. Kneeling down, he found the control panel and rewound a third tape he had made by editing the copy. Pushing the PLAY button, he began to run it, explaining to Janowski, "Every tape recording has a lot more information than most people ever imagine. I know because that used to be my job, putting together sound tracks for movies."

"In Hollywood, like?"

"Universal Studios, Warner Brothers, Tristar, Orion. Places like that."

Halleck heard him whistle. Impressed? Hard to tell. For once he wanted to see the expression on the man's face.

"On every master tape," Halleck continued, "the sounds are dubbed in one by one, at the right intensity. The actors re-speak their lines, fitting the words into the movements of their images on film. And as the action was happening, I did the rest, you know, breaking and flying glass," Halleck stopped and tried not to remember, "a roller skater coming in from the background, traffic noises like horns, screeching brakes, drivers yelling, all the sounds in all the places that ought to have sounds on film. And I had to make the levels of sounds, the intensities, right. If you have a motorcycle clearing a hill and zooming down at the camera, you have to mix the sound so it gets louder as the cycle approaches and so the sound you use is Doppler shifted to higher than natural frequency as the bike approaches, then suddenly shifts to lower pitch as it recedes, just the way it does in life."

"We ain't got no sound track here, Mr. Halleck. We got a kidnapper with a threat. I take that pretty serious. Don't you?"

Halleck wanted to grab the man by his lapels and shout, "Is it your niece?" Instead he counted to ten. Better. Calm now. Make him understand. "I know that. And I know that putting sounds on tape isn't going to get Janey back. But the process, Sergeant Janowski, of putting sounds on, of synthesizing a sound track, can be reversed. We used to do it all the time. If we used a sound, for example a rolling bottle that didn't clink when the bottle on the screen slipped, we could go back and erase it—not the whole sound track—just the bottle sound. And while I don't have that kind of control on these calls, I can, with work, get a lot of the contributing noises out of the composite sound track."

"So what?"

"The place where Janey is *right now* has what we call an accoustical signature. It's like a picture except that instead of being made up of lines and colors and shadows, it's made up of sounds. In fact the place where the kidnappers are holding Janey is characterized—made up—of all the sounds around that place, of all the things that move, pass, act on, or function in that place, from jet airliners passing overhead to dripping faucets inside."

"Again, so what if the place is on a flight path with bad plumbing, there's lots of places like that. Hundreds maybe."

"And there are a lot of places not on a flight path and without bad plumbing, like Lake Forest here. So even if you don't know exactly where to look, you know where not to look."

A wall of silence stood for about a minute until the big policeman sighed and said, "I think we should concentrate on the message."

"You mean the ransom demands?"

"Time and place, see where we are."

"We don't know." Halleck plucked up the cassette and chucked it over his shoulder, knowing it would land right in Janowski's midsection. "Right now, on this tape, you have a man's voice. Sounds a little like you, but it isn't you."

"I know that."

"But I can *prove* that," Halleck said, "because your voiceprint wouldn't match the kidnapper's. But his would. Now if you catch him, you've already got your first piece of scientifically acceptable evidence toward conviction."

"I think we should listen to Spike, Sergeant," Ellie said.

"This is a police matter, Mrs. Granville."

Halleck didn't know what else to say, so he said nothing, trying not to explode.

Finally he asked, "What are the chances, statistically, of getting Janey back if we do it your way?"

Janowski let another minute lapse before Ellie prompted, "Well?"

"Not very good."

"And the FBI will be notified, as required?"

"Yes, they will, after a preliminary report here."

"And what is the FBI position on ransom demands?" Halleck knew the answer.

"No negotiation. Make them an offer to leave the girl someplace in exchange for breaking off the hunt. That's the best they'll do."

"So the FBI will have no idea where to look, no pressure to apply, and will still make an ultimatum to release the girl or else?"

"That's it."

"Imagine," Halleck controlled his voice, "that you're the killer. How do you respond to that?"

Janowski let out another sigh, alloying his fatigue, annoyance and impatience all in one hard metallic sound. "What you got, Halleck? I can't make a recommendation without seeing what this amounts to."

Halleck pushed the PLAY button again. "I want you to hear three things, from highest to lowest confidence," he said, suddenly excited. In just an hour after receiving the rig from Midway Electronics he had used a multichannel analyzer and intensity integrator to give him three vital pieces of information regarding sound sources at or near the location that the kidnapper was calling from.

"Listen to this," Halleck whispered as the tape played. Because each sound was recorded at low levels, the background was an increasingly loud hiss. "Forget the static," he told Janowski. "We can get that out when the suppressor gets here from California."

"From California?"

"Coming in by Redeye tonight."

"California?"

"Listen."

The first sound leapt out, something between a ding and a struck cymbal, repeating at regular intervals, falling off and repeating without regularity. "Hear it?" he asked Janowski.

"Sure."

"That was inaudible in the original tape. It had to be isolated and enhanced."

"What is it?"

"Best guess? A wind chime."

"Wind chime?"

"Right. We had gust off the lake today, right? Sound is right, probably hanging from a window or eave where they're keeping her, something you could ask every cop in the city to look out for, report on. And it means she isn't in some high-rise or tenement."

Janowski's silence told Halleck he was either very interested or very skeptical.

"Next, this. I picked it up using a short interval percussive filter, nothing fancy but I got it at low level, then I ran over and enhanced. Here it is."

A sharp, faint, high-pitched, pulsing ring burst out, stopped, started again, stopped, came again, maintained, then stopped before the caller hung up.

"Recognize it?" Halleck teased.

Janowski said, "Not right off."

"Jackhammer on concrete, point blade."

He played it again, heard Janowski say, "Yeah."

"But the last one is most interesting."

He held his hand up for silence as the sound bled in, very faintly, a long, lamentable wail, a near screaming, but not human. A mechanical sound. It lasted about three seconds then stopped.

"I'll be damned," Janowski said. "It's the L."

"Sounds like braking to me. They've got her near an L station."

"How are you sure it's Chicago?"

"We make them a counteroffer on their next call."

"Is that safe?"

"Better to act than react," Halleck said. "Besides, it buys time. Time we can use to find a place with a wind chime near an L platform where a jackhammer is breaking up concrete. As long as they think they've got a chance to get the money, they won't quit. As long as we can keep Ellie and Brian apparently acting scared and cooperative, and persuasive, we can be sure they're not going to kill Janey, because we're going to make sure that as long as and until we actually drop the money, Ellie and Brian are going to want to talk to Janey, directly, and know that she, not a tape recording of her voice, is responding. That seems the best plan to me."

"And what about us? And the FBI?"

"I'll need you both. I'll need your eyes and your ears. And I've hooked this tape recorder into a digital clock now, with a headphone-isolated voice synthesizer for me. That means that whatever sounds appear on the tape will be imprinted with the time and date, which means that anything that moves on a schedule and makes a record on the tape will bring us that much closer to where Janey is."

"All right, Halleck. But it's just an angle. Ordinarily I would want to get out a picture on the news, to have everyone looking for her."

"Negative."

"What?"

"If Janey's picture turns up on the Evening News, they'll know that Brian and Ellie have contacted you."

"Still, I'd like to alert the docks and airports."

"Then get the picture to the managers. Ellie, do you have one?"

"Yes, Spike."

"Let Sergeant Janowski have it."

She rushed to the living room, plucked one from the fireplace mantel and handed it to the policeman, who was already retrieving his coat from the foyer closet. As he opened the door to leave he turned back and said, "I hope you can make this work, Halleck."

"You have any better ideas?"

"Not right away."

"And keep your search off the police band radio. Best to make the announcements in squadroom sessions only. If these guys are smart, they'll be listening in for any sign that something is funny. If they get spooked, they'll move."

"At least," Janowski said.

The kid was sleeping, or just out. The chloroform had knocked her cold and fast, as they hoped. There was no scene. Nobody worried, nobody interfered. Tim's attendant's outfit worked like a charm. They carried her to the closed restroom, slipped her into a plastic bag, then had Tim walk the bag of "trash" out back.

Under three minutes, start to finish.

Like clockwork.

He was fixing himself a cup of coffee when Tim pushed

through the door, pulled the muffler away from his face, put down the rented videotapes on the battered coffee table. Clint Eastwood in *Heartbreak Ridge*, Chuck Norris in *POW*, Arnold Schwarzenegger in *Predator*. From the bag in his other hand came a six-pack of Strohs, a pack of Slim Jims, and a bag of Pretzel Twists. Drinking could be a problem with Tim and he knew it. Turning to pull the whistling kettle from the stove behind him, he heard Tim ask, "When you gonna call back?"

"When it gets darker."

"Soon?"

Tim sounded nervous, anxious, so he tried to stay calm. "Soon," he told him.

"Sure as hell glad that jackhammer quit. Driving me fucking crazy."

Wonderful, he thought. Tim should love the dog next door.

"Girl awake yet?" Tim overeager, popped open the first can of Strohs.

"Negative."

"Maybe we killed her."

"Negative."

"Hey, can I go in there and play with her pussy until she wakes up?"

Tim, he thought, what am I gonna do with you. Still calm, quelling the rage he felt inside, he said, "Let's watch one of them videos, man."

"Then you call again?"

He nodded.

"Man, we're gonna be fuckin' rich. And she's gonna be fuckin' dead, man. So why can't I go in there and play with her?"

3

Halleck could just hear Brian's taxi pulling into the serpentine driveway, the door slamming, when the kidnapper's second call set the phone jangling. Before picking up, Spike turned and looked over his shoulder at the darkness where he knew Sergeant Janowski and Ellie were standing and said, "Keep him away. Let me handle it."

She whispered, "Okay" hoarsely and went to detain her husband.

Rejoining them after dinner, Janowski had been clear about the next stage, the critical second call. Talk to them. If they let the machine handle it, to buy time, they might panic. And anything that made her captors nervous could leave Janey real dead real soon. Still, Halleck had written his own script and would play it, struggling to remain detached, as if it were all an illusion. Or, as the caller had suggested, a business deal.

Brian Granville was a banker, a senior veep at First Chicago National, whose shiny new chrome and glass headquarters was etching out a new skyline where Lake Shore Drive spilled into the Gold Coast. Brian knew business, knew deals. A deal is where both parties got what they wanted. That's all, Halleck would insist, the father wanted. Janey for the money. But nothing less than a mutually agreeable exchange.

He picked up on the second ring.

The adrenaline lanced through him, the sweat began to flow, but his voice was low, firm, and, steady. "Granville residence."

"You Mr. Granville?"

41

"No. I'm Mr. Halleck, his brother-in-law."

A long silence intruded. Don't hang up, he thought. "I'm Mr. Granville's authorized negotiating agent for all financial matters of consequence."

"Then you know who this is?"

"I think so."

"And you ain't notified the cops?"

"Your message of this afternoon said not to, and we regard that as part of the deal."

"Smart. So let's talk."

"Please."

Halleck could not himself hear the electronic gear at work, the high-resolution tapes picking up every detail from the caller's background, the digital clock laying in time markers. And if *he* couldn't hear it, he was sure the caller never would.

"Two hundred thousand, like we said."

We. More than one. Another piece of information? Or just a figure of speech? No, it had to be more than one. This was a different voice than the first, sibilant and more slowly cadenced, heavily nasal and congested.

"We know the amount."

"Tomorrow."

"Not possible."

"You want the kid dead? Cute kid. Don't know why you want her dead."

"We don't. But not even the vice president of a bank can walk into a vault and just take two hundred thousand dollars, even in an emergency. There are laws that govern such transactions, federal laws. And no bank president is going to risk going to jail for five years to save a girl who may or may not still be alive."

"She's alive all right."

"How do we know?"

Shuffling sounds, followed by, "Mommy?"

"It's Spike, Janey. How are you?"

"Scared, Spike. I'm real scared."

"Are you hurt?"

"No. I'm hungry, though."

"Enough," the voice returned.

"Not so," Halleck said. "If we have a deal, we have a

deal. This is business, between you and me. I represent the Granvilles. You represent yourself and your partner. In two days, not one, we can have the money. Are you interested in an exchange?"

"Well, a'course."

"Then we must stipulate three conditions."

"Hey, now wait a—"

"First, we must know that you are in the Chicago area, not phoning from a distant point. So once this call is completed, you will go to a place where you can call from a public phone. You will call here, identify yourself as the party of the second part. Repeat."

"The party of the second part?"

"Correct. In the background of your call will be some Chicago sound that can be verified as real and live."

"This is a trick?"

"No trick. I'm not telling you where to go. You choose. Just make sure we can hear a live Chicago sound."

"Like what?"

"The waves pounding on Lake Shore Drive."

"You want me to go to Lake Shore Drive?"

"I want you to go where *you* choose. Just give me a Chicago sound."

"Fuck you."

Halleck held his breath, his heart raced. "Don't let one trip stand between you and two hundred thousand dollars," he said. "How long is two days?"

"I'll call back."

"Wait. Second, each time you call, we talk to Janey. And I mean talk. I don't want her to pop on and say, 'I'm okay' or 'They're treating me fine,' because all that can be tape recorded before you kill her. I want to ask her questions, not about where she is, because I really don't care. What I need to know is *how* she is. From now on, because it is a business deal, and only a business deal, we will talk about the merchandise and the payment, is that clear?"

"Merchandise?"

The line suddenly went dead, leaving Spike stuck with a dial tone. He looked around, or moved his head as if he could still see, searching the gray nothingness for help. From the corner Janowski said, "Hang up the phone, Mr. Halleck."

"What did I do wrong?"

"Just hang it up."

Spike did, asked again, "Where did I screw up?"

"He was just being smart, avoiding a trace."

"Trace?"

Halleck could almost hear Janowski nod, could hear him grunt. Again the phone rang. He picked up.

"You really *want* her dead, don't you?" the voice snarled.

"Never." Spike overreacted, regretted it. Stay cool.

"Then why you try to hang me up on a trace?"

"What are you talking about?"

"You got the police there, don't you?"

"Look. The police don't solve kidnappings. They only get hostages killed. We here want the merchandise. This is a business deal."

"I'll call back."

Again the phone went dead.

"What now?" The question was directed at Janowski.

"We wait," Janowski said.

"Wait for what?"

Halleck could hear the cop's tweed sports jacket shift with a shrug. Janowski made a guess. "How about a Chicago sound? That's what you asked for, isn't it?"

"I did, didn't I?"

"Which is no damn good to us," Janowski said, "because it takes us away from the sounds where the girl is being kept."

After a ruckus in the foyer, Brian Granville stormed in. "My God, officer, what's being done about this? What are you doing to search for my daughter? What the hell's going on?"

"Ask Halleck here."

"Spike"—Brian's voice was strained with tension, angry yet scared—"what is he talking about?"

"Calm down, Brian. I think I have a way to find Janey. I think that using the sounds from these calls, we can narrow down where she is to within a block or two."

"Are you crazy?" Halleck could feel Brian's breath, smell the liquor he must have had on the plane.

"Ask Sergeant Janowski if he has a better idea."

"Well?" Brian said.

"We usually wait until they pick up the drop after the demand for money, follow them, hope we can pick up the kid or cut a deal where they give us the location where the kid is."

"That sounds safer than trying to trick them. Give them the money and we get Janey."

"What's their incentive?"

"What?" Brian said.

"What's their incentive to return Janey? You give them the money, they claim they found her run down by a bus somewhere, use some other story if caught. But giving her back is producing the evidence for their own conviction, especially if she's seen them. If she's seen them, seen their faces, they almost have to kill her to protect themselves from the death penalty. Their only concern is getting the money *first*. And the only way we have to keep Janey alive is to play for time in getting the money to them, and to find where she is before it's time for the drop."

"Is that true?" Brian's voice shot off in Janowski's direction.

"It's one possibility."

"I don't know," Brian sighed. "I just don't know."

"We already know—"

"Know?" Janowski cut in.

". . . with high probability believe that Janey is being held in a place with a wind chime, maybe visible in the window, certainly where the wind is blowing hard, maybe near the lakefront, and in a place where a jackhammer is breaking up the concrete, within earshot, maybe two, three at the most, blocks from an L platform. How many places are there like that?"

"There could be hundreds!" Brian exploded.

Halleck stayed cool. "And there are hundreds of thousands of places in and around Chicago where she could be hidden. So we've already narrowed the search by a factor of a thousand in the first five hours."

"Needle in a haystack," Brian muttered.

Halleck wanted to ask if he had a better idea, but Brian felt helpless, was too emotionally paralyzed to analyze. That's where Halleck came in. He said, "I have to analyze the most recent tapes. Sergeant Janowski?"

"Yes?"

"We know something about how these men speak. There are at least two of them, each with regional inflections and certain speech pathology. Is it possible to trace the records for that sort of thing?"

"No, no records on that."

"So nothing?"

In the few seconds of silence that followed, Halleck could almost hear Janowski's brain grinding. After a full minute passed he said, "We could maybe ask the guards and wardens in the prisons. They live with these guys. They know how they talk."

"How soon?"

"We can move right away. But it might be tomorrow before we have anything."

"Try to hurry it along."

"Okay. Anything else?"

"All your patrol cars on the lookout for wind chimes and jackhammers within two to three blocks of an L stop. And if no jackhammers, look for sidewalks broken up, something the jackhammer has already done."

Janowski raised his voice and cut in. "There could be a hell of a lotta wind chimes hidden from sight, you know. I can't promise to turn 'em all up."

"I'm not asking for everything right now. I'd just like to have *something*," Halleck said. "So let's go with what we do find and see what turns up. Maybe we'll get lucky fast."

He could hear the tweed in Janowski's coat rustle as the cop said, "I'll get it out."

"Squad rooms only. Remember, they may have police band radio. Our deal says no police. Let's make everything we do consistent with that."

"Ever think you're in the wrong business, Halleck?"

Spike couldn't make out that tone. Admiration? Mockery? A mixture? He said, "Being blind is always the wrong business, if you have a choice."

"Then why is it you see things better than anyone else?"

"Ask me again after I've analyzed these last tapes."

"Better hurry," Janowski said. "I think you gotta another call comin'. And I think they're gonna prove to you what you already know. They're here. They're in the city."

"I know," Halleck said. "But where?"

Halleck desperately wanted something from the last call, some new and tangible clue that got them closer. For the first time the recording was marked with time clues, superimposed blips that indicated, every fifteen seconds, the local time. Now for the first time he was in a position to tie the occurrence of a sound to a schedule. But what he actually got was a wasteland. Nothing notable.

Or practically nothing.

There was something he thought was the wind chime, a tink, tink, tinking sound, but the timbre and frequency was different from the earlier sound. And instead of a cacophony of chimes, a noise for each plate in an array, there was only one ping, not as if tossed by the wind, but more or less regular. He *knew* that sound, knew that it wasn't the chime. It was louder, closer to the telephone. It was a different pitch. It was regular and monotonic.

Think!

What would the caller have, close to the phone, that made a sound like that? Why was it so familiar?

Ellie's shaky voice cut in. "Spike. What can I get for you?"

"Coffee," he said, "black."

"Coming up."

"How's Brian?"

"Having trouble. You know, wants action yesterday."

"And?" He could tell from what *wasn't* said that Ellie needed to say, "He thinks we should consider putting her photo out on the media. Television. Fliers to supermarkets, that sort of thing."

"What does Janowski say?"

"He says it's one approach."

"Diplomatic," said Halleck.

"What do you think, Spike?"

"I want Janey back, alive and well. That's all. Now maybe if we play for time, we'll get enough from these tapes to tell where she is, exactly. Then we can protect her better. Then we can go in for her. But even if we don't, Ellie, we can still negotiate with the money, make a drop, hope they let her go according to the arrangements."

"What arrangements?"

"The one I'm going to lay down. They hung up before that part, but they'll get it the next time we talk."

"So what do you want me to do, Spike?"

"Convince him, Ellie. He trusts you."

"I don't know, Spike."

"Sure you do."

"No, I don't!"

"Do you remember when I first came out here, after the accident? Do you remember how he insisted on taking responsibility, how he wanted to have me chauffeured all over the place, how he practically wanted someone to hold my dick when I peed?"

She sputtered a laugh. "Yeah, I do."

"And he wouldn't believe me when I told him I could get around. He wouldn't believe I could be safely independent. He just wouldn't accept that I wasn't going to get run down in an intersection. He just wouldn't take no for an answer from me, when it was my life, when I threatened to move away, but he *did* finally accept it from you."

"I remember."

"Now I don't know what you said to him or how you said it, because I thought I had made every possible rational argument I could think of. But he wouldn't accept. Now I may be blind but I'm not stupid, so I'm not going to try to fight him about his own daughter, because it *is* his right, not mine. But Jesus, Ellie, he's too close to it. And he's too stubborn. And on this one he just happens to be wrong. Because right now we are all powerless. Right now the kidnappers are holding all the cards and controlling the pace of the game. Unless we can change that it will play out exactly the way they have it planned for Janey, and we don't know what that means."

"I see."

"Then make Brian see it, too. Make him see that we're in a position like . . . like, well, walking along on a tightrope with nitroglycerine in both hands and we have to be awfully careful to keep our balance, not to slip, not even to breathe too quickly, because all we can afford to do is to take one step at a time, very, very carefully."

"I'll do what I can."

"You're not having doubts?"

"It's just . . . where is she, Spike?"

"Patience."

"Do we have time for a lot of patience?"

"Until the next call then."

"What's going to happen then?"

"You'll see."

"Spike, we have a right to know what you're playing at. It's our daughter!"

"I haven't forgotten that."

"I'm sorry, it's . . ."

"Hey. What does a guy have to do to get a cup of coffee around here? Beg on a street corner?"

"Okay."

Halleck heard Ellie pad off, head upstairs from the den, leaving him to focus on the second sound on the tape that might, just might, be interesting. It was very low, in the background, almost but not quite nonexistent. He asked the computer to bring it out, to enhance it to something, just to take any noise on that segment of the tape, to drop out the majors—meaning the voices—and bring up any signal out of the noise. What he got made him lean forward and strain with excitement.

Could it be?

He ran it back, then over again, normal speed. Still there, almost too good to be true. The high-pitched whining whistle, the whoosh, then the dull roaring sound. Jesus! It really was there. It was *real*.

It was, he was sure, the sound of a commercial jet airliner descending for a landing, passing nearly overhead, or at least close enough to exhibit the characteristic Doppler shift from the high frequency of approach to the lower frequency of receding.

And he had the time now.

The digital beep and synthetic voice annunciator placed the sounds as occurring at ten-thirteen and thirty seconds in the evening, or twenty-two thirteen and thirty on a twenty-four-hour clock.

Halleck was euphoric.

How many airliners could be low enough on approach to be heard overhead on approach to—his heart sank, but only briefly—would it be O'Hare or Midway? He would have to check both. Janowski's people would have to check that out. Still, now they had a beeline overhead, at most, since there were two airports, two. Halleck knew from making airport noises for films that federal regulations required approaching aircraft to be separated by, what? He tried to remember—one minute? And how many runways were working arrivals? More information. Still . . . Then his hope faded. Unless Janey wasn't in Chicago at all.

Upstairs the phone rang.

"Halleck!" Janowski shouted.

"Let me take it," Brian Granville objected.

"Brian," Ellie's voice said, "don't upset them with a new voice. Don't make it seem as if we're changing the rules."

Halleck found himself running up the stairs, swinging around the newel on the landing, leaping two stairs at a time, crossing the foyer and snatching up the phone himself, holding a hand high, a signal for all to be quiet.

"Granville residence," he said breathlessly.

"Listen," the caller told him.

The phone's receiver was filled with what sounded like a wild roar.

"What is it?" Halleck said. He honestly couldn't make it out.

"It's a Chicago sound, asshole. It's the *most* Chicago sound."

"What is it?"

"Turn on your television. Channel Seven. ABC."

The line went dead. Halleck's mind raced. What did television have to do with anything? Still, he said to no one in particular, "Turn on the television. Channel Seven."

Brian exploded. "What the hell has television got to do with getting Janey back, except maybe to get her picture out there, so someone can give us a clue where she might be!"

Ellie again padded into the adjoining living room, turned on the television to the ABC affiliate in Chicago, WABC. The picture snapped in sharply, as did the sound track. Frank Gifford's voice said, "And the Bears are at the Green Bay seventeen, on third down and two, fifty seconds to play in the first half here at Soldier Field on what is turning out to be a cold and typically windy Monday night in Chicago."

Halleck spoke up. "He was at Soldier Field."

"So what?" Brian demanded.

"So he's in Chicago," Halleck sighed. "I wasn't sure before this."

"Spike, this is getting nowhere," Brian fumed.

"*Au contraire*," Halleck shot back. "In the last two phone calls, we just got closer than I ever thought we would, at this point."

"How so?" Janowski said, his curiosity real.

"Get us a map of Chicago, a good one," Spike said.

"I have one in the kitchen, in one of the drawers," Ellie said.

"Get it."

Ellie was off again and back in no time.

"What time did the last call arrive?" Halleck asked.

"About ten forty-four," Janowski said.

"The exact time is on the tape," Halleck explained. "But for quick calculations, let's say ten forty-four for the last call, ten-thirteen for the one before that. That's a difference of thirty-one minutes. Which means what?"

Halleck waited for someone to figure it out. No one did, so he explained. "So the kidnapper, who was concerned about being traced, went from wherever he was holding Janey, to Soldier Field, in thirty-one minutes."

"How do you know he was at Soldier Field?" Janowski asked. "How do you know he didn't just put the receiver up to the speaker of a TV?"

"The crowd noise was muffled," Halleck said, "unlike the TV crowd noise. And the wind was rushing over the telephone mouthpiece. I figure he was outside, maybe in the parking lot. He may still be thinking we would run a trace, didn't want to actually get inside the stadium, where they could seal the entrances."

"Seal the entrances?" Janowski snorted. "Either he's been watching too much TV or this guy is crazy. How could you seal the entrances? And why? Who would we look for even if we knew he was there? Is this guy paranoid?"

"Maybe," Halleck said. "Maybe he's just scared. So we have to keep him very much at ease. We can't afford for him to get nervous. We have to assure him that we are moving as fast as we can, and that we intend to cooperate."

"And how do we do that?" Brian replied, his voice still angry but now flatter, more reasoned.

"We appeal to his greed," Halleck said. "We give him an incentive to stay in the game."

"How?" Janowski said.

"We act like good businessmen," Halleck said. "And offer him a bonus for his cooperation."

"Bonus?" Brian Granville said. "The guy wants two hundred thousand dollars!"

"Which we told him we can't have until the day after tomorrow, when he will expect it. But we can tell him that you have five thousand liquid in savings, available immediately. We ask him where, and when, and under what conditions they want it delivered."

"Just like that?" Brian scoffed.

"No, not just like that. I ask to talk to Janey. That's one of our conditions. This is business, remember? We stick to our obligations, they have theirs. That's the way we play it."

"Then we catch them when they go for the bait?" Brian asked.

"No. Then we let them have it. No tails, no surveillance, no suspicions."

"Let them have it?" Janowski said. "But we could set up surveillance they would never know—"

"Negative."

"How do you know they won't settle for the five thousand, kill Janey, and run!" Brian shouted.

"Because the five thousand was so easy. No mess, no fuss, no bother, no sign of police. And a man who can turn up five thousand overnight, has kept his promises, is worth half a million, can surely turn up the two hundred thousand dollars in two days."

"Risky," Janowski sighed.

"It's risky anyway," Halleck responded.

"No question," the cop agreed.

Halleck turned to the map. "Anyone have a grease pen?"

"I gotta Magic Marker, sorta," Janowski said.

"And now, sergeant, how far can a man drive from Soldier Field in thirty-one minutes on a Monday night?"

Janowski guessed. "You figure some of these guys drive crazy, even downtown, near the Loop, but still the traffic snarls things up, so even somebody wild about hoppin' lanes isn't gonna make any more than, what, maybe thirty miles an hour, on average, after you count for the time he gets hung up on lights. So thirty miles an hour, max."

"Times thirty minutes," Halleck said, "equals fifteen miles."

"So?" Janowski said.

"So draw a circle fifteen miles in radius around Soldier Field. How much bigger do we make it if he took the L? We know from the first call that there's a station nearby."

"The L would take him longer, because of walking time to the station, waiting for the first train and stops, and because he can't get close to the stadium as fast as he can in a car. So if he goes by public transport, the circle would be smaller."

"Then Janey is being held," Halleck announced confidently, "somewhere in this circle, near an L station, in a place near a broken sidewalk, in a place with a window chime."

Ellie arrived with coffee. "Spike," she said, "you wanted this."

He took it, began stirring, and froze at the spoon's regular clinking sound, suddenly knowing what the first sound on the penultimate tape was. "Held, incidentally," he said before sipping, "by someone who drinks coffee, or tea, or hot chocolate, something he has to drink out of a cup and stir with a spoon."

"How the hell you know that?" Janowski asked.

"The last call he made from the place he's keeping Janey had the sound of a spoon clinking against a coffee cup."

"What the hell good is that little piece of information?" Brian demanded.

"I don't know. But it could mean they're staying in a place that is furnished, has porcelain cups in cabinets. That narrows it, too. Could that mean they're not staying in a hotel room or condemned building, where they would have to bring in coffee in Styrofoam cups. Styrofoam doesn't clink."

"Maybe." Janowski sounded skeptical. Not healthy skeptical, which Halleck was able to accept. More like nervous skeptical, like Brian's nervousness. If so they were losing confidence. That was bad.

"Look at the circle," Halleck said, rapping the map, imagining it himself in his mind. He knew Chicago cold. They had done a film here before, something to add to the Chicago school of *Ordinary People*, *Risky Business*, *Ferris Bueller's Day Off*, *About Last Night*, and *Adventures in Babysitting*. So he knew what they would see. "Figure it out?"

Janowski was first. "Half of it's in Lake Michigan. They ain't there."

"Bingo. So we're down to a semicircle fifteen miles in radius, bordered on the east by the lake shore, centered around Soldier Field. And there's another important consideration."

"What?" Brian's voice. Sharp, impatient.

"The place where they have Janey is near, very near, a flight path. I don't know if it was Midway or O'Hare, but the circle says it has to be one of those. The digital timer on the tape has it happening at ten-thirteen. I'll need someone to run down that kind of information on arriving flights."

"Well, Janowski?" Brian said.

"We can get someone on it, early tomorrow."

"Early tomorrow is too late," Halleck said. "We need someone now. They don't have to be able to carry a gun. But they should know about computers, if possible, and information searches. Maybe a dispatcher, off duty, would do."

"I'll see what I can do, but no promises."

"Good, because I have some equipment arriving at O'Hare from Los Angeles in about twenty minutes. It's coming by special courier, a friend of mine, who will deliver it to my place, where I'm setting up a search center. I'd like an unmarked car to meet him at O'Hare, make sure he gets there all right. The night desk clerk will see that you get in."

"But the calls—" Ellie started.

"Can be rerouted to my place by call forwarding."

"I'll see that your friend gets escorted," Janowski said, picking up the phone. Halleck said, "Let's hurry up. We never know when another call is coming in. If they can't get through, they may figure we've set up a search head-quarters *here.* That means they may panic and, well, you know the rest."

Ellen snatched up the phone and activated the call-forwarding feature on the Granville's phone, asked Spike to repeat his number.

"It's 827–3756."

Halleck listened carefully to be sure she repeated the sequence correctly.

"We can't afford screwups," Halleck told her. "And this will be the last time you, Sergeant Janowski, or any of your men visit here, until after we get Janey back."

"What?" The word, pumped to bursting with astonish-ment, came from three sources: Janowski, with anger, Ellie, with astonishment, and Brian, with rage.

"Figure it out," Halleck told them calmly. "We've given them assurances that police aren't involved. That's part of the deal. If I thought we could make the deal without police, I wouldn't even want you to know about it. No offense, Janowski, but if Janey is lost because of something you do, who's affected? Not you. It's just another day at the office. Who's accountable? You? You say you did your best, you covered your ass, you played it by the book? So even if you do something that might be stupid, as long as it's authorized stupidity, there's nothing we can do to stop it. And authorized stupidity would include, for example, a daily parade of police cars coming and going from this address. How hard is it for anybody interested in casing out this place to drive by and see that? What keeps the kidnappers from doing it? Think about it."

Janowski sounded furious. "You can't do this alone, Halleck!"

He held up a hand. "I know. I'm blind and I *am* alone, and I can't even make mistakes in this city-wide search because I need your help, Janowski. Without your help, I'm not just blind, I'm something I haven't been since I got blind, and that's helpless. I can get myself across Michigan Avenue at noon without any help, but I can't find a little girl out there unless you help me. Is that what you need to hear?"

"Okay, Halleck. I like your angle," Janowski said. "But you're going to have to let me handle the official end, because there is a book on this. We're going to have to make it look like we're carrying something on, give reasons why we do and don't do things, reasons that are believable to people in the Police Department. You can't do that."

"No question." Halleck sensed the man wanted to talk, that he'd been silent too long, that he appeared, in the way he imagined himself, not to be in charge. And whatever it took to get his cooperation, Halleck was willing to do. At the same time, he really *didn't* want the police in charge, and that wasn't just because they were a plodding, disinterested bureaucracy. This was the Chicago Police, famous for being on the pad, for taking bribes to forget speeding on Lake Shore Drive, for racing to homes of the dying elderly to lift their cash before the estate attorneys could arrive to account for it. Janowski seemed and felt all right, but he was in with a pack of sleaze balls. Trying to forget that and focus on Janey, he half doubted the cop's assurance, "And we'll get you information as fast as we can . . ."

"And a large detailed map of Chicago, preferrably

contour, certainly something that gives the sizes and shapes of buildings in the search area, to hang on my walls. And grease pens and pushpins."

"Why?" Janowski said. "You can't see."

"No. But the assistant you're going to give me can. And whoever that is will be talking to you as we narrow the search."

"Anything else?"

"Coffee. Lots of black coffee. And amphetamines."

Silence. Janowski finally said. "That's illegal. I can't dispense drugs, Halleck."

"All right," Halleck said, wondering what would show up unofficially.

"What else?"

"Let's just get that equipment to my place, now that the calls are forwarded and get that map up. We need to plot the L stations in the search area right away. We can know that even before we get the info on the incoming flights. All we need is for that assistant to show up and start laying down lines."

"And I suppose you want him ready when you arrive?" Janowski snorted.

"Janey would appreciate that," Halleck shot back. Too much?

"Well, I'll see if I can arrange for a beautiful blonde, too."

"What the hell difference does it make? It's just a voice in the darkness to me. Just make sure this person can do computers."

"See what *I* can do."

"Thank you, Sergeant Janowski," Brian Granville said. "I can't tell you how—"

Halleck could hear Janowski's hand cut through the air, call for quiet. "Like Mr. Halleck here says, just doin' my job. Anything else?"

"Yeah," Halleck said. "To my place. ASAFP. For now let's bring the stuff I have already. Time's running out."

Stan Black arrived from O'Hare by special police escort ahead of Halleck, had already connected the uniquely sensitive recorders to Halleck's phone, leaving free the line the phone company had just begun to run in to coordinate the search with the police. When Halleck came through the door, everything he needed was set up, including extra button-sized earphones for the assistant Janowski was sending. From the shuffling feet, he could tell three people were in his apartment. "Who's here?" he said. "Stan?"

"Over here, Spike, just completing the hookup."

"Thanks for coming. It's important. Also confidential."

"Understood. I've met Sergeant Janowski but not—"

Janowski blew his nose, then broke in. "Halleck, I got you some help. Officer Debra Seraphicos was off duty, serving hot meals to the homeless, but I convinced her she might want to lend a hand here."

"She'll be paid. I mean, this is an assignment?"

"I can't officially recognize this, Halleck."

"I'll pay you," said Halleck, facing where he knew she was standing.

"I'll have to get approval for outside work," said Debra Seraphicos in a calm, clear voice, for a woman deep but gently modulated. A little nose in it, but no one but a Spike Halleck or Stan Black would ever notice.

"Then you shouldn't spend your time, unless you're compensated." Halleck knew he was pushing but it wasn't just ethics. He couldn't have someone working as a volunteer, so they could quit as a volunteer.

"There are other forms of compensation."

Halleck let it go. There was no time to argue. "Stan will show you the equipment, explain what you have to do."

"Okay." Haunting voice, what might be called seductive, but Halleck knew that didn't mean a thing. The voice he used for titillating phone calls in one movie called *Thrill Me to Death* belonged to a two hundred and thirty-pound, seventy-two-year-old Pasadena grandmother with one leg amputated above the knee. But it was so sexy it could prompt wet dreams in a coma ward. So he smiled to himself, imagined Debra Seraphicos as a three hundred pound, four-foot six-inch woman wrestler who would save Janey. That's all that mattered.

Halleck could almost see, certainly imagine, the way Stan Black would stand back from the gear, hold out a hand, raise his eyebrows, sigh—he could hold that much now—scratch the back of his neck, rub it, rub his forehead, blink, sigh again—there it was—then lead the uninitiated into the complexities of accoustical synthesis and analysis.

Black's voice said, "Here we have an interactive bank of instruments, all linked together but capable of working independently," and went on to show her how the system operated, including the button earphones.

After he finished, he gave her the down side. "The fact is that this equipment is very sensitive, but it doesn't interpret. It doesn't infer or attribute sounds to sources."

Halleck could hear Stan move, one step away, stop.

"But"—Black went on—"this little thing can. The IBM PC/X, taken in conjunction with the special interpretative software already loaded into in, can run frequency analysis and corresponding relative intensity profiles against existing archive sounds, comparing the unknown signals to those produced by various sources and give you, with a variable level of confidence, what it is. The more sounds in your library, the better it gets."

Stan Black handed Debra a checklist for operations. "I've written them down here. And, of course, Spike wrote the manual."

Again a sigh, the leitmotiv Stan Black sigh. "I've asked Cheryl to send you a library of sounds from LA tomorrow morning."

"But works only if you have the reference sound," Halleck said.

"Right," Black told them. Janowski coughed again.

Black went on. "What Spike is saying is that we don't have every sound in creation. As a result, sometimes the best guess comes from a sharp and experienced ear, like Spike's."

Spike Halleck said, "Explain the direct comparator feature to Debra. That's important."

"Direct comparison," Black told her, "is the ability to receive a sound directly and compare it to an unknown source."

"Let's do a demo on tape two," Halleck said.

"Using what?"

"Bring me a cup, fill it with water, and a spoon. From the kitchen."

After a brief slamming of cabinet doors, rattling of drawers, Black came back and gave it to him. "Countdown to record, three, two, one . . ."

Halleck began stirring, circling the spoon in the half-filled cup, continued for five seconds, stopped. "Run it back and key in a FIND search."

"Spike is asking the computer to locate a spot on the tape most like the one he's just used as input. Here it is."

The clinking noise on the kidnapper's call came right up.

"Run COMPARE," Spike said. There was some shuffling, as he guessed, Black was sitting Debra Seraphicos down in front of the keyboard.

"Spike and Debra," Black said, "are now asking the computer how similar the most similar sound on the tape is to the reference sound, which we just recorded. And, you see, the answer comes up, three ways."

"I see it," Debra's voice said, reading the first. "Ninety-five percent confidence."

Next, as Stan Black explained, came a tabular version of the analytical breakdown. "It has compared on the pitch of sound, the overtones and reflections, and, because it was a periodic, or pulsed sound, the relative frequency of the clinking. You were stirring too fast, Spike."

"Sorry, I was excited."

They both laughed, a welcome break in the tension.

"The final display, the part that looks like a bunch of craggy mountains all crunched together, is a visual display of the sound. The louder a particular sound is recorded, the higher the peak, or mountain. The softer any particular sound, the lower the dip, or valley. We can break these out using the multichannel analyzer and display each contributing sound in a complex noise and represent it, as you see, with a particular color."

"Neat," said Debra.

"Got it?" Black asked her.

"I think I do."

"If you have problems, call. Or ask Mr. Wonderful behind us here."

"Thanks, Stan."

"Don't mention it. Think I'll take in some Improv while I'm in town. Maybe *Second City*. Nice meeting you folks, wish it could be . . . well . . ." Black slipped out without finishing the sentence, leaving Halleck with his plans.

"I may need you tonight," he said to Debra without thinking.

"Say what?"

"No," he said, waving off the confusion with his hands. "We need to run distance calibration tapes using a telephone speaker interfaced to a portable cassette recorder, standing a hundred feet from an L station, then two hundred, until your recording light shows you get no signal."

Disbelief in her voice as she said, "Do you know what time it is?"

"Absolutely. It's forty-eight hours until Janey Granville dies."

Silence. Janowski: "It's seventeen fucking degrees out there, Halleck."

"Give me the portable tape recorder," Halleck said. "I'll do it myself."

"No, you won't." Debra Seraphicos, firm and angry. "*I'll* do it."

"See you back here soon," he said.

The door slammed, leaving Janowski's rasping breathing. "You're pushing it," he said. Then the sound of something rattling on his dresser. "What's that?"

"It ain't decongestant," Janowski said. "But I don't know nothin' about it."

Amphetamines. Uppers. Reds.

Old friends.

4

Debra Seraphicos came in gulping warm air and slammed the door behind her. "Shit!" she said. "It's colder than a witch's tit in a brass bra out there."

"Sorry," he said. "Put the tape recorder in a Ziploc bag for about ten minutes, then we can work."

"Any more calls?"

"None." He heard a shuffling of something small and hard, then the question, "What are these?"

"Amphetamines, I think."

"You think?"

"They feel like amphetamines, they sound like amphetamines when you shake them, and so far they work like amphetamines." Halleck was buzzing along on a celestial high, a strange stratospheric cruise in the realm of darkness where he was unnaturally alert, his ears and hands and tongue abnormally sensitive to everything. Especially his ears, as he wanted it.

A silence. Judgment? "You have coffee?"

"In the kitchen."

Cabinet doors opening, closing.

"In the freezer," Halleck said, touching the keyboard, listening for the beeper. Over his shoulders hung a set of SubInfra headphones, the kind used in human hearing research to determine how much, or rather little, a person could hear. They could produce intensity ranges down an order of magnitude below a dropped pin. With it, in conjunction with the blocking filters, he could hear the weakest sound that reached the kidnapper's mouthpiece.

"Where's the can?"

"No can. It's in a plastic bag."

"You grind coffee by yourself? You're getting to look like quite a guy."

"You should have seen me before . . ." He stopped. The shrink said that kind of reflection gets you nowhere.

"I didn't know you before, so it doesn't matter."

"What time is it?" Halleck asked quickly, uneasy with the drift of the conversation.

"One o'clock. How you feelin'?" Her hand worked on the back of his neck, firm but gentle. It felt good.

"All right. You?"

"Okay." She yawned. "I could use some coffee."

"Did Janowski confirm you would be paid?"

"No." Irritation in the voice. Why?

"I can see that you will be paid. What's your hourly, on overtime?"

"Mister, you couldn't *get* me to work overtime on the police pay scale at my grade. It isn't worth it."

"Then why?" The coffee mill roared to life briefly, he heard the powdered beans sluice into the perking basket, the percolator grunt to life. When it was whooshing water she said, "Janowski knew I would do it."

"But why?"

"What is this? Twenty questions?"

"Look." Halleck tried to control the modulation in his voice, to keep from wavering, to deepen it with authority, to slow the cadence to indicate confidence—the newscaster's tricks—but that's not the way he felt. He had a helper all right, a woman he knew nothing about, here for reasons he didn't understand. Was she incredibly ugly and fat, a social undesirable looking for a meaning to life? If so would she be temperamental and edgy, moody and unresponsive, clamming up when he needed to talk to her, storming out when she was tired, upset, or unrewarded? Or was she beautiful, just broken up with a boyfriend or husband, biding time, grasping for a bizarre straw to pull the moment together, to defocus on something that otherwise would, and still might, seize her attention. Either way it mattered. He wanted to know as much as possible that would help him control her. For Christ sake, he even wanted to know if it was her period. Right now, he knew squat, felt helpless, dependent, and vulnerable. Janey deserved better. Halleck continued, "We have a little girl missing and scarcely forty-eight hours to locate her before we make a drop. I think we have a good chance of doing it, my way."

"So do I." Sounded as if she meant it. Good.

"And I don't think the police approach is any better."

"I've seen it work out a lot worse."

"What?"

Long sigh, as if she'd been holding it for years. "Two years ago," she said, "I worked a kidnapping, Janowski in charge. We had a ransom demand, you know, a time and condition for drop. It got pretty complicated, because we had to figure that the first drop wasn't it, that they would hire a mule, a courier who knew nothing, to take the package from the park to somewhere else, maybe in a crowd, maybe a building, but that meant that if someone on the kidnap team could watch the mule make the pickup, they could also tell if he was being tailed."

"You had no leads at all?"

She apparently shook her head without saying no, expecting, he guessed, that he could see it. Anyway, she went on as if he could see that, saying, "Janowski was very nervous about that, because we had run a psychological stress analysis—"

"A what?"

"PSE. It gives the stress in a person's voice, so you can tell if someone is lying."

"Go on." Halleck was both listening and thinking. If they could get a PSE through Janowski and hook it into the system, they could tell whether the kidnappers were being honest, tell even things like the changes in the degree of apprehension from the first to subsequent calls.

"So Janowski tried to get clever. The gang was trying to extort money from a local broker named Calvern. Instead they kidnapped a tax attorney's daughter, last name Calvert, who went to the same school. The PSE told us that they didn't know the difference or didn't care. Everyone who sent their kid to that private school was rich, so the ransom demand stood, five hundred thousand."

"And Janowski decided what? Let me guess. To roll

up as many as they could at the drop, to get them to squeal on the others, to cop pleas for reduced sentences, then to bargain with the others they rolled up to disclose the holding place of the girl."

"You got it," said Debra, walking toward the kitchen, unplugging the coffee perker. "Things went wrong."

"Define 'wrong.' "

"Janowski decided that since the package was only a lure, we should layer over cut newspaper with a few hundred dollar bills. If the mule peeks in for inspection, it looks okay. Since he's not going to stay long, there's no problem in detailed inspection. He'll want to clear the drop area as fast as he can, sneak out where he can. That's where Janowski tried to be clever."

"Tell me," Halleck said. He would be working with Janowski, wanted to know as much as possible about how that man thinks.

"He put sentries on all the alleyways, even posted window washers to keep track of the mule's movement. It wasn't a bad surveillance plan, if everything went the way we hoped."

"But it didn't?"

"Lesson number one. Surveillance never goes the way you think. They always seem to know, almost like quarry, how you're going to try to hem them in."

"What happened?"

"As nearly as we can determine, the package was switched in a crowd. The signal we got from the bug inside put it heading off in a different direction than the mule was seen moving."

"And?"

Long sigh, very weary. The sound of sipping coffee. "Things just didn't work out, that's all."

"They never found the girl."

"They did."

"Dead?"

"Yeah." Almost inaudible.

"Kidnappers?"

"Vanished. Nothing."

"The mule?"

"Picked him up. Claimed he knew nothing. He probably didn't. That's security, like compartmenting intelligence operations. No one knows more than they need to, so there's no damage by discovery."

"Who hired him?"

Head shaking again? Timing was right. "No one knows. It may have been that he didn't. His PSE said he didn't. Maybe the thing can be fooled. Maybe he was telling the truth, because they dropped the kidnapping and murder charges on him as soon as they found the girl's body."

"Where?"

"Upside down in a trash can, head half off, downtown."

"And you saw it?"

"Yeah, I saw it. And I dreamed it. And I can't forget it."

Halleck let a minute bleed away before guessing, "And you think of this as as second chance?"

"In a way, I suppose. It's just something I have to do."

"Janowski learn anything from that little girl?"

"Janowski said, and I will never forget it, 'Sometimes it don't work. You're just playin' the odds.' "

"And you said?"

"I said nothing. I just glared at him. Who the hell was I, first year out of the academy? All I knew was that the father could actually have raised the money. I keep wondering if we had just given them the money, if that girl would be alive today."

"Janey's father *is* getting the money. If all fails, we'll have it. We'll deliver, if we can't find her. But even with that, there's still the possibility that they would kill her. There's no statute of limitations on kidnapping. They would need to be looking over their shoulders for the rest of their lives."

"Or just move on to the next job. Now, where do you want this map posted?"

"To me it makes no difference. I suggest you put it close to the accoustical analyzers, so it's easier to mark up the map."

The sound of paper crackling as it unfolded filled the room, as Debra struggled to tack it up.

"How tall are you?" Halleck asked.

"Why, am I trying out for the Bulls?"

"Just curious. Sounds as if you're straining to pin up the top corners of that map."

"It's a big map. Police inner-city tactical map. From the SWAT unit."

The word made Halleck wince.

Debra went on. "Five four, all right?"

"Five four. Sure it's all right. Nice height."

"These days you can take growth hormone if you're short as a kid. There," she exulted, finished with the map.

"Nothing wrong with five four," Halleck said..

"My mother hated the word *short*, insisted on being called petite."

"Short doesn't mean petite," Halleck said, almost incidentally. "Do you have those calibration tapes?"

"But she is petite, except for the bust."

"Oh," Halleck said. "You want to put your tape, the one you just made, into the cassette player that says ARCHIVE."

"Done."

Halleck reached over, struggling to find the shape of familiar controls, pushing the REWIND putton.

Before it clicked off, Debra said, "All fine to do what you can, but isn't that risky. I mean, couldn't you erase some of this?"

"Erasing requires that two buttons be pushed simultaneously," he explained patiently. He could literally work this unit in the dark. He used to do that by choice, before the accident, because eliminating distracting images allowed him to better concentrate on choosing, or modifying, the right sounds for films.

"Still, there must be things that I can do . . ."

"I need you as a police official, to run calibrations, to get data, as you did tonight, to get records when we get that far."

"You have this all figured out, don't you?"

"I have a plan."

"A good plan?"

"Let's see. Tape in, rewound?"

"Roger."

"I call up the program, CALD, for calibrate, distance."

He worked the keyboard, guessing that Debra was checking carefully on the entries on the screen, would scream if something were wrong. "Medium, atmosphere. Temperature, seventeen degrees Fahrenheit. Elevation, what?"

"Elevation at lakefront is five hundred and eighty feet, when the lake isn't running at us like a tidal wave, which it sometimes does. The city is flat as a pancake, so give it fifteen feet more. Why?"

"Elevation, five hundred and ninety-five feet above sea level. Barometric pressure?"

"What is all this?"

"The speed of sound in any medium depends on a number of parameters that affect the density and the kinetic energy of the air. From these parameters we can use a computer convergence program to tell us how far the receiver is from the source."

"Which in English means?"

Halleck rephrased. "Which means that we can draw little circles around each L station inside our bigger circle and say that Janey is being held inside of one of those."

"Okay. Go. You were losing me."

"Sorry. Hundred-foot intervals."

"Exactly."

"Do you mean, yes, I agree, or exactly one hundred-foot intervals?"

"No," Debra said. "If you have to keep being a pain in the ass, I mean exactly one hundred-foot intervals."

"How did you measure?"

"Using a laser finder on tactical binoculars, borrowed from SWAT."

Halleck finished the input and let the computer grind. The program finished with three beeps.

"Press the RUN key," Halleck told her, swinging away.

Halleck heard it click, explained, "The program is running your calibration sounds on the L against the kidnapper's first call, factoring in the exclusion for extraneous noises and the data I already fed in for temperature and barometric pressure on the recording machine tape—"

"But we already have time and temperature," she protested.

"For tonight. For the first call they were different. Using the physical laws that govern propagation of sound in air, the computer can make adjustments so that the calibration curve you ran under current conditions is converted to an applicable calibration curve at the time when the first kidnap call came in."

"Amazing," she whistled.

"Not so, but pretty neat. Here it is," Halleck said as four beeps pulsed at a long rate. "Here's where you earn your bread and butter. What's the number?"

"Where?"

"On the screen, under range. This thing doesn't do braille yet."

"You're a real comedian."

"My shrink thinks it beats suicidal depression."

A pause then, "Range is five hundred and seventy-two point three eight feet, plus or minus seven. What does plus or minus seven mean?"

"It means there is enough uncertainty in the data, including possible reflections and attenuations, to leave the computer with a figure it's unwilling to bet on by more than seven feet at . . . what confidence level?"

"Ninety percent."

"Raise it."

"How?"

"Key in ENTER, then C96, then ENTER again."

The keys clicked, a second passed before she reported, "Same figure, now plus or minus thirteen feet."

"Which means you go to the map, check the scale figure in the lower left-hand corner, take out the thread and measure out five hundred and seventy-two plus thirteen feet, or five hundred and eighty-five feet on that scale, anchor one end of the string with a pushpin at each L station inside the big circle, then circumscribe an area five hundred and eighty-five feet in radius around it. Somewhere inside of one of those cells, Janey is being held."

"Unless they've moved her."

"Unless they've moved her," Halleck affirmed.

"What else?" Debra said.

"The inbound flights from O'Hare and Midway."

"Let me call in and check."

Halleck listened to the numbers being punched in, the strange toy store tones when each one was hit, then her gravelly voice, "Marsha? Deb. What did you find out on those arrivals tonight?"

Except for a pencil rushing over a pad, silence, then, "I know it's late. Sorry. Yeah, it's important. I'll make it up." Pause. "Thanks."

More scribbling, dial tone, then, "We have a problem."

"Let's have it."

"You want the simple complication, or the complicated complication?"

"What?" Halleck said, puzzled.

"At ten-forty this evening there may have been three flights inbound."

"Three?"

"Two at O'Hare, one at Midway."

"Shoot."

"At Midway a Midland Air 456 arrived from Akron at 2241, approaching from the East and landing on runway 34S. The next arrival was two and one half minutes later."

"Well after the callers hung up," Halleck observed. "And at O'Hare?"

"At O'Hare they had a United 357 from Cincinnati touch down on runway 30N at 2240:30, followed a minute later by an Air Canada from Ottawa at 2241:35, then a Delta 71 from Atlanta, which landed at 2242:42."

"The last one is probably too late. This plane sounded low. It wouldn't have been airborne two minutes after the call. From the flaps whining and the Doppler, plus intensity, it might have had, if I had to guess, forty seconds left in a normal descent. We can run the track against some calibration curves that Stan Black and I did to dub the first scene of *Easy Rider* at LAX. Then we'll know better. So three? That's the complication?"

"That's the simple complication."

"Explain."

"The hard part is this: the pilots don't come in on a beeline. They fly the shortest distance from point to point to save fuel, then come around and bank to reduce speed for approach."

"How do you know all this?"

Halleck couldn't hear a shrug, but bet there was one. Her sigh was audible, and poignant. "My ex used to be a pilot for Braniff, before they were taken over."

"I see." Halleck couldn't get over using the expression. In fact, with the information coming in, he actually was seeing, creating mental pictures with lines and circles just as he did for chess pieces on a board.

"So, like I was saying, they come in on a bank, and from any compass point there is considerable variance in where they might be. It's the air traffic controllers' job to keep them all separated, not to keep them all lined up."

"So you're saying we don't know where any of these planes were?"

"Not exactly."

"Can't we get better data? From cockpit recorders, something?"

Angry here. "We're goddamn lucky to get what we've got this so fast."

"Oh?"

"Yes, oh. Marsha, my husband's—ex's—new wife, is a controller at O'Hare. I asked a favor, she came through."

"Speaking terms?"

"You don't have to hate everyone, Halleck." It was the first time she had used his name.

"You can call me Spike."

"I can call you shithead if I want."

"I thought you didn't have to hate everyone."

"Sorry. Mind if I smoke?"

Halleck didn't smoke, didn't like it in his place. The stale odor hung in the air, in the curtains, in the sheets, for days. But he had to compromise here. He needed her, and it sounded as if she needed a cigarette. "Please," he said.

"Thanks," she whispered, striking a match.

Smoke. Strong. Unfiltered Camels, he guessed.

"You don't smoke." Not a question.

"No," he said simply. No lectures. "You could tell?"

"No ashtrays, no butts, no burns on the furniture."

"A blind man who smokes doesn't need to burn his furniture," Halleck shot back.

"Don't get defensive, Halleck. Who's says a smoker has to be blind to burn their furniture?"

"Better?"

He could hear her inhale deeply, almost hear her nod, did hear her whisper, "Yeah." Then something, fingernails through hair? Maybe. Then, "Back to it. The planes come down, all the directions are known, and the approach corridors are set, but the actual wedge they fly depends on where they start from. Midland flight had a straight shot then had to dogleg and come in from the south. One of those puddle hoppers, he might never have gotten over the lake."

"And so was too far south of the big circle?"

"Maybe. But if he touched it, it was near the bottom?"

"South Chicago?"

"East Chicago, Indiana. The Dunes. Then around. I don't know."

"Give me something. Be generous. We still have time. Let's not start to narrow down too soon."

"Okay." He heard her move to the wall, the grease pen squeak. "Now for the others. Delta's out, right?"

"Right. We'll confirm that against the *Easy Rider* jet track as soon as we get that from Cheryl by modem, tomorrow morning."

"Tomorrow?"

Halleck nodded. Instinctive. He had been nodding for most of his life and all of his friends could see it, because none of them were blind. He saw no reason to abandon old friends because of the problem, no reason to flock to new ones because they shared a handicap. Hell, he wasn't a leper. "We should get them first thing, maybe by nine. That's seven on the coast. She knows the importance."

"And she couldn't do it sooner?"

"We have time."

"Then what the hell am I doing here?"

Halleck knew he should count to ten, keep the edge off his voice, couldn't quite. "Hopefully, what you want. Also what we need. We have plenty to do, to sort out, before then. What time is it?"

"Nearly two."

"Tired?"

"Coffee's working fine. What do we have?"

"Inbounds to O'Hare."

"The United flight from Cincinnati would have come north over the lake for approach, since they were landing to the south. That would have put it north of the tall buildings, midtown, before it got into its bank."

"Fits," Halleck muttered.

"What?"

"I said, was saying to myself . . ."

"You can talk to me, you know. I'd appreciate it."

"Sorry." He was. And glad she was here. Even at her worst, despite being jerked in after a day of normal duty, she wasn't, miraculously, much of a pain in the ass so far.

"I was just thinking that the United flight would fit. Look at all the L stations up there, the wind off the lake on the chimes, midtown construction and the jackhammer. It's another piece that fits."

"Fine," she sighed, frustrated. "Except you've got this Air Canada inbound from Ottawa, near enough in time and coming straight on in, doesn't have to make much of a bank, flight path brings it right over the city real near the United approach, so you end up with two wedges that overlap, not two lines, which is what you were hoping for."

"For now I'll settle for what I can get."

"Oh yeah?"

"Yeah," Halleck said. "We may not be as close as we want, but look at the map again."

"Spike, sweetie, you've got a lot of turf under these wedges."

"But look at what we've *eliminated*."

Most of the big circle around Soldier Field was gone. When they concentrated on the circles around L stations that fell beneath the flight paths, the search area shrunk to ten percent of its original size.

"Maybe we can do better," Debra said.

"We're doing all right."

"Back to the flights."

"Let's take a look at something else."

"No." Stubborn.

"Why?"

"We're missing something. Let me look at my notes. Here. So we have the Midland to Midway. And we got"—he could hear her break in a yawn, realizing she would have to sleep here—"excuse me. Jesus, I'm *not* really that tired. So we got the United from Cincinnati and the Air Canada both trying to stay ahead of the storm over the lake to the north . . ."

"What about a storm?"

"They were trying to land ahead of a thunderstorm."

"You didn't say that before. Now we've got something."

"What are you talking about, Spike?"

"The library has thunderstorm sounds. If our ears can't hear them, the computer program can tease them out of the background."

"You think?"

"The only problem is that the computer is just like us. If you ask it to look for a man in the moon, it will draw you one, even though no man in the moon exists. Same with sounds. But let's find out."

"Second tape is in."

"See it?"

"THUNDERSTORM shows nothing, Halleck."

"Impossible. We have it. It's fundamental stuff, textbook material." Halleck was stumped, suggested, "Try STORM."

"Got it! Here goes."

Halleck could hear nothing but the steady hum of the CRT, yet knew in seconds it should have an answer. Next came six long, steady bleeps.

"Bingo," he said.

"Hold on." Clicking keys, then her voice, "Go ahead."

"Now RUN."

Through the speakers came the sound extracted from the second call from the kidnappers. Out of popping static came the low growling roll of thunder.

"That's incredible," she said, clapping her hands like a kid on Christmas morning.

"What confidence level?" Halleck snapped.

"Seventy," she told him.

"Seventy percent confidence. Not bad for garbage. But not good either. Let's try something else."

"What?"

"Run the same routine on the Soldier Field tape."

She did with identical results.

"More hissing on this one," she said.

"What confidence level?"

"Not as good. Fifty-eight percent."

Halleck sighed with relief. "So we can rule out the Midway flight."

"Why?"

Halleck told her, "A storm in the north would send a weaker accoustical signature—the rumbling, the booming, the cracking—to the south. If the background sound had been from the inbound flight to Midway, which came in *south* of Soldier Field, you would expect the storm noises to be *louder* on the Soldier Field tape. They're *not*, they're quieter. You can hear that, and you can see that—if you can see—by the confidence level. Only a storm noise that originates north of Soldier Field would be weaker at the stadium and stronger along an approach path north of Soldier Field, which is what we get. That leaves out the flight from Cincinnati."

"If those noises are actually a storm," she added.

"I think they are."

"Why?"

"Because we hear them on both tapes, a half an hour apart, at comparable intensity levels and with identical patterns. If they hadn't been identical patterns, the computer wouldn't have matched them. That convinced me. At first I thought the first tape might have been a galvanized trash can rolling around in the wind, maybe a block away. It would have sounded almost the same to the ear, but not to the computer, which can run a sound forward and backward, matching the patterns of the source sound."

"All right, professor," she said.

Halleck realized with embarrassment that he was holding an expository finger in the air, let it down slowly, fell silent.

"Forget it. What next?"

"Let's run the library on WIND CHIMES against the first tape."

"If you're so sure, why run it?"

"The tape is so clear that the computer will do more than match the sound, it will tell us if the clappers on the wind chime are glass, metal, porcelain, or plastic. Give it more time and it could tell the exact material."

"And you wrote this program?"

Halleck nodded.

"Something," she whispered.

"It's never seemed more important than now. There were times after the accident when I wished that I could have traded all this for my sight. Not now. Not with what it can mean for Janey."

She put her hand on his shoulder, a soft, warm, yet strong hand, thin fingers, artistic it seemed. "You're doing fine."

"That's what they said in blind school. 'You're doing fine.' "

"They weren't wrong." Mellow voice, sincere. He ached to know what she looked like, wondered if he could ask to touch her face, thought better of it.

"It's funny, you know. During the times I was really concentrating on a sound, really racking my brains to think what would best imitate the noise made by some visual image, I would always close my eyes, sometimes even go into a dark room and close my eyes, to let the sounds flood my unconsciousness. And the right one would always come. After the accident I always agonized about those times that I could see and had chosen not to, had closed my eyes to colors because I thought I could always get them back by opening the lids, then suddenly couldn't. Bad enough that I had been cheated, I used to think. Worse that I had cheated myself."

"You couldn't have known . . ."

"Then I realized that if anyone could make it blind, it was better me than some schmuck who would lose sphincter control in the middle of a busy street, who would be lost in a world without images. For me, it had always been that I could close my eyes and tell exactly what was surrounding me, if there were enough sounds."

"You don't have to convince me," she said, her voice

punctuated by a sigh. A long day's sigh. Another one of those unmistakable noises. "Look, Halleck, I feel shitty. Mind if I take a shower?"

"Of course not."

"Down the hall?"

"And to the left. I promise not to look."

"Too bad," she said, her voice bouncing off the walls. "I've got a nice body."

5

About an arm's length away, the computer droned passively, a steady hum unable to distract him from the irresistible splash of water as Debra Seraphicos twisted and spun, herself humming, but soft, mellifluous, feminine, nothing like the computer. If she reported correctly, his showerhead was fondling a nice body with orgasmically pulsing jets of water. The thought of it made him hard.

He tried not thinking about it, not to respond, but was unable to relax, worrying that when she joined him at the machine, she would notice the terribly obvious, undeniable evidence that he had been fantasizing about her naked. She was the one who brought it up! Did she think he stopped being a man just because he couldn't see her? Was she a tease? Or was it just her way of trying to break the ice, to thaw the ruthless Halleck intensity? Who knew? All he knew was that he was hard and it wasn't going down.

Soon after the accident he discovered that women take more initiatives, when men aren't undressing them with their eyes. And they always tried to out-Teresa Mother Teresa, rustling up gourmet meals, making endless chatter about conspicuously nonvisual subjects, discussions so intentionally contrived they angered him. The politics of poverty. The morality of Star Wars. Or the audible, like the cadence of poetry. They asked about their perfumes or the nap of fabric, often guiding his hand beneath their blouses or skirts, delighting and torturing him as he fumbled at the modern fortress of clips and clasps and folds and tucks until, after angry ripping and tearing, orchestrated by a rising crescendo of "Ooohs," "Ahs," and almost terrified breathing, opened themselves to his ravishing fury.

Yet whatever sex became, it never got to love, not even tenderness. Always hot, sometimes brutal, never boring, but never intimate either.

And they all had the same adulations. Yet they came to him in pity or curiosity, neither sentiment wanted. Soon the fascination faded, the novelty wore thin. The girls vanished while his urges grew. Stan Black told him, "What you need, Spike, is somebody uninhibited, unjudgmental, a pro who will fuck your brains out and leave your body humming six hours later. What do you think?"

What did he think? He thought he wasn't horny enough to risk getting AIDS.

When he said he wanted acceptance, companionship, Stan said, "Sounds like you need a nice blind girl, Spike."

That depressed him.

Halleck remembered the blind as badly dressed and disheveled, their hair wild and dark eyelids squeezed shut, often fat and waddling, perpetually tentative, as if every step risked a fall. Basically, he decided, they couldn't hear constructively. By contrast Halleck's ears and mind worked through sounds almost as if he had evolved in a world where sounds, rather than sights, were the main source of information. Second came extreme heat and cold, as from fires or winds. Then more subtle clues, like odors, pungent and unmistakable—sweat, perfume, sewage, saltwater. For Halleck the world had become a cleverly designed puzzle where sounds, temperatures, scents, sometimes textures, were pieces that formed one unique shape. Belief and experience drove Halleck to conclude that he alone could find Janey.

The computer kept humming.

The shower stopped. The glass doors opened. He could hear Debra step out.

What time was it?

He would ask her.

Dependence. Some things were harder to find out. For these he felt resentful. Some he could solve. Technology was available, could be applied—would, he was now determined—that would liberate him more. Voice synthe-sizers, like the one creating time markers on the ransom calls, could be interfaced with computers to allow him access to information now only displayed on the screen, and to confirm the instructions he had keyed in. All that would be done. But now there was no time. Now he needed Debra Seraphicos, nice body and all. Now Janey needed Debra Serapicos, driven by guilt, to pin down where they were holding her.

"I'll be out in a second," she called.

"Time's up," he shouted back.

"This ain't Kabuki theater, Halleck."

In what seemed five minutes she reappeared, or must have reappeared to a sighted person. What Halleck got first, even before she padded across the wall-to-wall car-pet, was a scent. God, what a scent! He was afraid he would get hard again, began to fight it with tangible imagination. Think, he told himself, of jumping into Lake Michigan in February.

When he heard her arrive, he asked, "What are you wearing?"

"Bra and panties. Why? Can you tell?"

He felt his cheeks go hot. "No. I mean the scent, the perfume."

"It's called *Repechage*. French word, I think. Means second chance. Perfect scent for today's divorcee. Why? You like it?"

"Let's just say it has a real grab to it."

"You make it seem like a masher on an elevator."

"How do you expect me to keep my mind on my work when you're pulling my heart up through my nose?"

"That's a pretty explicit image, Halleck. What do we do, then? Carry on negotiations across a desexualized zone? I mean it's not as if I've violated the Geneva Conventions."

"Sit anywhere you want. Just don't leave. I need you."

"That's the first time a man has said that in some time."

"Janey needs you . . . Us," he corrected himself.

"Okay. Before we begin, tell me how you got this

crazy idea about sound and all. It seems, forgive me, almost as if you're working for them, the kidnappers."

"What?" Halleck let his voice go hard as ice.

"Wrong. Sorry. I mean, most people in these situations just go paralyzed, particularly if it's personal. They want the police to take over. How come you were . . . ready?"

"I've been through it before."

"My turn to say, What?"

"No, actually, it was a script we read, we had an option to do, and subsequently dropped. It didn't exactly go this way, but as I was reading through, I realized that there must be a treasure trove of clues in the sounds coming over the phone that the police and FBI, in this script, were totally ignoring. It was as if they kept trying to figure out, first, who the kidnappers were, then, who they might be staying with, then what they were thinking, then how they would react to a series of hypothetical situations. Essentially, they were trying to play psychoanalyst for the kidnappers while totally ignoring the evidence from the calls about where they might be holding the twin girls they had kidnapped."

"Was it a good story?"

"It was a shitty story," Halleck said. "But I learned something."

"You mean about sounds and all, the stuff we're doing?"

"No, I mean about police."

"And . . ."

"Most police," he corrected, trying not to offend. "People like Janowski, who is just like the cops in this script. They're all running around checking the book, making sure that what they're doing is procedurally correct, talking with their supervisors, trying to second guess the criminals, as if the whole business is a personal test of wits between them and the bad guys."

"A lot of cops see it that way," she said.

"But what they're focusing on is the consequences to them, not to the victim. The problem is that they look at it as if the victim is already dead, because statistics give little hope that she will come out alive, so they focus on setting and trap to make sure they roll up one of the gang, squeeze him until he pukes up the names of the others, and on sending them all to the electric chair. If they recover the victim alive, that's a nice bonus. But it's not the objective. The point is that they're not held responsible for the death of the victim. The kidnappers are, or will be. What they're held responsible for, if anything, is making sure what they do conforms to departmental standards. That's all."

"You want me to argue?"

"I don't know," Halleck said.

"Look, some organizations just bust balls to try to keep a killing from happening. Janowski's already notified Lou Scannon of the FBI, who's running twenty-four-hour computer searches on their VICAP program, trying to make a match. I tell you Scannon won't be taking any short days waiting for Janey to turn up dead, believe me. Still, to be honest I've seen it happen just the way you say. Why do you think I'm here tonight, Spike?"

"Sorry. I didn't mean it personally. I—"

"Shhh," she said, putting her finger on his lip, "I understand. And I think we're onto something here. Look at what you've done with the map already. Janowski knows he's nowhere right now. Why do you think he's pulling all these backstage strings? He may not give you the sun and moon but before you start thumping on him, just remember that he sensed you might have something, and for him that's a lot. That's why I'm here."

"I suppose." Halleck hadn't figured that before. Before, and to some extent still, he thought of Janowski as too skeptical, too slow, too uncooperative. But then it wasn't his little girl. It wasn't even his niece. But those suspicions, which he couldn't prove, got him nowhere. The only possible developments he could control would come from sounds on the tapes, some of which he couldn't even hear, some of which the machine couldn't even hear, at least on one pass. That would take hours. Turning to Debra's noises, the sounds that must be her moving around his apartment—still in her bra and panties?—he said, "I still have some work to do, thinking, mostly, but with the computer, too. Why don't you try to get some rest?"

"I'm all right," he heard her say through a yawn.

"I won't be using my bed tonight," he said.

"I can help, really. And if I need to rest, I'll use the sofa. What would your wife think if she came home and caught me in her bed?"

"Wife?"

"Sure. The ring . . . I just figured . . ."

Halleck laughed.

"Widower. What? I don't understand."

"No," Halleck said, "it's a joke. Everyone used to say that I was married to my work the way a nun thinks she is married to Jesus, so I began wearing a wedding band, as sort of a joke."

"Sends the wrong message to women," she said.

"Who's going to get involved with a blind man, married or not?"

Silence. A sigh. What was she thinking? What she said next had no connection to anything except Janey. That was enough. She said, "Halleck, why don't you show me what you're doing so I understand. That way if you keel over from exhaustion, I can take over. Because I think what you've done here is inspired. If what we're doing works, it may revolutionize antikidnapping strategy. Now it seems to me that all the other people who have supposedly been thinking about this crime are blind compared to you. At least you make them look stupid. And I'd rather be around someone who's blind than someone who's stupid any day." Another little silence intruded, then, "One woman's opinion. For what it's worth."

Halleck didn't know what to say, what he was supposed to say, how he was supposed to react. What she said could have been a lecture or it could have been a come-on. To know which he needed to see her eyes, the one thing he could never do. So he sat there in the forever darkness that would hold him until his last breath, feeling her energy, smelling her scent, listening to her breathing, and saying, at last, "We have to ask the computer to run a CAT on the tapes, to look for very low-level noises."

"CAT?" Her voices sounded confused, "Like the brain scans?"

"No," he told her, "Those CATs are Computerized Axial Tomography. This program is Computer of Average Transients. What it does is this: it plays the tape over and over again and records all the sounds, that includes the static, in digital form on the multichannel analyzer. But since background noise is random, it cancels out over time, giving a zero signal, a baseline. But the little sounds that are actually there at some point in the tape become stronger with each pass. In that way it can detect noises that the machine would never render on one pass."

"So how long does it take?"

"The computer will run until it is sure it has a signal, or until it is useless to keep looking."

"Or until we have another tape to analyze."

"Tomorrow," Halleck said.

"You think?"

Halleck nodded.

"How are you going to handle it?"

"Offer them five thousand dollars by the end of the day, their choice of terms for delivery."

"Think they'll bite?"

"Not if they think it's a trap."

"Janowski won't like it."

"He doesn't have to."

"It's not him. He would like to get what he can get while he can get it."

"He didn't learn anything from the mule?"

"I'm telling you, Spike, he's going to want something. Right now he's got the chief on his ass and the FBI, Chicago, pumping him for some action. He's in a frying pan."

"Then we'll have to insist he lays back. So far I've been able to keep the kidnappers playing because they think the police are out of it. Janowski could blow it, and there goes Janey."

"How are you sure, Spike," she said softly, hesitating as if to choose the next words, "that they haven't moved Janey?"

"I'm not, but will be."

"Huh?"

"Next call we look for replicates, ask the computer to match the sounds, even the low-level ones it gets on CAT, to the background on the next call. If we get matches, we know. If not, we start over."

"But if not, Janowski will want to have it his way."

"I know."

"And how will you know that Janey is all right?"

"Talk to her. That's part of our agreement. Part of theirs is that the police will not be involved. If either side breaks the terms, the contract is void."

"And Janey is . . ."

"Dead," Halleck said calmly, keying in the program, determined to see that before they had a chance to do that, he would have their hideout surrounded by police.

If he didn't need two men, Tim wouldn't be here now.

That's what he was thinking as he stepped out of the place for a walk, leaving his partner alone with the girl, confident that he wouldn't "play" with her, because even Tim wasn't that dumb.

Hiking the collar on his arctic fatigue jacket and lowering his head into the bitter wind, he pushed past the wind chime, the porch light behind him casting a long shadow as he moved down the steps and away, trying to think.

The problem was how to put two hundred grand in his pocket and leave two bodies without a trace. Two. First the one they had agreed on, the girl, as the plan made clear. Even Tim knew that, knew it from the start. Second Tim, which Tim certainly did not know.

Tim, loyal Tim, dumb Tim, would serve and die. But the dead Tim must also disappear because Tim's body could lead them back to him. And he couldn't risk that.

He kept his head down as he turned the corner and moved east, toward the lake, the wind coming straight at him, standing him up, shifting him to the side with its gusts. To his right was a bar, a laundromat, apartment building. Across the street a grocery store, shoe store. People were still out shopping. Christmas, he guessed.

How to do Tim.

And when.

His teeth must go, and his hands. No teeth or prints. Nothing must remain.

Nothing except him, the money, and the future.

But how and when, those were the questions.

The wind howled back, slapped him until his eyes watered, but did not answer.

6

Sergeant Ed Janowski stepped from the cab, handed the driver a ten, said, "Keep the change," and walked to the front door of the Granville home. As he rapped the gleaming brass knocker, he kept thinking about Spike Halleck, not knowing whether he was a genius or an idiot. He knew the type, understood that if they were right and if you used them cleverly, you could look like the modern messiah. On the other hand, if they were wrong, you could end up with your ass chewed off, no job and no pension. So most of the time it wasn't worth it. That was what he had come to tell the Granvilles.

It was Mrs. Granville who answered the door, froze momentarily at seeing him back, then rushed to let him in, saying, "May I take your coat?"

He let her have it, hang it in a front hall closet the size of his office, take him to the living room, where he found the husband pacing, working his hands together. When he saw Janowski, he sat down. The wife went over and sat next to him, put her arms around him, was still unable to bring his eyes back in focus.

Ed Janowski cleared his throat, adjusted his tie, an old habit that preceded speeches, then said, "Mr. Granville, Mrs. Granville, I know you have had a bad night, must have had a bad night. It wasn't a good one for me, or any of my people. For one thing, we came up with about two hundred and thirty-seven wind chimes and that may not be all of them. Even if it is, we got nothing to help us whittle that number down."

"Have you talked to Spike today?" asked the girl's mother.

"Well, no, because I want to talk to you first."

The husband looked up, hard. "You haven't got . . . something to tell us, have you—about Janey?"

Janowski held up a hand, shut his eyes, shook his head reassuringly, "No," he said, then added, "not yet. I mean that's what we have to discuss, because—"

"No word from the kidnappers?"

Janowski shuddered out a sigh, shook his head. "Talked to Officer Seraphicos. She says no. So we wait. I have to tell you I don't like this idea of Halleck's on the five thousand. Think it stinks, in fact, if you ask me."

The parents looked up, gave him an expression something between stunned and lost, asked, "What's the matter?"

"It could backfire," Janowski said. "I mean, here you have a couple of punks by the sound of it, and for them five thousand bucks is more than they hope to see at one time ever. So suddenly you say to them, here it is, come back for more next time . . . I just think they never expected it. I think they expected you to bargain them down, tell them you couldn't come up with the two hundred grand. Know what I mean? So here they are, not knowing what the hell's going on, being given five thousand free and clear, the only thing between them and scot-free is to, well, how do I say it?"

"Kill Janey?" the mother said, as if she wanted him to deny it, tell her they would never do something like that.

"Exactly," Janowski said, bringing an audible gasp from both of them.

Next it was the father who appeared to emerge from his stupor long enough to bark, "So what the hell do the police propose to do?"

"Well, if you ask me—"

"Who the hell else is there?" the husband exploded.

"Now, Brian," his wife murmured.

"If you was askin' me"—Janowski fingered the knot on his tie, tried to pull it away from a knotting Adam's apple—"I would have to say wait for their demands, buy some time, let them set the terms, then we deliver and roll them up after the drop."

"And what about Janey?"

"The exchange is part of the terms. They tell us where she's gonna be, we send someone there to cover."

"And what if she's not there?" asked the mother. "Do we trust these men, these people you called punks?"

"It has worked, this way," Janowski said.

"And has it failed?" The husband here, the businessman. Wants to know the odds. Jesus. His own kid and he wants to know the odds.

"It's the only way I've ever got a kid back, folks," Janowski said.

"Maybe there's something else you can do," the mother suggested.

"What?"

"It's just"—she looked anxiously at her husband—"maybe it's nothing."

"What is it, Mrs. Granville? Someone come to the door or somethin'? I mean, if you saw someone . . . Jeez, let's get you downtown, look at some pictures . . . What is it?"

"A-a-car," she stuttered.

"Car?"

"An unusual car for this neighborhood."

"Yes, ma'am." Janowski knew that in Lake Forest if someone drove through in a battered ten-year-old Chevy Nova it could cause the same reaction as seeing a flying saucer over Wright Patterson Air Force Base.

"A green car," she said.

"What kind of a green car, ma'am?"

"Old one."

"Yes?"

"With a grinning grill and . . . ?"

"A grinning grill?"

"Well, shit!" she exploded. "I don't know anything about cars!"

Outside of Mercedes-Benzes, BMWs and Rolls-Royces, maybe Volvos as a cheap second, Janowski was sure she was right. The point was that an old car was cruising through her neighborhood, probably had passed her house. How could he tell her that he couldn't arrest someone for something like that? He started to try when she interrupted with, "Both times it slowed down out front, as if—"

"Both times?"

She nodded.

"You see this?" he asked the father.

"The second time, yes."

"What kind of car, Mr. Granville?"

"I don't know. I don't memorize the styles of ancient automobiles, Sergeant Janowski. It might have been a Chrysler or Plymouth from what I remember. Don't you have any style books on these things?"

"Sure. License?"

"Illinois," she said. "I tried to read it but I was hiding—"

"Hiding?"

She screamed, "If it was them, I didn't want them thinking we had police here, with tapes, police looking out for cars, anything that could get Janey killed! Can't you understand what I'm feeling?"

Unglued. "Yes, Mrs. Granville, yes. But if we are going to follow this up, I need Mr. Granville, maybe yourself, down at the station to ID . . ."

She waved her hands back and forth, crossing one another, signaling no. "No trips to the police. No police. If they knew . . . We told them, Spike told them no police. They said if we told the police . . ." She didn't need to finish.

"Mrs. Granville, this is the first good lead we have."

"That's the point," her husband said, getting up. "It's the first lead you have and you know what? I talked to Spike Halleck this morning and he convinced *me*—not an easy thing to do—that he had narrowed the search area to something like three by two miles inland of north Lake Shore Drive. Now I want you to do only one thing, other than never again come back here, NEVER jeopardize Janey's life by showing up here where they might see you, Janowski, and that is to cooperate to the fullest with Spike Halleck or I can promise you, buster, if you don't, so help me I'll use every one of the well-placed connections I have to bust you down so far in the system that you'll be sloshing through turds every time you get up from your desk. Understand?"

Janowski knew it was a real threat, understood instantly that if this man's daughter died, even if it wasn't his fault, even if nobody could have been expected to save her, that he was going to take the fall. Suddenly the book went out the window. He had nothing. Less than two days to go and nothing. Halleck, maybe, had something. It was his only hope.

"Yeah," he said meekly. "I understand."

"I suggest, then," said the father, hissing his words in undiluted rage, "that you get the location of those wind chimes to Spike right away. And don't talk to me again, even by phone, until you have some good news."

"Yes, sir. Of course."

"And don't even dream about interfering with the drop today."

Janowski wondered if he could pull it off, give the man a reassuring lie then get his own investigation going out of surveillance. How could Granville ever find out? Even if he blew it, how would he ever know? Who could prove anything? And wasn't it the only time they would have to get that close to them? How could he defend passing it up to the chief? And wouldn't making that kind of a break in the case finally settle, once and for all, that the local authorities could make the best investigation. Christ, he would love to put Lou Scannon and the FBI in its place!

Nodding humbly to the father, putting his hand reassuringly on the man's shoulder, he said, "Of course, you're right. We'll stay away."

7

Asleep four hours, Debra Seraphicos kept gently suspiring when the phone rang. Halleck could tell from the buzzing and the location of the sound, that it was the new service they had connected, not the roll-over from the Granville number. Maybe Stan Black's girlfriend ready to transmit the sound library from LA. Snapping the handset he said, "Halleck."

"Spike, Brian."

"No calls so far. But I want to be ready. Can we make it quick?"

"Sure. First, lean on Janowski for anything you need. And I mean anything."

"All right." Halleck said. "What about the wind chimes I asked him to run down?"

"You want me to call him?"

"No, let me do it. Or Debra."

"Who?"

"Debra Seraphicos, an off-duty officer Janowski assigned. She's here for plotting the data."

"How is it going?" The tension in Brian's voice could crack a diamond.

"Right now, as of this minute, I'd bet they're keeping her within six hundred feet of one of three L stations about six blocks off Lake Shore Drive."

"Have you replayed the tapes?"

How did you answer one like that? Halleck had played, analyzed, reanalyzed, and replayed the tapes until his mind had *stopped* hearing what was actually there, numb from repeated concentration on the same source. However hard he tried, however heroically pumped up with uppers, Halleck was not a computer. He was human and tired, more than a little irritated. Still, it wasn't Brian's fault. His little girl was missing and only Halleck had given him any hope that she could be found.

"Several times," he said, not mentioning that he had been up all night.

"How does she sound?"

"She sounds scared, Brian. How would you expect her to sound?"

"Do you think she's all right?"

How to answer? From the sound, from the situation, from instincts? He might as well ask a psychic. Halleck took a deep breath, fought off a yawn, said, "As far as we know, she's okay. She just sounds scared." Halleck might just as well have said, without lying, that as far as they knew she was dead, but sometimes it's the half-full glass, rather than the half-empty one, that ought to be served. It would do no one good to have Brian come unglued, go hysterical. Halleck himself had some real concerns. Was she warm enough? Had they fed her? Would she be able to keep from crying? And if she couldn't, would they tape her mouth shut? If they taped her mouth shut and her nose got stuffed up, would she suffocate? It was pointless to speculate. You could go crazy with distractions that way, and that served no purpose.

"When do you think they'll call again?"

"I don't know. But when they do, I intend to make the offer, right up front, right away."

"The five thousand?"

"Right. You'll have it?"

"By nine-thirty at the latest."

"Good, I want you to stand by for instructions. We may have to dance a little to make their schedule?"

"Spike?" Hesitation, doubt? Something coming. He could feel it.

"Yeah?"

"Do you think you could hold them up long enough for a trace? I mean if we could set it up?"

"I don't even want to think about it. We're too close without that risk. And if I play for time"—he stopped, wanted to reword it—"if I even seem to them to be stalling, playing for time, we could blow the whole thing."

"But don't you see how quickly we could move on a trace?"

"This Janowski's idea?"

"No, mine."

"How come?"

"Look, goddamnit, Spike! You give them five thousand and think you're going to tail them, they could move someplace else before they make the final pickup. Then all your maps are useless!"

"I don't think so."

"What's to stop them?"

"Well, with pictures of lost and missing kids all over the backs of milk cartons, it's going to create some attention if they go dragging a kicking, screaming kid across town."

"They could drug her."

"That would look worse. I don't imagine these clowns look exactly like concerned fathers, or look even remotely related to Janey. You'd be surprised how people look for congruity in what they see, remember what isn't. That's how Richard Speck was caught."

"Great! After he killed eight student nurses."

"They can't kill Janey and make the big score. I've got to talk with her five minutes before the final drop, wherever and whenever that is."

"Did they agree to that?"

"No," Halleck admitted. "But they will."

"How can you be sure they won't move her?"

"For Chrissakes, Brian, no one can be sure, but I bet, in addition to being scared shitless, they don't trust each other."

"What does that have to do with it?"

"That means that they want everything as stable as possible. Both of these guys, or all three—it's got to be a small number to reduce the possibility of someone getting caught and ratting on the other—are facing the electric chair if they get caught. None of them wants to get caught. All of them want the money. Each of them wants his cut. You think the one who stays will trust the one who goes to pick up the money? And who do you think that will be? How will they decide?"

"I don't know."

"I don't either. But the five thousand deal gives them a chance to prove their honor to one another, to show that they can come through. Compared to two hundred thousand, five thousand looks like nothing. Even if they want a double cross, they can buy trust cheap simply by staying put, keeping a lid on things, make the pickup, affirm our sincerity, see, according to them, that the police are out of it . . ."

"I think they're already doing a little checking on their own."

"What?"

Brian told him about the green flivver that cruised by the house twice. When he finished listening, Halleck nearly convulsed. "I don't know if that's them but it might be, so be damned sure to keep Janowski and any police miles away. And I mean miles!"

"He wanted us to go down to the station, to try to pick out the style of car."

"Negative. Don't go to the police. That's our position."

"Just sit there, in the house, as if we're waiting for a call?"

"You or Ellie can leave, shop for food, look normal. I'm supposed to be there, at your place, where those calls are supposed to be ringing, to act for you. Play it that way."

"What if we can trace these guys through the car, Spike?"

"Did you get a license number?"

"Illinois. That's all. It was a blur, passed behind trees. I didn't get it," he admitted.

"How much closer can we get to them with no license, on a style of car that you may or may not be able to make? On the other hand, they may have another car, one you haven't seen and won't be looking for, that will follow you or Ellie right to the station, then the deal is off. Then where is Janey?"

"And what if the one that picks up the five thousand today decides that it's enough for him, that he's taken enough risk, that he wants the money and no more. What if he takes off, leaves his partner waiting. Won't the partner think something funny is up, maybe the police have got his partner and it's time to split? What happens to Janey then?"

Halleck had considered the worst-case scenarios more than once. In every one was a risk, a chance you had to take, an unavoidable uncertainty. And in the worst case Janey always wound up dead. But it didn't have to be that way. "Look," he said, "let's assume he splits. The partner still has the merchandise, still has a shot at two hundred thousand dollars the next day. For a while he waits for his partner to return. A lot of reasons can explain the delay besides getting caught. And the police don't come. That's critical because it isn't consistent with his partner getting caught. His partner is caught, plea-bargains down to life imprisonment for information on where Janey is plus the names of his partners. In that case the police would be there as soon as his partner could have, but that isn't happening. We've got to make sure that Janowski knows that. You're the father. You're in charge. He can't do anything to jeopardize your daughter without your permission. Just don't give it. Say no. The worst I think would happen is just what you suggest, Brian, the other guy moves, takes Janey with him. Then we still have a chance to pay two hundred thousand for her the next day. But if not, if the guy stays put because the place he has is secure—we've got to figure that they've planned this out but they don't have a lot of money. Otherwise they wouldn't bet their lives on two hundred grand. And he really is concerned with police, so he's not going to jump at changing locations."

"He'll *kill* Janey, then leave."

"We should know where they are before all this is set to happen."

"If I thought that, Spike, I'd get you the two hundred thousand and forget them."

"We're close. By next call, I'll have them."

"How can you be sure?"

Halleck told him. "Last night I ran some low-level analyses on the background sounds. On the second tape—

before the call from Soldier Field—I heard two people walking by, man and woman. Woman with high heels, the periodic click is unmistakable. It comes and goes, same cadence, increasing intensity, decreasing intensity, as she approaches and leaves. Then they laugh. It doesn't sound much like laughing until the damn computer makes it a laugh, forces the fit, but it's there, even unenhanced. It's a woman's laughter, unmistakable pitch and affectation, very feminine. Then they talk. The man says, 'Yeah, Jared . . .,' and that's all I can coax out. And the woman says, 'Very funny,' in the sense that something is very funny. My guess is that they've just seen or sat through something nearby that's very funny, that's what she's laughing at, and that, maybe, it involves someone named Jared, first or last name. My guess is that these two were walking from some kind of entertainment, movie, theater—something—to a parked car."

"What the hell difference does that make, even if it's real?"

Brian's impatience was understandable. He had no tolerance for seeing pieces of a puzzle fall slowly together while the pieces of his life were rapidly falling apart. Still, Halleck had to buy time, to prevent Brian from turning Janowski loose like a mad dog. Quickly he explained, "Where they're keeping Janey is within two or three blocks from a theater or movie house, something like that. And it's between that and a parking lot, or a street that's safe to park on. The two people are not in a larger group. They're alone, so we can conclude that wherever they've got Janey is in a pretty safe neighborhood. As soon as Debra gets up . . ."

"I'm up," yawned a voice behind him.

". . . I'll see what she can make of it."

"You'll let me know when they call?"

"Yes," Halleck said. "Just get me the five thousand."

Without another word, not even his customary adieu, Brian hung up. Halleck felt Debra stirring behind him, said, "Janowski has some wind chimes information, I understand."

"I'll get on it. Is that line free?"

"It is now."

Halleck heard Debra keying numbers in, listened. "Miriam," she said, "Deb. Janowski left some addresses on noise pollution infractions. Yeah, The wind chimes. No, no, no. Don't send anyone out with a meter. Let's just get the data base and locations. He wants me to handle it. Ready?" A pause, then to Halleck, "You got a pad and pencil?"

It hit him. He didn't. "No," he said.

"Wait," she said. "My purse." He heard the jangle of keys, compacts, eyebrow pencil, loose change, a pen slip out, wallet, pad.

"Is that big enough?" he asked.

"I write small," she explained, "and in shorthand. Yeah, shoot, Miriam." A pause, then, "No, not the whole list, we just want the offenders from the Near North Side up to maybe Lincolnwood."

Silence. Halleck hadn't worked out a signal for her to hang up if a call came in on the Granville line. Confusion was unaffordable. Still, she had to get these locations.

"How many?" Debra said. "Thirty-seven? Okay, read 'em off."

As she scratched out the addresses, the Granville line rang sharply. Halleck caught his breath, let it out, knew the recording machine was already running. "Keep working," he told her. "Just don't make a sound."

He picked up with "Granville residence."

"Is Ellen Granville available please?" calm, pleasant voice. Midwestern. No sense of alarm, no tension. Who? Of course! All calls were forwarded here, not just the kidnappers'. And there was no way of sorting them out. A perfectly innocent call from a neighbor might confuse or frustrate Janey's captors into a miscalculated move. He would have to dispatch all other calls quickly, but without raising alarm.

"Ellie is unavailable just now. This is her brother, Spike Halleck. What can I tell her?"

"Just that Janey is due, as she should remember, for the first rehearsal of this year's church Christmas pageant this Wednesday at eight o'clock. For fitting and the playbill picture. Will you tell her?"

"Certainly."

"If she has any questions she should call Marian Adams's on 314-2765."

"I'll let her know."

"Thank you."

"You're welcome."

"And Mr. Halleck? Could you ask her to have Janey bring that recipe of hers for fruitcake."

"Of course. Thanks for calling."

"Tell Janey I'll see her Wednesday night!"

"If I see her I'll pass the word."

"Good-bye."

"Good-bye."

Halleck heard Marian Adams' voice break into afterthought with, "And if—" when he locked the handset into its cradle. As in Ecclesiastes, there is a time for every purpose, even rudeness, under heaven. Now was the time. Under the circumstances it was hard to be concerned about Janey's missing a Christmas pageant. Yet here was another detail that needed consideration. While Janey was missing, her absences would begin to be noticed. They would have to devise a cover story, something credible but not too urgent. A cold. The flu. Anything to buy a couple of days but nothing to bring caring friends flocking in to see how she was doing.

As Halleck concentrated on how that would be handled, Debra scratched through the last of the addresses. Refocusing his thoughts, he once again ran through what he imagined would happen with the kidnappers in the next twenty-four hours. They would pick up the five thousand, split it. Coming unexpectedly as it would, the extra money would seem too good to be true. Beyond it and because of it, the pot of gold at the end of the rainbow would seem more real, more accessible, more enticing. Two hundred thousand dollars. That would keep the fish on the line. But it wouldn't land them. Because however they got their hands on that money, Janey's captors would all be forced to the same plan: kill the girl, then kill the others. Unless they found out where she was before the final payment, Janey was dead.

The phone rang again, a noise with a tangible stab to

it—the Granville line. Halleck picked up and said, "Granville residence."

"This is Mel Corvalis, City Desk, *Chicago Tribune*. We still have a few questions on this story we're going to run and need some more background information. Since you offered to fill in . . . hello?"

Halleck froze, unable to think. What had Brian done?

"What's this about?"

"The Granville story . . ."

"Sorry?"

"Brian Granville. Vice president, First Chicago National. Wednesday Financial Section. Remember?"

Halleck thawed, flushed. "Oh, yes," then remembered, keep the line clear. "What do you need?"

"This Mr. Granville?"

"His brother-in-law."

"You know Mr. Granville's age?"

"Thirty-six?"

"College?"

"Illinois, Harvard Business."

"And children?"

"One."

"Name?"

"Janey."

"Anything more on her?"

"What?"

"Something we can put in, you know, about hobbies. Human interest stuff, some project she's doing right now . . ."

"No, not now. Anything else?"

"No, that's it."

Halleck hung up, found himself shaking, took three deep breaths, rubbed the hot sweat from his palms. "What time is it?" he turned and asked.

"Eight forty-five."

"Morning."

"Yeah, morning."

A long silence, another deep breath, then, "I can tell."

"How?"

"Traffic noises from the street. Warmth of the sun on my face."

"How you feel?"

"Hollow, one-dimensional. I don't think man can live by amphetamine alone."

"Hungry?"

"I could eat."

"I'll fix breakfast. What do you have?"

"Eggs. Bacon. Cereal."

"How do you cook this stuff?"

"By smell, feel—consistency. A done egg is more cohesive than a raw egg. That sort of thing. Time helps. You set the burner on a mark, set the timer—they have them with ridges for the minutes, then cook. It can be done."

"You may be better than I am."

"Don't bet on it."

"Give me ten minutes."

As those minutes began to pass, aromas drifted in from the kitchen, attended by the sharp sizzling of strips of bacon frying, the whack of an eggshell cracking, its contents hissing onto a hot pan, butter, warm, some smoldering just short of burning, a "shit" erupting as a pan lifted from a burner was set into the sink with a clank. "This is why I lost my husband, you know," she said laughing. Sense of humor. Better than seeing, a vision into the human condition, humor.

"You want to come to the table?" she yelled.

"Better stay by the phone," he said.

"All right. Let me feed you."

"I can do it. Just give me the plate."

"Don't be an asshole, Halleck. *I* couldn't eat from a plate in my lap, was a disaster at dinner parties. Just"— she smacked his outreached hand—"relax. Bon appétit."

The eggs leapt into his open mouth. They were good. More than good. When he finished chewing, he said, "Man was a fool to leave this kind of cooking."

"He didn't leave it, really, to be fair. We just kind of kept missing. Me with police work, the hours and all. Him and the flying. The house was all we had in common, and not much of that."

"You don't have to talk about it."

"No, I don't."

Bacon this time, a couple of strips. Her turn to ask, "When was your last girlfriend, Spike?"

"The ring, remember. Wedded to my work."

"Don't give me the martyr shit. Some girl must have been smart enough to have gotten after your body."

"It's not exactly Arnold Schwarzenegger."

"God save the fairer sex from that. Eat."

Muffin, buttered. Blackberry jam. Shit. He'd asked the clerk for blueberry. Comedian. Even before he finished chewing he said, "I don't know how much you heard. Brian is getting five thousand for the first drop. Their terms. I'll need someone to carry it. Maybe Janowski could suggest—"

"I'll carry it," she said, placing a hot cup in his hand. "Coffee," she said.

"Negative. Too dangerous."

"What? You don't think we're trained to do this sort of thing? You may be surprised to know that I've actually done it a time or two before. And these guys, I can promise, don't even *want* you to be there. They just want someone, anyone, to show, drop the package, disappear, don't look back."

"I still can't let you—"

"Listen, Spike. You were the one who wanted Janowski out of it, right? And I'm not going to tell you you're wrong. Now there's no court order and no tap on the Granville line. The only person who is going to know their terms is you, and whoever else you tell. Now if you tell me, it's just me. One kid's death on my conscience is enough. I think Janowski could shrug it off forever. Don't let him know, I'm warning you."

"But—"

"As for the danger, it's the cost of doing business. Part of the job, all right? I'm not working for Walt Disney, you know."

Halleck sighed, tired of arguing. "You've got the job."

She left him with the coffee cup, walked away, started making pip, pip, pip, pip sounds. What was it? He didn't want to ask, couldn't stand the curiosity. Suddenly she said, "You're not going to believe this, but underneath the flight paths and inside the three circles around the L

105

stations we have sixteen—do you believe it?—sixteen wind chimes identified. So what are we going to do? We can't send patrol cars cruising by to check them all out, stake the place out. And I wouldn't trust Janowski with an unmarked. Unmarkeds all have the same license symbols, dead giveaway. So you know what this means, Halleck? It means I play door-to-door solicitor. What will it be? Chocolates? Magazines? All-purpose cleaning fluid?"

"None of the above. I just got an idea."

"Shoot, genius."

"Call a hack named Gerry Malone, works for Main Line Cab. Tell him it's time to pay up. Spike Halleck needs his services."

"What the hell's this about?"

"Never mind. When you get him, just give me the phone."

Debra dialed through and did what he asked her to, then handed him the phone. The voice said, "You da blind guy?"

"I speak for all of us, all of those fares you ripped us off on. Now it's time to deliver for those service fees."

"Hey, I got a quota t'make."

"Work overtime. I'm going to need your cab, but not you, tonight."

"You're fucking kiddin'."

"Never been more serious in my life."

"Fuck you, Mac!"

"Just a minute. I'd like you to speak with Officer Debra Seraphicos of the Chicago Police, and explain to her that you tried to overcharge a blind person." Halleck handed her the phone.

"This is Officer Debra Seraphicos of the Special Investigation Branch of the Chicago Police, badge number 7864. Mr. Malone, I have an official complaint here from a Mr. John Halleck that you did, on Monday night last, attempt to unlawfully overcharge him on a fare from downtown to Lake Forest. Is that true?"

"Hey, now, wait—"

"May I have your taxi license number, please?"

"What, you want I do what he asks? Why don't you just ask?"

"Under those conditions, Mr. Halleck, would you be willing to drop your complaint?"

Halleck took over the handset. "Bring your cab by my place, at eight tonight, not one minute later."

"Jesus!" the hack said.

"Think he'll do it?" she asked Halleck.

"Sure. Otherwise it's his license, or so he thinks. It's a pain in the ass for him, but compared to the alternative . . ."

"There's still no reason I couldn't do it right away."

Halleck shook his head. "Too suspicious. Some of those places might be walk-ups, places solicitors don't go. No one will think twice about a cab."

"How sure are you of those sixteen?"

"It's odds, that's all. Just odds," he whispered, thinking of the trips he had made to Vegas with Stan Black, the many times they'd lost, the few they'd won, how it was when you feel, actually *feel*, lucky, so that you know things are going to break for you. Halleck hadn't felt lucky in what seemed like a long, long time. And right now all he felt was nervous, nervous and tired.

"But we could have missed some," she said.

"Maybe." He hesitated. "Sure. But let's not give up so easily."

"Okay, like you say, Halleck, let's go with what we got. What next?"

He sipped his coffee, felt a small buzz, nothing to sustain him, but a lift. "We try to pin them down better. Have Janowski put undercover men, somebody in plain clothes, someone who looks like a commuter, maybe, at each of those three L stations. As soon as possible. And see they synchronize their watches on standard time and log in each train that pulls in and leaves. Each and every one, all three stations. Clear?"

Before she could begin dialing the phone rang and she gasped, then relaxed. "Your line, Spike."

He picked up. "Halleck."

"Janowski. What do you have?"

"Nothing more. You?"

"Seraphicos gave you the wind chimes?"

"Already plotted on the map."

"Good. Is she there?"

Halleck pushed her the handset. "He wants you."

"Seraphicos," she said.

Halleck listened.

Janowski said something that made her sigh. Impatience. "When I need a break, I'll let you know."

Silence. Janowski was saying something.

"No, I don't think it would be okay. Let me ask."

To Halleck: "He wants to know if you want someone fresh." Then she goosed him. Reflectively he jumped.

"No. No. He says I'm fresh enough for him."

To Halleck: "He wants to know if you wouldn't rather have Officer Kowalski sub for a while." He could hear her hand cup over the mouthpiece as she told him, "Kowalski is a big, hairy Pole with bad breath and the social presence of an ashtray. You want Kowalski?"

Halleck smiled, shook his head no, almost laughed.

"Janowski. Sarge. Listen. Mr. Halleck is a normal, red-blooded American male in proper working order, which means there is no chance in hell he would want Kowalski when he has a chance to work with me."

Silence. She laughs.

"Even if he can't see my tits, it's my brain he admires."

Another syncope.

"Go to hell, Janowski. All right. Listen, this is important. We're trying to get some time markers on arrivals and departures from those three L stations." She explained the plan and stopped, listened, then said, "Yes, I know all about your difficulties and all that stuff. So be a hero, Jano, just do it, all right. Fine. Yes, fine, I hear you. No, I won't be late. You said fifteen minutes at the Whole Donut. On Michigan Avenue. Sure, I got a question. How long are *you* gonna keep *me* waiting?"

To Halleck, her hand cupped again over the mouthpiece. "He wants to meet me. The patrol cars may have something on the green sedan. Big maybe. Will you be okay alone?"

"Go," Halleck said. "But try to be back in forty minutes, okay?"

"As soon as I can," she said.

"What does he really want?"

"When I know, so will you."

Her feet padded across the carpet, the temperature in the room fluttered as the door opened, clicked shut. Halleck turned in the darkness toward the Granville line and felt the adrenaline cooking inside him.

"Just hang in there, Janey," he said aloud. "With a little luck . . ."

A little?

8

"Absolutely not, Janowski!" she blurted out.

Only halfway through a puffy French cruller, Debra Seraphicos was mad enough to bust him in the chops. Beneath the scratched Formica counter of the Whole Donut she felt her fist clenching, then thought better of it. He was a big man, two twenty plus of past muscle now fat, a living tribute to what ten plus years of sloth could do to a former linebacker's physique. Still, the arboreal limbs and huge hands retained their power. Around the station he was not a man to anger. Even with her strength, the result of two years of power lifting, she was unlikely to do more than jar a few teeth loose. And after that, Janowski was likely to shake the stars out of his field of vision, massage his jaw and say, honestly confused, "What the hell you do that for?" So she didn't, which just left the anger roiling inside.

Beside her, spinning slowly back and forth on a stool, Janowski sat, hat still on his head, ready to roll if his page summoned. He just sat there, sipping his coffee, warming his cold hands on the sides of his cup, waiting for her response. That made her madder.

"You have no right, sarge, to put that little girl at risk."

She took out her agitation on her purse, fishing for her Camels, snapping one out, catching it in her lips.

Janowski scratched a flame from his Zippo, lit her up. "She's already at risk," he said. "And no one's seen her in nearly two days. That includes the wonderful Spike Halleck."

Debra offered him one but he shook his head, no. "Quit," he said.

111

"Since when?" she asked. She closed her eyes, took a long drag, let it slowly go.

"This morning?"

She had to smile, opened her eyes to meet his. "You got anything on the green car?"

Janowski sighed. "How many old green cars do you think there are in Chicago with Illinois plates?"

"In the areas of interest?"

"Who says she's there."

"You can do better?"

"Halleck is flaky, Deb. I thought you'd see that."

"Is that why you asked me to help him, because he's a flake? Or because you think so much of the professional value of my time?"

"You handle these things well."

"Define 'these things.' "

"The politics. The bullshit. All I wanted you to do was to sit there with Halleck, to humor him, to let him have his way, let his leads peter out, then bring him around. With Halleck on our side, we can bring the Granvilles—the parents—around so we do things our way at the drop. But suddenly Halleck has this screwy idea for an inducement."

"What are you thinking, Jano?"

"He's gonna get the kid killed, Deb."

"You think?"

"Possible. I don't know. I've gotta think he's playing with himself."

"What about you, sarge. You never play with yourself?" Janowski snickered.

"Listen, sarge, he's expecting another call. I promised to get back, so if you don't have anything else—"

"We've got a real chance if they bite on this five thousand thing."

"Make Halleck buy it, Jano. It's his call."

"He's an amateur. He's emotionally involved. He's unbalanced."

"No, he's not. You got those men at the L stations?"

"On their way, now, for all the good it will do."

"What's it going to take, huh?" she badgered him. "One more day. Whatever way it breaks, one more day. You so anxious, huh?"

"We can set up a good tail on the mule," he said.

"What is this, déja vu? Read my lips. N-O."

"So you just gonna let 'em walk with the five thousand?"

"Not my call. Not my five thousand."

"And so we get zip."

"We get time, we string 'em along."

"They won't spook, Deb?"

She shrugged. "What if they do? Either way you're covered. Let Halleck do it his way. If he wins, you take credit. If he loses, it was his call. You can walk away. What do you care?"

"I'm not in control. It's my investigation and I'm not in control. This is like using psychics."

"Compared to nothing, I'd take psychics," she came back.

"Maybe we got more than nothing."

"Like?"

Janowski drew a deep breath, held it, raised his eyebrows as he let it out. "Like maybe Lou Scannon. He keeps pinging me with questions like do I know so-and-so? Have I ever heard of what's his name? What do I think of the Japanese Red Army?"

"So what do you think of the Japanese Red Army, Jano?"

"Hey, you know I think that Scannon may be stiffing us, tryin' to sniff out what we have, put it together with what he has—and we don't—and beat us to the collar. Under the circumstances that makes me real nervous."

"You know what I think? I think you and Scannon are playing shadow games with one another and neither one of you has shit, that's what I think."

"Look, Deb. If you help, we maybe can roll this thing up on the next pickup." The images of the mule fleeing in the crowd, the chase, the little girl's mutilated body leaped into her mind.

"No," she said. "Halleck will pull it together or not in twenty-four hours. After that it's all yours." After that, she thought, we have no choice. After that we're playing the kidnapper's game.

"Halleck all macho about this, is he? Gonna make the drop himself?"

"How do I know? He tells me everything?"

Janowski shrugged. "Then who?"

Her turn to shrug. "He has friends, too, you know. Being blind doesn't mean you have no friends."

"You his friend, Deb?"

"Christ, Janowski. I'm a cop. You think I'm so desperate to get involved overnight with a blind man." As she said it, convinced, she wondered. Since her body had become more muscled, fewer men had found it attractive. More often they saw it as threatening. How long since she had been touched, except by herself? She tried not to think about it, said, "Look, like I said. A day. Give it a day, Jano. Don't sprout hemorrhoids over this."

"I want you to try to turn him our way," he said.

"If I see this map thing breaking down, maybe."

"And I want you to give me anything solid he does get, anything specific and useful, before anyone else gets it."

"Even the father?"

"Especially the father."

"I thought a minute ago you said Halleck was playing with himself. Now you say maybe he'll get something specific and useful, as you say. What is it really, Jano? You desperate? You curious? Or you jealous?"

Janowski's beefy face burst with color. "Look, I'm just keeping every angle covered, okay? I'm not stupid enough to look the other way if something pops up with all this electronic hocus-pocus bullshit. And in case you hadn't guessed I've got a few angles of my own. And right now they're maybe just as good, maybe better, than any Halleck has. I mean it's not as if I've been sitting on my ass."

"Then you followed his advice? Checked out those voices?"

"Fuck the voices." She was surprised at his vehemence. He went on, "All I know is that I've got two punks, suddenly kidnappers. So I ask the warden at Joliet if he has any ideas. He says he'll talk it around, knowing that maybe somebody they've sprung at Southern Michigan, maybe a gubernatorial parole, good behavior, whatever, will be involved. Anyway, he has this idea about kidnappings. Says it's the dream crime, the strike-and-disappear angle, that makes it so luscious. That's why the hard timers like to tease the punks into it, tell them it gives them control. After all, they don't have to walk into a bank, cameras all over them the second they go through the door, with a vault and armed guards to beat, stuck inside a building where alarms go off the minute they pull out their guns. No. Here all they do is knock down a grade-school teacher or bus driver, maybe just snatch the kid right off the street. How tough is that? And then they can name their price. Whatever the market will bear, right?"

Janowski stopped long enough to sip his coffee, then went on, "So every punk and short-timer that drains out, says, hey, I can do this. He already has some ideas, like this guy Granville, a bank veep. Hell, I mean his name is on the annual report, his address in the *Social Register*. How long does it take 'em to find the kid's school? They get her routine by asking questions, reading stuff. People like Granville lead structured lives, follow schedules, Deb. They *are* order. Everything is so neat, so perfect, till something like this happens to show 'em that no one is control. Forget nuclear war, forget tornados or lightning bolts, and just concentrate on getting across the street alive. You don't believe me, ask Spike Halleck."

"He does okay."

"You like him, don't you?"

"He's smart."

"I'm sure he thinks so. I just don't think he knows what he's up against."

"Maybe not," she sighed. "Maybe he's real green. And maybe there's a point where I'll say, Jano, Spike Halleck has taken us as far as he can with this noise thing. But not yet. We have a day."

"Do we?"

Janowski had a point. Everything Halleck was setting up was predicated on an assumption that the abductors would come back for more, that they would get greedy, that fear wouldn't drive them off. Looking into his eyes, old eyes filled with skepticism, she said, "Let me buy you coffee, sarge."

"I got it," he said, grunting as he fished into deep pockets.

"Forget the macho shit," she said. "I'm tired of it. Just let me buy you coffee. How much is coffee, right?"

He shrugged.

Debra put a couple of dollars on the counter, said, "How hard was that, Jano?"

"Huh?"

"You didn't think I couldn't afford to buy you coffee, did you?"

"No, I—"

"And you didn't think I would go hungry at dinner because I bought you a crummy cup of coffee, did you?"

"What the—" She could see the confusion growing in Janowski's eyes.

"And, you know, if we do break this case, you wouldn't think it absolutely impossible that I could take you out to dinner, the both of us, just to celebrate. I mean, I could spring for that, you think?"

"Yeah, I . . . guess."

"Then why don't you think that these guys would buy the idea that if Granville could drop five thousand on them one day, which is nothing to him, he wouldn't turn up the two hundred thousand, since what he wants is what they have."

Enlightenment filled his eyes, then faded. The skepticism had flooded in before he said, "Maybe, okay. But the warden at Joliet has turned up the names of a couple of guys sprung, one there, one from Southern Michigan, just three weeks ago, who we know got together to talk business in Chicago."

"A bit thin, no?"

"Hear me out, like you ask me to do for Halleck."

Her turn to shrug. He continued, "Couple'a guys, one a nickle and dimer named Nick Spiros."

"Nice Greek boy," she said smiling.

"Other named Danny Valitano."

"So?"

"Grew up bad together. Scuttlebutt is they were in a holding tank in Wayne County a few years back and overheard by the house snitch, subsequently cut up by the local population, to have threatened a real big score, then off to Brazil."

"Brazil? Why the hell Brazil? They speak Portuguese?"

"They don't even speak English," Janowski said. "But that's not what they're concerned about. They like the extradition laws down there, and the currency exchange. One strike, a big one, and they take a long vacation, pump up the local economy, enjoy the tits and ass in string bikinis at Rio, your typical convict wet dream scenario."

"And you think these are the guys?"

Janowski's shoulders move up, down an inch, his head tilts to the side. It wasn't much to go on and he knew it. "Let's put it this way. Since they were seen and heard in the Windy City, actually East Chicago, across the line, about two weeks ago, no one has been able to put them anywhere."

"Maybe they moved on," she said.

"And maybe they didn't."

"So what has all this got to do with Halleck?"

"Get him to hurry up, Deb. If these are the two guys, Nick is a sadist and pervert . . ."

"Like I said, nice Greek boy."

"And Danny thinks he's God."

"Now how can they miss with a team like that?"

Janowski got up, too. "Hey, keep me posted, huh? Let me know what's going on, and like I said, first and without delay. Anything solid, anything at all."

She butted out the Camel in the counter ashtray. "You, too, including anything you pick up from Scannon. And don't forget those guys at the L platforms."

"How can I? In thirty minutes they'll be bitching about the cold."

"With reason," she said. Beyond the rattling store window, the wind had picked up on Michigan Avenue, blowing scraps of paper at the pedestrians who advanced against it with raised collars. How would the kid be holding up in this weather? she wondered. Had she eaten as much as a doughnut? Was she still alive?

As she pushed through the door into the gust, she checked her watch, seeing she was late. "Shit," she said, and raised her hand, waving desperately for a cab.

As she stood at curbside, Janowski huddled inside the

warm bakery, eyeing her, thinking his own thoughts, thoughts he hadn't shared with her, or anyone. Now he had a lot already figured out that might actually happen in about two days, when the odds held that the kid would be dead or missing, the whole mess exploded, the parents outraged, the mayor mad, the chief pissed shitless, and who were all these folks gonna be sore at? Halleck? Of course not. The genius gave it his best shot. Blame goes where it usually does, to the official in charge. He knew who that was. So did Brian Granville. And it didn't help that the father kept him from openly mobilizing Scannon's men. So the FBI, sitting back and waiting, clear of any blame, would be delighted to take over if Janowski took the fall. And fall he would. He did not doubt Brian Granville's Republican connections or what failure would mean for him. Granville himself had been explicit. But if he was going to be fall guy, he didn't want it to be because an amateur like Halleck had screwed up. Janowski had been at this business a long time and knew the score. And he was sure he had enough cards up his sleeve to produce a good hand when he was called. But he wasn't about to sit back and let events that determined his future play out. He could do something Halleck couldn't, even if Scannon was stonewalling. He could look. What harm was there in that?

9

Behind Halleck someone entered his apartment, shut the door, shivered off the cold. To a blindfolded person, it could have been anyone, even an intruder. To Spike, who had always made full use of his hearing, and considerable use of his other senses, there was no doubt it was Debra Seraphicos. But it wasn't, of course, just senses. It was reason, too, the way the nonvisual clues held together in a pattern that led only one way.

First the tumbler clicked and rolled, turning smoothly, without force. Then the door opened and closed quickly, the way a woman living alone often learns to do, so that she alone gets in. The next clue clinched it. Wafting across the room came the scent, *Repechage,* that took him by the nose, reached inside him all the way to the secret place between his legs that started to twitch, something he couldn't stop. He didn't want to, really. He had no idea what she looked like. His picture of her was different, a series of sounds, a catalog of actions, an intimate history of smells, from her cigarettes to her perfume, the impression she had made on the couch, the unforgettable claim that her mother had been big busted, and finally, that strange, evocative blend of strength and softness in that so human gesture, so reassuring to someone like Halleck, awash in forever grayness, that says, I'm here. He turned around as if he could see her, something they had taught him to do, to acknowledge those of the sighted world on their terms, and said, "You're back."

"It's *still* colder than a witch's tit in a brass bra out there, Spike." As if agreeing, the wind shook the window facing on the street. "How can that be? It's sunny out there, for Chrissakes." Halleck lifted his face toward the window and could feel the warmth, just as he could feel the cold leaking in around the window frame. "Did Janowski put men at the L stations?"

"Either already there or on their way. More coffee?"

"And one of mother's little helpers," he said yawning. "They're due to call. No time to be falling asleep."

"Can you hold up under this?"

"It's only another day. I used to do this for exams at college."

"I did two years at North Park."

"And?"

"Lost interest. Nothing in there seemed to connect with the world I knew. Anyway—"

"When they call," Halleck interrupted, "I want you to stand right behind me. Plug in a button earphone so you can follow, but don't say anything, because we don't want them to be aware it's anyone else but me and the family.

"Watch the elapsed timer, the green LED display. Should show zeros now. See them? Right under the time of day."

"I see it."

Halleck told her as firmly as he could, "After the call comes in, I want you to tap me on the shoulder after each minute has passed, especially hard, almost squeezing, on the third. That will tell me to close it up, to hang up. I don't want them to suspect a trace."

"Now these guys are streetwise, if they've done time and traded bedtime stories, they would pick up on that right away. So it's better to come across like a terribly naive, honorable businessman who knows they hold all the cards on this hand, but who is trying to play into a better deal on the next, to close out the game with minimum losses."

"I hope you're right," she said.

"Janowski had other thoughts?"

"We both know he does."

"He tried to persuade you?"

"Of course. What do you expect, he'd tell me how he likes running errands for you?"

"But he *did* put the men at the L platforms."

"He said." Silence. "Yeah, he will. It's just when."

"When better be now. We need it now."

"He may be trying to split assignments between the green clunker and the other stuff. A guess. I don't know."

When the Granville line buzzed, they both jumped.

"Watch the timer."

She struggled to get the button earphone in, hissing, "Pick up the goddamn phone, Halleck."

He did, answering in a smooth, well-modulated voice, "Granville residence."

Slow breathing, stuffed nose, sniffles. A snorting sound, swallowing mucus, then, in the gravelly voice and cadenced breathing of the first caller came, "You know who this is?"

"I assume this is the Party of the Second Part."

"Whatever, yeah, right." In the background, Halleck could hear the jackhammer working again, had to calm himself. They hadn't moved her. As if in agreement, the tinkling of the wind chimes danced in the background. Still, he had only three minutes.

"This is the Party of the First Part. We are still very interested in your offer, assuming that the merchandise is undamaged."

"Wait."

Precious time ran off. How much? Debra, her hands lightly on his shoulders, had not squeezed off the first minute yet. Relax, he told himself. Be cool.

Janey's voice burst on, breathing hard, sniffling. A cold? What? No time to analyze. Later on that. "Spike, I want Mommy!"

"Mommy can't come right now, honey." Think. "She had to get your outfit for the Christmas pageant. She'll be back soon."

Suddenly he realized that all she had said could be a recording, played back on high-resolution tape. Halleck said, "What's the name of your stuffed gorilla, Janey?"

"What?"

"You know."

"Chombo?"

"Right." It was live. No way they could have anticipated that.

Debra gave him the first squeeze. One minute down, two to go. "Now give me the man back, Janey. We'll have you out in another day. You'll be home."

"Another *day*." To a kid, a day seemed an eternity. For Halleck, that same forever might not be enough.

"Okay?" Asking, by its tone, you satisfied, Halleck?

"Very well. As you know, we cannot have the total sum required in payment before tomorrow. Nevertheless, as an indication of good faith, and in recognition of your outstanding care of the merchandise, we would like to offer you a five-thousand-dollar bonus, deliverable anywhere in town, at any time and on your terms."

"What?"

"Five thousand dollars now."

"We said two hundred thousand. You want the girl delivered in a carry-out food box?"

Something icy lanced through Halleck's guts at that thought. Very quickly, still under control, he assured them, "We fully intend to deliver your two hundred thousand. I repeat, this is a bonus."

"I think this is a trick."

"How can it be a trick if we let you set the pickup terms?"

"You trying to get a trace?"

Second squeeze on his shoulders.

"None of our calls, as you know, has been long enough to get a trace." Halleck could hear something behind the man's adenoid rattle, something like—what—a child screaming? Janey! He almost yelled for them to stop before realizing that the sound was squealing excitement, kids outside playing.

"Five thousand bucks?"

"Wherever you want, today. And however you want it. The rest to follow. If you need time, think about it. Call us back. That's the offer. That's all the cash Mr. Granville could put together today." Halleck felt like snapping off, take it or leave it, thought better of it, waited instead.

There was a shuffling, a hand covering the mouthpiece, the muted sound of the one man yelling, listening, uncovering the mouthpiece, saying, "We'll take it, Halleck. Stick by the phone."

Then he hung up.

Five seconds later, Debra Seraphicos squeezed his shoulder so hard it hurt. "Ow," he said.

"Three minutes," she said back.

"He hung up. I think he has an hourglass or egg timer, or something, maybe just a digital stopwatch. I think he's controlling the intervals."

"Doesn't trust you."

"I don't think they trust anyone. It's their life they're dealing with, as well as Janey's. That can make anyone a little tense." She kept her hands on him, rubbing gently on his shoulders, up into the neck.

"Speaking of a little tense," she said, kept rubbing.

"That feels good."

"Your reward for being a good uncle."

"I'll have that when we get Janey back."

Silence, no confirmation. "Think they'll call back?" she said.

"Wanta bet?"

"I'm not betting against the kid," she said.

"I never thought you were. We're just betting on whether they nibble on the five-grand lure. One way or another they call back. That's the whole point, isn't it?"

"There's another point, Halleck. It's like any gamble. When the stakes get too high and the odds are bad, you walk away from the table. They can't buy another life, not even with two hundred thousand."

Halleck found no comfort in that. He had only the clues that came off the tape, his ability to put them in place, and the ability of his agents—the police, taxi drivers, bankers, and Debra Seraphicos—to run down possibilities, to narrow the search area. Hell, if they got it small enough, down to a block or two before time ran out, he would let Janowski throw up a cordon around that area and search, house by house. Still, he thought he could do better. Within the next two tapes, between the background noises and what they already had, he was willing to bet that, with luck, they could narrow it down to a two-by-two-block area. In fact he needed progress to defend his methods to Janowski, to keep the search going his way. Any excuse Janowski could find might be enough to cancel it. He couldn't let that happen. Not now.

Behind him came a knock.

"That must be Brian with the money."

She opened the door, let him in.

"Are you crazy?" she asked. "Walking down the streets of downtown Chicago with five grand?"

"Who knows it's five thousand dollars? It's just one of a hundred thousand briefcases. And that's nothing compared to what's at stake. What do we have, Spike?"

"Another call, just before you got here," he said.

"You talked with Janey? She's all right?"

"She's still scared, Brian. But she's settled. It's really her. She's still okay."

"And how much closer are we from the last tape?" Anxious, nervous, strained. But why not?

"We're just about to go over it. Before we do, why not check the map. The sixteen pushpins that Debra put in the three circles around L stations are places where we think, from the wind chime noises, Janey could be held. Right now Janowski has been cooperative enough to place lookouts at each station to log the times of trains arriving and departing. Unluckily for us I heard no train brakes on the last call. You, Debra?"

"No. I don't think so."

"Still, we can have the computer look for low-level track noises, maybe tease them out with CAT. If so, we can still confirm a train arriving from a couple of miles away—it shakes the tracks and makes them give off a characteristic rattle. If you screen everything else out, it shows up."

"But there's no marker, Spike," she said, quickly understanding how he was thinking. "There's no sound of brakes on this call, no specific noise at one time that would let us know Janey is near one of those L platforms."

"But that's the beauty of Janowski's men," Halleck said.

"I've never found Janowski's men particularly beautiful, but go ahead. So what? How do they help us if we get *no* braking sounds?"

"I need the times during the tape that L trains actually arrived at all *three* stations. If a train arrived during the call, and we didn't hear it, the place they're keeping Janey can't be near *that* station, so we can eliminate everything around that station and be down to two circles."

"I'll call Janowski on your line," she said, picking up.

"Wait, we could be getting a return from the kidnappers."

"Would someone like to tell me what the hell is going on?" Brian demanded. "Where do we drop the five thousand?"

Halleck held up his hand for patience, quiet.

"Janowski? Seraphicos. We need some times of arrivals for L trains at those three platforms, within the last half hour . . ." Silence. A clucking noise. "Now what the fuck do you mean, Jano, they haven't arrived. I thought you told me you were going to set this fucking thing up, sarge. Don't give me any fuckin—"

Brian Granville snatched the phone. "Goddamnit, Janowski . . ." Pause. "You know goddamn well who this is and you will remember that I said that I would hand your ass, basted and broiled, to the commissioners if you obstructed this investigation. Now get off your fat ass and make sure those men are at the stations, pronto. We're waiting on another call here, Janowski. We *need* this. Drive them personally, if you have to. But get them in place!"

Debra took the handset back. "You heard the man, sarge," she said. "Listen, don't tell me. I think he's right. I think you screwed up. Matter of fact, I think this could cost you big already, unless you can make it up. Yeah, sure, just an opinion. Yeah, sure, sarge, same to you. Don't forget to write." Halleck could tell she'd turned by the change in volume of her voice. "He's on it, I mean really on it."

For all the good it does us now, Halleck fumed. Forget it. "Let's see what else we can get from nothing."

"What do you mean?" Brian demanded, still hot.

"Street noises. Honking, squealing tires, revving engines, diesel engine sounds, that sort of thing. There's nothing like that. Now there's the jackhammer, which is louder than all that, but only by about twenty-five decibels or so. We ought to be able to hear something, but if, and only if, there's a lot of heavy urban traffic passing. If not, you get what we heard. Nothing. So we're looking for someplace without much traffic. A small, narrow cut-though street, a cul-de-sac, someplace, maybe, that's blocked off for repairs—that would jibe with the jack-hammer."

"Jesus, Spike, that's all guessing," Brian said, despair in his voice.

"Maybe, but there are three other things you're forgetting. One, from the jackhammer, which I bet will match up perfectly, *she's still in the same place*. As long as she is, we can close in. Two, we've got to listen to those kids playing, playing nearby, which could mean a park, or a playground, or a swing set, or it could mean that the street is shut off, barricaded, so the parents let the kids out to play, because there's no traffic."

"Still thin, Spike," Brian muttered.

"But it fits with the laughter of the couple, the people I said were returning from a party or movie or theater, who might have used the barricaded street for parking. For example, if it had a sign like NO THRU TRAFFIC posted, not many cars would go that way, unless they were stopping locally and wanted to avoid the high cost of parking. But only on a well-lit, settled neighborhood street."

"Maybe," Brian admitted.

"There's a lot to run down on this," Debra said. "But we can eliminate a lot from the map. We have the detail to ID things like parks and playgrounds, but we've got to get closer before we think of things like private swing sets. Remember the wind chimes? How many more swing sets are there than wind chimes? It would be impossible."

"Except that we were looking for wind chimes all over Chicago. We're just looking for playgrounds, or swings, or whatever, inside of three circles around L stations."

Brian objected. "But kids don't need a lot of fancy monkey bars. They prefer their imagination, and being together. It's as if, sometimes, they just have to get out from under their parents' noses, to get away from those monkey bars or swing sets that mom can see, to discover their world, their neighborhood. So don't waste your time looking for equipment. Look for the kids, themselves. Kids always call, they call to get attention, recognition. They call one another by name. I'll bet—maybe— that we could dig a name out of that segment on the last tape."

"Still, we can't check every kid in Chicago," Halleck said.

"Don't have to," Brian told him, "since there are a lot of places in those circles where kids aren't going to be playing. L Stations. Busy intersections. Bars. Think about it."

"All right."

"So why not start analyzing now?" Brian badgered.

The bottom line. Action. The clock was running. No one knew that better than Halleck. But there was another important consideration. "Brian, I can't analyze and record at the same time. It's not possible. The rig isn't set up for shunting. With this equipment—and that's what we're stuck with—we've got to record, then analyze. We can't both record and analyze. If we try analyzing what we have now we either have to lock out the recording of the next call, in which case we get nothing, or record over the disk that's being analyzed. Either way we lose. We have to wait for the next call."

"That could be hours!" Brian protested.

"I don't think so," Spike said.

"Why?" Father's frustration, anger.

"Because they're greedy."

"How can you be sure?"

"I can't. No one can. But for the first time since this thing started I feel lucky."

Then the phone rang again.

"Here goes," said Halleck, picking up.

"Granville residence."

"Yeah. Jan Steiner calling for Ellie."

"I'm sorry, Ellie is away just now. Could I take a message?"

Time. Halleck wanted to present the facade of normalcy, sustain the illusion that everything was all right, preserve the necessary privacy, if only for twenty-four more hours, that things were humming along normally in the Granvilles' life. So he couldn't rush callers off the line without creating the suspicion that things were *not* quite right. Still, there was a call coming in and he had to keep the line clear. Unfortunately, for reasons he never understood, Ellie had never expanded her service to include call waiting.

"Yeah. Tell her that aerobics is canceled tonight. Something about the instructor being sick, I guess."

"I'll do that." Come on, lady, finish up.

"And tell her I'm sorry about Janey."

"What?" Too strong. Jesus, she'd caught him off balance. But what did she mean?

"Tell her I hope Janey is all right."

"I will." What was it? Halleck still didn't know what the hell she was talking about, could only guess that she and Brian had decided on a cover story independently.

"If there's anything I can do, you know, let 'em know."

"I'm sure she will."

"You know, medicines or whatever. I can fetch them. Is she running a fever?"

Must be. "Not since we last checked," he improvised.

"Oh, good, because I figured, you know, that since she missed school this morning and all, that she wasn't feeling all that well."

"She's been better. I'll tell Ellie you called." Enough, lady.

"And ask her if it's still on for her and Brian for New Year's Eve at our place. She seemed kind of tentative about that."

"Sure. I'll ask."

"Something else I was thinking about, can't quite remember. Oh, well, I suppose it will come back to me."

"Can I have her call you back?"

"Yes, why don't you?"

"I will." By the time he hung up, Halleck was covered with sweat, his hands shaking, his breathing pulsed.

"Jesus!" he screamed, "I couldn't get that woman off the goddamn line!"

"You did good, Spike," Debra said.

"We could have missed it, you know. There's no way of telling. We could have missed it!"

He could almost hear Debra shrug. "If they're greedy, like you say, they'll call back."

"That's not my concern, or only part of it. The problem is that if they call and the line is busy, they wonder who you're calling. Police? FBI? Private investigator? For these guys, I bet every shadow has a badge. I want to minimize that fear. We have to control it. We *have* to keep them pinned down."

"There's no way we can stop the other calls coming in, Spike," Brian told him. "Ellie has a large circle of friends, active in charities and it's that time of year, you know, year-end tax deductions, Toys for Tots, that sort of thing. I'm surprised there's been as little as we've seen."

The phone rang again.

Brian said, "You see," as Halleck picked up again.

"Granville residence."

"Halleck?" Same voice, hard, a little slurred. Drinking? He hoped not.

"I confirm that. This is the Party of the First Part. Go ahead." Instantly Debra handed Brian a second button earphone, pointing to her own to show him how it worked, and slipped behind Halleck, her hand on his shoulder, ready to squeeze off the minutes.

"You've got five thousand dollars for us?"

"What kind of bills?"

"Hundreds. Fifty hundreds."

"Okay. Here's what I want you to do, so listen up." In the background came the sound of an L train squealing to a halt. No jackhammer, though. The chimes, as always, were there, too. And a dog barking, woffing, whawhawhawhawhaing. Something new. What did it all mean? Halleck was listening, all right, he was listening to everything, to anything that would give him the smallest, most seemingly insignificant clue.

"I hear you. Let me get a pad and pencil." He wasn't simply posturing, he was buying precious time. He could probably take their terms in under a minute, but that would deprive him of precious evidence that would help indicate, perhaps prove, where Janey was being hidden. "Got it," he finally said. "Go ahead."

"Take the money and put it in a mason jar, medium-sized mason jar, the kind you use for making preserves. Put three or four fishing sinkers—the lead kind—in with them—"

"Just a minute, I'm writing this down." As he spoke there were no clues that the call was being recorded—no beeps, no hums, no clicks. And yet incredibly sensitive. Stan Black once said this system could detect a flea's fart at fifty yards. Halleck didn't have to write down a thing, except to play the game. That he did superbly. "Go ahead."

"Next you fill the jar with water."

"Sorry?" Debra squeezed on his shoulder. One minute gone.

"You heard. Just do it. Fill the jar with water."

"Fill the jar with water," Halleck spoke as if the words could come from his mouth no faster than he could put them on paper. "Go ahead."

"Next you'll need a collar for the jar. You could use a dog's collar if you want, 'cept it might slip. Better is to use a real heavy rubber band, like industrial binder sort."

"Yeah, rubber band. Collar. Okay. Go ahead."

Up close, near the speaker, came the clink, clink, clink, not of the wind chime, but the spoon stirring hot beverage. Pause, sip, the sound, "Ah," then: "Now get yourself three of the green fluorescent tubes, the kind for scuba on night dives—get 'em at Morrie Magis, midtown, you know the place—then you tether 'em to the collar so they can't slip. That's real important. Make sure. You pull 'em couple a times, check it. Has to be tight."

"Go on," he said. Now something popped on all at once in the background, men yelling at one another, the sound of explosions, whistling of incoming shells, so real and yet not real at all. Halleck knew those sounds, had made a living from them. Movie sound track, but not movie house, not theater. So televison. TV or VCR. Check. Have to check schedules.

On the other end of the line, the man covered the mouthpiece and shouted, muted by unmistakable, "Shut that thing up," then came back, with the background sound track reduced. "Now, you take this to the Michigan Avenue Bridge over the Chicago River, you know it?"

"Yes," Halleck said.

"Near the Prudential Building."

"Yes, I know it."

"At three o'clock you stand in the middle, Halleck. On the side near the lake. You follow?"

"Yes."

"You crack the seals on the fluorescent tubes so they start glowin'. That's important."

"I understand."

"Then you drop the jar and five thousand and everything, like I told you, into the river."

"What?" Debra squeezed him a second time, but he was so dazed with what he just heard that he hardly recognized she had done it.

"Then you walk away. Don't turn around, don't look around, don't ask nobody for the time or nothin'. This was your idea. We never asked for no five thousand. It could sit there forever for all we're concerned. We just want to see if you can follow instructions. If you can, we keep talkin'. If not, well, you figure it out."

"Understood."

"We'll be watchin'."

"I'll be there."

"You better." Then he hung up, leaving nothing but dial tone. Ten seconds later Debra Seraphicos squeezed a last time, rustling her hair as she removed her button earphone and set it down with a click on the console. A second later Brian's earphone clicked down beside it.

"In and out in under three minutes," he said, almost to himself. "They still don't trust us."

Debra said, "Spike, sweetie, you don't know the type. They don't trust anyone. They don't trust their own mothers, these creeps."

"Still, we have a delivery to make."

"Suggestion," Debra said. "Let me get the stuff. I'm a shopper. And I'm a cop. I know every shortcut alley in town. So only another cop who knew what I was doing would be able to follow me. You understand?"

"Janowski," Halleck said.

"That son of a bitch!" snarled Brian Granville.

"Listen, guys, some things are like predicting rain in Seattle. Janowski is one of them. Just let me feel this one out. I report back, we'll see if we have a problem. Give me forty minutes, an hour on the outside. Right now it's twelve-thirty. Back by one-thirty. We make up the package here."

"And then?" the father asked.

"And then, if I've been tailed, we improvise."

"How?" Brian Granville was confused.

"Look. I know police stakeout procedures. And I know that they expect me to be Spike's eyes and legs. Found that out at the Whole Donut this morning. So when I leave here heading south like a bat outta hell with what they think is the package, they're all over me like a teenage boy on his first date. That's when Brian here, about twenty minutes later, sneaks out the back . . . you do have a delivery entrance . . ."

"Give Harold the doorman twenty dollars and he'll eat his own balls. He'll show you the way, Brian, let you out."

"And head for the real drop," she finished up.

"But they're expecting *me*," Halleck said.

"How the hell they gonna know the difference, Spike, especially you with your nervy bit about let me get a pencil and paper. They're going to expect someone who can see. They ever see you, Mr. Granville?"

"How would I know? Not that I know. Perhaps my picture in a trade magazine. I just don't know."

"Doesn't matter," she said. "Wherever they are from the Michigan Avenue Bridge is going to be far away. They're not going to stand right next to you and jump into the fucking river after this bottle. So you pull up your collar and wrap your muffler around your mouth. You don't want to get chapped lips in this weather, do you? And you wear your shades. Light glaring off the water like that on a nice clear day like now is like to give you migraine. And you pull down the brim of your hat, keep the warmth in your head, Mr. Granville. Now you do that, and keep your chin down, you could be Jimmy Hoffa for all they can tell. And who are you, Halleck, to worry? International celebrity? They'll be looking for Halleck and see Halleck because they aren't going to be looking for Halleck at all."

"You mean they're not going to be there?" choked Brian.

"I mean their eyes are going to be on what you're dropping into the river, not you. Now I don't know how they're going to get to it. That's their problem. But if it was me, and it is me, and somebody dropped five Gs off the bridge, I'd be glad I knew how to swim, because December or not I'll try to get the thing before it sinks."

"You think they're that desperate for five thousand dollars?"

"Five thousand dollars?" she shrieked, her voice cracking. "You think that's nothing? Maybe in Lake Forest that's nothing, Mr. Granville, but there's a whole big world outside those mansions where five thousand is more money at one time than anyone expects to see, ever. Don't underestimate what someone would do for that. And I'm not talking about hoods, either. You ever see some of those crazy housewives in these contests where they can get all the groceries they can carry up to five hundred dollars in ten minutes of racing up and down the aisles? Anybody would do that for five Gs. Believe me, anybody. They're not going to leave that money on the bottom of the river. No way. These are guys who maybe killed another punk for fifty in order to pay for their next fix. They're just betting that you, Mr. Granville, won't find it worth diving into the river to recover it. For you, it's easier to make it on the commodities market on a hot day. For these guys . . ." She let the lecture ebb. Enough.

"Either they can hold their breath a long time," Halleck said, "or they drag for it . . ."

"Too conspicuous," Debra said.

"Or they dive for it," Brian guessed.

"And that's why they need the fluorescents," Halleck said. "Remember, he said that 'It's important.' Why is it important unless that's the way they plan to use that to retrieve it?"

"We have to move on this," Debra said. "Back in an hour. Spike, anything you need?"

"Yeah," he told her. "I need to catch a train. Get that timetable for the stops from Janowski. We're going to be able to narrow it down to one L platform."

"An hour," she said, letting herself out.

After she had left, Brian Granville fell silent for a few minutes then said, "You think we're ever going to see Janey alive again?"

Halleck sighed in the gathering fatigue, rubbed his aching eye sockets, shook his head, and said, "Brian, my hunch is that nothing will happen to her until at least after you drop that jar into the water. That's three hours away. And less than a day before time runs out completely. Not much, but that's all we have."

10

In seventy minutes Debra Seraphicos burst into Halleck's suite, her shopping complete. Breathless, she said, "Plenty cold out there."

Halleck tried not to think about it, not with Janey out there.

Debra went on, "The puddles are frozen, not just crusted. The stuff is solid."

"You're not going to suggest it's too cold to go out." Brian tried to guess.

She must have shaken her head. Halleck heard the rustle of her hair brushing against the raised collar of a nylon jacket as she said, "The river. It's freezing."

Halleck got it right away. "Jesus, the jar will break right open if—"

"Nothing like five thousand dollars in hundreds scattered across the thin ice to grab a little attention. And we sure can't call these guys back and set something else up. So if we don't drop, we're screwed. If we do, well, what?"

"What?" Brian Granville had panic in his voice.

"How bad is it?" Halleck said.

"Right now? Ice around the shoreline, maybe on the pilings of the bridges. But the river itself is still running. I checked while I was out."

"So we can still do it," Brian sighed.

"You'll have to pitch the thing away from the bridge, so it doesn't hit any of the ice around the pilings, but it can still be done if it doesn't get worse. Or we could change to a plastic jar. That's why I asked about the time. Plastic won't break."

135

"They said glass, presumably because it doesn't float" Halleck reminded them, now wishing that he hadn't suggested it at all. "I don't want anything that makes them suspicious, like thinking there's some invisible molecule in the plastic that fluoresces under sodium vapor lights."

"There's a thought, Spike," Debra said, patting his shoulder. "Maybe you should be a cop."

"They don't hire my kind of handicap," Halleck said aloud, sounding, he hoped, factual, not morose, not angry, not defensive, not any of the things he was supposed to have felt and gotten over, according to his therapist.

He was surprised to hear, instead of the awkward silence that usually ends such pronouncements, a strong reply. "Like I said already, I'd rather have a good mind than a good set of eyes any day, Halleck. You can buy a good enough set of eyes at any kennel, right?"

"I guess," he shrugged.

"And how much help is Barkley on something like this?"

The silence seemed to answer by itself.

"Exactly what I was thinking," she said. He could hear her beginning to take charge of what she could, unpackaging things, heard Brian ask, "You got this stuff at Jewel?"

"I got the bag at Jewel, so you could have something to carry the jar in. You know how obvious you would be walking around Chicago with a glass jar full of hundred dollar bills?"

"I hadn't thought about it," Brian said.

"Now you don't have to," she said, continuing to take things out. The sound of the jar top being unscrewed was obvious. Knowing what needed doing, Halleck was able to pick out the noise of the lead sinkers going in, of the bills being pushed in, her steps to the kitchen, rushing water, rising meniscus, spilling, the top closing tight, even the low whining squeal of twisted rubber on the neck of the jar.

The next sound was Debra saying, "Trade?"

"But that's my briefcase," Brian protested.

"Looks Italian. Maybe four hundred dollars?"

"Five. Five hundred."

"Good, that's what I need."

"But—"

"Buy yourself a new one," she said curtly. "I walk out of here with this little gem and I'll pull everything Janowski's got ten miles south, dancing all the way. If I lose him, all right. If not, that's cool, too. Either way he's suckered. We wait until a half hour before the drop time. That gives him no time for comebacks. When I set the briefcase down and walk away, he's going to sit there watching the thing, tracking whatever idiot thinks Santa's come early."

"Then you come back here?" Brian said.

"No, then I head about ten miles west. I don't know where yet. Maybe O'Hare. It doesn't matter. It just spreads them out, makes them think that maybe the briefcase is a diversion, that I'm heading to make the real drop after, you know, picking up something that Brian had had overnight-freighted from Milwaukee. The point is that they don't know what the hell we're up to and we can use that. By the time they figure out they've been had, there's nothing they can do."

"And at nearly the same time I'll be making the real drop," Brian said.

"As scheduled. Now Brian and I've shown how we're making ourselves useful. What have you got, Halleck?"

"What about those checkpoint times from the L stations?" he asked.

"Almost forgot," she said, rustling through slips of paper in her pocket.

"Forgot? Jesus! Let's have it."

"Here they are. You ready?"

"You'll have to take them against the digital markers on the second call today. Let me rewind."

Halleck put in the most recent recording and let it run.

"This is it?" Debra said.

"Watch the numbers," Halleck told her.

The high-pitched squeal of train brakes filled the room, a piercing shriek so real in enhancement that they thought the engine had entered Halleck's apartment through the speakers. Synchronized with the sounds, the chronometer was displaying the corresponding clock times on the computer screen. "Here it is," she said. "Eleven fifty-four and thirty-seven seconds and running, thirty-eight, thirty-nine, forty, forty-one, forty-two, forty-three, forty-four, forty-five, forty-six . . . did we lose it, Halleck?"

"Taking on passengers," he whispered. "Resume the markers."

"Fifty, fifty-one, fifty-two, fifty-three, there it is, beginning to pull out."

"That's it," he said.

Debra sighed. The running and hours were starting to wear. "Let's see what the Price Waterhouse envelope has. You can tell from the map on the wall"—Halleck could hear her explain to Brian—"that all these L stations run through a corridor cutting north by northwest out of the city, passing through the Near North Side and into the suburbs. Three stations in a row surrounded by the circles. Now, when these trains passed, it wasn't rush hour. Still isn't. So they'll run every ten minutes, no more than that. In that conversation, the last one with the kidnappers"—more rattling paper—"lasting under three minutes, you'll see only one train. And with a run of two or more minutes between stations, you're not going to hear a train that's not actually pulling into the nearest station. Am I right, Spike?"

Close enough. He turned to point his dead eyes over his shoulder, where he knew, from the pacing, that Brian Granville was moving back and forth across the room, in front of the map, then said, "The train's braking was clearly audible on primary, which means at a level comparable to the intensity of the caller's voice. You'd never hear that from a distant station. Which doesn't mean it's not there, it just means we'd have to dig for it, using the recognition patterns and enhancement, the way we did with the thunderstorm noises on the Soldier Field call, or by pulling inaudible noises out of the background, isolating them from the noise, refining them, rendering them and playing them out, the way we did on that couple walking by. Speaking of which, we still don't know who Jared was—"

"Jared?" Brian's voice was puzzled yet curious.

"The couple walking by the place laughing, mentioned clearly the name Jared, then laughed again," Halleck explained.

"Couldn't be," Brian said.

"Couldn't be what?" Debra injected, impatient.

"Mike Jared? Canadian comic doing improv at *Second City*." To Debra, voice directed away from Halleck, "You may have seen him on *Saturday Night Live* or David Letterman. He's the one who does the skit where he bounces on his bed to reach a light fixture so he can change a bulb, is left hanging from the cord when his pants drop to his ankles, tries to get them back up when someone knocks at the door . . ."

"I don't watch much TV," she said.

"Well, it just happens he's at *Second City* now, two shows a night. Have to check the *Trib* for times."

Halleck mulled on that, wondered how, or if, it fit, how much of what they were doing was grabbing at straws. Their best bet was to stick with what he asked for now. Fighting off impatience and fatigue, he tried to refocus. "The spotters on the platforms. What do they report?"

"A southbound here. Passes through the northernmost station, says Adams, at eleven forty-five. He doesn't give seconds. That's the best he can do, says, on Timex. Still, that train, according to Goberman, who's at the next station south, the middle circle on our map, pulls in there at, what, to make sense would have to be southbound arrival at eleven forty-nine and about a half, say eleven forty-nine and thirty, then," rattling, looking at another sheet of paper, "Christ! I wish they made cops pass a legibility test. Here's the report of Officer Kowalski, the hairy Pole who's working overtime for us tonight, Spike. Now he's sitting out there on a raised L station in nineteen degrees of twenty knots steady off the lake . . . no wonder his hand is shaking . . . but this time it says, SB, southbound, AR, arrives, eleven fifty-four and forty-five seconds, by Kowalski's watch. Close enough?"

"Bingo," said Halleck, his heart racing. Too close for coincidence. "Draw a thick red border on the southern-most of those three circles. Janey's inside it."

"Are you *sure*?" Brian's voice.

"Where's *Second City*?"

"Right here." Debra Serpahicos and Brian Granville

139

spoke as one, no difference in the timing of their response. Halleck, sightless now but having worked in pictures, could see the scene, as both of their fingers went to the map, then their eyes met, so he delayed his remark so he could show them that he understood. Waiting only a second for maximum effect, he cleared his throat and said, just as if he could see exactly where they were pointing, "Inside the circle."

"On the edge," Brian said, "but within walking distance, even of the L. This couple, the one that said, 'Jared,' could have been walking to this same L."

"Maybe," Halleck said. "But inside the circle for sure."

"So we tell Janowski?" Debra asked.

"Negative," Halleck said. "The last thing I want is for Dirty Harry to take over, running unmarkeds through that circle like a microtome through a melanoma. We need to control this. We've got a couple of nervous guys out to pick up, we think, an unscheduled drop. I don't want anything funny to spook them."

"You're right," Debra said, sighing deeply. "Janowski thought he could move on the place with one of the guys gone, he'd do it. Best to keep him out, for now."

"How many wind chimes in our target circle?" Halleck asked.

"Five," she said.

"Tell Kowalski to get everything on those five. Everything. House types and occupants, moods and attitudes. If they're nervous or angry or indifferent when they answer his knocks, the condition of the street, any evidence of construction, jackhammers, and now dogs. No detail is too trivial."

"He'll be thrilled," she said.

"Why shouldn't he be?" Halleck said. "I saved him eleven stops."

"And now for this errand," Debra said, closing Brian's briefcase, snapping the locks shut.

"Give me thirty minutes. Then leave by the back," she told Brian. "I'm gone, for a couple of hours. You'll be all right?" to Halleck.

"Yeah. But I've still got to tease these last two tapes.

Got a feeling something's vital in there, something we've overlooked, something subtle."

"I'll be back." She pulled the door open, stopped and turned, and said, "Halleck?"

"Yes?"

"You really think these clowns are going to fish this jar out of the river?"

"No."

"What?" Brian Granville's voice, astonished, angry.

"You wanted my opinion. The least they're going to do is watch us make the drop, assure themselves that we do what we say we're going to do. You can bet on that. And they're not going to want to do anything as visible and haphazard as fishing. If I set this thing up the way they did, where they drop a fragile object into murky, freezing water, with a current sweeping it along, I'd want to be in place, tethered to the bottom, about ten feet below the surface, just away from the pilings, waiting, in a dry suit and double pack of eighties, listening for the splash, then looking, if I could see through the murk, for the three glowing bars as the object sinks. If I set it up this way, I wouldn't trust five thousand dollars to the mercy of fickle currents and zero visibility on the bottom. I'd like it dropped right into my hands. So when you drop the damn thing, Brian, look for bubbles. Don't stare. Lean out and chuck the thing so it doesn't shatter on the ice, but look for a trail of bubbles. Then walk away."

"To run down a scuba background on a con, Halleck," Debra said, stuck in the open doorway, "you're going to need Janowski to plug in the FBI."

"One step at a time," Halleck said, unable to forget that time itself was quickly running out.

11

Her watch showed two-twenty when Debra Seraphicos stepped from the elevator carrying the briefcase, heading for the revolving door. Clear across the vast lobby she saw Harold's eyes flicker like a hawk on a mouse as he approached, solicitous, his hands knotted behind his back, his narrow frame draped in a long maroon overcoat held closed by shiny brass buttons, themselves tucked into gold loops that ran laterally into runglike lines in a ladder pattern extending from his shoulders to his knees. She locked her eyes on him and sized him up. Atop his head sat a uniform cap that shouted his station to the seeing world, a cap with a gleaming black visor surmounted by the monogrammed logo of the Carlton Lakeshore North, the same model in smaller size that Idi Amin had donned in a short, terrible reign half a forgotten world away. So prepared and polished, Harold oiled his way across the polished lobby marble, an unctuous smile cut into his pocked skin, his white gloved hands suddenly too evident. Whether to laugh or throw up? In impression, now fully apparent, Harold looked like the last figure that the designing artists had removed from the album cover photo for the Beatles' famous *Sergeant Pepper's Lonely Heart's Club Band*; neither quite absurd enough to be intriguing nor quite mundane enough to be appropriately invisible, Harold had cast himself against context, forever ready to overact the few lines that life's play grudged him. Rushing at her, blemished and breathless, "Taxi?" was not a question but a plea, the groveling sycophancy of a badly chosen Romeo hanging on lines to a reluctant Juliet.

And Juliet Debra Seraphicos was not.

All business, she had braced against the cold in practical slacks, neither stylish nor frumpy, cut and fitted to make her body look as good as she had worked to make it, slender, strong, yet somehow, beyond the bulging muscles and forceful manner, completely feminine, as if Nautilus could never break asunder what a Raphaelesque God had put together. And put together she was.

That was why she had done it, in part, the business about power lifting and winning the black belt in Korean karate, to show the macho men in police work that they didn't have to worry about her carrying her end of the partnership, an end that always seemed to threaten them if they couldn't relate to it sexually. But as she said, "You're not my husband and you're not my father. You're my partner and if you screw up, I'm dead."

And if she could stand up under fire—and she could, had—she certainly didn't need a geek like Harold to flag a cab for her. Ignoring him, shouldering around, she headed for the door, for the street, her world. Out there all fares were equal. Hacks knew that doormen didn't pay the fare, and they certainly didn't pay the tip.

"Taxi?" asked Harold again, catching up at a run.

"I'll get it," she said.

She didn't know what he expected for a woman dressed in slacks and a ski parka, Nikes, and a four—rather, five—hundred dollar Italian briefcase. That kind of composite, where the parts didn't fit into any coherent whole, usually upset people like Harold, who expected their clientele to be well-behaved and equally well dressed. But she didn't care what Harold thought, even though she wanted his cooperation. Who could know? At some point they may even require it. Turning to him, she smiled, always disarming, and said, "Mr. Brian Granville will be coming down from Mr. Halleck's suite soon and will need some assistance. He will take care of you for both of us." From a nursery story she remembered, *The Three Billy Goats Gruff*.

"I'll remember that, ma'am," said Harold, tipping his hat.

Even as she whirled through the gleaming brass-framed revolving door, Debra was sure he would. Again she checked her watch. Two-thirty. In twenty minutes Brian Granville would be coming down, heading for the Chicago River. She wanted to be far away by then.

Once outside she stepped confidently to the curb into the stiff wind and raised her hand, one finger waving. One cab, then a second, pulsed by, their exhaust, like her own breath, a whitened smoke in the hard cold. Then a third one braked, banked its way across a lane of traffic and screeched to a stop beneath the scalloped green and white striped canopy outside. Without delay she yanked open the rear door, ducked inside, daring Janowski's stakeout to follow. Once in the back, she slammed the door and said, "Let's move. South on Michigan."

He looked back over his shoulder at her, his eyes clawing at her body like eager hands. "How far do you go, lady?" he asked.

"Just drive."

"I could take you as far as you like," he said, rolling a toothpick across a fence of teeth.

Cute.

"Just drive," she repeated.

"Where to?" he asked.

"For about ten minutes, it doesn't matter."

"What?"

"You choose. Get moving."

He shrugged. "Sure, whatever you say." The tires squealed, throwing her against the seat as the cab moved away, heading south. After ten minutes she would size up the tail, decide how to lose it, double back, switch and run, stop and wait. All the tricks. Now all she needed was to lead them off.

As the cab squeezed through the sluggish downtown traffic, her thoughts settled on the men following her. Cops. All so worried that little Deb couldn't take care of herself, all so determined to take care of her themselves, all so infuriatingly protective it sometimes made her want to scream. Why couldn't they accept it wasn't their job? They weren't her husband and they weren't her father. She had lost both of them. The husband was gone, as she alluded to Halleck, because there wasn't enough time or space for the two careers and too little lightning when they met under the sheets. She didn't say that but that was it, or part of it, or an important part of it, despite the fact that she knew there was more to life than a good fuck. Without a good fuck now and then, she could be pretty surly. And it had been awhile since she'd had one. But then she could layer over that, of course, if there were something besides the deadening routine of paperwork and desk jobs that seemed, inevitably, to lie at the gateway to larger careers, to a sergeancy, to more. This was different. This was urgent, alive. Halleck was exciting, more exciting, more animated, more visionary despite his blindness than the safe and sorry, ever apologetic, seemingly never successful investigators in the department. Janowski was neither better nor worse than the rest. The numbing certainty of a conspiracy of like-minded individuals is that they all act as clones, become as one and as none, acting on the book as if it were an end in itself and not a means to an end, afraid to improvise within the rules for fear that internal affairs would take them off at the testicles.

And the fear was real. Careers could end that way, so enforcement slackened. No one was aggressive anymore for fear of charges of police brutality, no one was prompt for fear of accusation that they hadn't been methodical in approval, in acquiring court orders, in seeking permission to pee during a stakeout, to paralyze the whole force, individually and collectively, leaving a sense of helpless ennui engulfing them all.

Tall buildings slipped by to either side as the cab galloped up a ramp, its hard tires thumping through the potholes. In the front seat the hack threw his right arm over the set, turned back and raked her with a stare. The toothpick rolled back and forth before he said, "Lady, come on. I *been* drivin' ten minutes already. We gonna be in Des Moines if I don't get more, so . . ."

Refocusing, breaking from her meditation, she looked around, saw where she was and started to freeze up, grabbing the door, bracing against the front seat, her breaths coming in short, hammering gasps.

"Hey, you all right. What? You want I pull over? Hey, lady . . ."

"Turn back, turn around . . . quick . . . just get me out of here," she choked, feeling syncope of blackness descend, lift, flutter, then fade.

This was the spot, the one they were approaching, where it happened, this, she closed her eyes as it snapped by, was where her father died.

The man who shot her father after stopping to watch him change a tire on the Eisenhower Expressway when she was seven years old, about the same age as little Janey Granville now, was never caught. The perpetrator was still, in the parlance of police officialdom, at large, wanted but not sought, exactly like Jack the Ripper, and with as much chance of being caught.

The funny thing, if the word *funny* can mean perversely ridiculous, about her father's murder is that the men who killed him were exactly the kind of people, poor, socially disadvantaged, underprivileged, paralyzed in a kind of caste of circumstances, that her father had studied, sympathized with, sought social programs for, testifying at City Hall and at the state level, and with success. He had decided that their limitations drove them to extremes and that they acted out of frustration, striking out in rage after becoming accustomed to violence, inured to its futility and human consequences, accepting it as normal and normative, and, unable to perceive anything injust about the ordinary, like children of war, getting caught up in the game. In one paper he called them "pawns moved relentlessly to the same positions by forces not of their choosing and beyond their control, unable to affect their own destinies for want of a commonly accessible avenue of escape, conspirators in nothing more than an inherited panorama of poverty, hunger, disease, drugs, violence, and crime." That was her father, the champion, the eloquent and legislatively effective champion of the Liberal Party line, a man inspired with the conviction of the rightness of what he was doing, who was perforated with six magnum slugs for giving too little to a couple of hoods offering to change his tire for him. And the irony of it was, or would have been, because he could feel or think nothing even before he crashed onto the shoulder of the road, his empty wallet cast carelessly before his dead eyes, that his death became emblematic of the conservative cause, an object lesson in the folly of decency in the face of hard crime. He would have hated that, spoken out against that as reactionary and ill-conceived, but he was silent forever by then. He was dead.

She never thought about it much, or tried not to. All those words, all those ideas he had didn't seem quite valid, exposing him and them as they had, like ritual lambs, to any slaughter convenient to the priesthood of terror. It was not, she was sometimes ashamed to admit, not just that she was shocked numb to see her father cut down. It was also, instantaneously, a second after he had fallen, that they were so helpless before the laughing, howling, leather-jacketed monsters who stood over his corpse, emptied his wallet, perhaps entertained, in the convenience that police laxity provided them, whether or not to rape her mother and kill them both. And while her mother kept referring to their safety as " . . . a miracle that proved, in a sad sense, that perhaps what your father was teaching was not all wrong, that, again perhaps, there was a twinge of guilt, of awareness that what they had done was senseless, yet they couldn't undo it. All they could do from that moment forward, was to leave bad enough alone." Leave bad enough alone? Or maybe, in her active imagination, Debra Seraphicos believed that what they were after was money, so they removed the one thing that stood between them and the money. There were no larger considerations, no other feelings, no deep social philosophies or moral twinges, not even an impulse of decency. They were simply done. If they hadn't considered raping her mother or killing them both, it had nothing to do with cosmic good as much as with convenience. It wasn't as if her mother wasn't attractive, she was and, despite the haunting vacancy that can at times fill her eyes, still is, not only in her own form but living on in Debra herself. They were just through.

Nor were the killers apprehensive about arrest or conviction. Two women, without the support of their man, suddenly alone, would not, perhaps they reckoned, tes-

tify against them. Or the description, clouded by terror
and shock, would be so diffuse that no one would ever be
picked up. What Debra remembered feeling, during and
after, was a complete sense of horror and helplessness, a
certainty that in this concrete world there were no knights
on white horses. It was and forever would be, it seemed,
increasingly as she grew, up to her.

Far beyond all reasons, including revenge, that was
why she became a policewoman.

It was, she would admit only in the privacy of her own
conscience, the only way she could have the means and
authority to protect herself as well as reduce the odds
against others. In self-defense she had three kills, each
followed by routine administrative leave, followed by
reinstatement. She had no guilt. Pulling the trigger had
become a kind of therapy. The men in the squad room
called her Dead-eye Debbie.

Her problems were over.

She no longer had nightmares nor any outward fears.
Still she wondered, again privately, whether the aggres-
siveness she had felt toward her husband, Al, wasn't
concealed and buried anger at what those two men did to
her father twenty-five years ago. And she supposed, equally
honestly, that she would never know. No one would.
Still, she doubted that was it, or at least all of it, because
she didn't hate men, generally. Nor did she fear them.
It, as it should, depended on the man. Like Spike Halleck.
She liked Halleck.

Why?

The obvious reason? Because he was, or she could
think of him, as helpless, and no threat, so she could relax?
Or was it because he was vulnerable and she could
help, she could really be a person of significance, one
undeniably essential to getting the job done? How completely different that was from Janowski, who worried
about owing for a cup of coffee! In truth, her feelings
about Halleck, whatever they were, were overpowered
by her empathy for Janey Granville. In Janey, she felt
vicariously the unfolding terror that she, as a kid, had
avoided. Abduction, threat, fear, the terror of not knowing if you're going to live or die. By six or seven most

kids these days are TV-wise. They've got a couple of
kidnapping movies under their belt. They know the skinny,
have gotten the pitch at preschool or first grade. Never
trust strangers. But strangers, hostile strangers, were all
Janey Granville had. So who did she trust? God? Now I
lay me down to sleep, all that crap? The voice of Spike
Halleck? The streetwise plodding vigil of Jano Janowski?
The steady shivering form of Ryszard Kowalski clocking
in trains three blocks or so from where you're held? A
lady cop walking through a hotel lobby with an empty
briefcase? Who?

She had no answers, only an instinct that Halleck's
tack was the best way in. She would go with it.

The cabbie crept forward, traffic rushing past on either
side, their blaring horns blurred as they whipped by. Half
turned around, the hack said, "You okay, lady? Hey,
you sick or somethin'?"

Looking up and shaking it off, she said, "Sure, sure.
Yeah. Look, turn it around, okay? Find me an L station."

"Lady, I can take you anywhere the CTA can."

"Just do it."

"You sure can pick 'em, Spike," Brian said, pulling
back the curtain as the cab pulled away.

"What?" Halleck was concentrating on searching the
sound track for cyclical sounds, like the ticking of a
clock.

"Always could," Brian said, moving away from the
window. "Did you ask Janowski for a beautiful woman
assistant?"

"And to think I gave up the option of a hairy Pole."

It was Brian's chance to interject a puzzled, "What?"

"Listen. She volunteered. If she's beautiful, how the
hell would I know?" And, Halleck asked himself, what
difference would it make? In Los Angeles, after the
accident and before moving to Chicago, he came to know
every tactile and olfactory delight, the fluxion of fleshy
curves one into another, the hot spots from the warm,
the warm from the cold, astonishing himself with his
hunger. Women seemed to turn on more for him now

that they could be privately exhibitionist, protected from sensual stares by his dead eyes, ready, more ready than he had ever known to take the initiative, to try things that for whatever reasons they had avoided or resisted while he had sight. Why? What difference did it make?

Gradually it began to depress him. Not because the women were unexciting. It might have been that they were so accessible, too accessible. And they tried, tried so hard to please, were so constrained by—what? pity?—to try that they were doomed, ironically by trying so hard, to failing so badly. Eventually he quit entirely and drank.

Without women and his work, work that he really did love, he filled himself with booze. And nothing is so totally numbing, so completely obliterating, as being blind and drunk. The room doesn't spin. You do. You are sure that the bed is moving in tight quick circles until you puke, then start to drink again.

A month that way was enough.

Then he was sure that he had to stop. Stopping itself became enough a goal to bring him back. It gave him something to aim for, something to accomplish. That done, he moved.

Then, with the move, came Brian and Ellie and Janey, a kind of family.

But not since that distant marathon orgy had he had a woman. Now he could think of little more than Debra Seraphicos. Brian's saying that, in addition to being funny, appealing, cooperative, and smelling great, she looked great made him ache to touch her. Being unable to see her, to appreciate her as other men did, undressing her in their minds, smiling, made him want her the more. But it was different. It was not the rage of lust, the trumpet call of the unattended phallus. It was very personal. She was already giving in ways the other women weren't. She was seeing him on his terms and, at least, accepting it. That was fine for starters. In a world where there are no guarantees ever, that was okay for now.

He was glad she was gone so he could focus on things without distraction. Janey deserved that, needed that. Brian's putting her back in the room, conjuring her in a way he never could have imagined without him, made him quietly furious. Remembering what his therapist had said allowed him to force a calm, breathing deeply, slowly.

His shrink, Herman Rathsmeyer, told him, "Spike, as long as men are captive to pornographic scriptwriters they chase impossible fantasies. Accept it and everybody feels bad. You think women aren't as concerned about their breasts and hips as men are about their penises, aren't just as threatened? They have no fear of inadequacy? You think the screenwriter's eternally receptive, graciously nymphomaniacal woman doesn't threaten them? Yet we all find the same trap, no? But we don't go out and change our organs. Spike, most handicaps in relationships are in the mind. You want someone indifferent to blindness, someone who likes Spike Halleck, so you can discover yourself. Everything else happens after that."

Funny that before he was blind Halleck had never asked himself what seemed a stupid question. Do you like yourself? Who asks that? What's the perfect answer? Yes, I adore myself. Ergo, narcissist. Or no, I hate myself? Ergo, psychomasochist. In the before time, the sighted years, it just seemed irrelevant. He loved his work, he enjoyed friends, relished women as company. He liked German whites, Mosels especially, Bernkasteler Doktor in particular, scuba with double eighties doing lazy weightless loops at a hundred feet in the Red Sea, the sighted darkness impossibly darker than any blind moment he had known, of black velvet twinkling with a majestic vault of lapidary stars on a cloudless night over the Chilean Andes, the haunting rhythms and enchanting words in metaphysical poetry, most of all John Donne's *A Valediction Forbidding Mourning*, playing violin, eighteenth-century chamber music for string quartets, and last of all, a good night's sleep. When he rattled off the list, his likes read like a personal ad. But did he like himself?

He liked life, the flux and flow of feelings and actions between and among people, the value of detailed analytical thought, despised the narrowness and slavery of superstition, realized some of it was inevitable, sometimes, ironically, good. There were things he couldn't understand, penetrate, like quantum mechanics and relativity, grand unified theory, and others, and there were things, he was convinced, that no one understood, at least yet, things that sometimes we get twinges about, hunches, inclinations that are irrational yet unavoidable, arrows of instinct that point the right way without any apparent underlying reasons. Call it luck. Halleck did not believe in God, although he was willing to accept that disproving God was as difficult as proving him. And he was willing to carve a large enough niche of doubt in his own skepticism about a supreme being to wish, even pray, that if He were a factor in ultimately balancing out the too evident wrongs with a counterbalancing set of rights, if for no other reason than to simply fuel the argument for his own existence, that He would consider here and now allowing Janey to get out of this thing alive, whole, well. And if this God, in whom he did not believe, was, as some suggested, the kind who helped those who really helped themselves, then He couldn't have any complaint that Halleck had not exceeded himself. But he wasn't counting on any deus ex machina descending into that final circle on the map just in the nick of time. He felt lucky, yes. Almost itchy with luck now. So close. But now it was time for thought, hard thought, not prayer.

The computer continued to hum through its search, beeped, indicating it had found something. As Halleck had requested, it would be a regular, patterned background sound, something in intensity between the voice of the caller, the principal imprint on the tape, and something much lower, like a metal trash can rolling in an alley three blocks away.

"Spike?" Brian's voice came in surprisingly, as if his mind had almost forgotten it.

"I've got something here."

"What?"

"I don't know. Let's see what the computer has picked up."

They ran it back and listened to it together, from the beginning of the tape, a percussive sound, like a drumming, repeating regularly every second or so, suddenly stopping, picking up again, same interval, running exactly the same number of counts, one a second for eight counts, stopping for the same interval, about two seconds, then resuming throughout the call.

"Tapping on the counter with a fingernail, maybe," Brian guessed.

Maybe? Halleck thought about it, rejected it. "Too intense. It's got the same click, you're right, but the level is wrong. And have you ever seen people who do that? If they're nervous, they're hammering away furiously. With this, it's just about one beat a second. So I bet it isn't that."

"What then?" Halleck could hear Brian's suit jacket cuff shift as he checked his watch. Soon he would have to leave for the drop.

"I don't know."

"Come on, Spike!"

Halleck held up his hand, listened again. Sharp but powerful. Click, click, click, click, click, click, click, click. Stop. Then again. Why the stop? What does it mean, the same number of beats? A limit. What kind of a limit? One way, then another? Direction. Turning? Turning around. The stop is for turning around?

Maybe.

Then the click would be, what? Footsteps? From pacing. Of course! Nervous men pace, change directions, pace again, and again. But why the sharp clicks?

"He's wearing taps on his shoes," Halleck said aloud.

"Play it again," Brian said.

Halleck did.

Brian whistled in astonishment. "I think you're right."

"One of them wears taps."

"What else is there?"

"Well it's regular, so he doesn't limp. Judging from the number of steps, if he's average height either the room he's in or the length of the telephone cord, whichever makes him turn around, is about eight yards long."

"Twenty-four feet?"

Halleck understood. "That is long for a cord. But you can get twenty-five foot extensions. And we have to reckon the cord plus the stretch on the coiled line."

"But twenty-four feet?"

"Could be cordless," Halleck mused. "But cordless sends out a radio signal. That would make it easy to pick up. I don't think they would want that."

"Speaker phone?" suggested Granville.

"No rise and fall in the intensity of the voice as he walks back and forth," Halleck responded.

"Long cord then?"

"Long room. At least twenty-four feet on diagonal, which Pythogoras would require to be—" he did the calculation in his head—"seventeen feet long."

"All very interesting, but I have to go. What damn good is all this?"

"Simple," Halleck said. "We know the size of the room, or one of the rooms. Anything smaller, in apartments, we throw out."

"We don't have floor plans." Granville slipped into his coat, picked up the rustling paper bag.

"Right now we don't need 'em," Halleck said. "We can use trigonometry to project room sizes using windows and walls, from the outside. Eratosthenes used the same trick with projected shadows at different latitude to determine the size of the earth three centuries before Christ. Shouldn't be too tough to measure the size of a room with a laser transit."

"We need something else, Spike, at least before we tip our hats. We need to be surer of where she is."

"I'm doing the best I can. You have any ideas?"

Brian was silent too long before he sighed and said, "I have to go." A second later the door opened, letting in a draft of cold air from the corridor. "Look for bubbles," Halleck said.

When he heard the door close, he got up, stumbled through the weight of a crippling fatigue to his bedroom, fished over the dresser top and picked up one of the small, ridged gelatin capsules that he remembered from his sighted years as red. Walking to the bathroom, he popped it in his mouth, filled a plastic cup with water, washed it down.

What had at first been a buzzing high, a brimming over of unnatural excitement, had dulled, first to a steady wakefulness, as if fatigue were wearing away at the chemical veneer, then, in the last few hours, despite his discipline, to a nearly trancelike stupor, awake but not quite alert, functioning but not really focusing. And for the increasing demands of decreasingly intense sounds, that kind of perception was bound to fail. Yet until the last few minutes it had still been enough, despite the sleeplessness, to keep him pressing on. Now he needed more help, perhaps for another twenty-four hours. In the end there would be a price to pay, but that was negligible compared to the one Janey would have to pay if he didn't come through.

So Halleck knew he had to stay in the game and in control until they actually got Janey back. If he had to sleep, to crash, to lose his ability to argue that his was not only the best but the only way, then with so little time and so much fear, he expected that Brian and Ellie would crumble and do it Janowski's way. What other choices would they have?

Wrapped in a long combed wool coat, a muffler thrown around his face, his breath condensing in baited puffs, Brian squeezed the Jewel bag under his arm, ducked from the taxi on East Wacker Drive and stepped toward the lakeside sidewalk across the Michigan Avenue Bridge over the Chicago River. The river was famous from films, some of which Spike Halleck had worked on, and from tourist books for its march of daring, cylindrical towers, their scalloped balconies cantilevered over the water, and the series of bridges that stood in graceful arches, one after the other, almost like mirror images, as the revetted waterway cut inland. It was *so* Chicago. Far behind him were the dizzyingly monstrous buildings, including the world's tallest, the Sears Tower, and its only slightly shorter cousins, each as impressive for its durability against the howling, demon winds as it was for height alone. Nearby and just behind was the Prudential Building, another giant, its offices filled with businesspeople like himself, men and women on another business day, some of whom he had worked with, lent money to, socialized with, in what now seemed another lifetime. West on the river, beyond the crook, out of sight, was the teeming Merchandise Mart and Apparel Center, another landmark crowding the waterway. Due east, before the river emptied into Lake Michigan, traffic coursed thickly along Lake Shore Drive, headed up past Northwestern University and Oak Street Beach, as empty now as it was crowded, summers, with near-naked bodies. The traffic moved in the direction of home, the place where now, especially now, he wanted to become more than a domestic sanctuary from twelve-hour days, where he never again would take the obligatory three minutes on a teacher's report, figuring he had all the time in the world, and say to Janey, "Real good, sweetheart, keep it up." The opposing traffic on Lake Shore Drive pulsed south, toward the city center, the Art Institute, Grant Park, where demonstrators had fled from tear gas and Mayor Daley's police during the Democractic National Convention in '68, toward the Museum of Natural History and Soldier Field, where Janey's abductor had made a call. Somewhere in this huge and suddenly cold city, two men holding his daughter were moving around freely in a huge swirling crowd of unknowing, indifferent humanity.

He took a step toward the bridge and almost stumbled over, what, a pile of rags rattling in the wind? No, a yellow-eyed man huddled against the cold, nothing showing over the tattered coat and cardboard shelter but a frayed glove holding a bottle, the short puffs of breath and those numb and numbing eyes. Having his own troubles, Brian stepped around, moved quickly. It wasn't his concern, not now.

Across the bridge, on the north bank of the river, a corner bank, a rival, had hung out a placard that flashed, every three seconds, consecutive messages in digital lights. 3:25. Time, 6°F. Temperature, 15 MPH. Wind Speed; Then: GO BEARS.

GO BEARS. Life was so simple, so stable, so routine for so many people that the matters of life-and-death urgencies, threats, the fear of cold and loss of loved ones never entered their minds. As he approached the peak of the bridge, faceless flocks of pedestrians, eyes watering and distressed, rushed on, bundled up and bent over against the gelid gusts, clutching packages and purses and brief-cases, one with a cased musical instrument, its twisted shiny brass bell and valves concealed in a textured black vinyl case, flowed across the bridge as evenly and unexpressively as muddy water flowed beneath them. It suddenly seemed to him obscene. All his life, from the time he was a kid, from the time of Gale Sayers and Dick Butkus, he had been a Bears fan. Who wasn't? Even in the lean years, who wasn't for the kind of football played in the Central Division. Hadn't he gotten the huge Mitsubishi forty-inch diagonal screen *just* to see the Bears, just to have parties of guys from the office and neighbor-hood where everyone could *see* Sweetness and the Fridge, McMahon and Willie Gault, Dent and Fencik? Yet sud-denly GO BEARS made him ill. How much better, how much more appropriate, if they should raise FIND JANEY! and all those faithful were put to scouring their neighbor-hood, reporting unusual, rousting the miscreants, deliver-ing her from the evil ones. Even to himself he was beginning to sound dangerous, distracted, a bit deranged. He had just suggested converting the whole city of Chi-cago into a huge Cuban block committee to watch and snitch on each other. Jesus!

He stepped ahead, clutching the grocery bag under his arm, feeling the awkward shape and weight of its con-tents, a mason jar filled with hundred dollar bills, fifty of them, about to get dumped into the drink. He remem-bered then what they had said and it made him feel colder than the wind, a wind that had begun to rake through the canyon formed by tall buildings lining the river, to whip the murky water into row upon row of combers, a steady, even march of whitecaps. Somewhere in one of the windows, maybe just at the end of a corridor, in one of the banks, perhaps, or on a street corner, one of them would be watching, watching him to be sure he did it right. So he looked up, not obtrusively, because he didn't want their eyes to meet, the knowledge to pass, the figure to disappear and with it, any chance of ever seeing Janey again. All he wanted was to make the drop on time and walk away. It was an expensive way, as

Spike knew, of buying time, but the accounts that seemed so important two days ago had no meaning to Brian Granville now.

Looking up again he saw the bank's digital clock flash GO BEARS again, then pass to 3:29.

Quickly he moved to the top point of the arched bridge, between and above two sturdy concrete pilings, each ringed, as Debra Seraphicos had guessed, with a thin sheet of ice. Between them, in the middle, where small craft would pass from inland moorings to enjoy the blustery lake on a summer's day, the water ran evenly, buffeted by wind, showing beneath the waves a current that twisted the brownish-gray sediment into strange ribbons, leaving deep patches of clear water, green and silent, then, in another second, washing it away with muck.

As he moved closer to the rail, a gust of wind picked up a page of newspaper and flung it against his face. Surprised, shocked, unready, he lifted one hand and flailed, spun around to see his attacker, felt the wrapping rattle off and flap away, when his foot, coming around to balance the sharp turn hit a slick patch of ice. Off balance, he began to fall, couldn't right himself. Instinctively he threw both hands free of the package in order to steady himself, or, if he were to fall, to ease his landing, to keep from breaking something on the hard concrete.

On his way down, the bank sign shouted GO BEARS.

On his way down, the Jewel bag holding the jar shot into the air above the same hard concrete. As his shoulder hit, he turned his eyes upward and saw through the corner of his skewed glasses the paper bag containing the mason jar begin to plummet, three feet above him.

GO BEARS.

Like Willie Gault he pushed himself violently, scuffling his Gucci loafers, jabbed one hand out like God's on the Sistine Chapel ceiling, tore the stitching from the shoulder of his Burberry overcoat and felt the crystal on his Rolex watch shatter on the pavement as he one-handed the teetering bag. As the wind roared down the river, louder than the crowd at Soldier Field, the air went out of him as he held the bag, jar enclosed, at the precarious end of one hand, two inches above the pavement.

A woman, her face pinched to a scarf with designer glasses, leaned over and puffed out, "You okay?" in frosty bursts. He surprised himself by shouting, "Get out of my way!" as he leapt up, clutching the bag, straightening his glasses, squinting through the wind and tears as the bank display snapped from GO BEARS to 3:30. Leaping to the rail, he held the package away, then snatched it back, suddenly remembering the fluorescent tubes tethered to the jar. They weren't activated.

Tearing into the bag, he grabbed the first of three plastic tubes, each now stiffening with cold. Panicked, he bent it too hard, snapping it, spilling glowing green solution all over himself.

"Shit!" he yelled.

The woman who had approached him after the fall began to inch away, sensing a madness.

The bank display said 5°F.

More gently he grabbed the second tube, cracked it, watched the solutions mix, too slowly, he shook it, saw the glow invade it, moving on to the third, carefully, snapping the inner chamber, watching it, too, mix. He shook them both. The Jewel bag fell away, whipped by the wind, first up and up on a spiraling vortex, then straight back across the water, headed inland.

Brian stood there with the mason jar, its attached tubes glowing, and threw another glance at the bank sign.

GO BEARS.

Just before it turned 3:31, he pushed the jar out and watched it fall. Fifteen feet away from the bridge it splashed cleanly, showed no signs of breaking, began to sink quickly. Below the surface the muted glow of fluorescing tubes slowly disappeared beneath the roiling murk headed for Lake Michigan.

And bubbles?

Quickly now, because he could feel their eyes on him and was afraid, quickly because he had no business there, this demented man who had shouted, "Get out of my way!" at a perfectly respectable woman, then "Shit!" at apparently nothing at all, quickly because he wanted no one to question him about what he was doing and why, because he wanted no police to meddle, because he was a businessman on a business trip completing a delicate transaction, and maybe, at some idiotic level because he felt improper, a bank vice president with scuffed shoes and torn coat, shattered watch, a step closer to the derelict he passed at the bridgehead, and mostly because he felt sick and relieved and confused and afraid all at once and didn't, as he felt he was going to do, want to puke. So he rushed off, too fast, perhaps, but it was the best he could do. As he walked away, the water in his eyes was not all from the wind. Mostly it was for Janey.

Flanked by two other detectives, Janowski stood outside a two-story brick building, its window slabs etched yellow by acid rain, and looked up, weary eyed, at the neon sign. If the letter L had been more than flickering, the red cursive letters would have said SAL'S, the name by which the place had been known to locals since long before anyone could remember. Now to the uninitiated passerby it was just SA 'S, which was the best most of the patrons could manage after each of the ritual nights they spent shooting pool with house sticks and downing Budweisers another neon sign promised were served.

Janowski lit up his cigar, opened his trenchcoat so he could get to the Smith & Wesson .38 snubnose nestled in his back, if he needed it. He didn't think he would. The regulars at places like SAL'S were now so well anesthetized from nonstop beer that their reflexes would make a wasp in February seem fast by comparison.

Before going in—he was in no rush—he looked around and reflected. Deb Seraphicos had danced them around the city, all right, leading big nowhere. After switching from taxi to L train to bus she had left a fancy briefcase near a bench in a courtyard of the Cabrini Housing Project. They watched and watched. Not many strollers around when the mercury drops, not many pick-up basketball games, not many kids crowding around ghetto blasters break dancing or shooting up. Too cold for that shit. No, Janowski had figured that whoever picked up that case was it. Or a mule at least. So when the black guy eventually came right through, looked quick right and left, and without missing a stride scooped the thing up, they put the tail on him, followed him home, came in guns leveled, you've never seen a more astonished gape. That's when they opened it and found nothing. Zip. Nil. It was empty. And that was clever. And Janowski was too old and too shrewd to put all his eggs in one basket. So he had Deb followed, bus, then L, to O'Hare, where she stuffs her purse into a baggage locker near a flight gate. Which they watch, and watch. By five o'clock, still nothing. But the flights are delayed, as usual, and it looks unsuspicious to have surveillance right there in eyeshot of the locker, a plainclothesman with carry-on baggage, checking monitors, asking questions at the flight desk, but by seven still nothing, and he figures something's wrong. Since any good cop can work a cheap lock, they hairpin it and go through the purse. Nothing. Not the drop. So where? So did they even use Deb? If not, who? Not Halleck.

Whatever happened, Janowski knew he'd been had, that somewhere the two hoods who pulled this off had reached the real pickup and were five thousand dollars richer. Being real punks, and probably real arrogant punks, they might have even hired a front-room, no-questions-asked baby-sitter and let loose. That would be typical. Score big, party away the same night, flashing big bills, buying drinks, impressing their asshole friends, pretending at what they'd never be: big shots. He could almost smell them now, not that he had any doubts. In Janowski's mind the question, as now, was rarely who, but where and when. From a stoolie, he now had that.

Then there was the jurisdiction problem. All right, so it was Indiana. East Chicago. But who cared? In Da Region, land of rusting steel mills and rundown three-room crackerbox houses, the state line was a convenience for lawyers and garbage men. Everyone else ignored it. Even police, normally the most territorial, relaxed. None of them wanted scumbags crossing lines just to save their own pathetic asses.

"All right," he said to his two men. "Let's move in."

The two men snapped the pump on their riot guns and fell in behind Janowski, who let himself down the three steps to the subground entrance and bulled his way through the door. As always in places like Sal's, the faces of the regulars came around clockwork fashion, their glazed eyes fixed on Janowski, cigarettes dangling from their slackened lips, pool sticks in one hand, beer bottles in the other.

The barkeep went rigid, his hands falling beneath the bar.

The two officers popped through the door and flanked Janowski, riot guns across their chests.

"Relax," Janowski told him. "Police."

"See some ID?"

Janowski flashed the badge, returned it to his sport coat. At the base of his spine, the sweat began seeping around his revolver, his heart began beating a little faster. Calm, he told himself.

"What'cha want?" asked the barkeep.

Janowski smiled, walked to the bar. "Why not a Corona?"

"Twist of lemon?"

"You got it."

"Anything for your friends?" The two detectives stood impassively at the door, their eyes playing over the pool tables, ready to respond to anything funny with a volley of double-ought buck.

"They're on duty," Janowski said.

"And you?"

"Social call. Looking for a couple of friends of mine."

"Who?" The barkeep, a man so fat his arms and legs were forced out from his body, wanted to seem cool, but glowed tension. Janowski tried to talk him down.

"Nicky Spiros and Danny Valitano."

The room hushed, temperature, already cool, seemed to drop twenty degrees.

"What'cha want wit'em?"

"Social call. Like to buy 'em a couple of Coronas."

"Twist of lemon?"

"That's what they drink, am I right?"

"You a friend of 'em?"

Janowski smiled, nodded. "Always, but always, looking after their best interests."

"You want I want, then?"

"Walk 'em over, set 'em down, say compliments of me."

"Thought you said you knew these guys." Sweat beads were growing in on the barkeep's bulging forehead.

"I do," Janowski said, his eyes hard. "I just want to see if *you* do."

"Can I see your badge again?"

"Just get the beers."

Bottles, glasses, and slices of lemon on a tray passed across the room. When they were set down on the rail of a pool table, all the men but two unknotted, leaving Nick the Prick Spiros and Danny Valitano saying, "Hey! Fuck's this 'bout?"

Janowski turned around, said evenly, "Drink the beers. Then maybe you can stand me a round. Even the whole house."

"You think we're stupid? Huh? Drinkin's a parole violation."

Janowski drew on his cigar, let the smoke out in expanding circles. "You're right. But what's a little drink when keeping each other's company is associating with known felons, also a parole violation, right?"

Across a gulf of twenty feet, the two sucked on the Corona bottle, squeezed the lemon slices above their mouths, let the juice drain straight in, fixed their eyes like turreted guns on Janowski, who watched their hands, making sure they were always in sight, away from the jackets, belts, or underside of the pool table.

Janowski kept staring and smiling and smoking.

"So what'cha want?" Danny Valitano finally said.

"To talk, is all." Janowski shrugged.

"So we talk. We'll talk, okay? Okay. Nick?" Valitano nudged his companion, who shrugged, said, "Sure. Why not?"

"Why don't we got downtown, where we can be more comfortable?"

"Plenty comfortable here, huh, Nick?"

"Humor me," Janowski said, acid in his voice, still smiling.

"Com'on, now. Whatcha want? I mean, what's this about?"

"We talk."

"We can talk here. Why not?" said Nick, bordering on a snarl.

"We do this the hard way?" Janowski came down off the bar stool, strolled toward the two, parting the silent crowd further. Two men muttered, slipped out the back; others, sensing trouble and knowing curiosity from stupidity, ducked into the men's room. The two cops with shotguns took one step forward, turned at the hip, and let the barrels down halfway.

Valitano now, both hands up, palms forward, conciliatory, saying, "All right, we just want to know what this is all about."

"What's the fuckin' charge?" Nick the Prick spat, hands in pockets. Janowski watched those hands, watched them as he would a coiled snake.

"Parole violation."

"Pa . . ." Danny Valitano laughed the first syllable before finishing the word, "Parole," then "violation?" his Adam's apple bobbing in disbelief. "Who the hell says it's a fucking parole fucking violation to play fucking pool, not even at the same table, not associatin' with nobody or nothin'?"

"Easy, Danny," Janowski said, stepping closer, keeping the line of fire clear between himself and his backup. "Don't want to add resisting arrest to the charges, not with all these witnesses."

"Come on, man!" Valitano stood anguished, clutching and unclutching his hands, his face now redder, the veins in his neck bulging.

"Finish the beers," Janowski said, right hand stretching around, contorting his face as if he had lower back pains, finding the handle of the revolver, waiting.

It happened so fast Janowski didn't have time to think.

Nick Spiros' hand exploded from his leather jacket.

"Knife!" One detective yelled.

"Drop it!" said the other.

But Nick Spiros didn't know or didn't care. He came at Janowski with a full arcing slash, fast and hard. The sergeant felt the air split under his nose, heard a high whistle as the blade zipped by, didn't know if Spiros had misjudged it or he himself had, instinctively, ducked back. His hand, full of loaded revolver, was just clearing its holster when the deafening roar of a riot gun ripped through the room.

Janowski watched in what seemed to his racing mind like slow motion as the blast flattened Spiros against the nearest wall, blood bursting from his chest and shoulder, and continued to stare, transfixed, as Spiros' eyes turned, hot and terrible as he grunted and peeled himself off the wall, then charged.

Out of the corner of his consciousness Janowski heard Danny Valitano screaming, "Don't shoot! Mother of God, don't—"

At the end of his arm, an arm that seemed to have a will of its own, Janowski felt his fingers squeeze off one, two, three rounds, right shoulder, chest, jaw below the ear, before the second riot gun blast roared out, decapitating Spiros, leaving Valitano screaming, "Jesus! Jesus! Jesus! How did you know?"

Janowski, huffing, quivering with shock, sucking air in quick, urgent bursts, turned slowly on Valitano, skewered him with a stare. "How did I know *what*?"

"Nothing," Valitano said. "Fucking nothing." His hands were high above his head, empty, shaking.

One of the detectives said, "This is going to be a mess."

Janowski said, "Let's get out of here. Get Valitano."

As they moved through the harsh cold, Janowski was glad he had done it his way, content that it was the most effective if not the most legal way of finding Janey Granville, and sure, now that they had Danny Valitano, that they would soon know where his victim was. The press conference could wait until tomorrow, but Debra Seraphicos could go home now. Halleck's plan would never have worked. The only reason he went along was to appease Granville and keep his own ass out of a sling.

Now there was no reason to worry about that. Within a few hours they would pick up his daughter and then there wouldn't be enough good things, enough praise, for Sergeant Ed Janowski.

He owed it to himself to establish the incontrovertible fact that while Lou Scannon and his FBI technocracts were still, like Halleck, playing with data banks and computer simulations, he had wrapped it all up where it always gets wrapped up—on the street. He felt good, great even, wondered who he should call first. The *Tribune?* WLS? Who? Somebody ought to know. What harm could it do, just once, to bypass Public Relations?

12

Five o'clock had passed when Brian Granville said, "It's already dark. The sky looks like snow."

"What's the forecast?"

"Four inches, maybe more."

Outside Debra Seraphicos turned back the deadbolt and let herself in.

"Where have you been?" Brian's voice, anxious.

"Let me get my breath. Really cold," she said.

"Did you fake out Janowski?" Halleck said, sitting down on his chesterfield sofa.

"Right out of his proverbial jock," she said, still panting. "Hold on." She took a minute to catch her breath, then went on, relating her deceptions in detail.

"How did the real drop go?"

"We almost lost Janey," said Brian.

"What?" Debra's voice, astonished.

Brian recounted the story he had already told Halleck. After he finished she asked, "But you did drop it into the water?" Despite its being Halleck's second chance to listen, it seemed that Brian almost had to tell it again, to exorcise the fear of what might have been, to convince himself that everything had finally gone right.

"And what about the bubbles? See any?" she asked.

"I didn't look too long, or too hard, but no, I didn't."

"So no one was there," she said.

Halleck broke in, "Absence of evidence is not evidence of absence. Like the ogre in *Billy Goat's Gruff* the diver could have been under the bridge, hanging on the pylons, waiting to dive as soon as he saw you drop it."

"The current took the jar out, toward the lake."

"How fast?" Halleck asked.

"Walking speed, couple of miles an hour, I guess."

"He could have gotten it."

Brian shivered, making so clear a sound that Halleck could hear it. "I was so cold on the bridge, I can't imagine how it would have been in the water."

"Warmer than you think," Halleck said. "Wet suits use the thin water layer between their skin and the neoprene for insulation. The water was moving, not frozen, so it couldn't have been much below thirty degrees. And if this guy had a dry suit, he would have been warm."

"We're talking a lot of money here," said Debra. "I mean, for gear and all. Does that make sense, to spend five thousand dollars to recover five thousand dollars?"

"If you assure yourself of two hundred thousand dollars the next day, why not?" Halleck said.

"How do we know they got it?" Brian asked.

"Not our problem," he replied. "We did what we said. Even if they didn't, Brian. Even if they just stood next to a window in a building and watched you drop five thousand dollars into the drink, gone forever, they would still know that you did what they told you to. And because I'm assuming that these guys know what to look for, they could spot a trap miles away. Am I right, Debra?"

"Right. A pro could pick out a setup. And he would know if there wasn't one."

"You think that's all they wanted, Spike?" Brian, plaintive.

"Maybe. I'm not inside their heads. You've got to admit that the five-thousand-dollar lure sounds like the thing the police would suggest."

"Right," Debra said, shucking her nylon ski parka. "That's why we had to take Janowski away, because he sees any chance as THE chance. The man has no patience."

"Patience is the luxury of time, and we have little," said Brian.

"Patience is also, Brian," Halleck added, "the luxury of progress, of which we have much."

"Apparently," Brian added.

"There's more," Halleck told him.

"Let's have it. Something from the tapes?"

"While you were away," he said. Behind Brian's voice he heard the scraping and banging of pots and pans, then Debra saying, "Dinner's on its way. Don't know about you two but I'm hungry."

"Ditto," said Halleck. "Stay for dinner, Brian?"

"I better be going."

"Have you talked with Ellie today?" Debra asked.

Brian said, "Yes, called her after the drop, said I'd have to wait to talk with you, then head home."

"By the way," Debra said, "to answer your question about what took me so long, try rush hour. It's still going on out there, as you're about to find out."

"About the stuff on the tape . . ." Brian insisted.

"We're still getting the jackhammer and the wind chime, and the L station sound, same intensity. I can't think of a single way they could have brought those same sounds to a different place, Brian, so I'm willing to bet anything that they haven't moved an inch. And I turned up something new—maybe significant—on the last pass. So basically it's just a matter of chipping away the unknowns, getting progressively closer and closer. And, damn it, we are! Look at how far we're come, how little we have to go. No, I'm sure they're set."

"Until the next call," Brian sighed. "It could be they, maybe, got nervous after the drop and changed everything."

"Not if they read it right. If they read it right, they're relaxing right now. They figure one more call and they're home free, two hundred thousand dollars richer," Halleck said.

"Whether or not they deliver Janey," Brian concluded.

"Right and wrong."

"What do you mean?"

"Right," Halleck explained, "in that it would be safer and easier for them not to have Janey around." Halleck spared Brian a more brutal expression of his fears for his daughter's life and went on. "Wrong in that, as we've agreed, we have a business arrangement. Nothing more, nothing less. For all appearances, the police have not been involved and we have presented them, at the very least, with a very expensive demonstration that we are not out to trap them. We have offered them an expression of our willingness to cooperate exclusively on their terms, and come through."

"But they don't know that unless they recover the bottle. If they don't," Brian droned, "it might have been filled with shit from shinola for all they know."

Halleck clasped his hands together and leaned forward to listen, suddenly alert to Brian's voice. In the last two exchanges it had slid from familiar, matter-of-fact conversation through low, dull, almost drugged whispers before erupting into an uncontrolled spasm of sobbing.

"I-I didn't mean to," he stammered, his voice cracking. "I almost dropped the goddamn bottle, oh, Jesus." The pressure finally hit him and he just opened up. Halleck froze, unable to respond. It was Debra he heard saying, "Hey, it's okay. Just sit down. Here. Sit down. I'm going to bring you something to drink, okay? Just sit down."

"You can stay if you want," Halleck said. "If it makes you feel like you're doing more."

"No," he said. "Ellie is at home, needs me."

"Not alone?" Debra said.

"Her mother is there. Still . . ."

"Get a cab home," Halleck said.

"Have Harold get one," Debra said. "We'll be working all night, Brian, I promise."

Halleck heard the ice crackle into a tumbler, heard it crack when the liquor hit it, a second later catching the scent of bourbon itself as it etched the air, guessed that Brian took it, heard him suction it down, hand the clinking tumbler back with a soft, "Thanks," then add, as he rose, "You will call if there's anything . . ."

Halleck raised a hand, said, "I promise."

"You said something about the tape, something else."

"Yeah," Halleck said. "It may be nothing, but it's new and it's real. It might help. I don't know how much, exactly, to make of it. In the background of the last tape, maybe half a block or more away, real low intensity, but nevertheless real, I got the more noises of some kids playing, which shows that kids *do* play in the neighborhood, that it's safe, maybe, again, a blocked-off street, but the sound was of a skateboard . . ."

"Not roller skates?" Brian asked.

"No. Roller skates alternate, a stroke, followed by a stroke, then another, cyclically. A skateboard is a steady sound, sometimes swerving, sometimes scraping. That's what this was. And there's another thing, too. A name."

"Name?" Brian said, "Not Janey?"

"No. The name I got is Regie," he said it the way it came out on the tape, REEGEE. "So what we're going to need, Brian, is someone to flush every president of every PTA of any school around that circle, to find some kid named Regie, or whose friends call him Regie. And we need it as soon as you can get it. We need not only the kid, but where he was this afternoon, whether he was at home or visiting a friend. And Brian, it's not something I want to trust Janowski with, not after today. Do you understand?"

Brian's voice was suddenly strong and clear, again recognizable as a man in charge. "Spike, Ellie is on the Greater Chicago Area PTA Council. She knows every PTA president in the city. *Every* one. We can do this. We can. Let me call . . ."

Halleck stopped him. "Take it home, now. I'm not sure Janowski hasn't tapped the phones."

"Spike!" Debra objected.

"It wouldn't be the first illegal wiretap you know of, certainly not if the FBI was informed," Halleck said. "Would it, Debra? Honestly now."

"No."

"But it's illegal!" Brian objected.

"Which only means that it can't be used to prosecute, not to narrow an investigation. And it only hurts if they get caught," he said.

"But doesn't it click or something while you're talking?" Brian asked.

"That's stone age equipment," Halleck said. "You can't even sell that to tribal Africans anymore. With the new stuff, you never know whether they're on or not. Sure we could sweep the phones, the room, but that doesn't keep them from tapping in remotely, either on the posts or at the switching stations."

"But why?" Brian said.

"To do his job," Halleck said. "To be there when the case breaks, to make sure that if we screw it up with what he considers an amateur arrangement, that he can pull our chestnuts out of the fire."

"But I told him not to . . ."

"And we saw, today, how well he understood," Halleck said.

"I'll be in touch," Brian said.

"Just call in and say you have something."

"Right."

"Because we're expecting an important call here. But we do want to know who Regie is and where he was this afternoon, because when we know that, we're going to be within a hundred and fifty yards of Janey."

"I'll find out. If I have to work all night . . ."

Spike Halleck shook his head. "No late calls with polite requests. You might have to make up a story."

"Like what?"

"Lost bottle of medicine, dangerous to everyone but the sick child. That always drives parents berserk. Tell them that and you'll have Regie in half an hour."

Brian laughed, a welcome sound, then fell silent. "I'm gone. Later."

"Better sooner," Halleck said.

The door closed and Halleck shifted his attention to the kitchen. "Looks like ham, broccoli, potatoes maybe— how do you like them?"

"I have a choice?"

"I asked, didn't I?"

"Mashed potatoes."

"So that will take awhile."

"We have time."

Halleck listened as she pulled things out of cabinets, banged pans on the stove, clicked on the oven, "Are we going to make it?" she asked.

"I don't know. We're close."

"Will Kowalski's information help?"

"I think so."

The oven door opened and closed.

"Salad?"

"What?"

"Do you want me to make a salad?"

"If it's not too much trouble."

"How much trouble is a salad?"

"Is this a trick question?"

"Anyone tell you that you're a wise-ass, Halleck?"

"Sure. People always used to before I went blind. That's how I knew things had really changed. Not because I couldn't see anymore, but because this great shock wave seemed to be rolling away from me that changed the people I thought I knew. It was as if they believed that I had changed in some fundamental and deeply personal way simply because I couldn't see anymore?"

"And did you?" The question came off easily, so Halleck had no trouble with it.

"Maybe."

"Bitter?"

"Some."

"Defensive?"

"Possibly."

"Self-pitying?"

"At first."

"And now?"

"Now I understand, or am starting to understand, through this therapist"—he almost tripped on the word but it came—"I went to—"

"Los Angeles?"

"Chicago."

"Still?"

"Occasionally."

"Me, too."

"Yeah?"

"Yeah. Why?"

"You just sound, well, so . . . ," he struggled. "You don't sound as if you need . . ."

"Something like that?"

"Well, yes."

"Neither do you, when you just be yourself, Spike."

"Meaning I'm all right for a blind guy."

"Not playing, Halleck."

"Well, you'll concede that you have an advantage in meeting the world on its terms."

"As long as you're looking for the world to approve you, as long as you lack the sense of self that can say fuck you, this is my life, to all of them, Spike, it doesn't matter if you're beautiful"—she slammed down a pot—"or smart," thumped down a head of broccoli, "or funny," hacked at it with a knife, "or even rich," yanked on the faucet, let the water fill a pan. Breathing hard, "As long as you'll do anything for approval, you're nothing. When you say what you're doing is okay, and how you are is okay, it really doesn't matter if you can leap tall buildings in a single bound, they've still got you as a mild-mannered reporter for a large metropolitan newspaper."

"Quite a speech," he said.

"Sorry."

"Don't be. You're right."

"Sure. But I'm not quite there."

"Maybe. But you're close."

"Forty-five minutes yet. Hope you can wait," she said, changing the subject, or was it shifting because she was uncomfortable, or just sensing that the conversation had run its course and she didn't want to bore him with her problems, or to seem in any way inadequate for the assignment because she could be perceived as possessed of what some still called a woman's set of problems? So Halleck just lied when he said, "Not so hungry I can't wait, no."

But he was hungry.

For her.

13

Halleck's suite had become maddeningly full of her, of her scents, her rushing movements, the pulse of her breath and brief touches of her hands, her funny, blunt, sometimes self-deprecating commentary, her intense curiosity, incessant hustle, her seductive openness. Strangely none of this distracted Halleck, who no longer felt alone. Suddenly and unexpected, like an epiphany, she burst into his world shining, melting away the inner darkness that had condensed from the outer darkness around him. Now he puttered intensely, his sightless body animated by fear and chemicals and mysterious excitement now yielding to a mind that, increasingly, was synthesizing visual images to communicate his analysis of what, exactly, contributed to the sounds from the kidnapper's calls.

It would be harder to convince Janowski, something that time would force him to do. Alternatively he could throw up his hands in frustration and despair. He was dwelling on these possibilities, not the savory aroma of dinner, when the phone rang. It unnerved him, made him fumble, scramble, until he realized, by the third ring, that it was not the Granville line. Too early for Brian? he wondered, as he said, "Halleck," who it could be.

"My name is Kowalski," slow droning voice suctioning mucus into its throat, then, "Debra Seraphicos there?"

"Yeah. A minute." Directing his voice to the kitchen, he said, "Phone."

"I'll pick up here, Spike."

He set the handset back in its cradle and returned to the couch, settled in, overheard the conversation.

"Yes, okay, great. Hold on. Let me get it straight. Just a . . . here's a pencil from my purse. Go ahead."

Silence, listening.

"No, nothing below the North Side. Forget all that."

Short pause.

"Just above that. Actually we're looking at something maybe seven blocks in from the lake, close to the L line northbound to the suburbs, but not that far out. No. Stop. Too far. Back up. Okay. Shoot."

Another pause, sounds of scribbling. Halleck had pencil lead, actually graphite, down flat. Its sound is nearly unmistakable.

"So just those two? No, not interested on the TriState. Forget it."

Blip of a pause then, "So those two."

What was she talking about?

"What about contractors, the way they go to outside contractors for overflow? That includes contractors. All right. Now that's those two in the area we agreed on. Right, I have it. Thanks, Killer."

Killer? What the hell kind of name was Killer?

"I know you froze your ass off at the L station. And you'll have another chance at martyrdom tonight. Much appreciated." A shriek. "Not *that* much appreciated, Kowalski, come *on*." Sputtering laugh, throaty, evocative. "I didn't see you on Janowski's little snipe hunt this afternoon. I see. You're right, you *are* lousy on tails. A little hard to hide six eight, right? Okay. Well, until about eight why don't you go home and thaw your frozen buns by the fire. See you then. Say hello to Gladys. And thanks."

She hung up.

"What was that all about?" Halleck asked, trying to stay cool.

"Another piece in the puzzle," she said.

"What?"

"Jackhammer noises," she said.

"We've already milked that one dry. I know it's the same jackhammer, even know that at the times we were recording that it was cutting up asphalt, not concrete, from matching against the library. And I don't think it's private construction because the sound has the echos of playing off buildings, of bouncing off facades after originating in the middle, or near the middle of a street. Which makes me believe, along with the absence of direct traffic noises, that the street is shut off, barricaded."

"So how do you prove it?"

The exact question Janowski would ask. No proofs. Playing the odds, still playing the odds.

"I don't know," he said. "How do I prove it?"

"Kowalski has been buried in paperwork, which he hates, ever since we sprung him from the L station, running down work orders for excavation, street jobs, down in Public Works, pulling the yellows, you know, seeing what he could find. And out of all that he got two inside or near our circle."

"Go ahead," Halleck said, leaning forward with interest as if getting closer would make him hear better. It wouldn't. He could hear her just fine. He just wanted to get closer.

"One of them is very near *Second City*, where Brian said this guy Mike Jared is playing, but outside the circle to the east, so on the lake side. The other one is inside the circle on North Park Avenue, about a block and a half west of *Second City* and east of the L platform where Kowalski was sitting near midday. When he makes rounds tonight, we'll see how close it is to the wind chimes."

"Ergo," said Halleck. "One match."

"Closest to the 1547 North Park chime. So let's look at the *Second City* thing again a little closer. You said the woman was wearing high heels, right?"

"Ninety percent sure."

"So why does she wear heels? Date, right? Night out on the town. Maybe dinner before, then improv. Now how do they handle that? Figure it out, Halleck. When you were driving, how far did you ever park from a theater?"

"Two blocks, three at the most."

"Your words. Three at the most. As for me, I would never park as far as three blocks, but that's a woman's choice, but this guy has a woman, right? So he would prefer to be closer rather than farther away."

"Figures," Halleck said.

"And they pick a good neighborhood unless they're going to park on a main drag, which isn't likely—not around there."

"That too."

"And if you check the map, when you start from *Second City* and walk toward the circle we have, the closest street"—Debra made an audible tapping on the wall—"is North Park. It runs north-south, Spike, so if you start at *Second City* and enter the circle at all, you almost have to cross North Park."

"What if they were headed for the L station?" Halleck asked.

"Then they'd be about three and a half blocks from *Second City*, still do-able, but to get to the L from the theater without crossing North Park makes you fly or go all the way around."

"Then maybe that's it," Halleck whispered.

"You want we check it out?"

"No. Not yet."

"Why?" she asked.

"Let's get what we can about the other places from Kowalski before we squeeze down any more. I don't want to rush and go right by something we ought to keep considering." Halleck also knew, both intellectually and from experience, that a body of evidence, as here, could be perfectly consistent with one conclusion without ruling out equally good alternatives. In those cases, the only thing driving a quick conclusion was another form of blindness called prejudice, or pressure to make a decision rather than wait, the rage, in whatever shape, to sweep away indecision for the sake of drawing a seemingly good conclusion. One of the prime failures of the human mind is its tendency to seek recognizable patterns quickly, whether or not they exist. But they were driven that way by the relentless ticking of the clock. Better than anyone did he know that they were pressed, but some time remained. The last phone call had not come, the one where they would need to negotiate, fairly and reasonably, for mutually agreeable terms for exchange. And whatever was decided then would start the final clock running. Until then, the only thing that both parties understood was that the money would be ready tomorrow. Unless, it suddenly struck him, the city was paralyzed by snow. Then what?

He decided to worry about one thing at a time. An arctic blizzard was beyond his control.

"Look," Debra said, "we're not any closer than we were this morning. Another suggestion. You ready for this?"

"Try me."

"We said, two, maybe three blocks away for on-street parking?"

"Agreed."

"Trust me on this one," Debra said, "that this couple is out for a nice evening. Everything supports that, Halleck. The evidence, as you say. Just put it together. They're out there walking by, just outside wherever they're holding Janey, a woman in high heels and her date, maybe husband, laughing about the show. They've had a good time. What do you make of all that?"

"I don't know. Pretty thin," he said.

"Trust me. I'm a woman. Here's the way it goes. You get all gussied up. High heels for sure, but I'll bet short skirt, knee length, maybe, but no longer, it's not the fashion, and if she has great legs, she wants everybody to know it, because not everybody has great legs. She wants to flatter herself and she wants to show what good taste her man has. But the problem, Halleck, is that it isn't always safe to walk in high heels in this great city of ours, and not because you may have to run from muggers—all right, you might, but you don't plan on it—but if you're a woman, you know that you don't want to walk for any distance on city streets in high heels. It's not, Halleck, just that high heels are uncomfortable, they are, but it's the cost of doing business, what you need to do to show off your great sexy legs to their best advantage. Everybody does it, so you can't get away with not doing it. But beyond discomfort there's risk. On the streets you have cracks and seams in the concrete, you have soft spots, dirt and mud, you have grates that will suck up a heel before you can shift your weight forward. A woman in heels doesn't want to walk three blocks. A half a block is too much. Now if she likes the guy, she humors him, okay. A couple of blocks, maybe. But her eyes are working like hawks, not because she's so cooperative or helpful, but because wherever he parks the car, she's got to schlepp out and back in this Torquemada footwear. But that's not the half of it. You know what kind of temperatures we're having out there?"

"I've been out," Halleck said.

"So this gorgeous lady is out in near-zero temperatures in a short skirt, feeling the arctic blast where no secrets hide. How far do you think she's going to want to walk with icicles crisping up down there? And if that's not enough, the wind is howling, throwing thirty mile-an-hour gusts at you, destroying a coiffure that just left you fifty dollars poorer. So the further you walk, the bigger chance you have of losing a heel, twisting an ankle, leaving your hair like a bramble patch, and getting your thighs so frozen together that foreplay with a blowtorch won't thaw them. Now this is your idea of a fun evening?"

"How does this help?" Halleck pressed her.

"Like I said. Trust me. If we don't want to take it down to the one place yet, let me draw a circle around *Second City*, a circle two and a half blocks in diameter, because I bet that's all this honey can stand. And I bet she's let the guy know that if he wants to get his jollies, like all men do, he better not leave her body too cold. If he wants to get close, he better park close."

"How do you know"—Halleck challenged her, a bit envious that she could get so much out of something he had missed—"it could be a fat woman with lousy legs who has a sexy laugh. We used to use them for sound tracks. They were great husky laughers, used them all the time. And they were sows. And the thing about fat women is that they have a lot of padding and stay warm, and they usually have stubby not-so-great legs that they drape in long, flowing gowns, which makes them warmer yet. So maybe those women wouldn't mind walking three blocks because they're glad to have any man at all."

"Listen, Halleck," she came back, hard and confident. "The fat ladies I know are bigger crybabies than the dreamboats because they feel so sorry for themselves. They just can't seem to muster enough energy to haul their huge carcasses the length of the hall to a rest room without huffing and puffing and needing to sit down. It's the fat ladies, Halleck, who send their skinny husbands to fetch the car from underground parking garages so they don't have to move more than a couple of steps from the warm vestibule of the theater."

"I wouldn't have thought of that," he said.

"And another thing—for a guy who's supposed to listen so well, Spike—is that a fat lady doesn't walk like the woman on that tape. Listen to the time between the heel clicks. That's a stride, baby. No fat lady steps out like that. A fat lady in heels sounds click, click, click, click, little teeny steps as if she's afraid if she steps out she'll pull a groin muscle. And another thing, too, you don't hear, because I *have* listened, Halleck, I have, honest to Christ, been listening and learning all along, but if we're going to keep going, it can't be Professor Halleck with his expository finger in the air all the time, because, Spike, you, too, have something to learn and I, too, have something to contribute, and I would sure as hell hate to find another little girl's body topping some godforsaken frozen garbage can down by the Loop just because to prove you're the world's champion blind man, that you're better in some ways than us seeing folk, that you were too blind and too proud and too arrogant to accept good help when it's offered."

"You're right," he said quietly, realizing, suddenly, chillingly, that he had been playing this, at least at some level, as a kind of blind man's bluff, a mental video game called Find the Lost Kid, where you kept filling in from clues, getting closer and closer, scoring more and more points with higher and higher degree of confidence, as if you would surely win, that there was no doubt, none whatever, that you would win, but in a false sense also playing as if when the game went wrong, when time ran out or you hadn't reached your objective, you could just drop in another quarter and start again.

"You're absolutely right," he said again, quietly.

"Goddamn right I am." She was crying, suddenly slowed down, choked back the sobs, went on, "So look, I say, believe me, this woman is not, absolutely not, going to get herself nice and pretty and warm and then let herself get edgy and tousled and frozen because some Bozo is too cheap to pay for garage parking and too stupid to find something any closer than three and a half blocks away."

"Ruling out the L," Halleck said.

"And puts the car within two and a half blocks. So we draw a circle that size, centered on *Second City*. It crosses into the other circle around the L . . ." He could hear her marking it in, the squeal of the grease pen.

"Making a football-shaped segment," he said, "inside of which Janey must be. How much is it? How long? A block?"

"Half block on either side of North Avenue."

"Including North Park Avenue?" he asked.

"Including almost nothing else," she sighed. "The only wind chime in the football is 1547. At least the only one we know of, Spike. Actually, nearby there's another one that may be worth looking at. But there's a whole semi-circle west of the L that's too far from *Second City* for walking. The other four wind chimes are over there. Toss 'em out. They don't make sense."

"I agree," he said. "But we should still wait on Kowalski. If what you say is true, what he finds will support it. And I have my own theory."

"Which is?" she asked, pacing near the wall.

"In order for this all to make sense, the neighborhood has to have a certain flavor. If you look at where it is, with *Second City*, close to the lake, not far from downtown, the real estate ought to be valuable. But if you look at buildings far north, most of them are still squat, two or three stories, sometimes seven, not the monsters that line Lake Shore Drive nearer the Loop. So what do I expect? I've never seen this place inside the circle, never will. There's no way I can peek at a picture book and cheat. But I'll bet you a hundred dollars that when we drive through . . ."

"Which I hope will be soon," she wedged in.

". . . that we're going to find a mixed commercial and residential district on the upswing. So what I'll bet we'll see is old bars, rundown laundromats, signs of the old neighborhood and signs of speculative investment, renovation and upgrades crowding others out. Some common wall reconstruction, some places just gutted and torn down. New services moving in for new clientele, the Yuppies, the parvenues. So you'll see gourmet groceries and flashy glass and brick office rentals either in place or going up. And trees lining the streets. This time of year there are no leaves, so I can't hear the rustling, no matter how hard I listen, or wind racing through the naked branches of saplings, but I'll bet you see them. Basically, you'll find decay falling away to new growth. And here and there you'll find an old frame house sitting on a lot it's held for fifty or more years, out of place with what's going on around it, owned by a slumlord who's agonizing between squeezing the last cent out of rent increases and selling out to developers. And with these places there are going to be maybe two, three, even four apartments cut out of crackerbox frames, occupied by students, itinerants, struggling actors, waitresses, pensioners, people who can't afford the rent elsewhere. That's where Janey is now."

"We'll see," Debra said, touching him lightly. It drove him crazy.

"Dinner soon," she said. "Mind if I turn on the news?"

"Radio by the toaster," he said, heard it snap on.

"In local news tonight, we just got this. Indiana State Police were forced to open fire where a parole violator at a Whiting bar called SAL'S pulled a knife and resisted arrest. Nick Spiros . . .

"Good Jesus," Debra interjected

". . . was shot and killed by officers after being told to drop the weapon and refusing. The officers involved including a full captain, have been

185

placed on routine administrative leave pending investigation. Spiros, who was recently paroled from Southern Michigan Prison in Jackson after serving five years on a sex offense, was being sought in connection with an unspecified ongoing investigation. We'll keep you updated on this story as it unfolds.

Now the weather. John?

Well, Mara . . ."

Debra snapped it off.

"What's up?" Halleck said.

"I should have told you."

"Told me what?"

"Janowski was working another angle."

"What?"

"It didn't seem to matter, I don't know," she sighed. "If you were aimed at the same thing, I figured you'd converge, pincer in on them."

"So what, I'm still confused," Halleck said.

"Janowski pulsed the wardens at the local joints about any recent releases who might have drummed up kidnapping as a get-rich-quick scheme. They went to their snitches and turned up the names of Nick Spiros, the now late Nick Spiros, and Danny Valitano. He was moving on them. Obviously he got a warrant out for arrest, maybe probable cause, maybe for questioning."

"Now wait a minute," Halleck said. "Janowski suspected—"

"One's dead," she said.

"Where's the other?"

The phone rang and they both jumped, relaxed when they realized it was Halleck's line. He picked up, guessing, "Brian?"

"Janowski," the voice said. "Can I talk to Deb?"

"For you," he pushed her the handset. "Janowski."

"Seraphicos," she answered.

"You can go home now," Janowski told her.

"What?"

"I've got Danny Valitano downtown."

"And Nick Spiros is dead, I just heard. Valitano tell you where the girl is?"

"Insists he knows nothing about it."

"You give him Miranda, Jano? Tell me you gave him Miranda, Jano."

"He's Mirandized, sure. He waived."

"He what?"

"He fucking waived. Doesn't want a C.A. Nothing. Screaming about false arrest. Claims he knows nothing about nothing."

"Find the money, Jano? Any of the bills? They should still be wet."

"None of the money. Figure they have it stashed."

"What about the girl, Jano. He seem ready to give up the girl?"

Halleck, who could only hear Debra, was getting the drift, didn't like it. He lay back, felt his heart race. What had Janowski done?

"Nothing on the girl. After all, it's his life, Deb."

"Can you co-opt your longtime buddy Lou Scannon at FBI, get them to press reduced charges?"

"We're working it. They don't seen too happy with the idea."

And the problem, Debra Seraphicos knew, was that kidnapping was a federal crime under the Lindbergh Act. Irrespective of state laws on the same crime, the Feds could still fry a convict if they wanted. Any plea-bargain had to involve both jurisdictions.

"You've got to find the girl, Jano."

"We're working on it."

"It's cold. Even if you're right, these guys were her custodians. They fed her, kept her warm, let her go to the bathroom. Without them she's going to—" She caught Halleck's face in the corner of her vision and didn't finish the obvious. Janowski may have blown it. Spiros, had he lived, and Valitano would now want to put themselves as far away from Janey as possible, to disassociate themselves from the evidence. With Spiros dead, Valitano didn't have to worry about a matching story. He could make up whatever he wanted, challenge them to prove him wrong. It was his game.

"Jano, you want I should come downtown and help out?"

"Go home, Deb. It's over. I'll call Brian Granville."

"Don't."

"What?"

"Until you have the girl safe, don't tell the Granvilles anything. They're not interested."

"So I'll squeeze Valitano's nuts off tonight. He'll give up the girl."

"Jano, is it him?"

"What you talkin' about?"

"Are you sure it's him? Has he confessed?"

"Of course not. He claims Spiros had set them up to hit First National Trust in Elkhart tomorrow."

"Possible?"

"Deb, it's him."

"Jano, you're talking a couple of nickel-and-dime hoods."

"Deb, go home." That said, he hung up.

Halleck said, "Janowski thinks he's broken the case?"

"He thinks so."

"You don't," Halleck guessed.

"Too easy."

"The guy on the news?"

"Yeah, and Danny Valitano, in holding downtown, talk big, lie a lot. There's nothing much to it."

"What about Janey?"

"Nothing," she said. "They . . . he, Valitano, denies it."

"Great."

"I'm afraid he's going to pull the plugs here, Spike."

"You're going, then."

"Officially, yes. I'm gone."

"Stay," he said.

"Do we have enough?" she asked.

"Maybe."

"We may have to do it on what we have, nothing more."

"Maybe not."

"What?"

"They keep tapes of interrogations, right?"

"Right," she said.

"Can you go downtown, get me one, bring it back here?"

"Spike, that's tampering with evidence, obstruction of justice."

Halleck shook his head. "No. We're not tampering, since we're not going to change anything. And it's not obstruction of justice if no charges have been filed, right? As long as he's under questioning . . ."

"I could get fired . . . go to jail . . ."

"All right," Halleck said. "I shouldn't have asked."

"Goddamn you, Halleck," she said, pulling on her parka. "I'll be back before Kowalski gets here."

The door slammed. She was mad, but she understood. If Valitano's voice didn't match the kidnappers, then Janowski would have to give it up.

Wouldn't he?

14

Magic 104 FM kept Halleck aware of the time while he dug deeper into the tapes for sounds, any sounds that might be helpful in locating Janey. Nothing more was mentioned on the shooting of Nick Spiros, just repeats on the previous announcements and promises of more to come. That and the weather, now calling for a gradual warming, into the teens, and an update on an earlier forecast, indicating that the winter storm that had already dumped an inch and a half of snow onto Chicago's streets wouldn't let up until it unloaded another six inches. Snow or no, Air Jordan and the Bulls were still on for the Knicks tomorrow night, the Bears to host the Cowboys Saturday at Soldier Field. Debra had been incommunicado two hours and was, Halleck had to assume, working as fast as she could. Nor had Brian Granville called, and since the Granville line was forwarded here, he could not call Brian without ringing into his own apartment. And Killer Kowalski, the conscripted off-duty cop, was out there somewhere, mushing around in the real-life territory staked out by the circle around the North Avenue L station, probably cursing at the cold, needing six stops at wind-chimed addresses plus full written reports in order to put the final picture together.

Unable to plan beyond that, numb with fatigue, his muscles weary and stiff, Halleck continued to dig for garbage. The last tape gave him something curious when the computer searched for periodic noises, like the clicking of taps as one of the kidnappers paced a room that couldn't be more than seventeen feet, or much shorter, either. In reexamining the tape, just toying, Halleck discovered something percussive in deep bass that didn't yield to straight periodic analysis. Instead, it came as a series of patterns, a very low hissing cluster of beat sounds, a cadenced boom, boom, boom, boomboomboom, with slow hard strikes, then faster, lighter ones, which repeated throughout the three-minute call. Start to finish, the pattern was either there, or someone was listening on a party line, with a record player on in the background.

Record player? What about that?

Playing what?

Halleck ran it again, using a headset to mute the traffic noise from Michigan Avenue. He cautioned himself that this was dicey stuff, that when you use artificial intelligence, there is always some degree of imagination exhibited that is not totally analytical. Asked to bring you a pattern, it will slavishly hunt down a pattern, without attention to its source, meaning, or sometimes, reality.

Still, Halleck had convinced himself that the pattern was real, not just a coincidental juxtaposition of background noises. But what was it, and what, if anything, did it mean?

Halleck was raising a monster headache chasing down the answer to that, because the extensive library of sounds from Los Angeles failed to provide a match.

But it was there every time, haunting and daunting, giving him no rest. In frustration he stopped, got up, went to pour a cup of coffee, heat it in the microwave, console himself like a student with a tough exam question, that nobody could get it and it probably wasn't that important. How much closer would answering the question get him to Janey? Could it possibly be that important?

Maybe not.

But what if it was? What if they failed, found Janey dead somewhere in two days and found, from fiber and follow-up investigations, that just this sound, properly understood, would have allowed him to zero in on THE place of all the possible places, where she might have been kept?

Obsessed with that, he waltzed his coffee across the room, placed it down on the Formica top of the work station and played through the pattern again. The radio was still on behind him as he took off his headset and rubbed his forehead, aware most intensely that the one thing that remained perversely the same, before and after losing sight, was a headache. From the radio speaker, a chatty local newscaster popped on and bubbled, "One group of locals not damped by the ongoing snowstorm, Milt, is these six seniors from New Trier High School, who call themselves *Total Toad*. They are out here, believe it or not, at the intersection of Michigan and Jackson, right behind me, with the wind coming off the lake in gusts of, I don't know, it's pretty windy when it blows, but they've gathered quite a crowd here . . ."

Halleck found himself unable to concentrate, irate with the drivel, unwilling to tolerate any disturbance. He got up to turn the damn prattle off, still hearing the rhythm of thuds, over and over again, until it seemed to keep pace with the throbbing in his head.

The commentator, a woman with more enthusiasm than sense, rattled on, ". . . as they have broken into a marathon rendition of their own composition, a little Heavy Metal number called "Dallas for Dinner," anticipating Saturday's game." The radio broke into a sound that made Halleck freeze. The thud, thud, thud of drums was clear now, as if someone on the tape he had just heard had knocked down an intervening wall. And there was the insane shriek of electric guitar, the lighter, more elaborate keyboard, but above and beyond that the sound that keeps apartment dwellers sleepless with anger, the heartbeat of rock percussions, the thudding base of the drummer crashing *through* walls like heavy artillery. Everything else got stopped, the guitar, keyboards, vocals, but the mighty drums always cut through. And that was it.

He didn't snap the radio off.

Awful, amateurish, offensive as it was to him as a virtuoso violinist, he listened all the way through "Dallas for Dinner," and would have liked an encore for dessert. That was it.

Someone next to where they kept Janey was playing Heavy Metal. And that told him that she was in an apartment or duplex or divided single-family home with more than one occupant. Ergo, not a deserted building, not a condemned structure. Ergo, a place with heat and, from the clinking of the cup, running water, plumbing. Ergo, most important ergo, even if Valitano and Spiros had taken her, Janey wasn't slowly freezing to death. She may have a cold, but she wouldn't fall into irreversible hypothermia.

Secondarily, still importantly, it told him something about the neighbors. Rock music at midday, a time and day when kids other than truants were in school meant unemployed, early twenties, perhaps, living at home with Mom and Pop, a girlfriend or boyfriend. Heavy Metal meant white, whereas Soul would mean black. Something here after all.

When the phone rang, Halleck jumped.

It rang again, the characteristic buzz on *his* phone. Turning sharply, he strode across the room, sat down, and answered, "Halleck."

"Spike, Brian. Good news."

What? Had that maniac Janowski called, told Brian they'd caught the kidnappers? His heart froze as he listened, saying only, "Go ahead."

"That kid you asked about?"

"Regie?"

"That's the one."

"Yeah?"

"Ellie came through!"

"You've got an address?"

"It took a little running. We've been on this thing like the edge of a cliff since I got home. We checked the elementary and junior highs in the areas, even the high schools to be sure, although to me the voice sounded young, immature."

"Right," Halleck told him.

"And we did use your story about a bottle of medicine misprepared, the dangers. Well, they went right out to the teachers, asking them. One of them came up with a kid named Percival . . ."

"Who the hell calls a kid Percival these days?"

"Percival Reginald McTavish, believe it or not."

"Regie."

"We think so . . . who keeps his skateboard in his locker."

"Locker means junior high, at least."

"Junior high. Lives with his mother at 1522 North Park Avenue."

"Bingo."

"Does that help, Spike?"

"I think we may have a lock on it."

"Shall I call Janowski?"

"No," Halleck said, hoping he hadn't snapped it back. The last thing he wanted was for Brian to debate the Spiros-Valitano conspiracy theory with Janowski and destroy the best chance of saving Janey's life.

"So where are we now? There's not much time."

"We're close. Very close, I think. Half a block or so."

"Then what in God's name are we waiting for?"

"An off-duty cop named Kowalski is checking out all six addresses in our target area. I want to debrief him, to make sure I'm not throwing something out that's obvious."

"When?"

"Three hours. Maybe less."

"You want me to come down?"

"No. But there is one thing you can do."

"Name it."

"See if you can get the time Mike Jared's show at *Second City* let out last night, to check against the tape."

"Done. I'll be in touch."

They hung up at the same time, Halleck going back to his coffee. It had gone cold. He got up to reheat it when Debra Seraphicos unlocked the door, spun through, refilling the air with her perfume, her gasping breaths.

"Still cold out there, Halleck."

"I've heard. How did you do?"

He heard a sharp clicking sound. "How do you think?"

"What is it?"

"Reels. Ten-inch reels."

Halleck's heart almost stopped. "They don't use cassettes?"

"You seen a police budget lately?"

Then it hit him. He said it without thinking, "Back closet, bedroom. There's a variable speed, programmable lock Akai/Roberts, something that got hauled out from LA during the move, by mistake, We're going to have to jump cables into auxilliary jack sockets to get analysis from the computer."

"If you tell me how I can do it," she said.

"No problem. I'm almost like a Marine fieldstripping a rifle. I used to thread this thing without looking while I was reading scripts, figuring out the sounds to use, the levels, the timing markers, that sort of thing."

"This isn't a competition, Spike."

He thought he understood, heard the softening in her voice, didn't want to lose her, to annoy her, to have her walk out. So he said, "Okay. I'll show you how."

"Good," she said. "Give me some new skills to practice once I've paid my debt to society for obstructing justice."

"You stole these?"

He could almost hear the shrug. "No. I just told Janowski I would take them down to the property room for him. They were sitting on Valitano pretty hard."

"Booked him yet?"

"Negative. And they wouldn't miss this until tomorrow, at the earliest. Maybe not until arraignment. It'll be back by then."

"Let's see what we have here." Halleck threaded the tape, told Debra how to wire it into the computer for analysis.

"Just run," he told her. "Push PLAY."

She did, producing Danny Valitano saying,

"I told you before, me and Spiros is thinkin' of maybe hittin' this little bank in Elkhart. Like I said, you're not listenin', as for a kid, I don't know nothin' about no kid . . ."

"That's it," Halleck said, stopping it. "We transfer the word *kid* from the Valitano's tape onto the comparator cassette, then run a match based on the word *kid* that the kidnapper used in his first tape."

Debra was quick with, "Here's the first tape."

"Put it in master, push LOCK."

She did.

"Now the same with the comparator tape, and push LOCK."

Again she did.

"Now run the police tape back to a point just before the word *kid*, either place."

Spike heard the high squealing blip of a tape running back, then the text run forward and stop, just before Valitano spat out the word, *kid*. Then a click stop.

"Now I push RECORD under comparator," she guessed.

"Right."

"And play on the Akai."

"Right."

They both heard the word *kid* and Debra said, "Now off."

"Good."

"Now stop."

"Right."

"And now what?" Strange question. She knew, or he thought she knew, the comparator routine. She had already done it with the library of sounds. Still, he walked her through. She sat down next to him. He could feel her heat, hear her breathing, wanted to touch her.

"Go into the Menu. Use the mouse for compare. Let's overlay with display. When it runs, it's going to throw up a voiceprint comparison on the screen. On the top you'll see Danny Valitano's voice, the way he says 'kid,' the exact combinations and intensities of the various frequencies required to make the sound the way he makes it. Underneath that you'll see the way the kidnapper makes the word *kid*. If it's the same person speaking they will be identical."

The computer automatically clicked and whirred, spinning through the first call to locate the sound on the tape most like Danny Valitano's word *kid* then automatically analyzing the distribution, intensity, and frequency of component sounds, instantly projecting the results as two voiceprints.

"What do you see?" Halleck said.

"Similar," she said.

"Everybody saying the word *kid* has to be somewhat

similar, otherwise the word doesn't sound like kid. If either of these guys had a Spanish inflection, for example, and said, *keed*, it would look substantially different, as would the word *kit*."

"Thank you, professor," Debra said, a little annoyance in her voice. "But what is the real lesson of the day?"

"Push INPUT," he said.

She did, bringing the two patterns into superimposition. From this, she could see, as she expressed it, "The valleys and hills are different. I mean, not in different places, but different shapes. Valitano's valleys are flatter, broader, shallower than the kidnapper's, but his hills, more like mountains, are higher, sharper, have little crags on them."

"They don't overlap," Halleck concluded.

"Not even close," Debra said.

"Then it's not Valitano. Janowski's got the wrong man."

"You're sure?"

"Absolutely."

"What do we do then?"

"We wait for Kowalski."

"That may be two hours."

"We've done everything else we can do."

"No we haven't," she said. Tone shift, Halleck got it right away. A kind of conversational non sequitur. It fit and didn't. He sat there paralyzed, wanting to dig his fingers into the Formica of the work station desk, afraid to hope.

"You hungry?" He got up, walked toward the kitchen, tried to change the subject.

She got up, followed, caught his hand with hers, laced her fingers through. "Yeah, I'm hungry. You hungry?"

She caught up his mouth with her lips, dissolved it in soft, firm heat, pulled at his breath.

He did not have to ask what she was doing. He wasn't stupid. And he wasn't impotent and he wasn't indifferent. It was never, hadn't been since the blindness, the what, but the why? And she must have felt him stiffen up with confusion because she said, as if she had lifted the question right off the top of his head, "Because you're a very sexy man, and I like that. But that's not all of it. Still, I don't know what to hope for."

She led him where he knew, tugging, her hands busy, urgent, determined, experienced, and persuasive. But Halleck needed no persuasion, none at all.

Halleck glowed with the familiar, the firm fleshy curves he now knew by their feel and flow, the secret openings by their smell and taste, the magic of two as one in the rhythm, the beat of the universe, like the night sky over the Chilean Andes, all endless black yet here and there in a sound she made, bursting off and twinkling in that blackness like a lapidary star, all wonder and magic at the bursting light and fading color coruscating through his mind as he pulled her taut buttocks against him, draped himself on the billowing pillows of her breast, his chest riveted by the hard-tipped crowns of her nipples, was suddenly swept, dizzyingly thrown into a spiral of want by as simple yet irresistible a plea as her whispered, "Yes," and buried himself in her soft, coiled, aromatic hair, was astonished, frightened by her strong, urgent hands, her fingers coiled and stroking, her mouth wet and wondrous, her tongue more than once almost, just almost and nearly too terribly undeniable, because as much as he relished that, it was inside her he wanted it, into her, first with furtive fingers, then the he of him that finally thrust in so deep he could not tell but didn't want to whether the long groan and rolling thrusts were not the counterfeits that he had so many times orchestrated with the fabulously convincing fraud of mighty sexual rapture, the sounds that dreams are made of, that he knew had come from the mightiest vocal orgasmizer of them all, the fifty-seven-year-old twice mastectomized one amputated, nearly, as *he* would soon be after the last time he talked to her, blind, grandmother of eighteen and twice divorced, chain-smoking, hard-drinking, self-described hard-farting, LaDonna Perez of Palo Alto, California, an emphysemic who would simulate a scream of coital ecstasy by abandoning her oxygen bottle, running up a flight of ten steps then screaming, literally, for dear life, all at a going rate of twelve hundred dollars a scream, grunt, or sigh. Halleck knew fakery, which made him know reality that much better. And the thing he could hate about reality was the very thing he feared about it, the chilling, deep-down, undeniable truth that you've lost control, that you're caught up in something that has a life of its own, something beyond you or your lover, beyond and above the heat and the sweat and the smell and salty taste of sex, something that could scare you so bad you'd run away or draw you in so tight you'd never be able to leave. And the funny thing about it was never knowing which way it would go. That was scary, too.

It built for . . . Halleck had no sense of time, the deep and urgent, cosmically rhythmic, ever-rising movement of their dance, the tune played outside unheard yet, in that silence, inside, between them, a secret. There were no words, words that seemed silly, awkward, ridiculous, even obscene. The sounds of love transcend words, he felt, because thinkers need words, build around themselves shells of words that only feelings break through, leaving something nonverbal, more vital, more true.

She built with it, knowing, feeling him in the blindness where lovers must learn by one body asking another, the other saying yes, or maybe, or no, or try this instead. Yet it was she who sensed the tide building, who rode it, crested with it, arched and grabbed him, both hands, fingers digging into his buttocks, both feet locked on his hamstrings, catching him fully inside her as he released, holding him as he throbbed, keeping him, as she did, impossibly hard beyond and beyond and beyond.

Releasing, slowly releasing, falling away, apart to either side, their lungs still pumping from effort, she laughed that so feminine laugh that means without saying it, "What have I done? Does it matter? Why am I asking myself this stupid question? It was wonderful!" Which came out between deep, quick breaths as just, "Wow." Silence settled in. A minute, two. He didn't know. Over and over he was taught that time, the time now so vitally running for Janey Granville, was not a sense that came to blind easily, not unless it was consciously tracked, deliberately counted. Yet however long it was that passed, he heard her shift, as if pulling herself up on one elbow to look at him and saying, "Why did they call you Spike?"

Another silence while he thought, wondering why this question now?

"Where did you get the name—nickname rather?" she rephrased it.

"Why?"

"Curious."

"Well, you know, for my work. Spiking sounds. Like spiking drinks, adding something to it that increases its kick. That's the point, to give the audience an accoustical kick. Like when they see a drop of water falling into a puddle in a half-lit room, with a sinister figure standing against the backlight, throwing a shadow. You can put more feeling, more fear, in those people sitting together in the comfort of that small theater by making that little plip sound just as if their own head is lying on the floor looking up at that figure, more fear than anything you can imagine."

"And so, Spike?"

"Yeah," said Halleck. "So, Spike."

"All right. But that's not why I'm calling you Spike," she said.

"What?"

"Not after this." She shifted over, her hair trailing, exotic smelling, evocative, in his face, her lips lightly touching his cheek, kissing it, pulling away, saying, close enough for her honeyed breath to condense on his chin, "For me it's Spike because you're as long and hard as a railroad spike. For me, lover, it's because you have an absolutely beautiful cock."

"You think?"

"I *feel* it. What I think, after this, is that you're going to have to stop thinking of yourself as handicapped."

Halleck felt himself blush. She certainly knew what she wanted. Or did she? What was all this about anyway? A break in the tension? His body felt strange. Exhilarated but strangely spent, something between the thrill of Olympic triumph and the agony of Sisyphean torture. It was what he wanted, but he still didn't understand it. And he couldn't afford to dwell on it. Regaining his focus, at the cost of distance, he asked, "What time is it?"

"Why, you want this to report it to *Guinness Book of World Records*?"

He sputtered a little laugh, quietly delighted by her humor. "No," he said, "we're expecting a visitor."

"Jesus, you're right! I almost forgot," she said, turning, grabbing at, what? Her watch? Must be. Halleck had no clocks except the obligatory one that came with the clock radio in the kitchen. What good were they to him?

He waited as she said, "Ten of eleven," and got up, rustling around. "Listen," she began to say, the sound of redressing filling the room, "I'll get ready if you can get dressed alone . . ."

"Been doing it for over a year," he told her, trying not to sound sarcastic.

"Sorry, it's just . . ." She sounded flustered, couldn't recover before the door chime sounded. "That's him. You'll be all right?"

"Three minutes," he said.

"I'm coming," she yelled, as the chime sounded again. "I can't see all your stuff."

"I'll get new stuff from the dresser, closet. Go."

"Okay. Brush?" she begged.

"Bathroom," he said, moving to put things on.

"We're coming," she shouted, running.

Halleck moved deliberately, fetching underwear, socks, walking confidently to the closet, selecting combed cotton slacks, a pullover sweater. Convenience. Not too many unknowns. He had his hair cut so he could just toss it to either side, run his fingers in either direction and it fell nicely in place. Slipping into loafers, he was ready. In the other room, he could hear Debra talking, projecting objectivity over embarrassment, sounding tentative. Five minutes ago she had been as vulnerable as a woman can be, as unguarded, as responsive. In that much time she had to change completely, become just as detached, professional. Now she had to deal with one of her own, a man Halleck knew only as a six-foot-eight-inch hairy Pole, nicknamed Killer.

Without the slightest uncertainty in his steps, Halleck strolled easily out to the living room, where the two were already speaking, hoping that Kowalski's nose was as poor as evolution could make it, as neglected as in most sighted people. If so he would not smell Halleck, nor would he smell Debra, who smelled of one thing and one thing only. Sex.

"Been cold all day and night out there," Kowalski groused.

"What'd you find out, Killer?" Debra asked.

"Mr. Halleck. Good ta meet ya. How ya holdin' up?" Kowalski's hand smothered his but Spike returned the pressure.

"Tired. What about these wind chimes?"

"Two places are unoccupied. No one home."

"You sure?" Halleck said, sitting down, clasping his hands together.

"One place on Michaels Street is a shell. Two walls standing, holes where the windows used to be. Bunch of bricks from the wrecking ball lying in the lot to one side. But in the second-story window frame, still hanging there—no window, mind—is this wind chime, sort of dangling thing of metal diamonds."

"Go on," Halleck said.

"No point in taking notes there, just moved on to the next place."

"What about the structure? Could anybody shelter themselves in there?"

"Shelter," Kowalski scoffed, barking laughter. "There's no floors!"

"Go on," Halleck said. "You said something about another one?"

"Greater Chicago Neighborhood Girls' Club, on Sullivan Street. Nice wind chime out front, underneath the porch. But it's empty inside. Felt like a real idiot. Walk up there, about to knock, see a sign, MOVED TO NEW LOCATION."

"Any sign of services?" Halleck asked.

"Nothing. Place is dead."

"Any sign of heat inside? Condensation on the windows maybe?"

"None of that."

"What next?" Debra said.

"Next I almost get killed. Next there's people there, people I wish wasn't there . . ."

Halleck leaned forward in his chair, urged Kowalski, "Go on. What kind of people?"

"Well, it was a smallish wood frame house, sort of crackerbox, you know, but bigger. Mighta been nice once, forty years or so ago. Kinda run down, now. Has a porch. I go up, knock. Say someone here called a cab. This big nigger guy—"

"Black," Debra interrupted.

Kowalski shrugged. "Like I say, nigger answers. Right away I can tell the guy is loaded. The eyes, you know, and breath would kill a water buffalo. He says, What the fuck I mean comin' at him this time of night? I crazy? Then I just give him the story, say somebody asked for a cab, this address. He turns around says, 'Verona, you call a cab, yo fuckin' bitch? Yo call a cab?' he says, 'Yo try to run away again? I kill yo, bitch.' Now by now I'm backin' off, saying there's been a mistake. He comes out, says, 'You bet there's a mistake, I'm gonna kick your white ass 'round the block,' and I am not about to stay to argue, you know, and have to explain to Janowski what I'm doin'? 'Specially when the dog—"

"There was a dog?"

"German sherpard."

"Address again?" Debra said.

"This is the one on the sixteen hundred block of Sullivan, two blocks west of the L."

Debra said, "Even a drunk black with woman problems is going to think twice about attacking a six-eight Pole, Killer. You're not dead and you're not tied up by a couple of guys who plan to kill you tomorrow, so I'm running a little low on sympathy." She took a deep breath, let it out slowly, went on it a low, cracking voice. "This place, the one with the black guy . . . Describe the rooms."

"Rooms?"

"Did you look inside?"

"Sure. Like we agreed, right. And I looked good because all the lights was on, upstairs, downstairs."

"Tell us about them," Debra pressed.

"Small rooms, you know. In the living room don't sit

down 'cause you break your knees on the wall, that sort of place."

"Not the sort of neighborhood our happy couple would want to walk through," Halleck guessed.

"Or a mother would let Regie skateboard through," Debra added.

"What about the place on Babcock Court?"

"Oh, that was a nice place. Like redone or something. Had to ring a bell on a box outside a high gate, you know, one of those ones made out of iron spears. Lady's voice comes on, real nice, says 'Yes, what is it?' and I'm there tellin' her that her taxi has come and she says, you know, 'What taxi?' Am I sure? and I tell her I only know what the dispatcher tells me as I stand there in the wind and cold really freezing my balls off, and here is this very lovely bitch I can't see, talking to me in accents, a little English, saying, 'I don't think Edward has called a cab but let me check.' So what can I do, right? I know good and goddamn well that Edward hasn't called a fuckin' cab, but I'm standing there, my balls beginnin' to fall off, waitin' for her to come back and ask me, Am I sure? I tell her again, 'Lady, I only know what the dispatcher says.' By now I *want* the fare, just to get out of the cold. I'm hopin', you know, this guy Edward remembers some place he's supposed to go, so I can stop freezing. Instead, I feel these little security cameras whirring around to take a look at me, while she says, 'I think you've got the wrong address.' And I say sorry. And that's all there is."

Halleck could almost hear Debra shaking her head no as she rolled into the final question, just to check. "Wind chime, Killer. Did you see a wind chime?"

"Sure, it was hangin' outside, off the brick pillar, just under a little cap, made the thing look like a pagoda or some Oriental shrine. This wind chime was made of . . . like blue china, you've seen the stuff, like real classy place settings for rich folk."

"Two more," Debra told him.

"There's the one just north and a little east of *Second City*, by the grocery market there, the gourmet place. You know, what's it's name?"

"Dominick's. I know the place," Debra said, "Go on."

"It's a walkup. Lots of little stores down below, first

floor. Then on the second is this window, wind chime is right there. Right above a window box, you know, for flowers. 'Cept there ain't no flowers, 'cause its winter. Only the snow, which by now is three inches. I can't find a place to park. Jerks behind me blowin' their horns. So I double park anyway. Walk up to the door, which is around the side. Now plenty of apartments, maybe twelve in all. Mailboxes inside. Outside are the call buttons. So I don't know what the apartment number is, 'cept it's on the second floor. What do I do? There's no light on in the place with the wind chime, so maybe nobody's home. What do I do, push the bells for everybody with a second-floor apartment, get everybody pissed off? Even if I get the right apartment, you know, get lucky, and they answer, what do I do, tell you what I think of their voices?" Kowalski sighed. "What the hell good would that be without the equipment? So that was the end of that."

Uneasy with the last report, Halleck said, "Any green cars at this place?"

"Lots of cars. None old and green. Not at this place."

"What about the others?" he pressed.

"Not as I could tell, with the dark and all. And sodium vapor lights make green like black, not much different from blue. Can't tell without a flashlight. Maybe that fancy place had a garage or somethin'. The only green car I really seen for sure, that I checked out, was at the last place."

"What?" Halleck and Debra said.

"Well," Kowalski said, "I drive up onto North Park and, you know, the street is blocked off the way I want to come in, so I have to circle the block and come in the other way, from North Avenue. I do that and can stop because there's no traffic. On the corner is a fenced lot across the street from the place, and on the street, right in front, is this dark car. Looks black at first. Then I get my flashlight out to check, it is really green. Chrysler Imperial—old one. Jeez, seventy-six maybe. Close, anyway, 'cause I remember what they used to do with the chrome back then. But hard to tell the exact year."

"Illinois plates?"

Kowalski nodded. "ZLP 213."

"Maybe," Debra said. "Tell us about the place."

"You mean, 1547?"

"That's it," Halleck said, feeling his heart begin to race.

"Got a dog," Kowalski said.

"You're sure?"

"Double sure," Kowalski said. "From the barkin' and from the chain link fence around the yard. Little yard, like the size of half a squash court is all I can think of. With a chain on for when they tie him up. Anyway. Dog barks inside, I ain't goin' nowhere. I can't get a new set of balls, know what I mean. Same thing with the nigger's dog. No way am I gonna chance it."

"So you didn't go up?" Halleck asked, controlling his temper.

"Now I didn't say that. You think this is the first time a cop goes to the door with a dog in the house. I go back and pick up my little jar of red peppers in case. Postman's trick. My brother-in-law's a carrier, give me the idea."

"So you went up," Debra corrected.

"Well, I kinda did," Kowalski said.

"What?" Halleck demanded, impatience cutting through the fatigue now gnawing at him like acid.

"I went through the gate and up the little cement path, up to the porch but there was a problem."

"Problem, Kowalski?" Debra said.

"In front of me was this real long room, kind of, with a door. Over the window to the right was where the wind chime was. But back to the left was another door, so the place was broke up into little apartments. So from the street it looks like an old house, still low, like a story and a half, probably old high ceilings inside—there's a lot of places like that around, but then, okay, I back away, start to walk down, and I notice, all right? there's a another little path going around back to the right, which I walk down, and what do you know? there's another place, like a basement room or somethin', down there. So some lucky landlord is squeezing three rents out of this place that he can't of put a penny into in the last ten years."

"So what did you do?" Debra asked.

"I went back up on the porch, at least to knock on one of the doors. Now the big place, the one with the wind chime is dark, blinds drawn, venetian blinds, 'cept there's a TV on inside. I can see it glowing, hear the sound of bombs, you know, war films, that sort of thing, but spooky because that's all there is. And I know this sounds dumb, and don't tell Janowski, but I get the chills, not from the cold, but because it seems so creepy, so quiet. Then I'm about to hit the doorbell, or the button, when the place next door just explodes in this rock music, almost like make me shit my pants. You ever done that? Been all tense and somebody surprises you. Well, I take my finger back real quick, like because I'm surprised and suddenly, out of nowhere, all around me is this voice, says, 'Whaddya want?' like if I don't have the answer he believes I'm gonna die or somethin', that's what it sounds like to me. So I say, you know, 'Hey, fella. Take it easy. I got a cab called to this address. That you?' He just says, 'No,' and backs off. Nothin' more. Just no. Scary, the look in his eye, I tell you."

"Anything else?" Halleck said. "What about street repairs?"

"Sure. That's why the street was closed off. Big canyon cut through. Too skinny for sewer. Looked like telephone work to me, I think."

"Describe the neighborhood," Halleck said.

Kowalski sighed. "What am I? Suddenly a real estate agent?" Shrugging he went on, "Not all like the house. At the corner, new place, all brick and windows. Then around the corner some bars, restaurants, mom and pop market, video store, laundromat. New office building and condominium just across North Avenue. Two blocks from *Second City*. A lot of change. Upscale. One lot was gutted, development sign already up. Gonna be nice soon."

"Thanks," Halleck said.

"Sure," he said in a way that Halleck could tell he was fighting off a yawn. "I gotta go. Else Gladys'll think I've been screwin' around on her again."

"Then go," said Debra, letting him out, closing the door behind. "What now?" she said.

"Let's take a look at this place," said Halleck.

"It's nearly midnight," she said, yawning.

"Good. They shouldn't be watching too closely," he said.

"Spike . . ." She sounded exhausted. And why not. She had been running all day, all over the city, stolen police property, made incredible love to him, all without the little red helper that kept him buzzing. What more could he want? In many ways it wasn't her problem. But she had the eyes.

"How about an amphetamine? I highly recommend them," he said.

"No, thanks. But let's go," she said, suddenly stopping, silent. "You don't have a car."

"I didn't pass parallel parking," Halleck came back.

"And mine is in the shop. How about a cab?"

"Too obvious," Halleck said.

"Wouldn't dare use unmarked, even if I could," she said. "They could tell."

"Too late for rentals?" A question.

"Not even O'Hare, this time of night."

"Harold," Halleck said. "He works noon to midnight today. Needs the money. Always seems to need the money."

"He'll lend us his car?"

"He'll *rent* us his car," Halleck corrected. "He'd rent us his *mother*."

"So where's Harold?"

15

"What if they call?" Debra said.

Halleck had thought of that, wondered, even obsessed about it, had concluded it was one of those very good calculated chances, like getting up in the morning more or less confident that you weren't going to be hit by a meteor on your way to work. "What time is it?" he asked.

"Ten past twelve," she said.

"They won't," he said, as much hoping as guessing.

They sat shivering in Harold the doorman's car, a fifty dollar an hour rental that had to be back by one. The car, like them, shuddered in the cold, its engine surging in viscous oil, struggling, like the Bears on the sideline in a Siberian front, to stay warm by simply jogging in place. The car suited Harold, running, as its owner did, with an audible chatter that might have been an arthritic transmission that poverty, neglect, or indifference had fostered, a mechanical problem given more and more to noise and less and less to motion by the day, which Harold had promised would, "Go away in a mile or two, maybe a little more in cold. Anyway don't worry about it. The car runs. My brother-in-law Andy had one like it, said the same thing. You know, a little noisy but the odometer on these babies will turn a hundred twenty thousand sure as the sun comes up tomorrow. It's just a little low on gas. So if you're goin' far, try to top her up, will you? Still, I wouldn't take it to Green Bay or nothin'." Sharing Harold's concern, the car emitted a high squeal as Debra turned the wheel to pull it away from the curb, her teeth chattering as she asked, again, "How can you be sure, Spike?"

"I can never be sure," he said.

"Then what if they do?"

"I left the answering tape on." He had the presence of mind to bring that along from Brian and Ellie's, knowing his limits, able to project that a couple would need to sleep, even if their daughter was kidnapped, or, given the excruciating tension, especially if their daughter were kidnapped, when their reserve melted away under pressure. The kidnappers might even suspect, if the Granvilles complained to their family doctor, not of kidnapping, but of stress, that he might prescribe a tranquilizer. Plenty of doctor feel-goods worked the suburbs, making a profit out of chemical comfort.

"Don't you think they will be suspicious if they get a tape?"

"I hope not. I hope, if our story seems right and they *do* call, it will seem consistent. We have a business deal, simple as that. Tomorrow we get the money and arrange for terms. Tonight we sleep. They take care of Janey until tomorrow and make us believe in an exchange."

"You think?" The car lurched left. Halleck felt it accelerate. Blind didn't mean senseless. He could tell they were moving. Around his toes heat was starting to flow.

"Remarkably enough they've played it straight. It had been just like a business deal."

"Maybe they were afraid of a trace."

"I hope so."

"What?" Debra said.

"I mean if they were afraid of a trace it means they wanted to hunker down in one place, not move. You're not afraid of traces if you're going to move after every call. All the calls and what Kowalski told us suggest they're sitting tight."

"You think you can convince Janowski?" The car decelerated for a light, running over a rough spot in the pavement, clanging on a metal plate left down during repairs.

"Maybe," he said.

"Maybe might not be good enough," she sighed. "He's so goddamn stubborn when he thinks he's right."

"But Valitano's not going to confess to kidnapping," Halleck insisted.

"No? Valitano knows the system, Spike. He knows that if they want, they can set him up, put him away. If they want they'll give him a going over that no doctor could ever turn up, things like rubber hoses, that sort of thing."

"That goes on, these days?"

"Police interrogator's most persuasive tool," she said.

"So Valitano might—"

"Plea-bargain on a crime he never committed? Sure. Happens all the time. Called Justice in America."

"But Janowski doesn't have Janey," Halleck said.

"He doesn't need Janey, Spike. If he gets a confession, he has a better case for conviction without her. He doesn't have to show the body. Just motive and opportunity," she said.

"He wouldn't—"

"He would," she cut him off. "It's a conviction. You know how many people have arrests, let alone convictions on kidnapping? He'll be a hero, even in the midst of a tragedy. And the public, in their paranoia, will love him for keeping this creep from stealing *their* little boys or girls off the streets."

"Jesus," Halleck whispered.

"Mary and Joseph," Debra finished. "But that's the way it is. The question is, do you want to be able to prove it?"

She turned sharp left, away from the lake. Halleck heard a distant foghorn cut through the snow, snow he heard slushing under the tires, swishing off the moving wiper blades. Before straightening out, the car shimmied and slid. "How?" he asked.

"I have an idea," she said, slowing for another light, turning in his direction, her voice no longer bouncing off the windshield. "So far you've been closing in using clues, all noises, and reason. And so far, so good. Maybe this place is it. Maybe not. It almost doesn't matter if Janowski's not buying because the local press is cooking on the Nick Spiros shooting and Lou Scannon and the FBI want some movement on the kidnapping. He's on the spot. So unless we give him something better, and I mean really better, he's going to run with what he has tomorrow."

"He'll book Valitano?"

"Even if he's wrong he can drop charges. It gets him off the hook, gets the chief off his back."

They accelerated away from the light, sloshing on Harold's bald tires.

"And you have this way, this proof?"

"I have an idea. It's worth a try. What if you could put a sound right on your tape, a sound *we* controlled, plugged right in at the scene?"

"Couldn't involve police band radio, no dispatchers," Halleck said.

"It wouldn't."

"What?" he said.

"My husband—ex—rather, Al," she said, "flies choppers now for one of the local radio stations, you know, carries around this Captain Jack on Traffic Skywatch. You've heard him. Except he only does that during rush hours. The rest of the time he's free. I was thinking that if he could find a pad a couple of blocks, no more than a half mile from this place we think Janey's being held, he could rev up and be over it in a minute and a half. And if we synchronized the timing, we could know exactly, from his observations, what time he passes over. That's when the chopper noise would be loudest."

"I don't know," Halleck said. "It could spook them."

"One pass. Right over the top. Nothing low and daring. Just a commercial chopper heading toward the Loop for a pickup. They do that all the time for the rich and famous. It's not an unusual sound. Hell, Spike, even if they look out the window, what do they see? A KCLI helicopter passing overhead without delay, moving on. What's so suspicious about that?"

"I see your point," Halleck said, understanding perfectly. If they actually injected a noise onto the ransom call, Janowski would have to believe it. The call would have to come before Janowski's press conference, but there was no guarantee that it would.

"So it's a go?"

"Can you arrange it?"

"If the weather clears, I think I can."

"You and your ex on speaking terms?"

She laughed, a warm, mellow laugh. "We're better friends than we were spouses. Sure, we talk. Why not?"

"He'd do this?"

"Not without knowing why."

"He could keep a secret?"

"That he could."

"Then let's pray for clearing weather."

"You religious?"

"Sometimes you hope there's a God. Sometimes you want there to be."

"You don't seem religious."

"Religion is leaving things to chance that you might otherwise influence. It's abdicating responsibilities, expecting God, if he exists, to alter the rules or patterns just for you. That's not faith, it's arrogance. Sometimes, if you've done all you can, you'd like a little extra edge, something you didn't count on, something to tip the scales in your favor when they're teetering with indecision. Then if a prayer will do it, why not?"

She remained silent. He couldn't read that, whether she approved or disapproved or was indifferent. The car hissed through the snow, chugging along, northbound. Halleck could not tell it was northbound except by knowing that was where they had to go, and by trusting Debra to get him there.

She was his eyes.

Soon he would ask her to paint him a picture.

"Two blocks now," she said, matter-of-factly. "It's gonna be tough getting in this time of night without being conspicuous."

"Just drive by," Halleck said.

"Can't, Spike. Road is closed. Barricaded. I'll bet a sign is up saying NO THRU STREET."

Of course. Was he too tired? Was it that? Or wasn't he putting the pieces together. Or was he so excited about actually getting Janey back that he forgot that if he were to succeed he would have to slow down near the end, to pay more attention to detail than before, not less. Yet he had covered so much in so little time, virtually eliminated all but a city block in two days, that it seemed that all he would have to do was to walk up, ring the doorbell, and say, "Here we are."

Still he knew that whatever he did, he must not cause them to move now. If he was right, and he believed he was, he had to devise a plan to get Janey out.

"If we prove this location to Janowski, can we expect cooperation?"

"You mean in getting Janey back?"

"What else could I mean?"

"You could mean what the book says, which is get the bad guy. Sure they'll minimize danger to potential victims, but the method is to cordon off the place, announce your presence, seem to negotiate, knowing that the clock is ticking. Now they aren't going to storm the place, but there's no place these guys can go. And like you said, Spike, they've had it. It's death penalty or life whether they kill her or not. So what difference does it make to them?"

"Janowski could promise reduced sentence," Halleck suggested.

"Janowski can't do shit. He doesn't have the authority. You think the FBI or Chicago is going to endorse a policy of leniency? Besides, these guys are bound to be streetwise. They're bound to know that a promise made under duress isn't binding, so they're on their own, with the odds against them. And it's hard to tell, Spike. It really is. Some of these guys would rather do anything than go back and get cocks shoved up their asses every day they do hard time. Some of them would rather die than do time. Really."

Halleck thought hard about that, had no ideas.

"Here we are," Debra said. "I'm pulling up across the intersection on North Avenue, just west of North Park. I can see through a chain link fence. The place is the third in—that is south—from the intersection. It's dark. And it's quiet. No rock music. It's twelve thirty-five. What do you want to do?"

"Case it," Halleck said.

"If I get out, I'll leave tracks in the snow," she said.

"Still falling?"

"Still coming down," she assured him.

"How about the wind?"

"It's Chicago. You have to ask?"

The car shook with a blast.

"Between cover and drift, they won't see anything, unless they're looking for it. I need for you to size up the place. Give me entrances, exits, windows. Let's verify what Kowalski gave us."

"Give me five minutes," she said. "But stay put. And stay low. This is a stakeout, Halleck. Remember that they can see you, even if you can't see them."

He tucked himself down, said, "Okay. Go."

And she closed the car door with a click, not slamming it, moved off into the storm.

Even through the wind he could hear her crunching off through the snow, sliding and hissing through unpacked drifts, even stop to let a truck—the low rattle and chained thud, probably a sander—pass. He sat alone but felt secure. A silly euphoria grew in him, left him with a sense of what he had done, gradually cut down a city of millions into one square block, probably to one house, all based on the characteristic noises made by background objects. With fewer sounds, depending excessively on any one, he could have been wrong, could have been unconvincing. But as the number of sounds increased, as they appeared at exactly the right times, and as they matched the corresponding sounds in the accoustical library, the chances of being wrong on a collection of sounds, on the local symphony of ordinary daily music that surrounds and marks a place, falls very quickly to zero. And he had shown that Valitano had not made the call, was not in fact connected with the kidnapping. And finally the only thing that kept Janey from getting safely home was finding a way to get her out of a place not one block away, a detailed plan with as great a chance of success as the probability that she was, in fact, there. But she was. He knew it. Not in the way he could absolutely prove, because there was always room for an inveterate skeptic to knock down any proof, even of gravity. But he had enough evidence to remove all reasonable doubt. And he felt lucky. Not since he and Stan Black had raked in sixteen thousand at blackjack in Reno had he buzzed with luck the way he did tonight. But he wouldn't let that cloud his judgment. He needed more than luck to get Janey out. And despite all the incredible sleuth work, or perhaps because of it, he could not count on Janowski.

In what seemed in Halleck's flawed sense of time about five minutes, Debra returned, huffing and mushing through the snow. Opening Harold's creaking driver's door, she let herself and a gust of the storm in and gasped with the cold, shivering hoarsely, "I've seen it, been around once, kicked the snow back so as not to show the footprints. No one is up. No noises, no sign of anyone awake." She stopped a beat, seeming to realize that Halleck would understand without elaboration that that could mean there was no one there, that, as they feared, the kidnappers and Janey had left, that the five thousand had been enough. Seeming to shake that off, she asked, "What do you want to know?"

"Doors?"

"Three. The two from the porch that Kowalski mentioned, and one to the cellar, maybe a basement apartment. Now there's a fire ladder coming off the upper floor on the side away from the yard, just below a window on a pitched roof, on the north."

"Dog?"

"Nothing."

"That's strange," Halleck said.

"Not so. Some people have to sedate their dogs at night. Otherwise the noise control ordinances would make them get rid of them. So they just dope them up to keep them quiet."

"Seems a bit counterproductive."

"They're not watchdogs, Halleck, they're pets."

"Wind chime?"

"On the porch, like Kowalski said."

"Car?"

"Still in place, on the opposite side of North Park. Under four inches of snow. Plow's been by, locked it in. Not going to make any quick getaways tonight."

"Windows?"

"Sixteen first floor, six around the top."

"Basement?"

"Four in the back, two on either side, near ground level, the kind that pull open on a hinge at the bottom. Curtains up on all of them, all floors, especially the basement. Real thick there. For privacy is my guess."

"Steps down to the basement, in back?"

"Four, and a railing, then a sump well, with a drain. Door is double locked. Dead bolt plus passage lock."

"Electrical meter?"

"Rear. Beside the door. Ganged in three. One for each apartment. Same with gas. Water seems common, one meter. What else?"

"Plans."

"I can't see through walls, Halleck."

"City Hall, from the tax assessors?"

"Old house, not likely," she said. "Tax assessors make a guess based more on neighborhood and frame than anything else. Rarely see the inside. Never need to unless they're challenged, which they almost never are. Maybe the architect or firm has plans, but this is an archive job. Architect is probably dead, firm may be dissolved. My bet is that the owner is not the original, not even the same family. This neighborhood has been up and down and is on the way up again. That kind of destroys stability."

"Fire Department. Inspection? They've got a fire escape. They didn't put that up out of philanthropy."

"You're right. When the place was broken into apartments, the landlord probably fulfilled the requirement, got a form saying he complied, which doesn't require submitting a plan, except maybe of the upstairs. You think that's where Janey is?"

"No way of telling. We have to locate the landlord. If he doesn't know, then we've got to get the plan from one of the other tenants, assuming they've been around long enough to borrow a cup of sugar."

"You crazy, walking in on the tenants?"

"Why not? Janowski would insist that we have to get them out anyway, don't we, if we're going to move on Janey?"

"Right."

"First thing tomorrow, as soon as the office opens, let's get the property tax records, locate the owner. We find out who his tenants are, see if we can isolate the apartment, which we probably can from size, to one extent. The upstairs seems too small, the basement too far from the wind chime. My bet right now is the middle one, the one right off the porch."

"It has windows on both sides," she said. "Meaning they can see both ways, except that the view north is blocked by a new wall from that redeveloped building. That's the way I got around back, just slipped down the alley. There's a path. On the other side is a yard, with dog shit, incidentally . . ."

"You should have said as much," he told her.

"Thought you'd smell it on my shoes."

"It's cold," he defended himself.

"Wait till the heater hits it. Anyway the view south is clearer, but still cut off by the adjacent house. Nothing directly on the front, since the other apartment with the door off the porch looks out on the street, probably has a set of stairs inside that goes up to the second floor. The point is that there are ways of getting in without them noticing, more if you decided to come up the alley in back. It's do-able, Halleck. The place can be taken. What's the plan?"

Halleck had been thinking about that since she left. So far it had been easy. So far it had been location, isolation and, finally, checking. Everything fit. He felt he had come as far as he could on his own.

"Sell it to Janowski?" he suggested.

"Possible," she said. "But what if he doesn't buy?"

"Another way," he said.

"I'm listening."

"If we can post someone here, someone we can reach without police band radio, we can tell when they leave for the pickup."

"Then we wait for the call," she said.

"That's the best way of getting one of them out of the house, improving the odds," he said.

"Who covers the drop?"

"Brian."

"Will he take the risk?"

"It's his kid," Halleck reminded her.

"Who goes in for Janey?"

"I do," said Halleck.

"No good," she said.

Halleck knew that she thought that because he couldn't see. "Suggest an alternative."

"I go in," she said.

"No good," he told her back.

"Why? Because I'm a woman?"

"No. Because I don't want to risk you," he told her. There was more than decency in his concern.

"It's my job," she said. "I'm trained for it."

"If it's by day," he said, "you go. By night, we take out the fuse box, and I go."

"Seems all right," she said. "Except if it's night, we both go. Two against one. Now what do we do to improve the odds?"

"We need one more person," he said. "Maybe Ellie."

"Forget that," Debra said. "Let me get Kowalski. He'll do it."

"Why?"

"Same reason he took the cab tonight. 'Cause he'll do anything. He's a little crazy but that's okay. And like I said, he'll do anything to avoid paperwork, since that's the alternative. For years they've kept him off surveillance since he's six feet eight inches tall. He'd love to do this. It's been a dream."

"Best if he could work it this way," Halleck told her. "First to confirm that one of them has left, second, locate the other."

"Locate?"

"Laser microphone. Point it at a window, you can tell if a person is in the room and even what they're saying. Assuming that Janey isn't in the front room, the one with the TV, that's where we want him when we move."

"All right."

221

"Except a laser microphone looks awfully suspicious. One look out the window and they'd know what was up."

"No way," she said. "Narco has a little van, looks like a TV repair truck, rigged for sound surveillance, directional, too. Just park it across the street, right behind the other car, that way if these guys try to move Janey, he's right there, can take them both."

"Risky," Halleck whispered.

"You've got to cover the angle that they take her, not leave her," she said, starting the engine. Harold's flivver rumbled to life. She pulled away. "If they're still there, Spike."

Halleck didn't want to think about it, knew he should. It was Debra who spoke first again, "You actually think they got that five thousand?"

"Possible," he said.

"But that means we're definitely looking for someone with scuba training," she said.

"Exactly," Halleck agreed. "Which would be an interesting question to ask about Nick Spiros and Danny Valitano. If neither one can dive, and both are so desperate for money, why do they ask for five grand to be dropped into the drink, where they have zip chance of getting it?"

"Jano's going to be tough to convince."

"It's going to be tough to resist the argument."

"Piss on the argument," she said. "I know this prick. He's got a suspect and what he thinks is a case, so tomorrow nothing is going to keep him from enjoying a fat cigar, a tall beer, and the Bulls-Knicks game."

"I don't believe it," Halleck said.

"Believe it," she snapped, throwing the car into a hard right, heading south. "Jano's like anyone creeping up on retirement, a little lazy, a little cautious, a bunch weary and unlikely to take any chances that he'll lose his precious pension because he makes a procedural error. Now I'm not saying that's right, and I sure as hell know that's not what we need, Halleck. But we'd have to be stupider than either of us is to ignore the obvious."

"Who then?"

"Like you said, us."

"Home," Halleck said. "To the telephone, to wait, then."

There was a long silence from the driver's side, a gap filled by gusting storm flaws, suspirating tires, now and then a horn, then nothing, the sound of her breathing. Finally she said, "You want that I stay?"

"Rhetorical question," he muttered, smiling.

At the next light she leaned across and kissed him deeply on the mouth, came away with, "I hoped you'd say that."

When the light evidently turned green he found himself with a strange fear that all this was just a fantasy sustained by the drama of Janey's abduction and that after it was over, Debra would disappear forever. So he wished, in a perverse way, that they wouldn't find her too soon, knowing right away that was wrong. He had to face whatever he was or wasn't. Whatever that was, whatever that could mean, whatever that implied for the rest of his life, he had to know. He could no more run from that than he could slow down the clock to gain time for Janey.

On both counts he was as frightened as he was determined. On neither was he the least bit sure. But he would soon know.

16

The phone rang three times before Janowski answered in a sleepy voice, deep and gruff, not quite through the morning's first coffee. Halleck pictured him from the voice, cadence, and conversational positions as a walrus of a man, a brimming handlebar mustache draped across his lip, droopy-eyed and bald, police regulations engraved on his brain, a predictable, mechanical plodder whose bureaucractic rectitude mirrored his failed imagination. Halleck would never see Janowski, of course, but the image fit, and lent itself to the next sounds, first one, then the other heavy heel thudding onto what was probably a marred wood desktop, a squeaky reclining desk chair leaning back as the walrus stretched out, awaiting the response, "Sergeant Janowski, this is Spike Halleck. I have some information you need. We have to go quickly, because we may have to break off for a ransom call. If so, I'll call you right back."

"I don't think you have to worry about ransom calls anymore, Mr. Halleck."

"You mean Danny Valitano?"

"Deb told you?"

"She did."

"I sent her *home* last night, damn it."

"She stayed anyway."

"Why?"

There may have been other reasons. Halleck hoped there were, but he said, "Because she found the evidence compelling and because you still haven't located Janey Granville."

Janowski's silence allowed Halleck to press on. "Valitano is *not* one of the abductors."

"I think he is. I've got a press conference scheduled—"

"Cancel it."

"Are you crazy? He confessed."

Stunned, Halleck's hesitation almost surrendered to Janowski. Snapping back he said, "How long did you grill him, Janowski?"

"Why?"

"Confessions made under duress, and fatigue is a form of duress, are not valid. Check that with your P.A." Halleck used the argot for Prosecuting Attorney, maneuvering conversationally for more authority, trying to make himself seem part of the team.

"The guy fuckin' *confessed*, Halleck. Understand?"

"A paper confession, Janowski. He wanted sleep."

"You have anything else?"

From the tone of voice, impatient, loud, and angry, Halleck was afraid Janowski would hang up. "Did either the late Nick Spiros or Danny Valitano wear taps?"

"Not as I know."

"That's strange, because at least one of the kidnappers wore taps. Now Danny Valitano was the mastermind, so he would do the calling. So what did he do, change his shoes to go out?"

Janowski exploded. "Goddamn, Halleck! I've been patient and gave you all the help I could. You know that. But this sound analysis is inadmissible."

"Inadmissible?" Halleck laughed because Janowski was so obviously wrong about things that Halleck knew so well. "What about wiretaps, Janowski? Ever seen an expert voiceprint a wiretap to prove who's talking? And what about shotgun microphones on surveillance? And what about the most inexact accoustical evidence in criminal law, sergeant? What about earwitness testimony? Ever sit through a trial where no witness ever reported on what anyone else said? Come on, don't insult my intelligence. What I've got here is the most sophisticated and scientifically defensible accoustical analysis you could hope for, so hear me out."

Silence on the other end, but Janowski didn't hang up.

"What about scuba? Either Spiros or Valitano know how to dive?"

"What difference does that make?"

"Strange that a couple of nickle-and-dimers would ask us to drop five thousand dollars into fifteen feet of murky water if they couldn't dive for it."

"You dropped the money into water?"

"That was the request."

"Shit, I don't even know if either of these guys could swim," Janowski told him.

"No?" Halleck said.

"Still thin, Halleck. What if all they wanted was to be sure you wasn't setting up a trap for them? That's possible, isn't it? They might have figured that five thousand was nothing to the Granvilles, but it was a good insurance policy against a trap. And they could have even done it just for now, to create a defense if they got caught, which they did. Their lawyer would say, I can just see it now—'My clients, your honor, can't swim! Why would they ask to have the first part of the ransom dropped where they can't get it?' "

"Did they have the money?"

"What?"

"Wet hundreds. Did you find it?"

"No, but I just covered that. Worst thing woulda been to get caught with anything incriminating before the big payoff."

Halleck shook his head to clear it, afraid if he heard much more he would begin thinking like Janowski, which was in some way a credibly bizarre, demonically inspired way of stepping around the straight path indicated by the evidence, explaining away what suggested itself as consistent and nearly obvious with a more inventive, even perverse, interpretation. Worse, he was attacking each piece as it emerged, forgetting that together they formed a pattern that was more compelling by far than any piece individually. Janowski was trying to make Halleck believe that it was unremarkable that no piece of accoustical evidence indicated Valitano or Spiros. But Halleck wasn't buying.

"We ran a voiceprint of the caller, the kidnapper, against Valitano, based on a match word, a word common to both vocabularies."

"Where did you get Valitano's voice?" Janowski's voice was very quiet, but unrelenting.

"That's academic," Halleck said.

"Not to me and not to the P.A.," Janowski said. "We could have you locked up for obstructing justice. You know that?"

"The P.A. has the evidence," he told him. "She can do what she wants with it."

"What?" Hard and cold as ice was Janowski's response.

"Delivered by courier to her office at eight-thirty this morning. It was signed for. And it shows the clearly identified voiceprint of Danny Valitano superimposed against the voiceprint of the ransom caller. No way do they match."

"Maybe it matches Nick Spiros," Janowski suggested. "But we'll never know."

For a moment it was as if Janowski had shoved a hard, cold blade through Halleck's body, making him shudder. He had figured, perhaps wrongly, that it had to be the brains, Danny Valitano, doing the calling. Maybe Valitano would have been sitting on a couch in the background, whispering directions to Spiros, who just paced nervously back and forth on that floor. Hesitantly he came back, "Maybe we will. Aren't videotapes kept of all suspect interrogations for use as evidence at trials? And wouldn't there be some of those for Nick Spiros?"

Janowski laughed. "What? You think we're Big Brother or something? You run the tape, take the evidence. Maybe the judge allows it, maybe he doesn't. But it gets erased, reused. Better use of public money, according to Accounting."

Halleck suddenly remembered, like a flash. "But we had two voices during our calls, Janowski! And it didn't match either one."

"Maybe there's a third," Janowski said.

"And Valitano won't give him up to plea?"

"Honor among thieves, maybe."

"Look," Halleck pressed, seeking a new tack. "Did you find where Spiros and Valitano were staying?"

"Sure? Little rundown slum place put up by an uncle of Spiros, Angelo, who runs numbers in Cicero."

"And no wind chime?"

"Coulda took it down. How do you know?"

"What about a jackhammer, street repair?"

"Not as I could see. But how do you know it was a jackhammer? I mean, could you convince a skeptic it was a jackhammer?"

"It sure as hell wasn't a bongo drum," Halleck countered, realizing, as he knew Janowski did, that you couldn't convince a skeptic of *gravity* if you broke his foot with a brick. To convince anyone, they had to be open to reason as well as evidence.

"Was there a dog there, or nearby?"

"No dog, no barking. No pets allowed."

"Was the place under an incoming flight path?"

"Can't say," Janowski yawned.

"Was the street closed? Remember, now, we have no traffic noises at all from close to the place."

"Maybe no cars was passing when you recorded. That doesn't mean there was no cars passing at all."

Halleck wanted to know the probability that in four calls from a busy section of Chicago there would be no traffic passing during each of the three-minute intervals. He reckoned that unless the street were shut down, it would be close to zero.

"What about *the* car, the green one that cruised by Brian and Ellie's house to make sure there were no police involved. What about that one? Did you see it anywhere? Did Nick or does Danny own the mysterious green car?"

"Who says the car has anything do to with it, anyway? It could have been nothin', couple of punks figure the closest they come to money is to tour it. That happens in Hollywood, right? People gaggle at the houses of the rich and famous? So why not here?"

"How far is the place from Soldier Field?"

"What does that have to do with anything?"

"How many L trains run through Cicero, Janowski?"

"Who cares?"

"Because all the pieces have to fit."

"You were workin' on the wrong puzzle, Halleck. Face it."

"And where is Janey Granville? Can you give me a 'who cares?' on that, too?"

"Hey, wait a minute. We're working Valitano, know he's confessed, to tell us where the girl is, okay?"

"What if he doesn't know?"

"You mean what if he forgets, because he doesn't want to give us the evidence we need to fry him?"

Halleck had thought about that, about the case that Janowski and the P.A. could make without Janey, how, ironically it would be stronger than the case they could make with a live Janey. A missing and presumed dead Janey could be used to whip the jury into a vengefully sympathetic mood that an ex-con who had conspired to the crime could actually have done it, then, watching Valitano squirm and sweat, watching his eyes shift and his Adam's apple bob as they hammered at him with circumstantial evidence, they would actually begin to see the kidnapper, then the killer in Danny Valitano, whether he was or not. A missing or dead Janey would convict and execute Danny Valitano faster than a recovered Janey, whose existence, survival, and health could be argued by the defense as responsible humanitarian stewardship. To Halleck it was becoming clear that at a deep level, beyond the bland protestation, Janowski was indifferent to Janey's safe return. Its greatest certainty would be reduced sentencing for Valitano. Which Janowski didn't want.

The prosecution smelled blood. If Valitano gave up the girl in plea-bargaining, they wouldn't get it. If Janey turned up and showed that the police blundered, or worse, fabricated a case, then Valitano could walk. Then the public spectacles of howling for and then taking vengeance would be thwarted. In the institutional perception, Janey Granville's reality had dissolved in symbolism. That forced Halleck into his last, most desperate move.

"The evidence is clear," Halleck said firmly. "You have the wrong man."

"That's not my view," said Janowski.

"We differ. I don't think the P.A. will bite."

"She may deny the significance of your information."

"That's possible, but it's now part of the public record, which means defense will have the right to see it under

230

full disclosure. Remember that all he needs is reasonable doubt to move for dismissal. The tapes and questions raise reasonable doubt. I'm an expert witness and I'll testify to it."

"He's confessed. It's too late."

"Torquemada would have been proud. You have a trumped-up confession. But he hasn't been arraigned and he hasn't pled. The confession is meaningless."

"Wait till the press conference. Watch it. Twelve-thirty."

"No chance. I have an envelope that contains the same information I sent to the P.A. Except this one is addressed to the city desk of the *Chicago Tribune*. That should bring some interesting questions to your press conference?"

"What do you want, Halleck?"

"Hold Valitano. No announcements of arrest."

"They're pressing upstairs, all the way to the mayor's office. Makes me begin to think the kid's father is getting impatient with your game. So what is it you want me to do?"

"Make something up."

"This is getting hairy, you know."

"I don't care. I need twelve hours."

"Maybe more," Janowski said.

"What?"

"Sixteen inches of snow on the ground out there, more in drifts when the wind gets it. And there's a lot of wind. Still falling. Nothing is moving."

"The timetable is set—"

"Hold on," said Janowski. "Got another call."

What seemed a minute passed before Janowski returned. Hurriedly, as if he were struggling with his coat, he said, "That was the coroner's office. The body of a little girl just washed up on Oak Street Beach. Report says white, blond hair, six to seven years old, estimated, been dead now about twenty hours. Looks like five thousand was enough."

17

Before Janowski could call, Brian Granville had risen, dressed, and left his Lake Forest residence. Nearly alone on the quiet suburban streets, he mushed neighbor Wally Pratt's Izusu Trooper into the gusting snow, rubbing his gloved hand furiously across the fogging windshield, wondering how much of the snow piled along the street was drifts, how many of those giant lumps covered disabled cars. Even in four-wheel drive the Trooper slid and shimmied as snow caked the wheel wells, layered the cold chassis, blanketed the hood. He snapped on the radio and got an update.

"Good morning, Chicagolanders. If you've got your eyes open you know what it looks like out there. So let's go to Andreas Vollenweider's *White Winds*, today's leitmotiv for the city. We've got sixteen inches on the ground just about everywhere, drifts to three feet in places. Just about blizzard conditions everywhere with Lake Michigan raked by gusts of forty miles an hour into six-feet rollers, friends. No day for Oak Street Beach, let me tell you. National Weather Service tells us up to five more inches on the way before nightfall with temperatures dropping below zero overnight. Nice conditions to have when we get Dallas here Saturday night. So hold onto your season tickets and hats, looks like we're in for another big one."

Brian clicked off the station, concentrating on trying to

find the road beneath the whiteness, checking his watch. Nine-fifteen. He was due to meet Sid Abrams at ten, downtown office. The paperwork would be signed, the money handed over. He would place it in a briefcase, move on to Spike's, wait for the call.

The weather made him nervous. Already it had closed most of the city, including the bank. Would the kidnappers act rationally, allowing for that, postpone delivery, do the reasonable thing in a businesslike fashion? Or were they edgy, nervous, impatient, feeling that somewhere a clock was running out on them, a clock they had to beat if they were to have any chance of walking away with the money? And what about Janey? How was she really? While Spike said he had talked to her, had offered to play the tapes of her responses, Brian didn't really want to hear it, to be haunted by those voices into even more sleeplessness. Already it was pure hell. Exhaustion had dulled his normally sharp social and calculational sense, now playing on his reflexes as he looked out on a white blanket, only slightly rippled at the shoulder of the road, staying in the middle, a sole vehicle moving through a wintry scene, evidently driven by a nut with too little sense to stay indoors. Someone, to the untrained eye, willing to throw caution away, to risk life or hypothermia for an avoidable trip to the 7-Eleven. But that was how it would have to be, to keep Janey safe from the two men suddenly gripped by a broadcast alerting the public to the recent disappearance of Janey Granville, a seven-year-old student at Branton Montessori School in Lake Forest. Any suspicion at this time could be disastrous. Even Wally Pratt, whose Izusu served as Brian's El Dorado, hubcap deep in snow and mud, couldn't, knew only that Brian had to beat "an unchangeable contractual deadline, an option clause that expires today, on a multinational deal, worth millions." That had been enough. Wally, too, was a businessman, used to pressure.

And when they last talked Janowski had his ideas, not convincing, not comforting, a little frightening, about a suspect but not about Janey. For that Granville had no sympathy, felt that Janowski, even if right, was temporizing. That's why he had asked the mayor to nudge the chief on "the zoning problem raised to me by Brian Granville." Spike was closer to his sentiments, exactly aligned in objectives. For the others there was no urgency for conviction, now or ever. If they got Janey back and the kidnappers disappeared, there would be no justice, but how often was life just? In terms of immediate pressure and eventual accountability, Sergeant Janowski had a very different set of priorities. He had to make an arrest, a case, secure a conviction. And he could do that without Janey. In fact, his best case for maximum sentence would be wheeling in a castered bier with Janey's body on it to enrage the jury. At this point, Janowski could screw himself for all Brian cared.

What he couldn't do was to screw Brian. As a banker he was too well connected with Janowski's bosses to allow Janowski the luxury of pissing him off. Unless the FBI's Lou Scannon had somehow threatened Janowski with obstruction with justice. Given the choice of unemployment or imprisonment, Janowski would make the predictable choice. To thwart that one, Brian had to call in a debt from the senior senator from Illinois, asked that he lean on the attorney general to have the Chicago FBI back off an investigation involving him, at least for a week. But he had no idea how fast the chain of orders was working. In any case, he had no direct leverage.

Unable to worry and drive, he gave himself over to the immediate, to clearing condensation from the windows, to pulling the sledding Trooper back on course, or what he imagined was on course. In plain fact, he could not see, not ten feet into the driving snow. In some sense, he might as well have been Spike Halleck, feeling himself, the snowy road on the tires, snowblind except for a few glimpses of familiar house shapes, the steep-pitched Tudor roofs of Mark Meehan's place sloughing snow into his front yard with an explosive poof, the colossal white oak at the fork of Plainview and Elm, defying traffic to venture ahead, the steady musical stanzas of ornamental streetlights, now ignited in the dim gray that enclosed the region. Looking down he checked his speedometer, dismayed to see that he was only managing fifteen miles an hour.

Perhaps Abrams would do better. He had called him this morning, found him up and alert, downing his second cup of decaf coffee, ready to shovel himself out, laughingly saying, "This better be important, Brian," being reassured that it was. Rare were people like Abrams who understood whom they could trust, took hard stands against the tyranny of regulations, went to bat for friends, and alienated opponents with equal force. Without Abrams he would not have been able to draw the two hundred thousand without justification, without the customary and usually prudent response to how the borrower intended to use the money. With Abrams involved, none of that mattered. He would owe him for that, but with a guy like Abrams, he felt, he would always owe him.

The drive to First Chicago National Bank was harrowing, the Trooper lashed by wind, snow driven through the curtain, minimal heat, and pursued more like a slalom run than a drive, working back and forth through stranded vehicles, their red-faced vapor-snorting drivers out and pushing. Brian drove along oblivious, one thought on his mind, only marginally concerned for others, who were no more than momentarily inconvenienced and who, if things got really bad, unlike Brian, could depend on the police to solve their problems. He arrived in fifty minutes, thrice the normal time, pulled up and through a ridge of snow driven up by the plows, hopped out shivering, clutched his coat, held his head down and charged through the whistling wind to the front door, where he fumbled for keys before letting himself in.

The lobby was cold, held at nighttime temperature to conserve energy, with no hope of change except the maintenance crew. In the systems they had chosen the thermostats were sealed against unauthorized tampering.

Once inside he shook off the snow, headed toward the elevator. Although he saw no signs that Abrams had arrived, no telltale trail of melted snow such as he was leaving behind, Brian imagined that he must be there. He lived only three miles away. Stepping into the elevator, Brian's stiff fingers loosened his scarf as his frozen lungs grabbed deep breaths of air, not warm air, but much kinder than outside. Impulsively he shivered, not with cold but with fear. The elevators shot up to the tenth floor, where he stepped out and headed down to Abrams's office.

Still dark.

Doubling back he walked half a corridor and opened his office, strode across to his desk and, without turning on the office lights, keyed in the speed call number for Abrams's home to verify that he had been able to get out. Abrams's Volvo had always served well in Chicago's heavy snows, but if he were stuck, Brian could shoot over and pick him up.

Three rings brought an answer. Immediately he recognized the broken voice of Rachel Abrams and said, "Rachel, this is Brian Granville. What is it? What's wrong?"

Sobbing flooded the line, followed by, "He was shoveling snow this morning and just fell over. By the ti-ti-time I found him he was . . . Oh, God, no, I can't believe it . . . he was dead."

Brian slowly went numb, could just manage, reflexively, through the icy panic that seized him, to say, "I'm so sorry, so so sorry," before hanging up. He should have offered to help, should have offered comfort, should have rushed right over, but he couldn't. Now there was nothing he could do for Sid Abrams. Or maybe, now, for Janey.

Automatically he dialed Spike.

"Halleck," came the answer.

"The money fell through." Brian choked out, unable to feel, unable almost to breathe, feeling dizzy and sick even as he said it.

"WHAT?"

"The approving officer died this morning. Heart attack or something, shoveling his way out to meet me. I don't know the details yet. So no money. At least not today."

"How long?"

"A few calls, maybe two or three days. Friday if we hurry. But we have to make a justification now. I have no doubt that the bank will stand behind me for it, if they knew how important it was. No question. But they would have to know. And even if they put down some euphemistic words to cover, someone would have to tell someone else. The secret would be out before we got the money."

Halleck understood. The silence told Brian he did. After it had hung a seeming eternity, Halleck said, "Forget the money. Just get over here. I need you. Janey needs you, because she's *not* dead."

"Dead?"

"Janowski has a body. Before I could get Ellie I think he reached her, dragged her down to the coroner's for an ID."

"No."

"I'll bet my life it's not her."

"Maybe I should—"

"No. I don't want you reacting to this. Nothing has changed. We're almost there. And I need you here."

"Why?"

"Because they're still going to call, soon."

"Even if Janey's dead?"

"She's not."

After a long silence, broken only by a sigh, Brian said, "On my way"

Armed with the information that Kowalski just phoned in from the City Records, Spike Halleck picked up the phone and listened, pushing in the numbers as he had heard them. The phone rang seven times. He was about to hang up when a sleepy voice drained through the static, saying, "Yes?"

"Mr. Ibn-Fahd?"

"Correct." The voice was flavored with minarets and markets, perfect for an Islamic terrorist movie. According to the records, Mr. Ibn-Fahd was none of those things, his only sinister characteristic being a reputation for ruthless bargaining on depreciated properties, his penury in restoring them to code conditions, the extortion he called rent and the negligence he passed off as maintenance. Of late the upstart imigrant had become a much admired legend among Chicago real estate moguls, notwithstanding the running debate on the status of his green card. Whether he had one or not now, in a few months he would certainly have baksheesh enough to get one.

"Mr. Ibn-Fahd, my name is Sullivan, Louis Sullivan of the Greater Chicago Metropolitan Rezoning Board. We are in possession of an application for rezoning that includes what our records show is one of your properties, a stand-alone residential structure at 1547 North Park. You know the property, sir?"

"What is this?" came an agitated voice. "You raise my taxes? I will protest!"

"Mr. Ibn-Fahd, we are not with Appraisal and Taxation. They're down the hall. We have no intention and, in fact, no power to raise your taxes."

"Then what?"

"We list your property through cross-reference to State Tax as a commercial rental—"

"You look at my taxes? This is invasion of privacy! I will sue!"

"Look." Halleck tried the bored, patient voice of the tired bureaucrat. "I'm just tryin' ta do a job—okay? We have to list the number of renters you have at 1547 North Park in order to complete an economic assessment of the impact of rezoning on the area. It's the law. So how many people would be displaced if the rezoning were permitted?"

"You would dare destroy my property? I will sue again!"

"Mr. Ibn-Fahd, I have no power to destroy your property, now or ever. But we need the information."

"I must talk to my lawyer about this."

"Mr. Ibn-Fahd, come on. Your lawyer is just gonna tell you to provide the information or answer a subpoena. If you don't want me to swear out a warrant and send a police car around to drag you in, you'll damn well provide the information, goddamn it!"

"Well, it is three apartments," said Ibn-Fadh. Halleck could hear the pages turning, as if records were being checked.

Ibn-Fahd let out a long sigh, as if even Allah's paradise could never compensate for this hell on earth. "You have in the front one, on the street, just there, a Mrs. Wellington and her teenage son, both unemployed. She is widow-pensioner, her son is nothing. You would put them on the street?"

"Go on."

"In basement is Chin Lo Ning, who is research in the cancer field at Northwestern University Hospital. Very good research, not much pay. You want what? People die from cancer for rezoning? Where does this man live if you pull the carpet from his legs?"

"And the other?"

"The other is problem. Mrs. MacDougal from Skokie, a circuit inspector from Zenith, takes on month-to-month. Then she cannot pay, so she sublets. Two weeks now to some men. I don't know them. They pay. That is all we care."

"So let's count heads here. Mr. Ibn-Fahd. Altogether that's five bodies, right?"

"You speak of bodies as if these people are dead, Mr. Sullivan. They are not! They are alive and poor! They have rights! Need living place! And what happens if they rezone? What of my investment? I will sue! Do you hear—I will sue!"

"Well, that's up to you. But city code entitles these folks to some minimum rights from you. Three rooms minimum. A place to sleep, a place to defecate and wash, and a place to cook. That's the law."

"You say?"

"All these places have that?"

"Except basement, where I have special signed waiver from Mr. Ning."

"He can't waive legally guaranteed rights."

"But this is America, land of opportunity!"

"That's why they have rights. Now what are you doing to protect the rights of those two subletters? Prove to me that those subletters have all the rooms they're entitled to and we just let this matter drop."

"But those men, they, they have"—Ibn-Fahd, whom Halleck was sure did not have a green card, was sweating, his voice breaking, cooperating as no legal immigrant would, gushing—"front living room, rear bedroom and very, very large kitchen, plus, as you say, bathroom, yes, and if you will, storage room leading into backyard."

"And what about animals, sir? What have you done to assure protection of animals and pets?"

"Chain fence around yard protect Mrs. Wellington's son's Airedale dog, called Chin to insult the basement tenant. This boy is a punk, you know. All the time horrible, loud music."

"And is this yard large enough to run the dog in?"

"Wait a minute, Mr. Louis Sullivan. This is snow, today. City Hall is closed. I hear on the radio."

"Some of us take our caseloads home, Meccatrekker! You never heard of the dedicated civil servant? Good day, Mr. Ibn-Fadh." Halleck slammed the handset down, fading badly with exhaustion, suddenly sorry for pushing so hard, surprised to find himself sweating heavily.

"So," Debra said, pacing behind him, "we have a living room, bedroom, kitchen, bathroom, and storage room."

Halleck didn't want to think too much about it. Not about the storage room, probably dark and unheated, hoping they didn't keep Janey there, nor about the bedroom, knowing that was where the abductors would be sleeping and understanding that if they never intended to let her go, they could be doing anything to her. Leaving the living room (where Kowalski had seen the TV), opening onto the porch, the bathroom, and the kitchen, the very big kitchen. From Ibn-Fadh's description, there was a door in, maybe one to the storage room, too, and windows in each of the rooms. A cop could get in through any one of them if he knew where the remaining kidnapper, the guard, was, when the other one left to pick up the ransom. Halleck's mind worked furiously conceiving an assault plan that couldn't fail, seeing it like a movie climax, imagining the breaking glass, barking dogs, shouting, imagining Janey's screams, then daring to imagine no more.

Just then the Granville phone rang. He could hear the machine click on, Debra say, "This is it," as her soft hand fell on his shoulder for only a second, then heard, "Don't pick up yet. I'm going to call Al from the bedroom phone!" Listened to her feet padding across the deep carpet, the Granville line ring again, Brian come through the door and say, "What is it? Is this it?" He held up his hand for silence, felt his heart thudding, his head pounding, the blackness in his eyes swirl with stars, heard the phone ring the third time when Debbie shouted from the other room, "He's lifted off. Go." Then he picked up, saying simply, "Halleck."

"You have the money?"

"Yes," Halleck said, deciding that he was certain enough of everything he could risk it all. The money was not important. They *knew* where they were and what they were supposed to do. Even if Janowski would not go along, they had enough to do it themselves. For guns, Debra and Kowalski, for extra hands, Brian and even Spike himself. The trick was splitting the men up, leaving one with Janey while the other went for the ransom, then moving, not from one point, but many at a time, enough to paralyze the lone kidnapper for a second of indecision, isolating him from Janey, then taking him. Nice concept.

"Here's the instructions," said the voice. In the background Halleck's ears, now tuned, heard the weak clicking sound from the taps as he paced, and the tinkle of the wind chime, as if just stirring in a light breeze.

Playing for time, trying to stretch the interval to hear the approaching helicopter, Halleck improvised, "Did you get the five thousand?"

Silence. "Wet, but yeah."

"Then you know we're sincere."

"You better be."

"Business, please. Our agreement. Let me examine the merchandise."

"What?"

"Speak to the package." This was the moment he needed, to show Janowski was wrong, that Janey was not lying on a slab downtown, but alive and exactly where she had been since the ordeal had begun.

"Just a minute." The handset went down with a clack, onto hardwood or Formica, something solid, unyielding. In the background came the percussive thuddings of *Quiet Riot* pounding on the walls, the yapping of Chin, the Airedale. Too much for coincidence. Halleck didn't need the helicopter to know he was right. There would be no jackhhammer, not now, not in the snow.

Next came Janey's voice, high, weak, shaking, and thick with sniffles, "Uncle Spike?"

Halleck strained carefully now, pressing for any trick. If Janey were really dead now and these men had recorded a set message, he wanted to know, but he did not want to alarm them, to have them feel that he was asking Janey to codify some information, to divulge something to let him know where they were keeping her. Anything like that would be particularly dangerous, now, so close to the exchange. And it would be particularly stupid, since he was sure that he knew where she was.

"Janey, how are you, honey?"

"Scared."

"Have you been fed?"

"Not the good food."

"You sleep enough?"

"I guess." Halleck heard a yawn, followed by a sniffle.

"Janey, what travels in the shape of the letter L?"

"What?"

"Remember our game?"

"Chess?"

"Right. What travels in the shape of an L?"

"The horse, Spike." Another sniffle, then a cough.

"And what do I call the horse, Janey?"

"You call it a knight, Spike."

"Hang on, Janey, we'll have you home in a couple of hours."

"For real?"

Halleck had never lied to her, didn't want to now, had no time for philosophical disgressions on the inability of good motivations to achieve the desired effect, so he dwelled for a dark, eternal moment on the irony that they either would free her or she would, in all probability, be killed, one or the other this very day, with no in-between, no long journeys around the country because if they didn't free her or if the kidnappers didn't, as they now couldn't, get their money, then the interstate police manhunt was on. Neither of these men could afford to have the evidence against them tag along, or walking free. In desperation, wanting to sound comforting, Halleck told her, "It will all be over soon."

At the same instant he heard the humming chop, low but real, growing. At the other end of the line, the handset changed possession. Now the voice of the kidnapper came on, saying, "Okay. Here it is . . ."

The chopper noise closed, coming dead on, growing.

"What's that?" the caller said.

"What?" Halleck replied, flooding the question with confused innocence, praying that shared confusion would defeat any growing suspicion that a police helicopter was converging on the hideout, ready to roll them up.

"Hold on," he said, clapping his palm over the mouthpiece. Halleck could imagine him going to the window, watching the chopper pass over, the radio call letters bright and bold, the mission evident: traffic report.

The voice came back, panting, "You still there, Halleck?"

"Still here."

"The money?"

"Yes?"

"Two hundred thousand?"

"We know the amount."

"We want it in a plain leather briefcase."

"Done."

"In hundreds, unmarked."

"Done, we already have it. Do you want the hundreds wrapped or loose?"

A moment of silence. "Wrapped?"

"In bunches with paper bands."

"Wrapped."

"Where?"

"There's a mailbox, a metal drop box, about a block north of the Michigan Avenue Bridge over the Chicago River. It's on Hubbard, do you copy?"

"Yes." Halleck's mind raced at that. Who says, Do you copy? Military. Former military. With the recovery of the five thousand from the bottom of the Chicago River it made sense. Maybe SEALs. And more than that, it made more sense. Two hundred thousand wasn't that much, not compared to Brian Granville's paper worth of a million three. So why hadn't they asked for more? Accessibility? Were they that smart? Did they know that the more they asked for the longer it might take? That's what Halleck had figured originally, that they wanted in and out quick, so if the police were involved, sub rosa, they still wouldn't have time to converge. After all, how had they given themselves away? In their minds, not at all. All phone calls under three minutes, everything clean, no sign of trouble, no surveillance, nothing at all until the helicopter and that only a traffic reporter. But suddenly, almost epiphanic, it struck Halleck that there was something else. The money wasn't it, or at least wasn't all of it. It was the mission. It was bringing the thing off like clockwork. It was some kind of a macho jolt, in and out with no traces, like a commando strike. Did he copy? Sure he did. And for the first time an aspect of the abduction shaped up almost visually, almost as if his eyes had once again ignited with vision.

"On Hubbard between Wabash and Rush, two blocks south of Grand. Do you copy?"

"On Hubbard between Wabash and Rush. Copy."

"South side of the street."

It was clear they had planned this carefully, that they wanted to communicate it without confusion, that it was important that they make themselves clear, that they appear and vanish in a twinkling, with split-second timing. Halleck had an almost palpable sense that they had done this, or something like it, before. It was too pat to be inspired, dreamed up over a shared fantasy in a prison cell just to chase boredom away. It was all so incredibly structured.

"The briefcase goes under the mailbox at four-twenty this afternoon."

"We can do that."

"Better. Then walk away."

"Say again?"

"Walk away. Leave the briefcase."

"Now for the merchandise," Halleck said. It was a deal, an exchange. They knew the terms. He was confident.

"After we get the money and count it, we will notify you of the location of the merchandise."

"No deal," Halleck shot back. He surprised himself with the vehemence, felt light with the terror that what he said might just doom Janey, but just as sure that if he didn't improve his negotiating position he would lose vital leverage. Even in a business deal he could never allow that. Here it was a life, a very special life.

"I don't think you're in a position to bargain," the voice menaced.

Halleck thought about that. Military. Special forces? What? Did it matter? If he was right, these men would not stop at cutting another throat, a skill they had been taught to perform so efficiently.

"We gave you goodwill with the five thousand," Halleck said. "And do want you to collect for your services. But promises are not services. Let's discuss an exchange."

"What do you want?"

"Is there a phone near your drop?"

"On the corner of Hubbard and Wabash, next to the Money Machine."

"Then we send our agent—"

"Wait. Agent?"

"The girl's father, for Chrissake."

"How do we know?"

"Picture. For Chrissake his picture is on today's financial section of the *Chicago Tribune*."

"We'll call back."

"Wait!"

The line went dead, leaving Halleck's head buzzing with dial tone. Jerked up, he felt Brian Granville lift him off the chair, his voice hot and angry. "You asshole! You incredible prick! You should have let them finish, you should have—"

"Calm down," Debra said, prying him off. "Chopper, Spike?"

"Right on time," he whispered.

"We know where she is," Debra said.

"No," Brian said. "We know where *they* are. We know where they are calling from—"

"I talked to Janey," Halleck said.

"Maybe they bring her in for the phone contacts, then take her back someplace else. You don't *know!*"

"No, I don't," Halleck admitted, realizing that there was risk, but there was always risk. He understood that better than a sighted person, that every time he stepped from a curb, even with a dog, there was a chance that someone wouldn't or couldn't stop, or was too drunk to react. Still, he did it because he had to go on. And they had to go on here. There wasn't any other choice. "But I do know that Janey wasn't taken by Danny Valitano and unless we convince Janowski, he's going to tell the press, in about an hour, that she was and that the dead girl is Janey. And unless someone stops him this is going to be on the air, at least by tonight. Maybe sooner by radio. So one of these guys, the one who loves TV, is going to get it, at the latest by six."

"So let's stop Janowski from blowing it," Brian said.

"I'll second that," Debra chimed in.

"What about the kidnappers?" Brian said.

"It was over three minutes, Spike," Debra said. "I wasn't squeezing your shoulders so you couldn't know. But it was. Maybe they were afraid of a trace."

"Maybe," Halleck admitted.

They all jumped when the Granville line rang again. Picking up, he said, "Halleck."

"Where can we deliver the merchandise?"

Debra was right. They cut off to kill a possible trace. Halleck spoke clearly. "We suggest that our second agent pick up the merchandise from a very open spot near a phone, then phone the first agent to release the money to you. Then he walks away."

"How do we know about the money?"

"We threw five thousand into the Chicago River. For nothing. We want the merchandise."

"Do this," the voice said. "We leave the girl, the merchandise, in this very open place, then your agent checks her out, but you leave her there and go to a phone. All the time he can see her, tells your agent to release the money. We pick it up, check it out, call back. Then you can pick up the girl, leave."

"Agreed."

"Where do you want the girl?"

Halleck was quick to respond. "We have no place in mind, because we have no trap. You name the place."

"We'll think about it, call you back."

"We have the money, waiting your call."

"If this is a setup, we'll kill everyone."

"All we want—" Halleck began, heard the click, the buzzing dial tone, then finished in a whisper "—is the girl."

Slowly he set the handset down in its cradle, stared off in blindness, the images of his thoughts and fears making their own pictures, like the one he used to see in screening rooms, except that this was real. If it went bad, the blood would be real and the screams, the haunting sounds of people dead and dying, would echo in his mind forever.

"What next?" Brian said.

"Next we call Janowski," Halleck said.

"Let me talk to him," Debra said, picking up Spike's phone, dialing through.

They listened as Debra explained. "Jano, Halleck was right. We just got another call, so it's not Valitano."

Silence while Janowski debated.

"No, Jano, that can't be right. The mother is wrong, didn't look close enough."

Another pause.

"Who would know?"

Pause again.

"No, Jano. We get only two voices, ever, even in the background. No sign of more partners. And that's too flaky. The more guys, the more chance somebody screws somebody else. No way."

Again a pause, Debra catching her breath on a sigh, impatient.

"Jano," she said, louder, "My ex—you remember Al? —did us a big favor. When we got the call, he took the KCIL traffic scout on a beeline over the place Halleck says they're holed up. And you know what? Yeah, that's right. We got the chopper noise, right on schedule. And we *know* the kid isn't dead because Halleck talked to her. I heard it."

Final pause.

"So are you in? What, you need for Moses to step off the mountain to believe? Okay, you won't do the press conference. But that's it? No, we don't have a place for a drop off. We're still waiting on a call. Sure, Jano, we'll keep in touch."

Halleck heard the phone click down.

"He'll cancel the press conference. That's it."

"So he won't help us take the place?" an outraged Brian yelled.

"Negative. Jano's an old mule. He's going back to the book, says that until somebody shows him that dead girl isn't Janey that he says she is, wants your permission, Mr. Granville, to pursue it *his* way."

"Can we take it ourselves?" Halleck asked.

The longest pause of all, followed by a longer sigh.

"We can sure as hell try," Debra said.

Without speaking, everyone seemed to understand that unless they took control now, Janey could slip away.

"You have a plan?" Brian asked.

"I sure as hell do," she said.

"Let's hear it," said Halleck.

"It goes this way . . . ," she began.

18

Ninety minutes after the ransom call, the three huddled in the produce department of Dominick's, across the street and half a block down from the intersection of North Avenue with North Park, checking the plan a final time.

"Kowalski?" said Debra. "You in?"

"Jano ain't gonna like this."

"Remember Jano's speech on initiative?"

Everyone who worked for him did. He told them not to sit on their ass unless they wanted to get bedsores or him to kick it. On the other hand, once you get up, do something. But while you're doing something, don't get your ass, the one you've just got up off of, caught in a grinder and expect him or any other cop to pull it out.

Kowalski shrugged. "I 'specially 'member the part about the grinder."

"Kowalski," she said. "Don't be such a pussy."

"Well, seein' as we don't know what they've got in numbers . . ."

"Figure two," she said.

"Two, three, four, whatever. What's a couple extra when you're trading lead?"

"We only have two voices on the tapes."

He shrugged. "And we got no idea what they got for arms. What do we make it? Peashooters? Zip guns? Saturday night specials? Magnums? Uzis? Sawed-offs with double ought buck? What? Bazookas?" Again he shrugged. "Makes me a little nervous, ya know, 'specially 'cause we can figure these guys is a little nervous, too. I mean, we ain't exactly gonna look like Jehovah's Witnesses, right?"

Debra turned to Brian. "You don't need to do anything," she said, "if you don't want."

"That's exactly why I have to do everything," he said.

She noticed a tremor, decided he would bear up. "You know what to do?"

"If there are shots and they get out, get to the car, ram it."

"We'll be right behind," she said.

"What about the others?" he asked.

Kowalski said, "The Chinaman, he's in the lab. Until late. No problem. Deb gets the Wellingtons out. Then we move."

Brian nodded, swallowed, unable to speak.

Debra Seraphicos tucked a standard S&W .38 Chief's Special, always enough for a head shot at close range, into an inverted underarm holster, took a deep breath and said, "Okay."

Kowlaski held up a hand, saying, "They moved the car. I can't see it."

"It could be farther up, or in the fenced-in lot down the street. They can't get out the other end. In the snow it looks open, but the ditch is too deep and there's not enough sidewalk to get by." Kowalski's eyes wouldn't let her go. "Listen. We know the kid's there. It's time to move, before they change the rules."

"Debra?" Brian said.

"Yeah?"

"Blind or not, Spike would be here, if he didn't have to mind the phone."

"I know," she said, squeezing his arm. "I know."

"So let's do it," Kowalski said, patting the .357 Mag concealed beneath his arm.

The three went out together, Brian Granville splitting and mushing to his car through the snow. It was still falling lightly in tiny gelid grains that bit the eyes. Against the powdery blanket already down the new stuff hissed like a hidden snake.

A few cars braved the storm, crawling along the once-plowed North Avenue, lights on, tires crushing grooves as they cut along, unable to do more than slide when they tried stopping, and thus not stopping at all.

The two cops marched forward, Kowalski falling off, going no farther than the corner bar, where he ducked in and checked his watch.

Alone now, head down against the gritty wind, Debra Seraphicos threw the scarf around her face, covering her nose, opened her parka and tucked it in, still slopping through knee-deep snow, opening the rusty latch on the chain-linked gate, letting herself into the quiet yard leading to the porch at 1547 North Park Avenue. Mounting the steps slowly, her hands tucked neatly into her pockets, with no intention of drawing her gun, she turned sharply left, slid three steps, and knocked on Mrs. Wellington's door. It opened to a puzzled look on the woman's face, an astonished and suspicious look of not expecting anyone or anything good, a look of eyes too often filled by too many parole officers, of ears too often filled by urgent and insistent solicitors or complaining neighbors, a look of too much time without any good news and no mind for any more of the bad kind.

"Mrs. Wellington?"

"And yes?" she said, as if expecting she knew not what.

"I'm Linda Savens of WVCR Radio . . ."

"This is something to do with Josh? The audition tapes?"

"No, actually Josh has won the free trip to Hawaii . . ."

Disbelieving eyes met her.

"For two . . ."

Changed to eyes wanting to believe.

"Maybe I come in, give you the arrangements?"

"Sure." A whisper. The door opened wider, Debra stepped in, feeling the fear all over her back, the side of her exposed to the apartment behind, where Janey had to be held.

Once inside, she ushered Mrs. Wellington to a faded floral design sofa, sat down, still smiling and said, "I know you just can't believe this." She reached inside for her leather shield case, pulled it out and gradually opened it, saying, "So I just want you to remain very calm while I explain—"

"It's Josh, isn't it?"

"No. Actually, it's not."

"What then?" Her hands worked anxiously at her buttoned collar as furrows creased her forehead.

"I do, however, need your cooperation *with* Josh."

Almost as soon as the name was mentioned, Heavy Metal roared down from the stairs leading to the attic.

"That's him," said Mrs. Wellington, wincing.

"You've both got to leave the house now."

"What?"

"Dr. Ning is already out and you must leave, too. In a few minutes we're going to arrest the men next door."

"I don't know anything about them. Only been here a week or so. I—"

"No one is accusing you, Mrs. Wellington."

"Josh never talked to them, never did anything except to bang back on the wall at them once."

"I believe you."

"I'll get him." She left and hobbled upstairs. Words exchanged. Josh got loud. No, she thought, not this. Not a complication.

Josh clattered down the stairs, ran his hand through hair of rainbow colors, snarled, "What you want?"

Debra held the badge up. "You'll both have to leave the house," she said.

"Am I arrested or what?"

"No arrest."

"Then fuck it."

Debra said. "Okay. Your mother and I are going to leave in two minutes. You can stay or go. I don't care. But you better hit the floor and keep your mouth shut, because when we return, a very large officer and I are going to put very large holes in anything that walks, talks, or does anything but lie down and put their hands on the back of their neck. That includes you. Are you staying or going?"

Josh turned whiter than the falling snow, muttered, "Get my coat. Jesus fucking Christ. Hey, wait."

In three minutes they came in together from the snow, entering the bar where Kowalski was waiting. Kowalski took a long look down at Josh, looked away and out, said, "You old enough for beer, kid?"

"Yeah."

"Let me buy you one."

"All right."

"Drink it slow."

"Okay."

"Real slow."

"Okay."

"Don't get up. Don't leave. Don't call nobody."

"Okay."

"How 'bout you, ma'am."

She shook her head.

"How 'bout a hot tea or somethin'?"

"That would be lovely."

"You drink it real slow, too. Okay?"

"Certainly."

"And you folks'll be back home before you know it."

"Fine."

"Sorry for the inconvenience."

"Officer?" said the woman, confused. "Are you supposed to have a warrant or something?"

"For them, yes. We have one. But we just wanted to get you out before we served the warrant, ma'am. That is, in case of unexpected shooting. Of course"—Kowalski shrugged—"you're right. We can't make you stay out. Why? You wanta go back before we do?"

Mrs. Wellington matched her son's snow-white color. "No," she said, simply. "We'll wait."

"Good," said Kowalski. "We'll be right back."

Together the two police officers left, their gun hands buried inside their coats, wrapped around the pistol grips, ready.

Back to front.

That was the plan.

If they were lucky and things went real smooth, the kidnappers would never know. Two of them would come in at the same time. If they reached the first checkpoints without gunfire, they would run off the few minutes, move as one at the appointed time. But that was a big if. First they had to get in.

They ducked together down the alley north of the place.

Two windows from the suspect's apartment overlooked the walkway. Actually, the facing wall, a redeveloped office building, butted up closely, leaving only four feet between them.

Kowalski would go in the first window, which figured to be a bedroom. The second, farther down the alley, was frosted, making it a good bet for bathroom.

Deb had set it that way.

She had reasons.

The calls had been from the living room where the chime was clinking steadily away. And one of them was a TV junkie, and the TV, as Kowalski knew, was in the room just off the front porch. Now there was the big, big kitchen Ibn-Fahd had described to Spike, which had to be fused to, or leading to the living room, both within earshot and microphone pickup of the wind chime, the TV, and the yard where Josh Wellington's Airedale Chin would be running.

Then it hit her.

Where was Chin? Where the fuck was Chin?

"The dog?" she whispered to Kowalski.

He shrugged, shook his head.

"I can't go back for it," she whispered again.

He nodded, shrugged, smiled bleakly, gave her his patented, "What the fuck?" and heaved himself up, using a water spigot to stand on. Tall as he was, he had no trouble reaching the windowsill. He tried it with a sharp push, heard a little shriek, drew back. Debra had her gun out, trained on the middle of the frame, waiting. Kowalski fell slowly back against the clapboards and waited.

A minute drained away. No one came.

Another minute passed as the snow fell, collecting heavily on his eyebrows, before he pushed again, felt the window move, looked down and nodded, checked his watch, and lipped the words, "Two," for the minutes before he would pull himself in.

Debra kicked the snow away as she raced to the back, finding a set of three stairs, dwarf-sized, leading up to a latched door on what must be the shed. Climbing it she was not surprised to find a small padlock guarding it. Even in nice neighborhoods certain precautions are taken. But cops know the tricks of those they catch. Often, that's how they catch them. Deftly she pulled a bristling quiver of lock picks and made short work of this one.

Checking her watch she saw she'd run off only a minute. But she was breathing fast, her mouth dry, her hands wet, her eyes filling with water. Reflexively she swallowed hard. Wait. Slow down. Calm. She stayed there on the top step, waiting for the time to run down, ready to go in exactly when Kowalski did. If neither made a sound, fine. If both made noises, fine, because they wouldn't know which way to turn. But if only one did, that was trouble.

Time ran out quickly and she stepped inside.

Kowalski would be pulling himself through the window.

Her foot went down in the darkness and began to move. She grabbed a stud and steadied herself. Still her feet moved. Looking down she strained to see, the transition from white light to blackness leaving her temporarily as blind as Halleck.

What? her mind screamed out. What was it?

Slowly the images began to condense out of the darkness, mostly lines and shadows, silhouettes against the wedge of light seeping through from the kitchen beyond. The luminous dial of her watch showed there was only another minute, before she had to burst through the door marked by that light. Looking down, then up, she saw an inverted U-shaped brace. What? Levers in silhouette. Handle, gears. Lawn mower! She was standing on the housing of a fucking lawn mower. Gently she braced herself on the stud, stepped down, around.

Like most sheds, this one had become the dark repository of things unwanted, unused, or unidentified. Aluminum foil crinkled beneath her feet. Couldn't they hear that? Or was it just that being with Halleck had made her so sensitive to the clues in noises, made *her* listen as he did. Perhaps the rest of the sighted world, including the kidnappers, were, by comparison, deaf. Brushing against a rake made the tines sing. She stopped and listened. Nothing.

Had they heard and gone silent, signaled to one another for silence, moved in her direction in silence? Were they waiting, guns ready, just beyond that thin, bright slice of light?

Or had they just as silently cut Janey Granville's throat at the first sign of intrusion and fled, sliding and drifting through the muffling snow? No way of telling. Just go with the plan.

Her heart was jackhammering in her chest, the rate and sound of the noise that Halleck had raised from the tape. Outside, in the snowy breeze, the wind chime clattered its telltale noise. This was the place. This is where they were.

Another step, this one free of noise.

Now closer.

Her watch told her.

The hand was sweeping away the last fifteen seconds before strike. No sound or trouble for Kowalski. Could he have been garroted as he lunged through the open window, trapped by his own complaisance that no response meant no detection? The fears hammered at her as the luminous hand gobbled up the last seconds and touched the top of the dial.

Crouching low, taking a deep breath and sharply exhaling, she lowered her powerful shoulder and burst through the fragile door, flattening on the floor, her gun coming up to eyeline, sweeping through the kitchen to the bathroom to the right, door closed, shouting, "Police! Throw down your weapons!" just as she heard a door beyond the living room splinter and Kowalski echo in deep bass, a sound that shook the walls, "Police! Throw down your guns!"

Then an awful silence, a sound of absolutely nothing that should have been roaring guns and exploding plaster, screams of pain and death, but instead the soft, almost inaudible hiss of hard snow against the window, the hum of an ancient clock suspended from the yellow wall, the metronomic drip, drip, drip of an old faucet, all subdued by Kowalski's yell, "Deb? Hey, Deb? You okay?"

"Right here."

"I got big nothin'. What you got?"

"Back me up," she said.

Kowalski whirled around the passageway, incredibly quick for a man that size, down low, so low, his gun two-handed, out front, an extension of his eyes. "Where?" he said, breathing tight, quick.

She nodded to the closed bathroom door.

"How do you want to do this?" he said.

She motioned with her hands for side-to-side positions, understanding that anyone beyond the door could hear them and, if they knew cops, understand anything they said.

"Okay," he said.

The doorknob was on the left, the door hinged right. It would swing back that way. Residential doors open inward. With stealth, inaudibly she slipped left, posted herself there. Unless they shot *through* the door, unable to see her or aim, she was safe.

Kowalski pulled himself around to cover the other angle. If anyone showed in his gunsights as the door cracked open, he would ventilate them.

Deb reached down and twisted her left hand, squeezing the revolver in her right. The doorknob, unlocked, turned easily. She shoved it and the door swung easily in, almost as if it had been counterweighted.

She snapped a look back at Kowalski, read his eyes, alert and fixed, watched his head shake, no, watched him shift and weave, slowly increasing his view, eventually revealing everything except what might be behind the door. Again Kowalski shook his head, no.

Against a small tremble in her hands she clamped down, almost unable to control the riot in her stomach, the raw fear gnawing at her, the formless terror that the thin slice of wood hid a messenger of death. Through the small space between the door and the frame, revealed as the hinges opened, she saw there was nothing.

But what else?

This was hers.

What had she told Kowalski? Don't be a pussy? "Right," she whispered to herself.

Exploding against the half-open door with all her force she drove it fiercely against the wall, knowing that if someone was waiting, he would go down before he could shoot upward, would lose his balance before he recovered it, would be seen off balance before he could get off the first shot. And she felt the door push back as she collided with it, was shocked at the force, swirled away and pulled tight on the trigger as it found the target.

Her eyes blinked.

Her breath left her deflated.

Her gun dipped slowly to the floor.

Kowalski spun through the door and beaded in on it before relaxing.

"Coatrack," she sighed. "Fucking coatrack. Who keeps a fucking coatrack in a bathroom?"

Kowalksi shook his head, added, "Nobody home."

"Let's look around," she said.

"Don't touch anything," he said. "before Forensics."

She turned slowly and saw a form melted in the folds beyond the shower curtain.

"Let me," Kowalski said, stepping in between her and whatever was resting, lifeless, in the tub.

"Come on," she said. "You can't spare me this . . ."

He looked at her, then down, using his pistol grip to pull back the vinyl curtain. She looked down and saw, saying "Thank God," a wrinkled neoprene wet suit, double scuba tanks, regulator, air hose, mouthpiece, hood, goggles.

"Bingo," she said.

"Or bathtub diver," Kowalski cracked. "Real popular in northern cities." He holstered his Magnum before sighing, relieved, "What else?"

Debra was already out of the bathroom, into the kitchen, her eyes on the thing the tension had made her ignore before. It was right on the counter, right out, as if they hadn't a concern in the world that anyone would find it, or them. Disbelieving her own eyes, she just pointed.

Kowalski said, "Is that it? Part one of your installment plan?"

Debra shook her head, yes, moved closer to look. It was all there but the money. The mason jar, the heavy leaden sinkers and, the Lite-Ups tethered and still in place, now exhausted, their chemical reactions spent, completely without light.

"Halleck really was right," she muttered.

"Oh, great, Deb. Now you confess your doubts! What if this had been the local chapter president of the NRA?"

"Anything in the bedroom?"

"Junk food cartons. I wasn't minding detail."

"Let's look again."

They walked back, past the TV set, video machine attached, passed a sofa, end table, saw the phone, the twenty-foot cord. She sized up the room, found it to be just the dimensions that Halleck described. "This is exactly like he said it was."

She went on into the bedroom, saw mattresses, two twins, flopped at angles, a futon nestled in the closet. On that were a pair of girl's panties.

"Oh, no," she said. "Pray God not."

She picked them up, found a long brown stain, smelled it. Not blood. She'd had an accident.

"Crapped her pants," Kowalski said.

"She's scared!" shouted Debra.

"I crapped my pants once. Domestic dispute. Got there with my partner. My turn to go first, so I ring the bell. The door flies open. I don't expect it, so I freeze. Time just drifted, as if I had all of it in my life just draining away into a few seconds. The shotgun came down. The guy pushes it in my stomach, pulls the trigger. And I imagine my guts spread out forty feet behind me. And I shit."

"You got hit with a shotgun at that range and lived to tell about it?" said Debra.

"It didn't fire. Defective cartridge. By then I wasn't even reacting. My partner grabbed the barrel before he pulled the other trigger, blew half the door frame away. That's what happens when you're scared. You freeze. You can't react."

"Looks like we gotta find her then, doesn't it?"

"Yeah," he said, nodding, "it does."

"Time to bring Janowski in," Debra said. "This is them. Even he has to admit it."

"Yeah. Jano's a stubborn asshole, but he knows the scent when you rub his nose in it."

"But we're back to zip and just as much time left. I hate to say it but we may need all the technology that Lou Scannon's FBI guys can throw at this place. And fast. All we got left to run down is the car. Let's check the street," she said, holstering her gun.

"So why not have Jano put out an APB on it?"

"And sit on this place, too, in case they come back."

"What are you gonna tell Halleck?"

"That he can't give up on this one yet. He has to hang in. Absolutely must."

Kowalski pushed back his kinky hair with a huge hand and shook his head. "They've disappeared. We're nowhere again. A couple of hours to the drop and we're fucking nowhere. What the fuck do we do?"

"I don't know." She shrugged, numb with despair. Then she turned and said the first thing that came to mind, "Why not ask Halleck?"

19

Halleck jumped, spilling his coffee, hissing, "Shit!" as the Granville phone rang, for the first time not knowing how to handle it. It might be the nervous Sunday school teacher, wondering if Janey would be well enough to rehearse the Christmas pageant, or it could be the chatty neighbor after the fruitcake recipe, or it could be the handyman wondering when he would be able to finish the upstairs bathroom, or it could be a wrong number. But Halleck sensed it was none of these. Instinctively he was sure this was it. But he let it go through a second ring, even as a new cassette was chewing up tape. Grasping the handset, he waited for a third ring, hoping to keep one of them busy at the other end with the promise of money when Debra and Kowalski came charging in. It was near enough time for them to strike, according to his reckoning. The news station that droned subliminally from the kitchen had reminded him instants ago that it was three-fifteen, overcast, and windy.

He picked up, answering as he always had, "Halleck."

"Party of the Second Part."

In the background, something was wrong. Adrenaline lanced through him, leaving him cold, almost unable to speak. Halleck had become so used to the familiar clues— the idle tinkling wind chime, the clinking spoon in the ceramic cup, the barking Airedale, the clicking taps as the caller paced, the deep, weak thudding of heavy metal drums, the background soundtracks from the television— that panic seized him when he didn't hear them. Not one of them. Instead there was a low steady howl, the sound of wind.

They had moved.

Of that much he was sure. His heart hammered, his palms sweated, his voice cracked as he finally managed to say, "What are the arrangements?"

There was another silence, a long deadly interval when the handset banged as if hammered, when Halleck didn't know what had happened or what they knew about what had happened, when he imagined that they might, just might have returned from an outing with Janey, the final outing prior to the exchange, when they were feeling particularly insecure about losing their golden goose, only to see two figures floating around inside their sanctuary. Or, as Debra had suggested, they could have planned this all along, fearing that somehow an unseen noose might be tightening, or they were at last spooked by something—the helicopter, perhaps—into bolting. He couldn't tell. Now he had a completely new situation and hours, not days, to converge.

"This is it," the voice said, followed by a scratching sound then a long hiss. Match. Lighting a match. Smoker, too. Why not before? Lapsing? Someone who had given it up before and returned from nerves? Certainly the tension was enough to crack a diamond. Maybe.

"I'm ready for your terms," said Halleck, knowing the recorder was getting it all but not willing to let them suspect, even now, that they had been gathering evidence, evidence admissible in a court of law, saying, "Let me get my pencil. All right."

"Same drop, Hubbard west of Wabash, south side of street. There's a mailbox. Put the briefcase under it. Walk away, but only as far as the revolving door at the corner. You'll see it. Have the father stand under the canopy until you pick up the girl, Halleck. By then we'll have the money, verify it. By then you'll have the girl and can call the father. There's a phone stall just around the corner from the revolving door. The number is 813–9010. Repeat."

"It's 813–9010," Halleck said. The caller's voice was grabbing for wind, the way a person does in the cold. Outside. Janey, too? If so, how was she dressed? On the day she was abducted the weather had followed the meteorologists' call, starting above freezing and going into the forties, light and variable winds. Ellie had dressed her accordingly, thinking she would only be outside for a few blocks and not more than ten minutes. A few days had changed that so cruelly that Chicago today might have been an outer planet, its skies choked by heavy, gray clouds, swept by steady, relentless, howling winds that, even as he spoke, rattled his window, the temperatures dipping into the low teens, expected to drop near zero tonight.

"Let me check the merchandise," Halleck said.

"Soon enough," he was told.

"Our agreement," he responded.

A sigh, a sigh that wouldn't put two hundred thousand tax-free dollars at stake for a squabble. Not when they were both this close. Janey's voice came on, "Spike?" Teeth chattering. Not good.

"You okay?"

"I'm cold."

"A few more hours."

"You said that last time!"

"Soon enough," he told her. "Let me talk to the man."

The voice came back on, "Satisfied?"

"Get her some warm clothing," Halleck demanded, surprising himself at his vehemence.

"It's only a couple more hours, Halleck."

"We don't want her dead, we don't want her hypothermic, and we don't want her sick. Undamaged condition. Remember the terms?"

"We'll see what we can do."

"Do *something*."

"All right!" Angry now, realizing that he was losing control?

"Time?"

"Five-thirty?"

Halleck was surprised by the tone. It wasn't a statement but a question. He was asking for approval of a proposal, not demanding an agreement to terms. Halleck let the idea hang, looking at it coolly, figuring out what it might mean. The first thing it meant, in Halleck's view,

265

was that they had planned to evacuate the North Park Avenue hideout prior to the exchange and that they hadn't tried to go back. There was, in the voice, predictably, nervousness but no anger, no rage at betrayal or trickery. They evidently had no idea that their hideout had been identified or assaulted, nor any idea that they couldn't go back there.

Did they ever plan to go back there?

He didn't know. If they thought it was safe, there was no reason they *wouldn't* return, unless it didn't look safe, in which case they would drive away. Or they might not want to retrace any of their steps, preferring instead to get away with the money as soon as possible.

That made more sense, getting away from any and all connections to the crime, including Janey.

Janey.

Which way would it go?

If they wanted to break the chain of evidence connecting them to the kidnapping, they would certainly want to put distance between her and them. If they were clever, as organized as the scuba recovery suggested, they might actually have developed solid alibis and have no reason for *needing* to kill Janey. In fact, a *live* Janey Granville could so badly derail the momentum of pursuit that it would take police hours to resume the hunt. A live Janey Granville would so preoccupy parents and press with the story that they would not, emotionally or rationally, be able to focus on assisting in the pursuit of her abductors. Halleck was playing this scenario to a private audience of one, making it as plausible as possible before realizing the crucial flaw, that Janey had probably seen them, unless they wore masks whenever they brought her to the phone or unless they had blindfolded her the whole time. But what if they had? Now they were out on the streets and, unless they had ski masks—a possibility in this weather—then she certainly would have seen them. The question was, with their lives on the line, could they afford to take the chance? Halleck thought not.

So how and where they decided to kill Janey was all that was at issue. What to do?

"Five-thirty?" he repeated the question, disbelief in his

voice. Fewer than two and one half hours from now? He had no idea, none whatever, where they were, except, with chilling certainty, calling from an outdoor phone. Even if he could put a tap on this one it wouldn't matter. Within minutes of their hanging up they could be blocks away, in any direction. And with the streets so empty, it would be too obvious to converge police, even now. Yet if he didn't agree to five-thirty, that would leave the whole basis of negotiation at risk. They might take it as delay, as playing for more time to learn more information so as to intercept them. And if he delayed he had no idea how long Janey would be out in the cold. In a very real sense Halleck was suddenly playing God. Brian, who was out supporting Debra and Kowalski in a futile rescue attempt, was not here for consultation. Ellie, sedated after Janowski's insistence that she ID the dead girl's body, was in no condition to respond. It was Halleck who had to decide, as he suddenly did, that it was better to pin down a chance at recovering Janey than to risk her slipping away forever if they discovered that the whole process of discussion had been a ruse for pinning down where they were holed up.

Halleck figured that if he could close the window to two hours, a number of advantages were his. First, Janey certainly would not freeze to death in that time. Second, for two hours, if as he suspected Debra and Kowalski had found evidence tying the North Park Avenue address to the kidnappers, Janowski could afford to cover that place with a trap, in case they showed. Third, if the terms were cleverly structured, they really would have a chance to rescue Janey. On the other hand, if the deal soured, if they discovered that their hideout had been raided, they could panic, or they could follow what might have been an integral part of this apparently intricate plan all along—to grab the money, kill the girl, and run. The down side of agreeing to two hours was that it could be a death sentence set in motion, with no way to stop the clock. But what other choice did he have?

He couldn't recover, sit on tape after tape, sifting through clue after clue, ever narrowing the search and plotting success on a map. When they stayed in one place *and* Halleck had been as lucky as shrewd, it took nearly three days to verify the location. Now they were on the move, with no indication they would settle in anywhere before they wanted to close the deal, two hours from now.

"You agree?" the voice said.

Halleck didn't want to lose them, to trip over the three-minute interval that allowed a trace, saw no alternative, so he said, "Agreed."

"Fine," the man said. "Here's what we do. The father drops the money, stays near the revolving door on the corner, looking in. We pick up the briefcase, check the money, call you, tell you where the girl is, then you pick her up."

"No," Halleck said quickly, realizing they would immediately know that the money wasn't all there and either kill Janey then, or have her dead already. Under these terms there was no way to balance collection with delivery, a condition essential for business in a once-only exchange.

"What?" More disbelief than anger.

"Two hundred thousand dollars in a business deal is a lot to lose without any assurance that the package will be delivered. As you describe it, the delivery is in your hands *after* the money is. That is not an exchange. We agreed to an exchange."

"What do you want?"

"Something we both agree is fair, that protects both equally."

"Agreed," the voice said. He lost nothing for agreeing to an arrangement in principle. This was only foreplay. No one ever got screwed at this stage.

"Here's my proposal. You arrange to have the merchandise placed in an open delivery area, an area unapproachable for several hundred yards in all directions, an area exposed to the weather so it is cold and we must agree to the exchange on those terms, and we are forced by circumstances to accept or the merchandise is"—Halleck struggled for a euphemism—"spoiled. So once you have announced the pick-up location, entirely of your own choosing, we must satisfy you with delivery of the money."

"How do we know the money is there?"

The crucial question. It had to come. Halleck had an answer. "The money will be where you want it first. Under the mailbox. Then you will make the call letting us know the location of pickup. We do not need to be at the pick-up location. We only want to verify the package is intact. Now if we can see the merchandise, say with binoculars or telescope from the top floor observation deck of one of the downtown skyscrapers, you will be free to pick up and check the money before we can ever reach that location. It could be miles away. We just have to see . . . the merchandise before we give you the money. Then you get delivery."

"How can we recover if you trick us?"

"Take the merchandise back," Halleck said.

"The police could get there as soon as we could."

"No police," Halleck said flatly.

"Maybe. Just suppose."

"The girl is freezing, if you understood my suggestion. You think we're going to risk her life on it?"

"Just suppose."

Halleck drew a deep breath and said, "I don't know this but I suspect you or one of you knows how to use a high-powered rifle, a long-range, very accurate high-power rifle. And I don't know but suspect that in a city like Chicago, you can put your hands on just what you need in two hours."

"I see."

Halleck believed that he understood perfectly. "But it has to happen this way. One of you will keep this rifle trained on the merchandise until he gets a call from the other that the money has been received."

"Roger."

Roger? What kind of man says 'Roger'? Halleck's mind was screaming military all over again. "So you agree?"

"Yes."

"Final condition," Halleck said, confident.

"What?" Doubt and impatience, more of the latter. This was the stage when professional negotiators started a process called nibbling, asking for ostensibly small, sometimes important concessions. It happens at the end of a long bargaining session, when the other party is due to catch a plane, when they have invested too much time to say no.

"I will be moving to inspect the merchandise before we okay the transfer of funds."

"Say again?"

"From a distance the merchandise could still be recognizable and spoiled." Meaning they could kill Janey, keep her eyes open, the blush of color still on her cheeks, and prop her up in a field somewhere.

"That's a change." Nervous.

"No major change. Just an adjustment."

"I don't like it."

"You still maintain control of the delivery zone. We know nothing—no one can—until you are ready. You name the place. Your call will be forwarded at this number to an observation post you must identify in the next thirty minutes. From that spot I will make preliminary confirmation of delivery. At that moment I will phone the father, who will place the money, in a briefcase, under the mailbox, or deliver it to *any other* location you specify at that time. There are no tricks here," Halleck insisted, astonished at his own desperate conviction. "Immediately after preliminary notification, I will move, alone, to confirm the condition of the merchandise. I will appear, in the open, possibly, if you choose, in your gunsights, where I will stay until you have confirmation of the funds. As we know the transaction must occur quickly because the girl is exposed. For that reason, when I arrive I will be carrying a thermal blanket with which I will cover the merchandise. I will then move to a phone nearby, which you will specify, and make a call to the corner phone you designated at Hubbard and Wabash and instruct the father to leave the money anywhere you want."

"But then you have the girl and we have zip."

"Negative," Halleck insisted. "Then you have the terms. If the money is not delivered as planned, you can have me and the girl in your gunsights and the father, too, sitting on a street corner, ready to die."

"As long as you know the rules."

"Understood."

"And that we're playing for keeps."

"So are we."

"I'll call back with instructions."

"Soon," Halleck told him.

The line clicked dead an instant before his own phone rang. It was Debra. "Spike, she's not here. She *was*, we're sure, but no more. They've moved."

"I know," he told her. "I just got the call."

"How soon?"

"Exchange by five-thirty."

"Listen. We have Jano on board now, and Lou Scannon of the FBI to go over this place for prints, anything else. I think we may need him, since we're back to square one. We found the scuba gear and the mason jar we dropped. It's them. I don't know where they got the training—"

Halleck broke in, "I can almost smell military. Their last conversation had phrases like 'roger' and 'say again' in it. My bet is SEALs or something—"

Debra interrupted. "My bet is on a dishonorable discharge, maybe a transfer to CIA then out for dirty dealings. We don't have a chance without federal computers and service records."

"Okay. Try to get psychological profiles."

"I'll see what can be done."

"No sign of Janey?"

"Some underwear is all," quickly adding, "but no sign of blood. I figure they've taken her for insurance."

"She's alive. I just talked to her," Halleck said.

"Two hours?" Debra whistled.

"Only two. If they play, I think I've isolated her."

"How?"

"I'll explain later. Can you come right back? I'm expecting a call on delivery instructions."

"On my way."

"If I'm not here, if I have to leave, pick up my message on the gray cassette recorder by the door, the same one I use for messages to the front desk. If you can't find it, ask Harold, but it's right inside the door on the table to the right." Halleck rang off and turned to the Granville line just as it rang again. Snatching it up on the first ring, he said, "Halleck."

"Go to the observation deck, top floor of the Sears Tower. Put your calls through to a phone, any phone, there."

It was a trick. He knew it right away, played it right. "Wait."

"What?"

"I have absolutely no way of knowing what the number of those pay phones are, or of finding out. I'm all alone on this. It's going to take me at least an hour, maybe more in this snow, to get down there from Lake Forest, find out, to call in the number to the girl's father so he can switch the calls down here."

"Then you don't have much time."

"Okay, I'm gone. Just understand I'm moving as fast as I can."

"Just get there. You may have to wait."

The line went dead. Nothing to do now but have Harold the doorman get him a cab. After he left directions for Debra he phoned the front desk and said, "Harold, there's a twenty in it if you can raise me a cabbie."

"Sure, sure, Mr. Halleck," panted Harold. "But how was the car? You want to rent the car again today? If it was okay, why not take it? It's fine."

"No thanks," he said.

"Why not I drive, huh? I could take some time for lunch?"

Harold was like a puppy badgering a tired master to play. "Call a cab," Halleck said.

Passing the twenty to Harold, Halleck felt the door move aside as he hit the cold wind, the voice of the doorman shredded by its howl, "Bundle up, now, Mr. Halleck. Like to catch your death from cold out there."

As he stepped across the sidewalk he could hear the cab idling, the hack shuffling on the salted street, the radio in the cab echo off the smoky upholstery and leak out the open door, could feel the heat and smell the sulfurous cloud of exhaust rap itself around him as he ducked and entered the cab. His door slammed, then the hack's, who said, shivering, "Where you goin' on a day like this, my man?"

"Sears Tower," Halleck said.

At the Sears Tower Halleck overtipped the hack, forced the cab door open, and fought through the wind to the building entrance. He had seen the Sears Tower when sighted, knew its appearance from memory, the way he did the notes in Beethoven's Fifth, could see its forms in projection in his imagination.

That plan in his mind's eye, Halleck pushed his way through the hinged double doors, preferring them to the ones for handicapped, the kind that rushed open and waited like courtiers until you passed. Actually touching and moving the doors located him in space, prepared him for next steps, gave him more confidence, allowed him to pace more evenly.

As he advanced into the lobby, he heard the rattling casters of a trolleyed cleaning bucket, the dripping of a retracted mop, the swish of its tendrils across the slick floor.

Another voice caught him from the side, said, "Sir. Where are you going?"

"Observation deck," he said.

"I'm sorry. The observation deck is closed today. Weather."

Halleck felt something colder than the wind cut through him, pulled up his courage, tried a trick that had worked, "It's all right, I'll only be up there a few minutes. I was told to meet someone who works inside the building up there."

"Who is it, sir? I can call him."

Halleck improvised, "Actually, he was just visiting on business. I'll bet he's on his way up. I'll catch him."

"He'll just be sent back," the female voice sympathized. "I'll bet he'll come here to meet you in the lobby."

"Brian Granville will be meeting us, too. You may know him. He works very closely with the Sears vice president for Finance."

"I may recognize him but I don't know him. I'm just sorry, sir, but the observation deck is closed . . ."

The doors snapped open and closed behind Halleck as he tried to think his way through. There was always a way. Next he would try to say that he had remembered something about an upper-story office, get that far and run the rest of the way up. He could run, was in good shape, and that was one thing where rhythm, more than sight, was important. Trying to run stairs by putting your feet where your eyes tell your mind they belong is apt to cause a fall, whereas just letting your feet rise and fall without looking for anything but turns at the landings will keep you steady. He opened his mouth to try that angle, felt the waft of cold from the opened doors, and heard a breathless voice say, "The observation deck just opened."

The receptionist's voice said, "Yes, ma'am," weakened as it turned away from them to say, "Bobby, you have keys?"

"Yup."

With Debra's hand tucked under his elbow, they moved to the elevator. "You should have waited," she said.

"Is this a nag?"

"When you act like a little boy, Spike, expect a scolding."

The elevator shot them up halfway, where it stopped to break what engineers call a chimney effect. There they changed and continued to the top, where it let them out. Halleck could almost feel the height, could easily hear the wind beating on the glass, feel the chill that had flooded the unoccupied deck.

"Where are the phones?"

"Let me look." She released his arm, leaving him feeling, strangely, much more alone than he was used to, and wondering what she was to him and whether this was just adrenaline or more, torturing himself with the question that troubles all handicapped people, asking himself what she could see in a man who couldn't ever be completely normal, pushing the flood of feelings aside and just listening, numbly, as her footsteps echoed away on the huge floor, hearing her voice ring back. "Over here," she shouted.

Halleck used the echoes to avoid walls, walked in her direction, said, "Try one."

He heard her pick up, drop in a coin, slap it with her hand. "Thief," she said. "Dead thief at that. Next."

Another coin dropped. "Something. Wait." She held the handset away, let Halleck hear that wailing noise, a strange rising and falling that sounded something like a European police car siren. "Scratch two," she sighed, moving to the third.

"Shit," she muttered. "You have coins, Spike?"

He always did. They taught you that at blind school. Coins for phones, how you could always get an operator to help, how they could always find you if you just kept the line open. He said, "In my pocket," began to reach, only to feel her hand fire in first, pluck out a quarter, deposit it, and sigh, "Miracle of modern technology."

"Call Brian at home," Halleck said. "Have him refer calls here." In a minute it was done. Halleck said, "Now call the receptionist downstairs, have her call Brian and Ellie's number, to be sure the system is working."

She did and the phone rang. Halleck reached for it, felt Debra grab his hand, say, "It may be them."

He nodded, answered, "Halleck."

"This is the call you wanted," came the voice.

Relieved, he said, "Thanks," and hung up.

Halleck had no sense of how long the silence hung, shroudlike, in the air, before Debra cut through it with, "Don't blame yourself. We almost got there. And you were right."

"You think that would make a good epitaph? 'Uncle Spike was right, just a little slow. So here I am.' "

"It's not over," she told him, squeezing his shoulder.

"We lost the initiative. It's their game now."

"But you said—"

"Yeah, they have to show us Janey, but we could still all die. Janey, Brian, and me."

"Jesus, Spike. What can I do?"

Halleck's mind spun out of depression. It was a good question. They were sitting here waiting, each second a seeming eternity, but there was something, there must be something they could do. In a minute he was sure there was. They could prepare.

"Body armor?" Halleck said. "They make it in coats, right? Like trench coats?"

"We have in downtown. Why, you want some? What's your size?"

Halleck waved his hand, indicating she had misunderstood. "For Janey. I told them I was going to cover her with a blanket until they counted the money. But we don't just have to keep her from freezing, we have to keep her from being shot!"

"I've got a car blanket, Spike. We could sew it under the thing."

"Next we need to know how long it takes a child of seven or eight to freeze to death out there. That limits how long we have to get there once they point her out to us—"

"Point her out?" Debra was understandably confused.

"That's the reason we're here," he said. "They picked it. Some time before five-thirty they're going to call. At that time they'll tell us where to look to find where she's sitting . . ."

"Sitting? Outside?"

"Things have to happen fast from then on and they know it."

"Where will they put her?" There was clear deliberation in her voice, as if she were trying to eliminate possibilities so they could focus their thinking on a few places. It was the lesson she'd learned, and learned well, from Halleck.

"You tell me," Halleck sighed, exasperated. "That's why I need you, Deb. They said to come here and they would tell me where to look, high-power binoculars or telescope—"

"All we've got up here is these tourist telescopes," she said.

"And a quarter's worth of time. They know that."

"How many quarter's you got?"

Halleck jangled the change in his pocket. "Six," he said.

"Give me one," she said.

"Why?"

"Let's have a look. See what we can figure out."

Halleck heard the coin clunk in, the meter rushing off time, the collar of the telescope pivot madly back and forth, Debra swinging it, here, there, looking, checking things out. When the timer stopped whirring and the coin dropped, he heard her whoosh out a breath and say, "On a clear day, as they say, you can see forever, all the way to the western Michigan shore. Today we have weather. Clouds, even here. I think they must be hanging on the building, I swear. Everything is blurred. South along Lake Shore Drive I can see as far as Thirty-first Street Beach, when the ground fog isn't patching things over. It comes and goes. A lot of that is low and the lake is running. Can she swim?"

Halleck was iced by the question. "What?" he said numbly.

"Can Janey swim?"

"Yes, she can swim. In a pool, when nobody jostles her."

"Because if they put her on one of the beaches when the lake is running, she's going to have to be able to get herself away or she'll drown."

"Bastards," Halleck exploded, let himself go for the first time since it had started, hammered his fist into the wall, hit something shallow but sharp, started to bleed, sucked it.

Debra's voice was flat, factual, as she said, "We need the Feds. They've got tons of info. Us, we got zip. And they can tell us exactly how long Janey can last out there."

Halleck heard the mounted telescope squeal through a half turn, Debra say, "Let's look again. Most beach south of here is below Lake Shore Drive. So we can't see anything. Ditto as far up as North Avenue Beach, which I can hardly see at all."

"How long will it take to get to either of those places?"

"Once on the street? Ten minutes, maybe less running Code Three—that is—with sirens."

"No sirens," Halleck reminded her.

"Right. Okay, no cops, no sirens. Twenty-five minutes?"

"How about a flasher, a little portable rooftop red light, no sirens, then we pull it in a couple of blocks away?"

"Ten to fifteen, depending on how we hit the lights. Sirens clear intersections, flashers don't."

"How about Al? Can he get us closer faster?"

"Choppers are grounded, Spike. You felt the wind."

"Just about knocked me over. What else did you see?"

"Open spaces?"

"That's the idea, so they can see we're not trying to trap them."

"All of Northerly Island, that's big, isolated, plus Grant Park, very open, and maybe the area around Ohio Street Beach, near the Water Filtration Plant, but I doubt it."

"Reason?"

"Navy Pier is right nearby. I think this guy, the scuba diver, is spooked of the service, never liked it. And it's much tighter in there. They can't see as far."

"Inland, to the west?"

"Douglas Park and Garfield Park, but again I doubt it?"

"Reasons?" Halleck again demanded.

"Both hemmed in by roads, easy to isolate after the exchange. Like box canyons, they're hard places to get out of. And if this guy is planning on popping Janey if you don't deliver, he wants a clear shot from far away. He's not going to get that in Douglas or Garfield parks. Too many trees. In these other places he can make like Lee Harvey Oswald and shoot from tall buildings, even across the water."

"How far?"

Debra sighed, thought, answered, "A good scoped sniper rifle with a strap, on a clear day without wind can put a single shot fifty-millimeter round in the center of a man's chest at a thousand yards. And the Soviets have a rifle with more range than that."

"He could be a thousand yards away?"

"Anywhere, at any point on a circle, a thousand yards from the center, where Janey will be sitting."

"I might not even see him," Halleck mused, almost to himself. "Even if I could see him."

"That's why we go for the body armor, for both you and Janey. And for Brian, unless you want Jano to walk the money in."

"He'd do it?"

"Volunteered."

"Can't," said Halleck.

"Huh?"

"They may know what Brian looks like. I told them about his picture in today's *Tribune*. If it isn't him, they may bolt."

"So we go with Brian," she said.

Debra kept swinging the telescope, thinking out loud so that Halleck could follow. "Most places on the Lake Front are a few blocks from the L. From a sniper position a thousand yards off, one shot, maybe two and they put down the rifle, walk onto a train, and are gone."

"L is running?"

"Best in snow, sloughs the stuff like a pitched roof. No L stations close to the other parks. They'd need to use the roads, meaning a car. Easier to follow a lone car on a snowy road than a man in a crowd on the L"

Halleck nodded, listened as she continued.

"Remember these guys don't trust one another. Look at the pick-up spot. Don't think that Janey will be dropped far from there because after they do this little dance of phone calls, if the one guy confirms the money, the other is going to be off like a bat outta hell tryin' to catch him before he splits. Believe it. It may even work that the gunman isn't going to quite believe the other guy, so if the bag man—the collector—calls him and says, 'Pop the girl, there's no money,' he won't. That was the genius of the five thousand, Spike. You already showed you're good for it. So what does the gunman do?"

"I don't know," Halleck said.

"I don't either, but I bet he hesitates, even after he gets the word, before firing."

"What does that mean?"

She shrugged. "It means we have a little extra time. What are we going to do with it?"

"Keep her covered, keep her low."

"What about Jano?"

"When we learn, we should post him a few blocks away, out of sight. Unmarked cars."

"Agreed."

"Keep him out of sight until the first shot is fired, then turn him loose."

"Code Three," she said.

"As many cars as fast as possible, as visible and audible as possible," Halleck told her.

"We don't know where he is, where he will be hidden," she reminded him. "A circle two thousand yards across is a lot of real estate."

"It doesn't matter," he told her. "As you said, his partner has the money, he is up to his ass in alligators. I think he's going to get the hell out of the swamp pronto, wherever he is."

"Or whoever he is," added Debra. "Which brings in the Feds. Let's see if they can't find out who these schmucks are."

"And how long we have to get to Janey before she freezes to death."

20

Lou Scannon, Chicago FBI, slipped his palm against his lower back and stretched, wincing with pain, pulled it away and rubbed his thick neck, shook his head and resumed circling the squawk box, impatiently waiting a connection. As he passed a bronze ashtray, Scannon retrieved a smoldering cigar, replaced it between his lips, drew deeply and exhaled, marbling the office air with choking smoke. Looking down at a young agent, his eyes wide and anxious, Scannon barked, "Well?"

"He's responding to a page, sir."

"These scientists get paid? For what?" he huffed.

Through bursts of static he heard a throat being cleared, then, "This is Chip Fraunt."

"Naval Research Station?" Scannon said, needing to be sure.

"Yes."

"Lou Scannon, FBI."

"But I had my clearance run last year. It's not up for renewal—"

Scannon cut him off. "That's not it. We need your expertise."

"Yes?"

"We need to know how long a person can survive at about five to ten degrees Fahrenheit, wind going steady fifteen to twenty."

"First, are you asking for a temperatures Fahrenheit of five or ten degrees, or an average, or do you want a range? Second, is your wind speed in miles per hour or knots? Third, what is the relative humidity of the ambient air?"

"What the hell difference does it make?" Scannon exploded, checking his watch.

"A substantial difference," Fraunt said evenly, without a trace of emotion. "If you want to know how long a person will survive, especially relative humidity, since we cool evaporatively and the wetter the air, the more slowly we lose heat."

He made what seemed to represent the outside conditions and said, "Make it seven degrees Fahrenheit, wind speed twenty miles an hour, relative humidity seventy-five percent."

"Man or woman?"

"Woman, girl," he snapped back. "What difference—"

Fraunt responded in a flat, even, dryly factual voice and said, "Women have an extra layer of fat, are better insulated, last longer. Body weight?"

"What?"

Fraunt was thorough, if aggravating, explaining, "The higher the body weight, the smaller the ratio of surface area, or skin, to mass, and the better the body protects itself in core temperature."

"You got a girl here, what, Myles?" He snapped at the young agent, "Sixty pounds?"

"More like fifty," Myles suggested. "Same age as my daughter."

"Fifty pounds," Scannon shouted.

"Dress?"

"I don't know if she was wearing a dress or slacks that day. Myles?"

Before Myles could answer, Faunt cut in, "I don't mean exact attire, but the degree of body surface covered and the insulating power of the fabric."

"She was dressed for school on a day that was maybe twenty-five degrees and sunny. Help me out, Myles!"

Myles swallowed apologetically for failed anticipation and replied, "Files say she had a pleated wool pinafore, Black Watch pattern fabric, white knee socks, blend polyester and wool, patent leather shoes, low flats with buckle strap, overcoat a pleated hip-length fiberfill with an inner zip flap and outer crossover buttons, plus a pullover hood, waterproof, like the rest, but not insulated. That's all we have."

"And she's dry?" Fraunt asked.

"She's not taking a goddamn shower, man. Of course she's dry!" roared Scannon, again checking his watch.

Fraunt responded firmly, still apparently nonplussed, "No, that's not what I meant, Mr. Scannon. It's just that children, unlike adults, tend to roll around in the outside, snow in particular, which then melts into their clothing. When they get wet this way, the water begins drawing heat away from their body at an abnormal rate compared to the air and wind. That's why fliers downed in icy water only last five minutes."

"I don't need a goddamn lecture, Fraunt, I need an answer."

Scannon could hear Fraunt sigh, as if he were dealing with a child, then explain, "Your little girl, fifty pounds, dressed that way, not wet, will be okay, as long as she's moving, at seven degrees and twenty miles per hour wind, seventy-five percent relative humidity, insulated by her overcoat, for maybe thirty minutes before she begins to be challenged."

"Challenged?"

"Before the body's heat-producing mechanism can't keep up with the environmental drain."

"Thirty minutes?"

"If she is dressed as you described, her legs will get cold first, because they're not protected."

"Anything else?"

"She should avoid getting wet."

"Or else?" Scannon demanded.

"Or else she begins getting in trouble sooner, maybe only fifteen minutes."

"What's the Jesus Factor on this?"

"Once she gets past the first threshold, you haven't got much time."

"Define," demanded Scannon, chewing on his cigar like an old dog on a bone.

"Five to seven minutes more," Fraunt told him.

"You're sure?"

"Dead sure," Fraunt said evenly. "A lot of our data

comes from the Korean War, where we knew exactly how long men were out, what dress, what weather."

"Thanks," Scannon said, no gratitude in his voice. When Fraunt rang off with a perfunctory, "You're welcome," Scannon told Myles, "Let Janowski know. Tell him to relay the message to Havlechek."

"Halleck," Myles corrected.

"Whatever," Scannon said, waving his cigar. "Now let's get back to DOD on those discharges, see if they've run the prints from the hideout, what they have."

Myles said, "I have a call to the Pentagon working now. Ringing."

"Switch it over to the squawk box. You call Janowski. Go."

Myles hopped up and hustled off as Scannon took his place, reclining in the chair until the ceiling filled his field of vision, listening to the ring, the voice answer. "This is Colonel Brighton, Armed Services Personnel Sector, for the Secretary of Defense. What can I do for you, Mr. Scannon?"

"Like to know the names of any recent dishonorable discharges, or servicemen working for CIA and dismissed, over the past, say, year, maybe year and a half. Scuba experience. Clandestine. Infiltration. Commando. Anything like that. And unfavorable psychological profiles. Especially like to know if you have one or two matching the prints we wired you."

"We copy receiving your transmission of fingerprints, are working them on urgent, but have only manual searches. Can you help us narrow? I take it you think they are among the two hundred and twenty-seven dishonorable discharges from all services in the last fiscal year."

"Two hundred and twenty-seven? That's too damn many," fumed Scannon. "But start lookin' there. And scratch Air Force. Drop everything in the Army except for Special Forces, too."

"Let me check this," Brighton said. "Roger yours for listing dishonorable discharges from Army Special Forces, Navy, and Marine Corps?"

"Commando stuff," Scannon said. "With scuba, clandestine, like I said."

"Suggest we look at Navy SEALs and Marine Recon, plus Army Special Forces, to narrow it."

"Go, go," said Scannon, checking his watch.

"Working the descriptors on the terminal, now," Brighton said.

Silence, then, "Coming up, here, we're down to twenty-two."

"Still too many," barked Scannon.

"Suggest if you're interested in scuba experience that we drop the Special Forces entirely, which shows none with that background."

"Do it."

"Fifteen."

"Too many."

"We could try dropping all the Marine Recon except those showing scuba training."

"Go," said Scannon.

"Five."

"How many with Midwest backgrounds, maybe Chicago birth or upbringing, high school."

"Let me pull those files."

Silence. Scannon checked his watch, found himself whispering, "Come on, come on," until Colonel Brighton said, "None."

"None?"

"Roger that."

Scannon was stunned, hadn't expected that, wondered if he should go back further, asked, "Is this file up to date?"

"Reports filed in, revised, and verified electronically two days ago."

"Suggestions?"

"Are you looking for a criminal, sir?"

"What?"

"Are you seeking a criminal?"

"Yes," Scannon admitted, not knowing what else to say.

"Shall we roll over into Section Eights"

"What's that?"

"Section Eight is a discharge for mental instability, specifically psychoses, deep neuroses and delusions of grandeur, sociopathic behavior or extreme insubordination interpreted as the exhibition of spontaneous mental dysfunction."

"Crazies?"

"A range of mental problems."

"Give me a list of crazies, see if we can match," Scannon told him, rubbing his neck, closing his eyes, feeling time drain away.

"Reading," the colonel told him.

Scannon drummed his fingers.

"Humm," the colonel said.

"Humm what?"

"I have here a Navy SEAL, section eighted two months ago, originally from Skokie, trained for arctic diving in the Great Lakes, described by instructors as shrewd and resourceful but too independent. Resists orders, finds his own way. Very goal oriented. Problems with structure, authority. And impatient. Exhibited violent reactions to frustration, deep fears of betrayal, and basically pathological feelings of distrust."

"Paranoid?"

"Suspected but unconfirmed temporal lobe lesions."

"What does that tell us?"

"That was the same condition afflicting David Berkowitz, the Son of Sam killer from New York. These people hear voices, believe they've been sent on divine missions, see success as preordained by divine forces, their missions as ways to save the world, themselves, sometimes, often, as agents of God, or destiny. This man served and lived as a military adviser to the Mujaheddin in Afghanistan, saw his mission as prophet and savior against the communist heathen, tried, according to reports, to assume leadership of the guerrilla forces, had to be recalled. When his replacement arrived, this man tried to assassinate him, had to be evacuated under sedation. Was released without fanfare to private facilities."

"Where?"

"Chicago. Actually Cicero."

"And who is this guy?"

"His name is Wade Barnes Hansen."

"Can he shoot?"

"Record says expert rifleman. Sniper trained. Expert in stealth, infiltration, exfiltration. Says he picked up expertise with a 7.62 millimeter Dragunov sniper rifle, captured from Soviet Elite Forces."

"Range?"

"Dragunov? A good marksman can put a single round in a one-foot diameter target at eight hundred meters."

"Good God! That's almost a half a mile!"

"That's the good news," Colonel Brighton said. "If you're concerned about assassination—which is none of my business—but just let me warn you that the Dragunov can fire a round every three seconds on semiautomatic. In other words, he doesn't have to kill with one round. Every three seconds he gets a chance to add a hit."

"And he can do it?"

"*Anyone* with that kind of training, Mr. Scannon, can put a round somewhere in the human body at a thousand meters."

"And you think he would kill?"

Silence. Then, "Mr. Scannon, Hansen wasn't pamphleteering in Afghanistan. I can't tell you how many coffins he filled. Let's just say he was busy."

And now, Scannon thought, this busy, paranoid killing machine, or someone very much like him, would be out there now, waiting distrustfully for a drop of money, waiting with a finger on the trigger of a rifle aimed at the heart of a little girl six-tenths of a mile away, from a position no one knew in a place as yet unnamed, for an appointment less than an hour away.

"See if you can match one of those sets of prints we sent you to our boy. And put anything else you can on the wire to me, here, colonel. Pronto."

"It's done."

"Thanks," he said flatly and hung up.

Myles raced back into the room as the handset clicked down, saying, "Janowski's been informed, Mr. Scannon. He said he will see that Halleck knows."

"Wonderful," Scannon said. "Get in touch with him again. Tell him we may have a real suspect this time, a man out there with a rifle that can kill somebody from more than a half a mile away, a man trained in concealment and escape, a regular superRambo. Tell him we've got an hour to locate him. And Myles?''

"Yes, sir?"

"Ask him how long he's going to let Amateur Hour run?"

"Sir?"

"Myles?" Scannon grunted mightily, scratched his chin and smiled. "In case you haven't figured it out, we are standing directly downwind in a hurricane from what is about to be a megaton shit explosion. If it happens, nobody's gonna walk away smellin' real sweet. Get my drift?''

"Yes, sir."

"And tell Janowski I'd like to hear his plan."

21

"Thirty minutes," Debra told him with a sigh. "Maybe thirty-five."

"That's all?" Halleck said.

"So say the experts in Washington." She placed a gentle hand on his shoulder, squeezed. "Hey, you okay?"

"Been better," he said.

He heard her light up, smelled the acrid smoke, stopped himself from telling her that it was going to kill her. She coughed, drew again, coughed again, exhaled. Then he asked, "*You* okay?"

"So-so."

"What time is it?"

"Four thirty-five."

"How's the light?"

"Holding. The clouds hurt. There's a lot of ground fog."

"How long are we going to be able to see anything?"

"Half an hour?"

"They'll call soon." A logical assumption but also a prayer, a desperate hope that there was still a way to play the game out so Janey would live. This was the part of the plan he thought they would never reach, the exchange of money for a life. Yet he had planned for even that as a last measure. How was he to guess that a snowstorm and a heart attack would leave them playing poker, bluffing, trying to bring her in without leverage, without, in fact, a goddamn thing to broker for her.

"Spike?" Something different in her tone, less musical. Instantly he felt it and stiffened. Could it be? Could they already have found Janey dead?

"What?" He snapped back at her, his head turreted to where he knew she must be standing.

"Jano wants a stand-in."

She got right to the point. So did he. "Can't," he said.

"Spike, you gave it a great shot. Just bad luck. Now it's police work."

"Even if I agreed," he said, pacing on a short leash, "which I don't—we can't run it that way."

"Sure we—"

He cut her off. "This little girl has spent the last couple of days enduring the most terrifying experience of her life in the hands of strangers. Now we're going out there to bring her back, having no money to exchange and what she needs most of all, to be under control, so as not to run away, a moving target for both bullets and cold, is to see someone she knows and trusts."

"I see your point." She punctuated the sentence with a hard draw on her cigarette.

"So let's go with the plan." As they'd discussed, they would use an unmarked car and roof beacon to move them within a few blocks of the collection site, wherever that was. The waiting cab would be right behind. Before they reached the site, Halleck would switch to the cab, which would take him the rest of the way, drop him off, and depart. He would be carrying the body armor disguised as a blanket, walk it over to Janey, tell her to cover herself in it completely, to keep warm. Then he would walk back to make the final phone contact, buy time, and—here the plan ran into so many uncertainties it broke down—then just see what happened. Whatever that was, if he got Janey covered and backup was on the way, she was safe. That was all that mattered.

"You're going to be all alone out there," she said.

"We tried another way. It didn't work out."

"Not your fault."

"Fault or no, that's the way it is. There's no way to change that now."

"You're up against a sniper, Spike."

"Nothing I can do about that either."

"Look." He could hear the final exhalation of smoke, the frustration barricading unexpressed anger, her voice trembling on the edge of control. "I've got eyes and I would be scared to death out there alone, with someone beading in on me from a half a mile away and I don't know where, won't know, even to look for the wisp of smoke after the first shot and then it may be all over. Look, Spike, they think they know who this guy is—"

"I've heard that once before already."

"I thought we weren't doing blame."

"Sorry." He didn't know if he was. The Valitano–Spiros lead had been stupid, a concoction of convenience. He thought, even now, that both Janowski and Scannon knew that all along.

Debra picked up right where she left off. "He's a crack shot. He could be anywhere. And he's more than a little paranoid. If he feels betrayed, he'll shoot."

"You have another plan?"

"Let me go in for Janey?"

Halleck shook his head.

"Can't you hear what I'm saying," she sobbed. "Jesus!" He reached up, wiped her cheeks.

"Some professional, huh?"

"Still the answer is no."

"Spike, I have eyes! I can see a muzzle flash or smoke. I can hear—"

"I can hear, too," he snapped back, "and put a direction to it. If I'm not hit, and someone has field glasses on me, you look to where I'm pointing as I lay, facedown in the snow, somewhere out on that line, in that direction, is where the sniper will be. And after all is said and done, I've got to be out there."

"Why?"

"Because I can't live with being on the sidelines if both Janey and you get killed."

"You, too?"

He nodded his head, smiled. "Hell of a time to fall in love, huh?"

"We do what we can."

"Let's just stay alive for another hour."

"They're going to give you tactical support."

"Meaning?"

Debra sighed, tried to explain. "As soon as we know,

before we move, we give Janowski the location. He's got a command center. Using unmarkeds, he dispatches fire teams. They occupy surrounding points, start surveillance. Maybe they pick up the shooter before he opens fire."

"And maybe not," Halleck said.

"They're good," she said.

"I don't want them screwing things up, spooking the guy."

"They won't. They plan on tying a noose outside his effective range. Wherever he is, he'll be inside their circle."

"What else?"

"They're going to Halleck him."

"What?"

"You've made believers of them, Spike. They're going to use directional microphones and triangulate on the first shot. What the hell do you think of that?"

"If I'm not dead, I'll think it's great."

To the left, just beyond the reach of his arm, the phone exploded in ringing. Outside the wind battered at the tall building, rattling the windows on the observation deck. Janey was out there. He snatched up the handset and said, "Halleck."

"Point the telescope southeast. Do you see her?"

Halleck covered the handset, whispered the directions to Debra.

"No. Be more specific," he said.

"Northerly Island. On the playing field. May look like a dot."

Again covering the mouthpiece he whispered, "Northerly Island. Playing Field." Then to the caller, "Hold the line. I'm alone here and the cord doesn't reach the telescope. Give me a minute. I'll be right back."

He walked to where he knew Debra would be standing, swinging the lens assembly in the right direction, scanning. "Okay," she whispered. "I see her. Or I see something. Confirm. And let's move."

Halleck walked back, tried to conceal his fear, said, "Confirm."

"Get moving. There's a phone on the observatory wall,

on the east wall. After you check the merchandise, make your call. I'll give you twenty minutes."

"Twenty minutes?"

"Right."

"We're at the top the Sears Tower!"

"The roads are empty, Halleck. Just drive fast. We're waiting." The line clicked dead.

"Let's move," he told her.

"Call Jano," she insisted.

"Go!" he said.

She punched in the numbers, said, "Northerly Island. Meigs Field. We're moving."

Cupping Halleck's elbow tightly in her hand, she dragged him to the elevators and hammered the DOWN button. Almost instantly one appeared. They shot in and pushed the button for the break halfway down, switched on the run, and ducked into a waiting unit, dropped quickly to the lobby.

As the elevator fell to street level, Halleck's hope began to sink. As if submerged by the descent, fear began seeping in, racing his heart. Before he could recover, the doors popped and Debra yanked him forward, whispering, "Come on, Spike. Hang in."

Halleck's mind spun. Not two miles away, on a lonely peninsula raked by savage winds, Janey was sitting in a blanket of snow, waiting. For rescue? Or would a bullet and the cold get her first? Which?

The building doors snapped open with an electronic hum. The cold slapped and stung him, pushed him up, froze him motionless, so hard he could not move without dipping his shoulder, turning sideways, slipping the force. Flecks of ice pecked at his face, numbed his lips, set his teeth chattering, all in a few seconds. Despite his full coat, the chill was merciless, unremitting.

Debra still tugging, her voice broken in the howl, just audible. "Let's go," she said, pushing down on his head with a "Duck!" squeezing him into what must be a compact car.

"Kowalski here, Mr. Halleck," said a deep voice from the front seat, followed by, "gotta drive now."

Kowalski must have hit the accelerator, flattening him

against the seat. Beneath him the tires lost purchase, fishtailing the car in the dry, powdery snow.

"Cherry top," Debra told the driver.

"Here goes."

"East to State, then south to Roosevelt, near the marshaling yards. Don't lose the cab."

"Lose a hack?" Kowalski snickered. "You kiddin'?"

"You ready, Spike?"

His mouth said, "Ready," but the turmoil in his guts said something else.

Debra said, "At Roosevelt we switch Spike to the cab. Once he drops you off, tell him to leave."

One less target, Halleck thought. Impulsively he asked, "Can't we try to get Janey back to the cab first?"

Kowalski's deep voice penetrated his hopes. "Figure the shooter's got Teflon-coated slugs. Go right through an engine block. Taxi's no cover. We've got to get the man."

"I thought you said the bulletproof coat would protect her," Halleck said.

"From copper-jacketed rounds," she said, still holding his arm. "Hell, I don't know if you can even get Teflon slugs in .762."

"Had a little chatter with Scannon's man Myles," Kowalski said. "KGB makes 'em."

"You figure he could have picked 'em up in Afghanistan?" Debra asked.

"Souvenirs," Kowalski said, yanking hard on the wheel, throwing Halleck left. He threw his hands out, keeping his head off the window glass, then pushed himself upright again.

"Just get me there," Halleck said.

"The phone's gonna be ringing for you. We got the number and will keep buzzin'. Head for it right after you cover up the girl. Unless you do that, he'll think you're playin' for time," Kowalski said.

"Are we?" Halleck wanted to know.

"Bet your ass," Kowalski told him. "Five minutes from now there'll be a dozen IR scopes sweeping that area, trying to pick him up."

"How much time does that give me?" Halleck asked.

"Don't count," Debra told him. "Don't hold your breath. Just walk through the plan, as if we don't exist. Check Janey, cover her up. Tell her to keep down, for warmth, for cover. Walk to the ringing phone, make the call to Brian. Order the drop at the other end, but slow. We'll let Scannon move on the mule, once he picks the briefcase up."

"How long?" Halleck still wanted to know.

"Jesus!" Kowalski screamed, jerking the car into a spin. Behind them, the cab's horn bleated. "Assholes like that, we'll be lucky to get there at all," he roared.

"Come on, big guy," Debra said. "How long?"

"Seven minutes to the switch."

"Any way they could see us?" Halleck asked.

"None," Kowalski said. "All clutter, high-rise."

"Just tell the hack to goose it," Debra said.

"Elapsed time?" Halleck said. In his head a clock was running, its units measured not in minutes but in heat loss, the cost not in passing time but passing life. He had brushed only briefly with the cold but it had numbed him through. Now, right now, Janey was sitting in it. Whatever the calculations, he knew that even now, sensitive to cold as she was, she must be suffering. And slowly, unremittingly, freezing. How long? He clutched the stiff ersatz blanket in his lap, suddenly as grateful for the wool lining as for the armor. A gunman was intangible, somehow still unreal. He could not quite imagine what kind of monster would slaughter an innocent child for money. But the cold? The cold was very real. And very deadly.

Debra told him, "Nine minutes since the call, now ten."

"How far?"

"A block to the switch," Kowalski said.

"Ready?" Debra said.

He grabbed a breath, let it escape. "Ready."

The car pulled over and slowed. The hack pulled up beside them, rolled down his window and asked, "You folks ready?"

Halleck in, the hack turned, grabbing for air. "Where to?"

"Northerly Island, the planetarium," Halleck said.

"Christ," he responded. "You could freeze to death out there."

"Right. Let's go. And step on it."

Once on Northerly Island, the cab's tires continued to claw through the heavy snow, breaking drifts, eat up time, time that Janey didn't have. Halleck could almost feel the hack looking around as he said, "Hey! Somethin's in the middle of the field."

"A package," Halleck said. "I'm supposed to pick it up."

"Package shit, it's movin'."

"Get as close as you can to drop me off," Halleck told him. "Then drive away."

"But somebody's out there, freezin', man!"

"Not your problem. Just drive off."

"But you can't *see*, buddy. How you gonna—"

"Forty bucks more"—he pushed the money at the driver—"to drive on."

"What the—"

"Drive on."

"Sure?"

"Sure," he said, letting himself into the blow.

"Good luck, man. You're gonna need it."

Halleck crouched down, stuffed his hands in his pockets, and crabbed forward in the biting wind, hiking his knees to make way through snow that had drifted, in places, up to his thigh. Behind him on the planetarium wall, he could just hear the steady, regular buzzing of the telephone, a beacon in his private sea of darkness, a point on which he would fix his return journey. Ahead of him was Janey, a Janey he could not see. Hearing nothing from her, he shouted, yelled as loud as he could, "Janey."

"Uncle Spike!"

She was alive!

"I'm coming!"

"I can't see you."

What had they done to her? "What?" he said.

"I'm blindfolded. I'm like you."

"Keep talking, Janey. I'll get to you."

"I can't move, either."

"What?"

"They tied me up," she cried.

"I'm coming. Don't try to move now. Keep talking."

"I'm here, Spike, I'm here! Right here!"

Halleck dipped his shoulders more, fought his way through the biting snow, blown and chipped from the night's fall, cold and hard as death, howling at him, slapping and pummeling him like a barroom brawler, a force larger than life yet perversely alive with empty, pointless anger, hitting him again and again with jabbing bursts while his feet slipped and dug and twisted a path in the cold grit that crunched beneath him. Crouching lower he pushed on, wheezing on air suffocatingly cold.

"Spike, hurry! I'm *so* cold!"

"I'm coming," he shouted, his teeth now chattering, the invisible wind a monster ripping at the armored blanket he clutched beneath his arm. He held it as closely as his own life. Still following her chirping voice, he could hear her chattering, "Over here!"

How far, Halleck? They played this game in blind school, this business of training your ear for direction and distance, that seemingly pointless exercise that they said could someday save your life, now was helping save another. Quickly he corrected his approach, judged her to be about twenty-five yards directly ahead.

"Talk to me, Janey."

"Here, Spike. Here!"

He mushed ahead, mired down by deep snow, each step a struggle, his feet being the first since the storm to touch this exact part of the field. Now he was regularly hiking his knees to clear the crest of snow with each new step. If he didn't he would trip, fall down, or mire in place. Clutching the blanket high, keeping the windbreak and refuge dry, he pushed toward Janey, now right ahead, five yards off.

"I hear your feet, Spike!"

In two steps Halleck crashed into her, fell down, still holding the blanket, let his hands find her, hug her, pull the blindfold down, reach for her wrists, loosen the rope, rub the circulation back. Then the bonds on her feet. And perhaps for the first time since she had been taken, she let herself cry. "I was *scared*, Spike. I was so scared."

"I know," he whispered.

"Can we go home *now*, please?"

"Not right now. A few minutes, that's all."

"But I'm *so* cold."

"I know. Just a little time more. Right now I want you to listen to me very carefully, as carefully as you have ever listened to me."

"Okay," she sobbed.

"Are you listening?"

"Yes."

"While I make a phone call, Janey, just one phone call, I want you to wrap yourself up in this blanket" he handed it to her—"and lie down in the snow, as flat as you can. Cover yourself completely, keep warm. Stay out of the wind. Especially your head, Janey. Even keep your head completely covered."

"Okay."

"And wait right here until I come back."

"Okay."

"It will only be few minutes, I promise."

"Okay."

"Have I ever broken a promise?"

"No."

"So wait right here. And whatever happens, whatever you hear or feel, stay under that blanket!"

He got up and trudged off toward the ringing phone, realizing for the first time that it *was* his responsibility, that he had waited too long to act, that he had tried to make himself too cleverly, too obviously, too completely right, that he had, at some level played for Janey's life as if it was a token on a board game, actually thinking, at some unconscious level, that if things didn't work out he would somehow put the pieces at the first square and start again. But that wasn't it at all, never had been. Now he was out, alone, exposed, vulnerable, and next to helpless, wondering where the advantage was, what he could do, out here, to save them both from a sniper's deadly bullets.

Reaching the ringing phone, he picked up and heard Debra's voice say, "She okay?"

"Cold but okay."

"And you?"

"So far . . ."

"Make the call," she said.

"Right."

As she hung up, the dial tone resumed. Maybe Lou Scannon and his FBI men could buy some time. Maybe, but Halleck wasn't counting on it. Carefully, one by one, he pushed in the numbers to reach Brian Granville, wondering if, as he walked away, a bullet would tear through his heart.

"Talk to me, Kowalksi," Janowski said, his eyes poring over Meigs Field from a command post in the press box of Soldier Field.

"Ain't got shit," the big cop said. "Got tracks near the girl, a few, but most of that's been drifted over. Have no idea whatever where this dude is planted."

"Work out in circles, from the center, where the little girl is sitting. Give me anything suspicious at ranges of a hundred yards or so, any place where he could be squatting."

"Can do, sarge," said Kowalski. "But you think he's gonna be on the point at all? I mean, one muzzle flash, we pinpoint that noise with that accoustical array Scannon got us, then he's there, no way he can get off. I see no boats, nothing. Not that he could work a pleasure cruise in those swells. Nothin's gonna fly in there either. That leaves two ways out, if he's out there. He drives or he swims."

"Don't guess, Kowalski. Find him."

"First hundred yards away is all snow. That's it."

"After that?"

"Two hundred yards, nothing 'cept couple trees, not even enough to hide behind. And the water in the yacht harbor and the lake on the other side. Inside of three hundred yards we got the planetarium building, where

Halleck's callin' from. I see him, nobody else. Four hundred yards takes us all the way down Solidarity Drive, the rest water. Nothing there 'cept snowed-in cars."

"Anybody in 'em?"

"Negative, Yano. No objects, no movement, no heat sources."

"Keep going. He's still got a lot of range in that rifle."

"Five hundred yards spills Solidarity into the outer of Lake Shore Drive. Some cars snowed in, abandoned. One looks like the owner tried to dig it out, gave up."

"Have somebody check it out."

"Roger that. At five hundred yards we get a lot of water in the lake and the lake shore down to McCormick Place. Squat there. Again, no objects, no movement, no heat. From shotgun mikes, no accoustical sources either. Zip."

"Keep going. He's somewhere out there, the bastard. How do you think the girl got there? Angels from heaven?"

"Six hundred yards gets interesting," Kowalski said.

"Say what?"

"Six hundred yards we start biting into Grant Park around us here at Soldier Field. I don't see anything but I can almost smell him."

"Talk to me, Kowalski. You're drifting."

"Jano, friend. Six hundred yards is what I would take for a clear shot. Beyond that it gets tougher, unless he's real good."

"Scannon's seen the dossier, Kowalski, and the prints they took at the hideout *do* match. We have a positive and believe me, he's good."

"I still see nothing up to six hundred yards."

"Go to seven."

"Seven gets tough. We start picking up traffic, movement that's normal, and heat sources like buildings, steam grates, the noises that go with 'em. It only gets tougher at eight hundred yards, you get near rail lines and more buildings."

"You say rail lines?"

"Yeah."

"Where?"

"South, inner Lake Shore Drive."

"What's the nearest street you can park on and see Meigs Field?"

Kowalski looked out of his glasses and checked his map before saying, "Calumet."

"How far's that from the nearest L station?"

"Three and a half blocks."

"Perfect," Janowski said. "Check it out."

"Sarge! That's an eight hundred yard pop!"

"I know," Janowski said, "Get going. And another thing . . ."

"Yeah?"

"He'll be near a pay phone. See if Deb can run us a list of all the pay phones within a half mile or so of Meigs Field."

"You think he's gonna put himself in the open like that?"

"What else can he do?"

Kowalski shrugged. "He's a crook? Break into a building. Hell, lots of empty buildings today. A city full of empty buildings, and lots of phones."

"Or he could be right out there, sure as hell we'd bet he'd never dream of doing it," Janowski barked back.

"On my way."

Janowski turned back to working his old eyes over the terrain again, instinctively sure of what reason and evidence had also suggested, that the shooter was not bottled up, but would take his marks from a considerable distance, betting on his skill and the number of rounds in his clip to make a kill, but also limiting the number of rounds he fired to a minimum, as with each shot the chances of locating him increased. Muzzle flashes, parabolic microphones triangulating, the direction the snow would burst as the rounds fell in around the target. Target? A little girl. He checked her out through the field glasses, noticing how remarkably low she was. Nothing vertical. What had Halleck said? Evidently she understood, because she was really hunkered down, not much of anything at all. Unless the marksman were above her, perhaps shooting from a building or raised road, it would be hard to see her at all in the failing light. But if he did, could he hit her? Maybe. The target was still within range, but just barely. Standard copper-jacketed rounds, fired from a range of eight hundred yards, revolving two hundred thousand times a minute after a muzzle velocity of twenty-seven hundred feet per second, could still kill her if they hit her without the Kevlar protection. But she was covered in it now. Unless the sniper had Teflon-coated bullets it would be a tough chore. With them it was only a matter of being on target. If the man was braced into a sniper's harness with the barrel butted against a wall, he wasn't likely to miss his aim. But there was one thing he couldn't control—the wind. Gusting in bursts of twenty miles an hour, it could bump a bullet fired from eight hundred yards by as much as four inches. And for a small target four inches can be the difference between life and death.

Still, for Janey Granville he could only pray. Odds were against the first shot missing. It wasn't his job, he reminded himself, to save her. He had no power to stop the slug in mid-flight, to deflect the bullet from its course. His job was to apprehend the criminal. And whatever happened to the little girl, he was sure they would get the shooter. One round, they would know which direction to turn their eyes and instruments. Two rounds, they would have his position. Three, officers would be moving in, Code Three. Four and he would have to drop the rifle and run—all the roads to escape would be cut off. Five rounds and they would be returning fire. SWAT snipers topping Soldier Field needed only a firing order after they confirmed his position to return the favor he was doing for the Granville girl.

But five shots ought to be all he needed. He could miss one in the wind. But with five both she and Halleck would be dead.

Payoff time. And time to vanish. He tried not to think about the money, tried not to worry about what Tim might think about when he got it, wondered if Tim would be stupid enough to try splitting on his own, decided that Tim knew he would always screw up unless someone held his hand. So the shooter nestled down in the chill of the Continental's interior, his breath bursting into frost, knowing that in the gathering dark the tinted windows made him invisible, thankful for a lucky snow that forced some lazy Yuppie to abandon his car in a roadside drift on Calumet, just inside inner Lake Shore Drive, still awed at how it could have been so perfectly serendipitous, the car, the position, the tinted glass, the cellular phone, which he had used to make the last call to Halleck and the one on which, in minutes, he would get the prearranged signal, "Roger, Jolly Roger," from Tim, letting him know that the easy life had just begun. Still, even now, he wasn't sure. A business deal? A *straight* business deal? With a kid's life at stake? That simple? Or that stupid? Was that the way rich people thought, that everything has its price? Maybe it was. How could he know? He had never been close to rich, until now. Two hundred thousand tax-free dollars. The thought of it made him dizzy.

So he tried not to think of it, to keep the night scope's cross hairs of the Dragunov rifle pinned to the image of the girl as the man who should, if this were just a business deal, be Halleck, stumbled awkwardly toward the girl, holding the blanket he said he would bring for her. Touching thought, though she would need more protection than that. Checking his diver's watch, he assured himself that everything was on schedule, as planned. And soon it would be over.

Five o'clock was drawing close, sapping the light from the sky. Still twenty minutes away, the clouds and winter had already begun shadowing the land. Only the uniform whiteness of snow rendered his target unmistakable. Yet it was that same whiteness, piling here and there in crested drifts, that exploded when struck by hard gusts, throwing up impenetrable curtains of flakes and shaking the Continental so vigorously that the Dragunov's muzzle, steadied against a window brace, shook with the force. How much difference could it make, when he began shooting? Shrouds of snow, up and down in seconds, no hiding place, a hundred and more yards to run, through thick, yielding powder. There was no escape. She hadn't a prayer. The rifle was entirely enveloped by the Continental's cabin, the four-foot length would be braced steadily at both ends, against his shoulder and where it peeked through the front window. The range gave something away. At eight hundred yards the round could play a lot if he didn't compensate for the wind and the drop, and, as he knew, the rifle's own tendency to pull rounds a little left. Still, the position, off the peninsula, if these honest businessmen had brought in the police, would take a lot of looking to find, even without the tinted glass. From here he had quick access to the L, three blocks away. If he drove, it was only seconds. Running, a minute or more. Then lost in a crowd.

As for success, there was little chance he would close the transaction on this end. A clip was already loaded, the rifle set for semiautomatic fire, able to place a round inside a six-inch circle at six hundred yards every three seconds. No one shot mattered. He had ten, if he needed, to finish the job. And, police or not, they couldn't know where he was. How could they? The muzzle flash would be inside the car. And the report would seem to come from nowhere, broken up by the clutter of buildings surrounding him. Knowing that, sure that they didn't have any better chance of finding him here than they did from the short phone calls he had made from the hideout, absolutely positive of that, he began to relax a bit, allowed his heart rate to drop, wiped the sweat from his hands. Calm. He forced a calm. Nothing ruins markmanship like tension.

Taking and releasing a few deep breaths slowly, he held the target in the bright circle of the night scope, watching the man who should be Halleck drop the blanket, the girl crawl under it. Why? Maybe to escape the wind? That must be it. Now the man was starting back to the planetarium wall. All as planned. So far, so good.

Nothing to do now but wait, wait until the money was in Tim's hands. That much they needed. After that, nothing.

On the console between the Continental's customized bucket seats was the cellular phone. Tim had the number. He, on the other end, had the target. Simple business, as Halleck said. So far, no sign of cops. Cops now? What difference could it make? Squeeze the trigger, the girl's gone. Halleck, too, for good measure, since he was the only one who heard my voice. All in a twinkling. Before they could figure out where he was, he would be gone, too. Money or not, he was safe.

Then a chill ran through him.

What if they got Tim?

How to deal with that? Ten minutes after Halleck lifted the handset on the planetarium phone, he had to pop the girl. If Tim didn't have the money then, it was too close. If his partner had the money and ran, he would need to catch up right away. As long as the girl was in danger, under fire or wounded, they would run to her, right? That should give him enough time.

Halleck was too nervous to dial the numbers, though he knew them by heart. His fingers were numb, his mind uncertain. With every heartbeat he felt a rifle pointed at his back. So he pushed *0* and explained to the operator, as they had taught him in school, that he was a blind person, would she put through a number for him. The answer was always the same word, "Sure," in the same condescendingly anodyne tone. Right now he would take it.

One ring only at the other end before Brian's voice said, "Spike?"

"Janey's alive, Brian. She's fine," he chattered.

"Thank God!"

"But I've got to get her out of the cold, soon."

"She's exposed?"

"Under a blanket now, but that won't help for long."

"What are you going to do?"

"Go back, use my own warmth for her, shield her, walk her in." Since it seemed ridiculous for a criminal to trap himself here with only one road out, Halleck figured that if he could walk her back toward the planetarium, shielded in the blanket, stay behind her, the sniper couldn't get to her unless he got him first.

"Any sign of the shooter?"

Although Halleck could not know what Janowski had discovered, he could half feel the rifle barrel trained on his back. Still he said, "No. Just make the drop now. I've got to figure there's some kind of clock running here that requires your pick-up man there to call back in a certain number of minutes after I hang up here, or else he starts shooting. We've got to make it seem as if we're holding up our part of the bargain."

"Right," Brian said. "Be careful."

Halleck didn't know how a blind man was supposed to dodge high-powered rifle bullets. Still he said, "You, too. Walk away from the briefcase as soon as you put it down. Don't even look around. Let Scannon's men handle it."

"Okay. Good luck."

"Yeah," he said, wondering above his fear how lucky he was now, pulling up his collar and shoving himself back into the wind, shouting, "Janey!" hearing her muffled response from under the blanket, "Still here, Spike!"

Lowering his head, he pushed himself against the wind, toward the weak voice, oblivious of anything else. The surest way she could die, irrespective of who was out there or what they did, rifle or not, was freezing. If she were to avoid that, she had to move, the sooner the better.

Lou Scannon sidled up to the pillar and looked out, his stubby hand deep in his pocket clutching the walkie-talkie. Behind him the waitress in the near-empty restaurant asked, "More coffee, sir?"

He smiled and said, "Not just now, thanks," annoyed that she had not taken the big tip as a signal to go away. Unheedful, she smiled some more, pirouetted as young girls do, swung her hips vigorously, and marched back to the kitchen. When she was gone, Scannon extracted the walkie-talkie and told the dozen men on its dedicated channel, "Dropping now," as he watched Brian Granville, as instructed, place the briefcase under the mailbox located in the center of the block on the south side of Hubbard between Wabash and Rush, turn without looking, and walk off. Perfect form. He could be running drugs, Scannon thought.

Except for gossamer steam vapors bannered on the cold wind, the street Brian Granville left behind was deserted, empty of people or cars, without sign of activity or interest, a monument to the hard arctic cold that had the city in its grip. People didn't want to go out, cars failed to start. As a result, nothing moved without a need.

Two minutes passed before a four-wheel drive vehicle, a Bronco, mushed by, slid to stop at the intersection of Hubbard and Rush, waited out the red light, then moved off in the direction of the lake. Surveillance? Scannon had time to be patient. "Hold your positions," he told his men.

So they waited, on loading docks and behind doorways, unseen and nearly undetectable.

Three more minutes passed before an old woman, bundled in layers of old clothes, her head scarfed, face cloaked in a muffler, pressed by on the wrong side of the street, stopping, looking confused, moving to the corner of Hubbard and Wabash before turning north into the full force of the wind. "I don't think so," Scannon told his men.

He began to think that the mule might be taking a wait-and-see attitude. Maybe today he could afford it. Not many people out. Nobody but city workers, street people, and someone like him, who had no choice. When you're thinking about electrocution or life in the slammer, anything looks suspicious. But then if he doesn't move, he must know that some bum is guaranteed to walk off with it, just as happened for Janowski at Cabrini yesterday. And this guy can't expect Halleck to keep the girl out in the cold while he twiddles his thumbs. Something's gotta happen soon.

He checked his watch.

Closing in on five-twenty, streetlamps popping on. Soon.

Seven minutes had passed since the drop.

Skewered from afar by five pairs of binoculars, the briefcase remained of no apparent interest to anyone.

Suddenly a man in a fatigue jacket and McMahon sunglasses popped through the brass revolving door at the Hotel Excelsior at the corner of Hubbard and Rush, north, jaywalked quickly, hands jammed into pockets, face hidden in a black and gold ski mask.

"Any bets?" Scannon asked his men.

Now Scannon could do the job his way. Forget Halleck. He never had it right. This is the way it would have come down, sans FBI. Not as a business deal, money for a girl's life. No way. The bag man would pick up the cash, pass Granville heading east, blow him away as he stood there, and by the clock, as soon as they confirmed the cash, have the sniper take out the girl and Halleck at Northerly Island. Maximum cooperation from a hostage family, minimum vulnerabilities for apprehension. For the businessmen Granville and Halleck, zero return on investment, zero chance of survival. But for the kidnappers, take the money and run, three dead, no leads, free and clear to do it again.

At least that's the way it shaped up to Scannon.

"Stand by," he told his men.

The ski mask swiveled up and down as if addicted to the soaring chrome and glass architecture around him, his eyes always coming back to the mailbox. He finished slanting across the street, stepped up onto the sidewalk, and headed toward the briefcase.

"As soon as he touches the handle"—Scannon breathed into the mouthpiece—"get Granville inside, fast. Then let's take this asshole."

"If he's armed, boss?" Fabrinelli's voice.

"You guys know how to shoot off a kneecap, for Chrissakes. Take this prick alive. He's got a phone call to make, tellin' his partner how rich they are."

"Right."

The ski mask dipped at the mail-box and swept up the briefcase as the free hand dipped into the fatigue jacket, retrieving a small automatic pistol.

"Move," said Scannon. "All stations close. Let's not wait for engraved invitations here."

Instantly the street corners surrounding the mailbox flooded with agents, hand-over-hand on service revolvers. One held a badge high and yelled, "FBI. Drop your weapon and lift your hands over your head. NOW."

The ski mask swirled, turned to the corner where an

instant before Brian Granville had stood, now occupied by two men, their eyes sighted over pistol barrels, focused on him.

Scannon stood sheltered in a doorway, directing, and said, "Don't fire unless he does."

The trapped man whipped his head around, spun, vaulted the hood of a parked Mercedes and ran for the door of a closed bakery in the middle of the block.

"Got him," Scannon said, until now fearing there could be a driver involved.

Without stopping the man blew off the door handle with a single shot, splintered the wooden frame, and began pulling on the door. Then, very slowly, his hands went up, the gun rolling off his fingertips. The agent who had been concealed inside the bakery was heard on the walkie-talkie to say, "Surprise!"

Scannon waddled up seconds later, saying, "Martinez, read him Miranda, and quick."

Martinez pulled a laminated card from his suit pocket and recited, "You have the right to remain silent . . ." as another agent cuffed him. At the end, Martinez asked, "Do you understand these rights as I have explained them to you?:"

"Of course he does," Scannon said, ripping off the ski mask.

"I wanna lawyer," the man said.

Scannon pushed his nose up to the man's face and said. "You're gonna make a phone call, all right. But for you, we make a special exception. You we treat special. You we're gonna give *two* phone calls. You understand?"

The man shook his head, no.

"You want not to fry? Call your buddy. Tell him you got the money, like you planned."

"Don't know what the fuck yur talkin' 'bout."

"No? Guess what? I don't know what the fuck you're talkin' 'bout when you say police brutality." Scannon seized the suspect's nuts and squeezed so ferociously all the man could do was gasp. When he got his breath back, he whispered, "You fucker!" Scannon smiled sharply, turned to Martinez and said, "Martinez, I think this suspect is resisting arrest. Help me out on this. Am I confused or—"

"Looks like he's resisting arrest to me, boss."

"You remember the number, scumbag?"

"Okay," the man gasped, still doubled over.

"There's a phone on the corner, as you advised Mr. Granville. Let's move."

The man slumped and tottered toward it, Martinez supporting him with an arm, the other agents clustered in.

"Tell me the number first," Scannon demanded, shaking the man until his teeth rattled.

"IM2RICH"

Scannon reached for the man's nuts again.

"I swear, it's the same as the license number on the car!"

"Car?"

"Cellular phone."

"Tell Janowski," Scannon said to Martinez, "the shooter's in a fucking car!"

Turning his eyes hard on the bagman, Scannon said, "Now let's make this call and make it good."

"What do I say? I'll say anything you want. Just don't smash my balls again."

"Tell him you got the money."

"I got the money."

"Right."

Scannon punched in the number, handed the phone over, and pulled out his revolver, placing the barrel against the man's temple before smiling.

His eyes locked onto the kidnapper's as the man said, "I got the money."

Scannon nodded, for very good. What he couldn't hear was the sniper's agonizing moan on the other end.

He dropped the receiver into its modular cradle, picked up his rifle, tightened the sniper's harness, and braced himself against the far side of the rear seat, his mind racing.

Not "Roger, Jolly Roger," the code, but "I got the money."

So Tim got shit and they got Tim.

No time to cry over busted pipe dreams, he told himself, pushing the first round into the chamber, wondering how long it would be until they knew where he was.

Long enough, he said, to cut losses.

And long enough to get away.

Hit and run, hadn't they trained him for that? And hadn't he shown them, even Soviet pursuit teams, that they could never get him?

The muzzle rested steadily on the Continental door, pinched in place by window glass, beaded in on a small target surrounded by a white background, knowing that the girl would be necessary to establish his guilt, beyond a reasonable doubt. So first the girl. Then Halleck, the liar.

Simple business deal, my ass.

Tim would crack like a melon dropped from the Sears Tower, would spill his story and the rest, but then Tim, as his military record showed, was a nut case too. Hardly an unimpeachable witness. That's one of the reasons he had chosen Tim. That and Tim's rage to follow. He was like a sheep that way, but a sheep on the way to slaughter.

Sayonaro, Tim.

Even from eight hundred yards, the flattened image of the girl half filled the bright disk of the night scope, her dark blanket clearly outlined on the snow. Quickly he tried to size up the target, wanted a head shot, the kind Oswald used on Kennedy, could find nothing. Everything beneath the blanket was just flat, as if she were trying to escape the wind. Never mind something under there is her. And, another part of his training reminded him, something under there is nothing, just snow, substrate. Where to shoot? Shoot the highest point or the bumpiest point. No guarantees, but people look up and out with their heads first, to see.

Why would she raise her head at all?

To see Halleck.

Unless Halleck told her to lie flat. But then this is the kid's uncle, right? Her first friend in days? Her saviour? Her only chance? The only person, as far as she knows, in miles. How is she going to react if he goes down? She's not going to think. She's not going to obey instructions, she's going to get up. She's going to get up and run to help him.

So take out Halleck, flush the girl.

He brought his sight around to Halleck, lumbering almost blindly through the alabaster wilderness, lurching first one way, then another, slipping in up to the hip, getting up. Sure does move a lot. But all in one line, head-on.

He brought up Halleck's image in the hatched cross hairs of the magnifying scope, drew a bead on his heart. If he hit within a six-inch circle, he still would kill him. It was the best shot when he allowed for margin of error, gave him a Jesus factor. After the first shot the target would stop moving, sit still for him. The second should do it, once he had finished the girl.

He took up the aim, closed his finger down on the trigger, took a deep breath, and started to release it, slowly, squeezing gradually.

Janowski was frantic. "All stations, all stations. Find me a 1988 Lincoln Continental, custom job. Illinois plates, believe it or not, IM2RICH. Tinted glass, cellular phone. Christ, wet bar for all I know. Our shooter is out there in it. And he's within range."

Kowalski's voice burst through the static. "Not in traffic, Jano. No way he's gonna make a shot like that movin'. He's parked. That means he's outside Lake Shore Drive. And that means he's got a eight-hundred-yard shot."

"You wanta just *find* him?"

"We're on it, boss."

The blast of air hit the Continental like a hammer, just as the Dragunov's firing pin struck the bullet's primer. As the first round fired, he lost the target in swirling snow, cursing, bringing the rifle back. But when the wind dropped, the target had fallen.

The round hit Halleck like a Mike Tyson punch, knocking him backward, leaving him sprawled in the snow, his wind gone. He shook his head, trying to clear his thoughts, touched his left shoulder, felt the hot wetness that must be blood, understood instantly that he was going into shock, would be unable to assess his own condition, but would fight for life until he lost consciousness.

How bad was it?

No idea.

His coat was soaked around the shoulder, but nothing low, in the stomach or heart, not even lungs. He was breathing fine, no coughing, nothing trickling from his mouth. His heart was racing, undamaged. His intestines seemed fine, undamaged. His hand felt low. No blood, no pain. Only his shoulder, which burned and ached, throbbed, failed to respond when he called for support from that side. Rolling the other way, he kept flat and thought of praying.

Why not?

If there is a God, please show yourself. If not, pardon my delusion. But I'm not asking you to save me. Janey maybe, but not me. They gave me the score in blind school and he remembered it well, memorized it, recited it like a prayer, when he went to bed. "The seeing world," it went, "sees, and looks for solutions in what it sees, even when what it sees misleads or deceives it. The advantage of being blind is that you cannot be misled or deceived by what you do not see. And you will look to solve your own problems in ways the sighted cannot see, not only because you must, but because you can. Instead of being dominated and tyrannized by one sense, you will make use of every one you have. And you will, above all, think. You *will* find, in your search, the solution that remains unseen to those who can see. And you will find it not in looking for it, but in thinking for it."

In thinking for it.

And how do you outrace a bullet from an unseen killer?

You don't, he admitted.

Why hadn't the shooter finished it? Halleck was lying in the snow, a sitting duck. No. No, he wasn't. He wasn't sitting at all. He was lying. A minute ago, when the bullet blew through his shoulder, he was standing. No more. Maybe, just maybe, the sniper couldn't see enough to be sure.

"Spike!" he heard Janey scream.

Suddenly, for the first time since the nightmare began, Halleck filled with terror. Janey might panic. Realizing he had been shot, seeing that, she might instinctively get up and run.

He had to stop her.

"Get down," he shouted, rolling his head her way, projecting the words as loud as he could. "Stay under the blanket, Janey!"

"Spike, you're *hurt!*"

"I'm okay, Janey."

"Spike," she sobbed.

"Janey Granville," he yelled, trying for anger, feeling light with effort. "I've never lied to you in my life and if you don't get under that blanket and stay there until I say so—"

He heard the second shot ring out.

"Janey!" he screamed.

It was a clean shot. He figured the bump in the blanket that stuck up after Halleck went down was the girl's head. The sight was perfect, the squeeze even, the muzzle steady.

Everything was clean and perfect.

So it surprised him when the round hit two and a half inches right of where he aimed it.

Then he realized it was the wind, gusting over twenty knots now. But the wind doesn't explain why the bullet appeared to skip off the blanket, rather than ripping it to shreads. Maybe it was a ricochet angle, so low it was bound to skip. He lined it up again.

"Halleck's hit," Janowski said.

"I'm going," Debra Seraphicos said.

"Stay," Janowski said.

"I'm going," she said again.

"Stay. That's an order."

"I quit," she said.

"Great. Would it help if I said please?"

"Eat it, Jano."

Then she was gone.

"Great," Jano grumbled, raising the field glasses, seeing something that he needed. The second round skipped off the Kevlar blanket. Working his eyes back along the line of snow kicked up by the slug, he said, "Kowalski, he's somewhere down this side of the McCormick Place. Try Calumet." He raised his field glasses and waited for the snow to clear, scanning in the right direction, spotting the Continental for the first time, shouting, "Calumet, Kowalski! I've got a dark-colored Continental with tinted glass parked on Calumet! Move your ass!"

22

He saw Halleck fall, swallowed up by icy mists, sure he had killed him. Instantly he switched his sight to the girl, saw what must have been her head pop up beneath the blanket and fired, saw the round pushed off by wind, seem to skip when it should have burrowed. Could his trajectories be that far off?

Why hadn't she bolted, gone to help her kin?

Unless he warned her down.

Unless he was still alive, told her, even though hit, he was okay. And unless the little girl, obedient, believed him. Then the only way to flush her out, if she was looking, was to gut-shoot Halleck, to leave so much blood spilled across the snow that the little girl would run to him, as she would without thinking, as she would after a puppy flattened in the street, mindless to the dangers of traffic.

How long?

It should only take two more shots to kill all the witnesses or participants. He couldn't afford impatience.

Away from the girl he moved the scope, found Halleck flattened and low, a bad target, but good enough. In the cross hairs he centered the forehead, drew a breath, let it out slowly, began to squeeze the trigger.

Halleck, dazed but still alert, screamed at himself to think. Of course there was no running from bullets. But was he left with nothing? Pushing himself to one side to relieve the pain in his shoulder, he felt the powdery snow slip neatly through his fingers, almost as if it weren't there.

As he moved, in the very second or less, he felt something snap by his skull, grazing his flesh. It passed in a high-pitched whirl, followed less than a second later by the crack of a rifle firing. Supersonic round, got there before the report. He had heard it before. If you don't dodge until you hear the sound, you're already dead.

Reaching his fingers up he touched the side of his head, felt the warm blood oozing, knew that if he didn't do something, the next time he could be dead. Even if lucky, luck doesn't last if you don't help it out. Janowski, Kowalski, and all the SWAT police in the world could never undo the terrible damage from a well-aimed high-powered rifle.

"Spike," Janey screamed again.

"Stay down, Janey!"

Then it hit him, as hard and certain as the bullet would have, had it struck.

Dig.

Burrow, Halleck.

Here you are in twenty inches, enough to bury a prone body easily, enough to deflect or slow rounds perfectly aimed and enough, more than enough, to hide a dark object from detection, especially with the light failing, with the sifting and drifting and swirling of snow in the wind.

Working feverishly with his hands, he burrowed madly into the snow, forcing his damaged arm to help, to flick snow away, while the other one did yeoman's service, hurling buckets of snow into the air. In seconds he had easily displaced enough to form a shallow trench, slip in, kept hurling snow out, wedging himself deeper and deeper, moving below the surface, out of sight.

Another curtain of snow raised and lowered before the high-powered scope cleared, showing . . . nothing.

Where Halleck had been was solid white.

Scanning the area, figuring the target had risen to run, to escape the incoming fire, he again found nothing.

Where was he?

Checking back, he found some speckles of blood from the first shot staining the snow, but nothing else.

What the hell?

It didn't make sense.

Shaking it off, he moved his sights back to the girl.

At the same instant he heard the wail of sirens.

Easy, easy. Get it right.

The combat sniper night scope drew its hatched cross hairs onto the blanket, saw the bump higher now, as if she were looking for something, as if she, too, thought that Halleck had, well, just disappeared. Patience.

A second more, another, and the blond hair and crumpled bow showed, her mouth moving, maybe shouting. Didn't matter. This was the shot, the only one he needed. The wind went calm, the field cleared.

Perfect.

Drawing a slow breath and exhaling, he slowly squeezed the trigger, fully focused on his aim, forcing himself to ignore the slow, almost inaudible hushing sound to his right.

The cross hairs were pinned perfectly on the foramen magnum, back of the skull, when the firing pin hit the cap and the bullet left the chamber. Bingo! he thought.

Not knowing what had happened, the skirl of shattering glass struck him cold with shock.

Pulling his eyes up from the scope, he heard the pickup's driver swearing, "What the fuck's going on, you asshole?" as he skidded to a stop, throwing open the door, storming toward him.

Out, his mind said.

Unlatching the Continental's door, he threw himself backward, falling on the sidewalk, struggling awkwardly with the sniper's strap, pivoting to bring the barrel around, watching the man's hands go up as he said, "Shit!" and turn, unable to see the round discharge that exploded the base of his skull, flattening him in the road.

No witnesses, he reminded himself, unable to quell his racing heart, knowing that the pickup's headlamp had taken the lethal bullet intended for the girl, knowing that if the girl was up, mushing through the snow to save her uncle, it wouldn't take much of a shot to kill her.

Using the Continental's roof to brace the long barrel, ignoring the approaching sirens, he lined up a shot, filled the night scope with target, saw the little girl half exposed, was distracted by something else, closing. Not Halleck. Who? A woman? Who?

Never mind, shoot. Kill the girl.

He was bringing the target into focus again when the first squad car fishtailed through the intersection of Calumet and Cullerton, two blocks to his right. Sidearms extended through the windows, two uniforms firing.

Bullets sung off the ice, whined off the Continental's roof, forcing him to swing his weapon their way and fire, exploding the patrol car's windshield. The driver apparently blinded, the car swung wildly his way, impaling itself on a fire hydrant fifteen yards away.

The policeman riding shotgun rolled out of the listing car, clutching a riot gun, and was cut down, his hands gripping his own throat where the round had hit.

Before he could re-target the girl, a second police car arrived, this one to his left. From the scream of sirens, he knew that more were coming fast.

Sighting in, he blew out the windshield and began to run, thinking only of escape, too afraid to drop the rifle as he had planned, knowing more than fearing that he would need it to protect his retreat. Double time, he raced due west on Twenty-first, heading for the L.

Kowalski coordinated the hunt, stationed on the top of the stair of the nearest L station, taking and relaying information to Janowski, who was on his way. "Two cars down, two officers down, one apparently dead, another incapacitated. Two other officers on the scene, vehicle immobilized, are in pursuit on foot. Report suspect armed and dangerous, last seen heading west on foot. We have the area bottled up with vehicles, Jano. North on Eighteenth, south on Twenty-first. Only one way we're leaving open and I'm here."

Looking east, Kowalski muttered, "Come to Papa," and gripped the pistol in his heirloom greatcoat.

Halleck heard Debra Seraphicos yell over the wind, "Spike!"

Pulling himself up in the snow he said, "Get down!"

"It's over, they're in pursuit," she said, falling down beside him. "How's the shoulder?"

"Hurts like hell," he said. "Where's Janey?"

"Spike!" said the little girl.

"Coming," said Halleck, turning to Debra. "Could you help me?"

"I think so." She smiled back, knowing he couldn't see it, content that she knew the man well enough to understand that he heard the smile in her voice. "How long are you going to require these services?"

Draping his good arm around her neck, they pushed into the snow. "How long is the offer good for?" he came back.

"Day at a time, Spike."

"Sounds fair to me," he said.

In two minutes they reached Janey, who peeked up and said, "Who is this lady, Spike?"

"A friend," he told her.

"A friend with a blanket, honey. I'll bet you're cold," Debra said.

"I can't wait to tell Chombo about this. He won't believe it."

Halleck realized suddenly that neither could he. Forgetting that, he drew Debra closer so that together they formed a shield against the wind. "Nobody can complain about you not being able to take care of a kid," she yelled, keeping her head down, bucking the gusts, turning slowly to her side, again smiling. "You ever think of having any?"

"Not until now," he said, feeling her arm tighten around his waist.

From between them he heard Janey shiver, stuttering, "I-I-love you, Spike. You never break a promise. Ever."

"Bring him in slow," Kowalski said. "Give him room. We got civilians up here."

"If we get a shot, should we take him?" The voice of one of the cops crackled over the walkie-talkie.

"He's got a scope and special training. We have two men dead. Don't push it. Let's try to make him think he's escaped, just give him the track to the station. Let me take it here."

"You need backup?"

"Got units up and down the line, in case things go wrong here," Kowalski said. "But let's see what I can do solo."

"All yours."

Kowalski, never a reader, pulled in a copy of the *Trib* to break the wind, looking over the top to watch for company. He had the description from the first contact and hell, not even a Kabuki actor could change that fast on the run.

"Come to Papa," he said again, checking his watch. Only minutes now. He started to clank down the latticed steel stairs to street level, needing to follow the fox to the right platform.

At street level he raised his collar against the swirling wind, flecked with shards of ice, cutting at his face, narrowing his eyelids until he could barely see. An instant later the street lights flickered on, casting the intersection in a hard pale yellow, lining Cullerton with buoys of glare, illuminating an approaching figure.

He wasn't hard to spot.

No one else was out, except one lady, underdressed in a housecoat, a small dog tethered on a long leash, barking and whining at his bursting bladder, frantic to yellow the fresh-fallen snow, tugging on his mistress, nearly toppling her on the slick steps.

The approaching man, over six feet, huddled in an arctic fatigue parka surmounted by a lined hood, swirled in surprise, his hand half-leaving the pocket in which it was tucked, showing, only momentarily, what Kowalski was willing to bet his life was the handle of a service automatic. But when the man saw the hapless woman, the yapping, peeing dog, he relaxed, dipped his head and shoulders into the wind, resumed his trek west on Cullerton toward the L station, looking up, squinting to see if it was all clear.

Not wanting to spook him, Kowalski had to decide the role he was to play. Quickly he decided on the irate husband, one he knew well, waiting impatiently in foul weather for a spouse who had probably become hopelessly mired in deep snow, and would never arrive. He raised his head and turreted, looking both ways on Archer, then back along 19th, shaking his head in disgust, pacing furiously back and forth, slapping his sides to exorcize the cold. And, in the corner of his vision, he watched the man approach.

There was no sign of the rifle, which by now, Kowalski bet, lay abandoned, perhaps quickly buried in deep snow or chucked far into a narrow alley, somewhere east of his present position. So it was man against man, pistol against pistol, waiting for the right moment. Kowalski had no idea whether the man would give himself up. He had to be ready to accept that he wouldn't and prepared himself for what needed to be done.

Half a block to go.

Suspect approaching.

Kowalski's left hand had submerged the walkie-talkie in his deep greatcoat pocket while his right held his weapon, almost toylike, his huge index finger filling the trigger guard.

Close now, seconds.

The man ducked his head, dipped his shoulder, and battled a gust of wind crossing State, oblivious to the blaring horn of a passing car, feinting, dodging, moving straight ahead, as if he had no time, none at all, to lose. Without delay he headed for the northbound platform, briefly spinning full circle, checking his rear.

Kowalski began sidling that way, slowly, a natural movement, only ambling, seemingly aimless, muttering muted curses, railing at fate, the kind of undirected noises that vent growing anger and frustration. "Jesus, where is she?" he said, loud enough for the passing man to hear.

He slowed, turned, as did Kowalski, going the other way.

No cop is going to give you his back as a target, is he, shithead? Kowalski thought.

When the suspect clanged onto the first step as he ascended to the platform, Kowalski turned to follow, but slowly, cautiously, giving him room. South of him came the whirring, rattling, thundering sound of an approaching train.

Now.

Ten steps behind, his steps quieter, Kowalski wondered where to take him. Above him on the platform twenty-five or more people had gathered, their eyes anxiously turned south, fixed on the approaching headlights of the train, their breath pulsing plumes. Too much risk there. From here on, whether on the train or off, there would always be more people. Now it was him and the kidnapper alone on the steps.

Now it was time.

Kowalski took a deep breath, tightening the grip on his pistol, beginning to reveal it. He had the man's back. All timing now, just the right moment, but soon, real soon.

He didn't have that choice.

Suddenly the walkie-talkie in his pocket exploded with Janowski's voice, "Kowalski, hey! You have him?"

It was loud enough for the suspect to hear.

Time seemed to slow down, drag, and flow. Kowalski could hear his own words as if his mind had raced ahead of events, was looking back at what had already happened, and that mind heard him scream, "Police! Drop your weapon!" as the man spun and dipped, his hand, full of pistol, clearing the parka pocket.

And almost home! his mind roared as he spun.

No surrender.

Never surrender!

Wasn't that what they had hammered into him? Wasn't that, wounded and bleeding, tortured and nearly broken, the creed he had always followed? Why was it suddenly different now?

Did they expect him to simply put down his gun and walk into the electric chair? Or if they were "merciful" to rot away a lifetime in a holding tank, his ass daily fagbait? Did they really?

And hadn't he always, but always, made it?

Why different now?

Why?

Just shrink your enemy's target and make your shot.

One shot.

One shot only.

That's all.

All in a second.

What was a second?

His mind, fast as the thoughts whipped in, was still behind his twisting body, its arm extending, the barrel of the automatic a deadly integral part with that mind, that body, that arm, one reflexive killing machine without hesitation, confusion, or mercy.

The gunsight quickly crossed the right shoulder of the target and began to move into the center of the chest as his finger closed on the trigger.

Kowalski heard the round explode, felt the bullet all through his arm, as it left his gun. He didn't know why the man had tried to beat the odds, didn't know what he could have been thinking. By the time the suspect started to swirl, the cop had his mark, hand over hand, center of the back just below the head.

He couldn't miss, even with the turn.

He was so close.

Eight feet, maybe less.

What did a few inches matter?

Nothing.

He was so close.

When the bullet struck, the twisting body spewed blood across his coat, up on his neck, under his chin. As if it were alive, an organism of its own, the platform exploded in screams, was joined and overwhelmed seconds later by the shrieking L brakes, the same sound, the very same, that Halleck had picked out on the tapes.

Breathing quickly, life somewhat crisper than a second ago, and somehow infinitely more precious, Kowalski suddenly realized that in this moment he, too, was hearing more, almost every snowflake falling on the metal handrail to his left as the kidnapper's body tumbled, thumped down three steps, and jammed against his legs, the eyes open, lifeless, astonished in death at the irrevocable reality of fatal error, somehow so filled with terror and, at the same time, yearning, that the man, or what had seconds ago been a man, looked poignantly pathetic. It was a look which, it seemed, was supposed to make Kowalski ashamed of his actions, his self-defense, his profession, himself. Those eyes, so wide, so disbelieving, eloquently pleaded that there was, or might have been, a life worth living, somewhere deep inside.

Taking a deep breath, exhaling vapor, pocketing his gun, he looked down, deep into those pleading eyes and said, "Too late now," then stepped aside, letting the corpse cartwheel down the stairway.

Into his ears, their sense heightened by his brush with death, came all sounds, the skirling, howling, wailing sirens, converging from all directions, the still screaming passengers on the L platform, the hoarse barking of Janowski's voice filtering through his pocket, saying, "Come in, Kowalski. Do you read?"

Slowly he pulled the walkie-talkie out and responded, "I read. Kowalski here. Suspect resisted arrest. He's dead."

"You okay?"

Kowalski smiled, letting his pistol dangle at his side, looking around as the flashing beacons condensed around him, lifting his eyes to see the two L security guards bracketing the newels at the top of the stairs, beyond them the curious, horrified swarm of eyes peering down at the lifeless body sprawled at the base of the stairway. Clicking the switch to speak, he said, "I'll make it. How's the girl?"

"Cold, but untouched. She'll make it, too."

"But he got Halleck?"

"Halleck was hit, but he'll make it."

"Jano?"

"Yeah?"

"Does this mean we get to watch the Bears game this Saturday?"

23

Halleck heard the crowd detonate with cheers and lurched forward on the sofa, turning to his left to ask Debra, "What happened?"

"Walker coughed up the ball. The Bears recovered."

"Who on the Bears?" He was trying to visualize, to image what must have happened from what he knew. Using his mind this way, he had recently discovered, was the second-best thing to seeing and infinitely better than brooding in the darkness.

"I can't tell," she said, pressing on his thigh to get a better look. "It's a pile of 'em."

Halleck could see that, too, and laughed. Three days had passed since they pulled Janey from the snowy field on Northerly Island. Nearly two had passed sleeping off the uppers he used to push himself to exhaustion. Still a bit woozy, he had joined the other "heros," as his sister Ellie had called the FBI and police, to celebrate Janey's safe return by watching the Bears destroy the Dallas Cowboys on the frozen tundra of Soldier Field. He could imagine them all, gladiators armored in high-impact pads, layered in thermal underwear, their breath pulsing white plumes as dragons would fire. Because he had seen it all once, he could almost see it now.

"It's the 'Fridge,' " Debra said.

"Nah," Kowalski said. "It was Dent. The Fat One stole it from him at the bottom of the pile."

"How do you know?" Debra laughed in astonishment at the suggestion.

Kowalski must have shrugged. Halleck could almost hear it. After a pause that was just enough time for a shrug, he said, "Just seems like something he would do, y'know, to impress Ditka."

Halleck laughed at his imagination, good as a sighted person, projecting a huffing, puffing, heaving mountain of flesh squirming and pulling on inflated pigskin.

"So how's the shoulder?" Kowalski said.

"Still sore," Halleck answered, chafing at the strap that held his left arm against the body. "Throbs an ache, nothing really intense."

"Well, I promise you he'll never shoot you again."

Or never try to steal another kid away from her parents, he thought. For reasons he didn't understand, but perhaps because he lacked confidence in the courts, he told Kowalski, "Thanks."

"You're welcome. So what did they put you on, painkillers?"

"Nah," Halleck imitated Kowalski. "I wanna enjoy this."

"Me, too. Have you tried the dip? Great dip."

"Down in front." Janowski yelled at the big cop, moving next to Halleck, whispering, "I never been'ta Lake Forest before, Halleck. I mean this is something. The Granvilles must of really busted the piggybank for this shindig. There's everything here! Booze up the cazoose, chips and dips, hors d'oeuvres, little sandwiches without crust, with toothpicks stuck through 'em . . ."

"Don't eat the toothpicks, Jano," Debra said.

"I know that!"

"Just relax, sergeant," Halleck confided, responding in the same guarded whisper that Janowski had used to express his wonder. "Lucullan extravaganzas are de rigueur for this neighborhood."

"*De* what?" Janowski stuttered.

"Standard fare." Halleck laughed. "No extra charge."

"Here come the Feds. No place for a small-town cop with them around. I gotta get me another drink," Janowski said. And Halleck could almost see, in his mind's eye, the big sergeant shake his head, half wonder, half confusion.

Halleck could feel the shape of sound change as Janowski was displaced by Scannon, who knelt down, laboring for breath, paying the price of years of inactivity. "How'ya enjoying the game?"

"Fine," Halleck said, not knowing what to expect. Unlike Janowski, who just wanted to muddle through, Scannon sounded right away like a man with an agenda.

"Everybody here for the Bears?"

The room roared approval.

"How about you, inspector?" Debra asked.

"I love to see Dallas lose," he said. "And I can take the Bears, except when they play the Redskins. That's different."

An instant passed as Halleck listened to Scannon gulp down his drink, rattle the ice, clear his throat, inadvertently losing alcoholic vapors. His nose told him what others wouldn't—or couldn't. It sorted through the odor and concluded that the inspector had settled on Chivas Regal, accepting an opportunity that might not come again for some time.

Finally he said, "You should be proud, Halleck."

"Why?"

"You did what I thought was impossible. You took a collection of background sounds and by using your brain, and your knowledge of this city, you located where they were keeping the girl."

"It was too late," he said flatly.

"Not in the end," he said. "Besides, in truth, and off the record, half of that was our fault. We just didn't believe it could be done, so we hung you out to dry. If we had pulled your way, maybe we could have closed in sooner. You never know."

"You never know," Halleck said.

Brian Granville, sounding like the happiest man in the world, swooped in, leaned down. "Spike, Spike! How about a beer?"

"Yeah, okay."

"St. Pauli Girl okay?"

"Sure. Fine."

Brian whirled off, picking up a few orders along the way, yelling to Ellie, who hushed him back.

Scannon started to say something when the TV exploded in cheers again, forcing Halleck to turn once again to Debra and ask, "What now?"

"McMahon to Gault, touchdown. Gault made Dallas buy the inside move turned the corner around, then took it to the opposite post. They didn't lay a glove on him."

"Love to see Landry's face," Halleck said with a chuckle.

"He's like always, figuring his investments or something, arms folded across his chest, that little hat on his bald head."

"Hey, watch that about bald," Janowski yelled from the bar.

Everyone laughed but Scannon, who got back to the point, asking Halleck, "Did you read the coverage in the *Trib*?"

"No," Halleck said simply.

Brian Granville swept by, announced, "Beer," and shoved it into Halleck's outstretched hand. He took it to his lips, savored the simple flavor of a good thing.

"Well, the article said nothing, except the girl was recovered, one kidnapper was killed, the other in custody. No specifics."

"That's good. The family appreciates the restraint," Halleck said.

"Restraint?" Scannon scoffed, almost choking on his ice. "The press would have eaten this up whole if we had given them the skinny. If we had given them the details you'd be set up for a tickertape parade down Michigan Avenue, Halleck. You know that?"

"No," he said.

"But there's more here than just the comfort of getting Janey back," Scannon said.

"Not for me there's not," Halleck said, sipping the beer.

"Halleck," Scannon whispered. "You've opened up a whole new dimension of forensic investigation. You've perfected a way of using the telephone to locate a criminal. Think of the implications! We're not just talking about kidnappings here, we're talking about terrorism, extortion, about locating the collaborators of drug kings by analyzing incoming calls from legal wiretaps. There's no limit to what we can do!"

"Feel free," Halleck said, his turn to shrug.

"But you're the expert," Scannon said, almost whining.

"Lots of people can do sound effects, backwards and forwards. Stan Black, for example, who helped me set up here."

"I talked with Mr. Black, who said *you* were the best, who said that you, blindfolded, used to identify the most bizarre sounds at parties."

"True."

"Then what do you think?"

"I've got an interest here in Chicago." He reached over and squeezed Debra's thigh.

She said, "The man is not lying, inspector."

"You don't have to leave Chicago. I can use you as a consultant, as an expert . . ."

Halleck shook his head. "Stan Black is just as good."

"You want to know what Black said? He said that he was just like everyone else who could see, that they refused to stop *looking* for things in order to start *listening* for them. He said, in his words, 'Ironically, only a blind person can escape the distractions and focus on the evidence.' "

Halleck snickered. "Stan just doesn't want to get taken away from films. That's his love." And was once mine, he thought, shaking it off to say, "That's what he does. That's how he makes himself useful."

"And what about you, Halleck?"

Janey rushed in, jumped on his lap. "Uncle Spike!"

"Pumpkin!"

"Here's Chombo," she explained to Debra.

"He's nice," Debra said.

"Feel him," she insisted.

"Very nice."

"He's cuddly."

"Sure is," Debra agreed.

"Spike, you feel Chombo."

"Nice," he said.

"Spike can feel things but he can't see anything," she explained to Debra.

"But he can see things with his ears," Debra said.

"How can you *see* things with your ears, silly?" she said, giggling.

"Don't you tell where things are in front of you by seeing them?"

"Sure," she said.

"Now if Spike can tell where things are by listening to them, how is that different from seeing?"

Halleck could almost feel Janey's face screw up with confusion. "He can tell where things are but he can't see," she insisted. "He can't see how pretty you are, no matter what kind of sound you make."

Janey hopped out of Halleck's lap, asking her uncle to defend her. "Right?"

"Pretty is as pretty does," Halleck told her.

"What?"

"You'll understand when you're older," he said.

"Daddy always says that and I always say I'll never get old enough to understand all of this."

"Then you'll never be alone," he said.

"Uncle Spike, if you don't stop talking in puzzles I'm going to have Chombo steal your cane!"

"I'd find him," Halleck snarled back.

"No, you wouldn't!"

"Yes, he would," Debra said. "He found you."

"I love you, Uncle Spike," she said, jumping onto his lap.

"Ouch!" he said. "The shoulder!"

"I'm sorry," she said.

"Come over here," Debra said, "so you can get used to me."

"Are you going to marry Spike?"

"I don't know," Halleck and Debra said at the same time, then laughed, Halleck finally saying, "I just guess it depends on how lucky I get."

Scannon, who had endured the silence like a stoic, found the chance he needed to break in again, saying, "So, is Janey going to be the last little girl to get rescued this way?"

"Not necessarily."

"Is that a yes?"

"A maybe. How long do you think you can keep this secret? How long do you think it will be before the callers start using accoustical isolation booths and shut us out?"

Scannon said, "I don't know. Even if they do. Black tells me we can learn all sorts of things about the caller without any background noises. We can tell where he was brought up, where he moved while he was growing up, a sinus condition or harelip, a lisp, asthma, whether he smoked, lots of things, all from the voice. And we could use the voiceprint in court if it came from a legal wiretap. In other words, Halleck, we could know who we're looking for, we could always or nearly always, tell that, even if we could tell nothing about where he was."

"That's approximately true," Halleck admitted, hedging.

"So that's yes," Scannon said.

"No. I'm not going to think about it," Halleck said, "until we've got Debra a job."

"Janowski said he'd take her back, that, as far as he's concerned, she never quit," Scannon said, cracking his knuckles.

"No," Debra said. "Not that."

"Then come to work for us, at the Bureau. Chicago Office."

"Really?" said Debra, suddenly intrigued.

"Yes."

"Doing what?"

"Being Spike's eyes, for one thing, when we send him out to other offices to teach them how to use this technology. As for the rest, you can write your own job."

"You can do that?"

"As Halleck has shown me, Ms. Seraphicos, you can do anything, as long as you really believe you can. Do you believe you can?"

"That's a rhetorical question, right?"

"And how about you, Halleck?"

"Yeah." He smiled broadly. "How about me?"

ABOUT THE AUTHOR

A Cornell graduate with a doctorate from Purdue, the author was a university researcher, then a government energy technology expert before turning to full time writing in 1990. He lives with his wife in Washington, D.C. and is just finishing a novel about biological warfare.